MAX LAGNO

# THE CITY OF FREEDOM

*You're the chosen one!*

*Max Lagno*

ADAM ONLINE
BOOK TWO

MAGIC DOME BOOKS

The City of Freedom
Adam Online, Book Two
Copyright © Max Lagno 2019
Cover Art © Vladimir Manyukhin 2019
English Translation Copyright © Alix Merlin Williamson 2019
Published by Magic Dome Books, 2019
All Rights Reserved
ISBN: 978-80-7619-056-6

ALL BOOKS BY MAX LAGNO:


*Adam Online* LitRPG Series:
*Absolute Zero* (Book 1)
*The City of Freedom* (Book 2)


*Level Up: The Knockout* LitRPG series
(with Dan Sugralinov):
*The Knockout (*Book 1)

# TABLE OF CONTENTS:

# Chapter 1
# White Spots

I WALKED ALONG a broad street in Liberty City, guided by a map on my tablet. I saw a multitude of NPCs and players along the way, most of them humans, supers and androids. Liberty City was their city. Mechanodestructors didn't feel at home there. They had their own world in Rim One, the capital of which was the city of Mechatron; an imposing conglomeration of highly advanced structures designed specially to support mechanicals.

I didn't know what bizoids did in Liberty City. I knew little about the race; in my day, few would have thought to become such a strange, inhuman creature.

Angels also inhabited their own worlds. Possibly the same worlds people visited when they chose magic over technology. Those dreamers deserved each other.

This didn't mean that there was racial segregation in Adam Online. Mechanodestructors could easily visit Liberty City and the surrounding zones. The question was more in why they would need to; the quests and infrastructure they needed to level up were in other zones. You could buy or find all the same magical items and spellcasting consumables in Liberty City, but they weren't as numerous or as good as in magic zones. By the same token, there was no point looking for UniSuits with fifty upgrade slots in the stalls and taverns of the magical worlds of Himmelbleu or Heroes of Magic.

That said, the grinning maws of some creatures did appear through the crowd from time to time, almost like gorillas or bipedal reptiles with dinosaur heads. I also saw mechanodestructors in the form of small arachnid robots.

The security of Liberty City was uplifting after that spate of anarchy in Town Zero. Sure, I got punched in the face as soon as I got here, but at least I was alive. The local law-enforcement agencies were tough, and were always dozens of levels above people who just moved there. No matter how hard you tried to fight them, the cops still always won.

Rim Zero was a world around two thousand miles long by two thousand miles wide. Rim One consisted of another eight squares of that size surrounding Rim Zero. Eight worlds, all different from each other.

When Adam Online first came into existence, the worlds of Rim One were enough for everyone. Time passed and more and more players arrived. Those that had leveled up demanded changes, new worlds, new quests. And so appeared Rim Two: another sixteen squares. As the years went by, eventually all those worlds had been explored and settled as well, so Rim Three was added, twenty four squares of unclaimed virtual land. Then Rim Four added another thirty two cells to the already huge world. That was enough for a long time, but by the time Olga and I came to Adam Online, Rim Five had also been added. An entirely unimaginable extra forty squares, not counting their vast and numerous dungeons.

History repeated itself. The opening of new Rims caused a race between players. Back then, not all the worlds of Rim Four had been explored, not all the zones had been discovered, but people flocked to Rim Five. It seemed to us then that we could spend our whole lives exploring a world like this. Myself, Olga and millions of other young adamites greedily discovered new zones, named them after themselves, filled the world map with white spots.

Olga and I unlocked one of those unexplored squares, an entirely mountainous world with odd gravity effects. Islands of earth had risen up into the sky. Some floated low, others soared above the clouds. We even staked our claim on a flying island with a whole lake at its center. The island had no monsters and no quests. It was a true virtual limbo. We liked that flying island so much that we built a home on the lake's shore. Around it we built workshops where I crafted weapons and perfected my skills. That was the house where Olga spent her final days in Adam Online, before the i-entropy destroyed her mind completely.

Even all this wasn't enough for people. They wanted new worlds and adventures. So Rim Six was launched, and from what I understood, something strange happened to it. It was if the virtual world itself was rising up against human greed. If you imagined the control systems as real characters, you could picture them crying out: "When will you finally eat so much that you burst, you leeches?!"

I wondered if our island and home were still there. I didn't even remember which cell they were in. I doubted that my search for Nelly Valeeva would take me to that world, but I wanted to visit it. I remember that I didn't even sell the property, I just left Adam Online and promised myself I'd never return.

I guess ten years is long enough to break my

promise.

My hearing slowly adapted to this noisy new world.

Rim Zero was intentionally made relatively ordinary — with deserts, junk heaps and half-destroyed buildings to remind players of the real world.

But Liberty City was too flashy for me, too overwhelming. And this city was nothing in comparison to Londinium, the capital of Rim Five.

A couple of players tried to catch my attention as I walked, offering to sell me stuff; a map to a supposedly secret zone, miracle pills that would restore 'a thousand percent health' or 'the fastest jeep in Rim One.' These shysters thought I was new. I tried not to upset them. I shot them a dumb smile and walked on.

The Lakeview Estates living complex was a group of two-story buildings on the shore of a small lake. A few people sailed catamarans at its center. Hmm, a pretty good place to start with. It was strange that the driver and his family lived in some dump in Rim Zero when they had property like this in Liberty City. The lives of NPCs were full of logical flaws. You could go crazy if you thought about them too much.

I quickly found building 1884, and the right apartment on the second floor. An open staircase led up to it on the rear side of the building. Two stations stood in front of the apartment buildings in a square covered by an awning. They both looked like snack vending machines.

The first was a Projectoria station, a system for fast travel between zones in a Rim or city. To use a station, you first had to find it and then it appeared on your map. Each teleport cost money depending on the distance. These stations also served as respawn towers, where you could revive after death for ten thousand gold. If you didn't have enough money, you'd go to an ordinary respawn tower.

The second station was a Respec-T system. It provided 'respec-tification,' which was a chance to redistribute your base stat and skill points. A useful procedure when you had to quickly strengthen a certain stat at the expense of others. It also had the ability to strengthen any stat or level up a skill for twenty four hours. Respec-T offered boosts of one, five and ten points.

These stations were usually close to each other, but were sometimes far apart. It all depended on the zone. Numerous vending machines for weapons and ammo often accompanied them. There were single-brand vending machines and multi-brand types too.

To refresh my memory of how all these systems worked, I approached the Projectoria station and selected a map. It lit up on the front of the machine. I had two teleport points available: this station itself, and another one between the respawn tower and Lakeview Estates. They were automatically added to the map when you walked within thirty feet of them. You often didn't even notice. I'd have to walk around the town for a while before I'd be able to teleport everywhere. I could have invested in my tablet and bought maps with the Projectoria stations marked on them, but I needed the money to upgrade my weaponry and UniSuit.

I moved to the Respec-T station and saw that one respec cost two hundred and fifty thousand gold. An expensive pleasure. Boosting one stat by one point cost a hundred thousand, by five points — five hundred thousand. Ten points didn't cost a million as you might expect, but ten million.

I left the stations alone and went up to the second floor, opened the door to room number four and entered an empty apartment full of sunlight.

Three large rooms with pristine white walls. Both large windows opened out onto the lake. Next to one window was a white chair. That was all the furniture. I opened a window, sat on the chair, put my feet up on the windowsill and faced the morning sun. A warm breeze brought in the scents of the lake, and a barely audible whisper of waves and birdsong.

It was pretty cool. How much would it cost to buy real estate in this district? Five hundred thousand at least. If it weren't for the quest from the driver, I'd have had to get a room in some stinking hotel, in a stinking district with high criminal activity, which meant a high chance of some headhunter trying to cash in on the price on my head. That 'Whitelist' again. So much needed attention, I had so much to do...

Anyway, the Whitelist wasn't a serious problem. And those were for people too afraid to think about the serious ones...

The longer I looked at the world through the window, the more afraid I got. How could I find Nelly Valeeva here? If she'd been a player, fine, I could have easily found her through a search. If it were as simple as that, the Moscow Security Bureau wouldn't have set up a whole clandestine operation and spent a fortune to level up this character.

If she'd been an NPC, that would complicate the search a little, but it would still be possible. But she was an old binary array that the CSes just never deleted for some reason. Although... Wasn't the reason obvious? For them, Nelly was a player, an adamite that was outside the control of their algorithms. The fact that this player has stuck around in the game for a hundred years doesn't bother them: the QCPs are responsible for kicking players off when their time runs out, not the game algorithms.

I jumped up from my chair. My idle thoughts might have thrown up something potentially useful. Nelly Valeeva was an anomaly. That's exactly how the MSB detected her. They were the ones who said that because she's an anomaly, she appeared in anomalous zones in the generation of new worlds. After all, it was the control systems that created those worlds, and nobody knew what exactly happened at the moment of creation.

But all this could be wrong. If Nelly's anomalous ghost existed in Adam Online, then it existed everywhere, or more precisely — might have existed everywhere.

Alright.

I rose from the chair and walked around the room, glancing at the lake shore where a group of girls lazed around in the sun. Some of them took off their swimsuit tops, exposing their breasts to the morning rays.

There was a possibility that the MSB agents weren't the only ones to see Nelly Valeeva while deciphering a random chunk of code caught in the unimaginable ocean of traffic in Adam Online. Players might have seen her too. After all, adamites didn't have to decode or convert anything, they just had to be in a zone where Nelly Valeeva might appear.

I had to search for messages from players about odd missions or strange phenomena that might originate from the conversation that Makarov showed me, the one between Nelly and the unknown stranger.

It was easier said than done. There were millions of players, and they generated millions of messages. Nearly a third of them kept blogs where they wrote about their travels, shared their leveling experiences or just posted an endless stream of porn with various NPCs or players. There was no way to properly process such a torrent of information. You had to be a CS, and even the CSes only processed local information in the vicinity of a player or players.

The corridor of puzzles led to a dead end. I'd missed something. But what?

I watched as two cops approached the naked girls and made them put their clothes back on.

Adam Online was a game, a form of human activity built on already defined conditions. How could I use those conditions to solve this problem? If, for example, I started randomly wandering the world and questioning players, there would be a certain chance that I'd happen upon a description of something similar to Nelly Valeeva. It'd only take five to eight hundred years.

Even if I put up ads on all the noticeboards, few would reply. People posted trillions of ads that nobody had ever looked at or read. People only read ads that offered some kind of reward: money, gear, weapons, maps to secret zones and quests.

If I put up a reward for the information, then the ad would get attention. And firstly, I'd be drowned in replies from all kinds of psychos, fraudsters and weirdos. I'd spend my entire taharration rotation sorting through messages. Secondly, I'd draw attention from people I wouldn't want attention from; competing security services.

No, looking to the community for help wouldn't solve the problem, it would only make it worse. I returned to the window and leaned out, looking at the lake. The girls, whether players or NPCs, looked nice even clothed. My Eagle Eye let me admire all the details.

I turned away from the window to keep my thoughts on track, but it was too late. I was tired of all this thinking. Yes, I'd felt out some kind of path, but it wasn't a path to my goal, it was just a possible way out of the dead end of previous conclusions.

# Chapter 2
# Floating Range

MY TABLET had been signaling me about events for some time. I grabbed a Penny Packer bottle of whiskey from my backpack and took a swig. I'd probably gotten a debuff or buff for drinking, but my Knowledge was too low to see the details. I had to increase it. I had to level up everything, I had to hurry. I was too weak to find Nelly, who might be in places where even the grass or a frog could kill me. There are such zones...

I switched on my tablet:

*Welcome to your new home, Leonarm.*

*There is nothing here, but after all, a house is a reflection of its owner's internal world. Is your internal world really so empty? Don't you want to start some interior design?*

Sure, I'll get right to it, sounds essential. Although... it actually was. I needed to buy wardrobes for my clothes, safes for weaponry. Where would I keep my loot? I could throw it on the floor, but I wasn't some tramp.

I'd need to buy a bed too. What if I brought a girl

home? I couldn't expect her to indulge in the joys of sex on that chair. Although I'd be up for it. Life in the real world wasn't exactly full of dates with the opposite sex. Most of the women in my country lived out all their fantasies in Adam Online, so I could only look for a partner among people who didn't play Adam Online. That was a very small group. Very, very small.

The second message was more interesting:

*From: Liberty City Police Department.*

*Dear Sir, our colleagues from Town Zero have reported that you provided assistance in eliminating a gang of dangerous criminals. They have transferred 10,000g as a sign of their gratitude. We will transfer this sum to your account without delay as soon as we receive your bank details.*

*The department needs people like you, sir. Our door is always open to you. Liberty City is a fine place, but it has its flaws, one of which is a hydra of organized crime that rears its ugly head in certain districts of the city.*

*We hope that as a new resident of the city, you will respond to this call to fight against the criminal underworld. I have a special quest for you.*

*Yours truly, Detective Joshua Culkin,*
*Chief at PCPD Third Detective Department.*

*'PCPD — Preserving honor since 1877.'*
*You can find us at:*
*Central Park, 23rd Street, 105.*
*Open every day from 9 to 19.*

Money in Adam Online could be stored digitally in your tablet or neurointerface, but that meant that you could be robbed after death and left with nothing. It was better to store large amounts in a bank. Many of the banks in Adam Online were representatives of real banks. A player's virtual and real accounts were synchronized when they left taharration. The local currency was converted into real dollars, and then into rubles or yuan. People in virtual reality earned money so they could pay off bills and loans for their pods and dissociative fluid in real life.

Considering that the only thing associating me with Leonarm was the nickname, I wondered where the money I earned would go after I emerged from the pod. Hmm, now that's a question... What if I became a millionaire? I had to link Leonarm's account to my bank account. But was it worth putting my bank details in the spotlight, transferring cash from the account of a player called %Username%, who had entered Adam Online through an illegal landing?

The trouble was that until I opened an account with one of the banks or linked my real-life account to Leonarm, I wouldn't get the reward from the Rim Zero cops.

My quest list opened:

*True Detective.*
*You should visit Detective Culkin and find out what he needs.*

I opened the map, found Central Park and put down a marker — it was a long way from me.

The other message read:

*Furnishing Lakeview Estates Apartment.*

*All you have is a single chair. It's shameful. What will your neighbors say?*

*Bonus: create the ideal combination of interior design items and get a bonus reward.*

*Completed:*
*Kitchen furniture — 0/5.*
*Weapon safe — 0/1.*
*Bed — 0/1.*
*Table — 0/1.*
*Chairs — 1/5.*

And so on — there were another ten or so interior items, from pictures on the walls to paint for those walls. After this, the tablet squawked a series of signals and I got over a hundred messages from furniture stores. Each of them offered 'an exclusive choice of furniture to suit any taste.'

I tapped on an offer from the middle of the list at random. I certainly had no plans to start studying trends in interior design.

On the other hand, since I was planning to woo NPCs to get at least someone into bed with me, that meant I'd need to buy the right bed. I had no intention of seducing players after my experiences with Amy McDonald and Vildana.

I examined the advertisements more closely, chose a store called Sensuality. Their vulgar pink and red tones caught the eye. The store immediately offered a bed called the Sexodrome, which was, of course, shaped like a heart. It was accompanied by a gleaming red sheet and all the trimmings. The Sexodrome cost 3999g.

I aimed my tablet at the wall and dragged the bed

from the tablet screen. The Sexodrome appeared in the room and thudded against the floor, taking up most of the space. I aimed the tablet at the floor and chose a color — black. I dragged the skin of some furry animal off the screen and dropped it on the floor. I put heavy burgundy drapes on the windows. The bright apartment was immediately plunged into darkness.

I found a fireplace and put it opposite the bed. Its soft light battled the darkness, but it was still gloomy. I placed red lamps in the corners. Candles on the mantelpiece, a painting of some virtuous Renaissance orgy above the bed. I couldn't show too much obsession and scare off my guests.

These preparations reminded me of another game setting that I wouldn't be able to change... I opened my settings to check it.

*Sexual realism — [maximum]*

Hmm, not quite what I wanted. The process would be recreated precisely, down to every last physiological detail. How could I have been dumb enough not to check the part of the MSB contract about control over settings?

I put a Belorussian-made wardrobe in a corner, a place for me to store my civilian outfits. I was done with the bedroom. I moved to the room that would be the kitchen. I decided not to flaunt my lack of taste here. I put in some light and cheerful Ikea furniture. It all cost around three thousand gold. I moved nine bottles of whiskey into a cupboard and put one on the table, grabbed a glass and drank.

Ice wouldn't hurt, but for that I'd need a refrigerator. Drinking and eating wasn't essential in

Adam Online, though many enjoyed the pleasure. The food here was far better than what we ate in real life, which was mostly synthetic pasta and meat from soy and unknown animals. Food restored health a little. Some rare foods gave buffs, but you couldn't rely on food in battle: eating a chocolate bar gave you plus one to health, but it took so much time to eat it that you could die three times over before you finished.

I drank some more whiskey and moved to the third room, which was marked Study on the tablet. I actually intended to turn it into something between an armory and a toolshed.

I approached my choice of a gun safe a little more seriously, studying the offers on the market. But with my funds, my search was over quickly. I was limited to the cheaper options.

I had my eye on the Vault Slim Fit gun safe with a built-in durability regenerator. It restored one durability per hour to weapons inside. Not a lot. There was a safe from Tula manufacturers called the Old Master. It restored ten durability per hour, but cost ten times as much.

I aimed my tablet at the wall and dragged the safe onto it. It appeared in the room with the clang of metal, its doors invitingly open. It could store one of each type of weapon apart from heavy weaponry like grenade launchers and shoulder-mounted rocket launchers. Liberty City was a relatively quiet place, so I could get by with just a knife and a standard Glock.

Incidentally, when I got to Rim One, my booklets updated to 'Guidebook on Rim One of the Adam Online Universe' and another standard Glock appeared again. Phew, it's a good thing the previous booklets updated. I was afraid that error would come back and make the booklets multiply and fill up my inventory.

I moved my Uzi, Marble sawn-off and Tesla revolver into the corresponding slots in the safe. They could restore durability and save me some money on repairs.

I picked up my tablet to keep decorating. I got the decoration progress bar up to seventy five percent, and a message popped up:

*Decorator skill learned: +10 XP.*
*Keep leveling it up and people will ask you to arrange the furniture in their own homes!*

One last interior item remained. I scrolled through the list and dragged a LockerDouble cupboard for special gear into a corner of the room. It had two sections for storing two UniSuits. One section was also equipped with a durability regenerator. I put my UniSuit in there right away.

The other section of the cupboard could store one helmet, a pair of gloves and a pair of shoes. There was a funny conditionality to it: if you put one helmet on the shelf, then you wouldn't be able to fit another in even though there was plenty of space. An invisible wall just blocked the second one.

It wasn't always easy for the CSes to combine maximum realism with maximum playability.

My decorating quest showed that it was ninety five percent complete. Strange. I thought I'd added all the items from the list. I probably had to figure out for myself which was the last missing item. I took a swig of whiskey.

I walked around all the rooms, looked at the walls. What was missing? A trash can? An ottoman, a nightstand, a table lamp? A pet? A statue? Loud neighbors?

A strange unevenness on the wall next to my crockery cupboard caught my eye. Hmm, what was that? I ordered paint for the walls, wasn't leveling out the walls included in that service? I aimed the tablet at it:

*There may have been a hole here that was poorly patched. It's probably a hiding place.*
*Eagle Eye skill increased: +10 XP.*

Naturally, I kicked the spot on the wall. A chunk fell off. I kept kicking until the hiding place was completely revealed. Inside was a metal box nearly four feet long. I pulled it out, afraid that I might need lockpicking skills, but the locks on the box turned out to be simple latches.

Inside the box was a sword in a scabbard wrapped in rags. I took it out and read:
*A beautiful sword of an unknown design.*
*Composition: iron and an unknown quantity of unknown components.*
*Slashing damage: 50 or 900.*
*Cutting damage: unknown.*
*Strike damage: unknown.*
*Block: 50 or unknown.*
*Durability: 500/100.*

*Enchantment: unknown.*
*Unknown property.*

*Unknown property.*
*Unknown property.*
*Unknown property.*
*Value: 250,000g or unknown.*
*There is a high chance that this item is a rare collectible, but this is not guaranteed.*

At this point, the word 'unknown' was practically seared into my eyeballs. It indicated I didn't have enough Knowledge.

But the fact that Slashing Damage was still shown in a floating range was a result of my Blade Combat skill.

The two-hundred and fifty thousand gold value was a nice surprise, but I still wasn't sure that it was accurate, and not higher or lower.

You didn't have to be an Adam Online veteran to know that there was a quest behind this sword. I unraveled the rags around it and found a scroll of paper attached to the round pommel. I unrolled it, but couldn't read it. I waved my tablet over it to find out why.

*A scroll of text in an unknown language. Maybe it's Elvish?*

Well, what next?

I could just palm off the find at the nearest Curiosity Store, a chain specializing in items like this. Considering that I knew nothing about the sword, I could sell it for half a million or for peanuts. There would definitely be someone in that store who could read the scroll. If it was an NPC, I'd have to be certain that they wouldn't take advantage of me. After all, my Reputation was only a few points higher than someone who should be taken advantage of. I could look for a player who could read the scroll, but as a perfect stranger, they'd definitely trick me.

I decided to leave the mystery of the sword for later. Judging by the fact that my tablet had fallen silent, it was clear to me that I wouldn't get a quest until I could read the letter.

I ordered some more paint for the walls to cover up the hole. More costs. And the quest to decorate the apartment still didn't want to finish. What was going on? What was the problem?

I looked at the sword... what if...

I looked through the catalog and found a 'Hanger for Paintings or Other Decorative Items.'

I placed it above the bed and put the sword on it in its scabbard. The tablet squawked in satisfaction.

*A great detail! You appreciate the value in subconscious phallic symbols, Leonarm.*

*Sword above bed: +10% chance to seduce an NPC of any gender.*

*Decorator skill increased: +10 XP.*

*Quest complete: Furnishing Lakeview Estates Apartment!*

*Earned: +100 XP.*

*Congratulations, Leonarm, you leveled up!*
*Your current level: 12.*
*Obtained: stat points (1), skill points (1)*

I decided not to spend the points for now. The future would let me know where best to invest them.

*The Sensuality store appreciates the brazen lack of taste in your bedroom and has given you a Sixth Sense lamp. +10% chance to seduce an NPC of any gender.*

The image of a lamp shaped like a person on their knees appeared on the tablet, with the option to choose between a man or a woman. I chose the woman and put the lamp on the nightstand by my bed. A dim pink light emanated from the girl's open mouth.

I looked over my bedroom with satisfaction: this was a real Lothario's pad! Yes, I'd rather call myself a Lothario than desperate.

I drank the rest of my whiskey to celebrate my victory and got another message:

*Achievement: Reveler.*

*Are you alone, with no family, job or friends? You're in the perfect position to become an expert in alcoholic beverages.*

*Alcoholic brands tried:*
*Spirit: 0/1*
*Whiskey: 1/5*
*Vodka: 0/5*
*Cognac: 0/5*
*Wine: 0/5*
*Port: 0/5*
*Champagne: 0/5*
*Beer: 0/5*

Achievements were best ignored. The idea was that they'd complete themselves as you lived your life in Adam Online. Anyway, it was time for me to go out. I was already starting to think that I could forget about my military skills and just live in Liberty City, enjoy all its pleasures, level up to level three hundred in peaceful professions and ship off to Rim Six.

Of course, I didn't seriously consider it. Interior

decorating skills didn't exactly mesh well with monster battles.

I left the apartment and walked down the stairs.

On the other hand, what if I did level up a peaceful character? Went into business, got into real estate, financial machinations? Selling the Lakeview Estates apartment would provide some starting capital. If I got rich, I wouldn't need to fight. I'd have enough money to hire an army of powerleveled warriors of all races and creeds. I could even hire players or a whole clan.

Dreams, just dreams. I knew from past experience that I didn't make a good capitalist. I remembered that I'd tried to play the stock exchange once, even opened my own stores, sold crafted weapons. If it weren't for Olga, I'd have ruined myself and been in debt. She managed all our finances, and thanks to her we only ever got richer.

I walked away from Lakeview Estates and looked around. The sun had already risen and it shone gently, rather than burning as it did in the planes zones. Alright, where to first? To the detective or...

My gaze was drawn to the lake, where three times as many girls were already sunbathing. But no. I had to get myself tidied up, I couldn't wander around this magnificent city in standard scrub gear.

So first things first — I had to earn money. The Liberty City Police Department was the main goal of my outing. I'd check out some stores on the way.

Aside from clothes, it was also time I upgraded my tablet, got some augmented reality goggles or at least a voice assistant. I was sick of having to wave some prehistoric device over stuff to get information.

I threw a farewell glance at the naked NPCs and

walked toward Central Park. It was a long way to go.

# Chapter 3
# Middle Class

YOU COULD BUY clothing the same way I'd bought furniture, through special advertisements that materialized the items you ordered. But there were two advantages to buying them in the stores instead: variety and social opportunity. Items from the stores were always better than from the ads. You only found rare items in the stores. And, of course, visiting a store was more fun than just scrolling through adverts.

It wasn't as if I was desperate for a social life... but then why did I spend so much money fitting out my bedroom?

That was why, when I found a whole street of stores, I turned onto it even though it wasn't on the way to the police department. The Projectoria station flashed a soft green, marking itself on the map.

Centerline Avenue was a broad and long street full of people. This was a rare day; there were almost as many people on the street as NPCs.

I hadn't been on this street before. I'd once known Liberty City well, but Adam Online was a living universe. Everything had changed here since my time. The city lived like a real city, constantly rebuilding and updating itself. Although the proportion of different districts was the same as before. There had always been slums full of gangland mayhem, and elite districts guarded by the police or even the military.

And something else hadn't changed: Liberty City was an amalgamated image of a megapolis of the mid-twenty-first century, before the wars and cataclysms that made our world look more like the Mechanodestructor Heap. A happy time for humanity, when you could enjoy the pleasures of life and trips to real tropical islands. The architecture, car design and fashion in Liberty City fluctuated from 2007 to 2041.

Bars plays songs from that era, the cinemas showed its movies, the stores sold its games consoles so people could play archaic games. Liberty City conserved that era: many adamites were content to live in the city and never bother with other zones. Although in Rim One, there were a few more zones that recreated the life of that time.

Swiftville, for example, a place not far from Liberty City. It was a city zone where everything was built around racing with different forms of ground vehicles. Or the aeronaut city Aerial, where nobody walked on the surface, everyone flew, at the very least with jetpacks. Or other zones where historical battles were reconstructed, such as the Siege of Saigon, the Germano-Russian Occupation, the Ukrainian Secession or the Capture of Syria.

Needless to say, in the real world many of those historical places no longer existed. They'd burned up in atomic flame like Saigon and Beijing, or drowned like London, or they were now highly radioactive as in the case of Mecca and Jerusalem.

I walked past window displays, trying to choose a store.

I needed to make the right impression on the chief of the detective department, and I shouldn't dress too smart. My choice fell on a store with the alluring name Middle Class.

A very cute salesgirl greeted me at the entrance, probably an NPC. It wasn't that players couldn't work in stores. There were plenty of opportunities for that, especially if you preferred to play a peaceful life simulator. You start as a simple sales rep, completing quests like 'serve ten customers in an hour' or 'sell goods worth X amount.'

Something else gave away the fact that she was an NPC. The girl looked too good. To get an appearance like that, a player would have to not only reach the required level, but also pay a large amount, and that means it's unlikely they'd be working in a store.

The salesgirl's hair was tied back in a bob and she wore a humble uniform that looked a little like a maid's outfit.

"Need any help?" she said.

"I'm just browsing," I said, glancing over her figure. "But you can help me."

I wanted to add, *'What are you doing tonight?'* but thought better of it. Without the right skills, I doubted I'd achieve much except a drop in Reputation.

Instead, I said I had a business meeting to go to, but I didn't want business-style clothes.

"Alright, smart casual. It's over here."

She moved nimbly through the aisles and I followed her. I aimed the tablet at her at the same time:

*Irene Laggan.*
*Level: 32*
*Class: unknown (requires 12 Knowledge).*
*Occupation: saleswoman in a Middle Class store.*
*Interests: unknown (requires Insight skill).*

Irene stopped next to a clothes rack and pulled out a jacket, then grabbed some pants from a nearby stand. "These go well together."

I aimed my tablet and read the clothes' stats. The saleswoman froze helpfully.

*Furr Velvet Jacket.*
*Increases NPC trust by 20%.*
*Improves relationships with NPCs of the opposite sex by 30%.*
*Worsens relationships with NPCs wearing a cheaper jacket by 5%.*
*Unknown property (requires Seducer skill).*
*Unknown property (requires 12 Knowledge).*
*Price: 5,999g.*

*Gap Pants.*
*Increase openness of NPCs in conversations about their personal life by 10%.*
*Unknown feature (requires 15 Knowledge).*
*Unknown property (unknown requirements).*
*Price: 1,999g.*

Hmm, that was a great jacket, but I wasn't planning on seducing Joshua. He was most likely a brutal old cop that wouldn't be very tolerant to same-sex love.

"Irene, the person I'm going to meet doesn't care

about fashion. I need something to show him I'm a good guy. I need to convince him that I can be trusted."

Irene Laggan shook her bob teasingly. "You don't earn trust with clothes."

Uh-huh, the CSes had gotten involved, activated their creative functions. The girl wasn't just a bobblehead showing off clothes to customers now.

"Sure, but clothes might help make a good first impression."

The salesgirl put the jacket back.

"Alright, what kind of impression do you want to make, and who're you meeting?"

"He's a cop. I need to get a job from him."

"Oh!" the salesgirl cried. "Then this is what you need."

She pulled out a long leather jacket that looked somehow worn. I raised my tablet uncertainly:

*Max Payne Leather Overcoat.*
*+1 Agility.*
*+1 Strength.*
*+1 Pistols and Revolvers skill.*
*Improves relationships with military-type NPCs by 15%.*
*Improved relationships with feisty NPCs by 5%.*
*Unknown property (requires 10 Knowledge).*
*Unknown property (unknown requirements).*
*Price: 4,999g.*

I tried the overcoat on right away.

"Well done," I praised the salesgirl. "Just what I need! And it looks awesome."

The girl averted her gaze shyly.

"No problem, it's my job. Although I actually have

bigger dreams than being a salesgirl."

"What would you rather be?"

Instead of answering, the salesgirl sighed and offered me a shirt that was so colorful it bordered on the obnoxious. I had my doubts, but Irene encouraged me.

"Don't worry, you don't want to look perfect. You need a flaw."

Alright, why not listen to her? The overcoat almost completely hid the shirt anyway.

*Bershka Shirt.*
*Worsens relationships with stylish NPCs by 25%.*
*Improves relationships with NPCs indifferent to fashion by 5%.*
*Price: 99g.*

"You didn't tell me about your dreams," I said to Irene.

The girl offered me some thick-soled boots.

"I want to move to Swiftville."

"The car city? Why?"

The girl answered with another sigh, indicating that she didn't want to talk about it. I must have needed some higher skill to get her to talk.

I put on the shirt and the overcoat above it, then the boots.

*Dr. Martens Boots.*
*+1 Agility.*
*Unknown property (requires 10 Knowledge).*
*Price: 1,999g.*

I twirled in front of the mirror. Needed to change my haircut. Then I wondered, should I buy the velvet jacket too? It had a really good bonus to relations with the opposite sex. I counted my money and decided against it.

I paid, nodded to Irene and walked toward the exit.

"Wait!" the girl caught up to me at the door. "This will really complement that outfit."

She rose up on her tiptoes, entwined her hands around me and clasped a medallion around my neck. I took it in my hand and pointed my tablet at it.

*A simple medallion bearing the Middle Class store logo.*

*Provides a 15% durability boost to all clothes bought at the Middle Class chain.*

*Price: free.*

"Actually, we give one to all customers who spend five thousand or over. Heh heh, and we tell them all it complements their outfit."

The girl winked and went back into the store. Now it was my turn to shout "Wait!". Irene turned.

I took a risk. "What are you doing tonight?"

"Getting ready for bed. See you later."

The girl disappeared into the store, and I nervously checked my tablet, which had flashed after Irene's words. I expected to see a Reputation drop, but instead:

*Insight skill learned: +10 XP.*

*Now you can evaluate the mood of creatures around you.*

*Level up this skill to recognize other character features and learn to influence mood as a result.*

*Unlocked additional NPC stat: Character.*
*Unlocked additional NPC stat: Mood.*
*Attention: the accuracy of these measures depends on your Knowledge and Reputation in combination with your Insight skill and others.*

At this stage, knowledge of an NPC's character didn't really help much. You could figure it out anyway, the same way as with players, through behavior. But knowledge of their current mood and influence on NPCs' emotional behavior would come in handy. It wasn't that I couldn't influence them just by talking to them, but the influence wasn't as extensive as I'd like.

The more the influence, the better the quests and the more generous the rewards.

# Chapter 4
# Hundreds of Fine Braids

CENTRAL PARK was a little old park at the center of a business district of the same name. It was ringed by roads packed with cars on all sides.

I decided to cut across the park to the police department building. Surprisingly, there were plenty of players in the park.

They weren't doing anything, just lying or sitting on the grass, watching the sky. Some drank beer or ate sandwiches out of picnic baskets. Probably the same hedonists that enjoyed the virtual world of Adam Online without chasing after levels, skills or other perks.

I wondered whether it was worth it for them to go into a virtual world just to fool themselves. The fact that they couldn't see their stats or level didn't mean they weren't playing the game. Every one of them probably had a bunch of achievements. Like 'Beer Barrel' — drink two hundred pints of beer. Or 'Garfield,' eat a million calories.

As I walked past, one of the hedonists called out to me.

"Hey, dude, catch!"

I turned and just managed to catch a bottle of

beer thrown at me. Damp and pleasantly cool.

"Thanks."

"No worries, bro."

I opened the beer and took a swig so as not to offend the player. He could be anyone. My encounter with the laughing gentleman in the top hat was enough to keep me wary. Nearly getting sent back to the respawn tower with one punch will do that.

I waved the bottle at the player and moved on. I liked the fact that there were places where you could just relax and keep your hand away from your holster, where you could just live and play a simulator of real life. A beautiful version that you couldn't get in the real world.

Another endless traffic jam blocked my path when I needed to cross the road at the other side. A bright blue race car came up to the back of it. I could tell from the style that it was a player's personal car. Instead of numbers, the license plate was stamped Swiftville and bore the nickname Hasty. The car's windows were black mirrors.

The player tried to get around the traffic jam. The car rolled onto the sidewalk, violating the highway code and scaring passersby. I barely managed to jump back behind the protection of the park fence. The bottle slipped from my hands and smashed. Then I heard a police siren and saw cops on motorcycles appear from between the rows of cars. They chased after the lawbreaker.

The racer and the police disappeared around a bend in the street, spreading panic and destruction, but I had no doubt about it: the cops would catch him. A helicopter thrummed in the sky, and several police drones flew by overhead. Even the best racer in the world wouldn't shake that tail. If Hasty didn't kill anyone on the road, he'd get away with a large fine. Otherwise he'd lose his Reputation and be hunted until he was killed or left Liberty City. He'd only be able to return to the slums, the gangster districts. In civilized districts, the cops would start tailing him again as soon as he got into their field of view, or the view of an upstanding NPC that would immediately call the police.

Even without the plate, it was clear that Hasty was from Swiftville. There everyone drove at ridiculous speeds, and the police didn't chase them, they chased people who drove slow and got in the way of everyone else. This Hasty didn't seem to be a man of great intellect, since he'd decided to flaunt his racing skills right in front of the Liberty City Police Department.

The department building was noticeable: tall, decorated with columns and a long broad staircase. Its facade was dark brown marble, but that made it look solid rather than gloomy. You could see it right away — this reliable institution stands up for law and order in Liberty City. At least in those districts where there are no criminal gangs to stand up for lawlessness and disorder.

I ran up the long staircase and pushed through one of the heavy wooden doors. I found myself in a big hall, part of it cordoned off with a barrier. The floor was covered with plastic sheeting. Several workers stood on gantries and painted the walls. Renovations?

A police robot stopped me. It was a ten foot tall mech standing on two legs. Its knee joints were bent backwards as if the robot was preparing to leap at any moment. Its arms ended in two machine guns fitted with silencers.

"Purpose of visit?" the thing rumbled.

"I'm here by invitation of Detective Culkin. He sen..."

Some small police drones descended on me from the ceiling, scanning and checking me. One started flashing in alarm and exuded a red projection of my Glock, Lefaucheux musket and knife.

The robot clattered backwards from me and aimed its machine guns. "You must surrender your weapons."

I took out all my weapons. The drones grabbed them and carried them off.

"Proceed to the registration desk," the robot ordered, waving its machine guns toward a row of windows with police officers sat behind.

I walked up to a window with a cute black policewoman behind it. Her nametag read Heylia Grant.

"You got some serious security here," I said.

The girl took off her cap. Her hair was woven into hundreds of fine braids.

"Sorry for the inconvenience," she smiled. "Ever since someone brought a bomb in here, we've been forced to take precautions."

"Woah!"

Now I saw why they were repairing the hall.

"Several officers and civilians died. Mayor Weinhardt even declared a time of mourning. You new to Liberty City?"

"Arrived today. Who was the bomb from?"

"It was an act of vengeance by the Golden Piranhas syndicate. We arrested their leader's chief assistant recently. Incidentally, it was Detective Joshua

Culkin who led that investigation. You're here to see him?"

I nodded.

The girl closed the window and stood up. "I'll show you the way."

"I can find it myself."

"All visitors have to be accompanied by police officers. But if you prefer, I can send him," she nodded at the police mech.

The robot clicked its paws in readiness. "Civilian, walk ahead of me at a range of no more than ten feet. Do not turn or make any sudden movements. I will shoot to kill."

I turned back to the window. "No, I think I'd prefer you."

Heylia left the booth and walked ahead of me, not only showing me the way, but also showing that her police uniform did a great job outlining her inviting curves. We walked along a corridor and began to climb some stairs. I couldn't take my eyes off her back and legs. Eh, no guts, no glory!

"What are you doing tonight?"

"What do you mean?" the girl said in surprise. "Getting ready for bed."

I sighed helplessly, but then she suddenly helped me out.

"On the other hand, why sleep when the weather is so good in the evenings now?"

The Max Payne jacket had an effect on military-type NPCs. Now I had to continue the conversation and not mess it up. If I let on that I'd built a whole love den, Heylia would be unlikely to agree to come and see it. She mentioned the weather, which meant she'd rather take a stroll in the great outdoors.

If I'd had skills for deeper discussions with NPCs, I'd have known exactly what kind of exercise she wanted to get. I'd have to guess.

"Want to meet in Central Park after work?"

Heylia stopped smiling.

"In the park? What would we do there? Drink beer? Feed the birds?"

"We'll just meet, then I'll tell you where we'll go next. I promise you'll get to enjoy the weather in full."

Heylia Grant shook out her thousand braids.

"Alright then."

The tablet gave off a signal:

*Insight skill increased: +5 XP.*

*So uniforms do it for you, huh? Or do you just want Heylia Grant to use her handcuffs on you?*
*Reputation with Heylia Grant increased: +1.*

Then a second signal:

*Seducer skill learned: +10 XP.*

*So you want to crush the shards of broken hearts beneath your feet? Careful, someone might break your heart too.*

And a third:

*Congratulations, Leonarm, you leveled up!*
*Your level: 13.*

*Attention: you have unused stat points (2) and skill points (2). Spend them wisely!*

It was odd that I didn't get a quest like Seduce Heylia Grant. I probably hadn't met some condition or other just yet. But I'm sure the quest will appear when we meet in the park.

Heylia led me through several large rooms full of tables covered in the transparent screens of old computers, from back in the days of Nelly Valeeva and gyrorbs. The decor here underlined Liberty City's association with those times.

Police employees scurried back and forth, spoke on the phone or on video links, opened maps of the city on the screen and marked things. One closed door was marked Police Archive. I stopped still for a second. Here it was — a way to find information on Nelly Valeeva. There was a small chance that she might have left a trace in some archived cases. I didn't know yet whether my guess was right, but all the same, it was a lead. What if...

"Why're you standing there?" Heylia asked. "You can't just hang around, come on." We moved on.

We entered an empty corridor with a row of doors. We stopped by one of them.

Heylia turned to me. "Josh will meet you soon, please wait here."

"So see you tonight?"

"Yep, see you tonight."

Heylia flashed me another gleaming smile and walked leisurely back down the corridor. A police drone flew into the corridor and hovered above me. Safety measures, I guess.

# Chapter 5
# Stimulation of Choice

AT FIRST, I patiently waited five minutes. Then I pulled at the door to the office... It was locked. I listened: I could hear someone speaking quickly and quietly behind the door.

"Mr. Culkin, sir?" I knocked. "It's Leonarm, you invited me..."

Silence. Then I realized that it wasn't a conversation I could hear behind the door — it was just the Free Adamite radio. I recognized the intro music.

I frowned. Why had I flown into radioactive zones in Chinese Kazakhstan and risked my life? Why had I pulled my consciousness out of my body and put it into Adam Online, where I'd told myself I'd never return? Was it really to wait around for some virtual cop? What was this, a bureaucracy simulator?

I pulled on the door one last time and decided to go back to Heylia. I'd rather flirt with her than hang around here. The door at the end of the corridor opened, and a heavyset middle-aged man in a white shirt with suspenders came through it. He pulled up his zipper as he walked. I read:

*Joshua Culkin.*

*Level: 102.*

*Class: Defender.*

*Occupation: Chief at PCPD Third Detective Department.*

*Character: unknown (requires level 102).*

*Mood: unpredictable, positive and several other unknown configurations (requires Insight level 3).*

The detective walked along the corridor, dominating it up with his body. He reminded me of the NPCs in the Minecraft zone: square head, cubic torso and legs like two blocks.

"Are you Leonarm?" he asked.

I just nodded, hinting that his absence had annoyed me.

The detective opened the office door and went inside first. It was gloomy, and stank of coffee and cigarettes. Joshua Culkin walked to a table by the wall, poured a coffee from a filter coffee machine and put the cup in front of me. Then he poured his own, sat at the desk, and gestured for me to sit opposite.

I took a swallow, gagged and put the cup back down. Disgusting.

Joshua noticed my grimace and chuckled.

"Our coffee is just like our budget. Shitty."

*Coffee Break.*

*The detective can find criminals, but can't find good coffee. Will you help?*

Joshua Culkin picked up a pack of cigarettes from the table and lit one. "Listen here, Leonarm, I don't want you to get the wrong impression about me. Sure, I was polite in my message and I congratulated you on a job well done. But here's my personal opinion: you're an ass. Just like everyone who hasn't proved otherwise.

Joshua paused, judging by reaction. When I kept a stony expression on my face, he continued.

"Want to work for me? The money's good."

"You said you had a shitty budget. Not enough for decent coffee."

"Paying professionals is different."

"O-kay, keep going."

Joshua sat back in his chair, stuck his thumbs behind his suspenders and clicked his tongue.

"That's all. Like I said, you're an ass until proven otherwise. How do I know if you're a professional or not? Villagers from Town Zero think any punk with a pistol is a hero if he shoots the bad guys. First you have to convince me that you're capable of real work."

"Hmm, you're the real ass here. No point trying to prove otherwise."

"Well now, don't forget, I'm a cop. I can insult people. You're nobody yet."

Strangely enough, my tablet squawked in response to this squabble.

*Insight skill increased: +5 XP.*

*Your new boss doesn't like asskissers. Or maybe he just needs to be kissed a certain way? You found that special way, Leonarm!*

*Reputation with Joshua Culkin increased: +1*

*Your overall Reputation: 6.*

So Joshua liked cocky subordinates? The main thing was not to get too cocky.

I nodded. The quests would start now: kill this many members of that gang, arrest a black marketeer, bring in ten illegal guns, chase streetwalkers...

Joshua took a folder of papers out of his desk drawer and threw it across to me.

"Get up to speed. This is your first case. It'll decide whether you get promoted from an ass or not."

I skimmed through the case materials: suspect photographs, interrogation protocols, stills from security cameras during the shooting. This was a little more interesting than playing fetch.

"Did you know that the Luxor District is the safest place in Liberty City?" the detective asked. "It's a weapons-free zone. You have to hand over your weapons at the checkpoints, and hundreds of autonomous police boats patrol the water around the island, intercepting any attempts to smuggle in weapons."

"Yes, sir, that's why L.D. has the highest property prices and all the bank headquarters."

Joshua leaned across the table and tapped the crime scene photo I was looking at: criminals in masks aiming assault rifles at hostages, making them lie on the floor.

"Trouble is, kid, things have changed recently. These shots are from the Liberty City Exchequer bank. It's in the center of our city's safest district."

"There's a gang of armed bank robbers operating in the Luxor District?"

"Highly armed. Not just assault rifles. They have explosives and weapons for taking out helicopters and police drones."

"Who are they and how'd they get the weapons?"

"At first we suspected the Yellow Piranhas, even went and pointlessly arrested one of their higher-ups. But the interrogation revealed he knew nothing about the gang. We don't know who is organizing the attacks. Each new assault has new members from the Blacklist. Whatever's going on, we've sent an agent to infiltrate the group of raiders, who seem to be preparing to rob another bank in the Luxor District. The agent got in touch with us recently and told us where and when the next raid would be."

"What's my job?"

"Be in the bank when the robbery takes place and get some information from our agent."

I was puzzled. "Why not just catch the whole gang?"

Joshua Culkin sat back in his chair. "We don't need the contractors! We need the organizers, we need to find out the delivery channels to L.D. Don't let me down, kid."

My tablet spoke of the detective's displeasure:

*Ugh, Leonarm, did you forget that dumb questions get you dumb answers? Watch what you say.*
*Reputation with Joshua Culkin reduced: -1.*

I continued nonetheless, "Why can't the agent convey his information the same way he informed you about the time and place of the raid?"

Joshua Culkin sighed. "You don't think we asked him? The group members are getting their weapons right before the raid. Until then, they'll have no contact with the outside world. We aren't even sure what kind of info our agent is going to give us during the robbery. If we're lucky, we'll get a hint about where they got the guns. Of course, I'm sure the weapons go through a middleman. But if we find out who that is, that's progress."

The tablet gave off a signal:

*I have no words... And you have too many to keep your mouth shut when you should.*
*Reputation with Joshua Culkin reduced: -1.*

Slowing as if giving me time to read my messages, the detective pulled a badge out of his desk drawer and unwillingly passed it to me across the desk. "I don't even know whether I should trust you with this."

"Don't worry, you made the right choice."

I picked up the weighty badge and admired it. There was a big star at its center surrounded by a ring of smaller stars. At the top of the badge was the crest of Liberty City, and in the lower half it said Special Detective.

I moved my gaze to my tablet.

*LCPD Detective Badge received.*
*Rare item.*
*+3 Perception.*
*+5 Insight, allowing you to see not only NPC moods, but much more besides.*
*+2 Pistols and Revolvers skill.*
*+75% chance to get information from positive NPCs.*
*Reputation with criminal NPCs lowered to 95%.*

*Unlocks the Communicative skill.*
*Sometimes you'll know what to ask an NPC, instead of talking nonsense like you usually do.*

*Badge bonuses:*
*Ability to summon police reinforcements: one car.*
*Receive data from police drones within 1600 feet.*
*Use of LCPD armory: one UniSuit upgrade, any weapon, any ammunition.*
*Use of LCPD gunshop: prices for repairing weapons and equipment reduced by 50%.*
*Use of LCPD hospital: medicine and healing prices reduced by 50%.*
*Use of LCPD garage: police car.*
*Improve your reputation to unlock other vehicles.*
*Improve your reputation to unlock other LCPD capabilities.*

*These bonuses are only available in Liberty City. Improve your reputation if you want your badge to carry weight in other cities in Rim One.*
*Improve your reputation to unlock new bonuses.*

Now that's what I'm talking about! This I understood — encouraging people to choose the right side of the law.

As I was about to put the badge in my pocket, the detective shouted, "What're you doing? Had a good look? Now give it back."

"But..."

"Don't 'but' me. We don't give badges to just anyone. Complete the job first. We'll see how that goes and then I'll decide if you can be any use to me."

I unwillingly returned the badge. That sure was some logic; it wasn't like I'd stop being just anyone after completing the quest, or at least just someone who completed the driver's quest.

Joshua Culkin tossed the badge into a desk drawer, cast a condescending glance my way and stood up from his chair. "By the way, about the money from Rim Zero. Open an account at Liberty City Exchequer. The more believable your presence at the robbery is, the better."

"When is the operation?"

"I'll let you know. Don't leave town."

"But can I..."

Then Detective Culkin jumped, fell into his seat and rolled into the wall. I barely kept my feet as well: the floor was shaking like an old washing machine. Cupboard doors slammed open and folders of documents fell to the floor. The windows shattered, showering us with shards.

Only then did I hear the explosion. The sound traveled through all the walls, reached my body and shook it with a low-frequency power.

The detective jumped out of his seat and ran past me. "Follow me!"

# Chapter 6
# Double Strike

THE SQUARE JOSHUA CULKIN fit into the square corridor perfectly. He ran with unusual speed for his size, sweeping away all in his path. The corridors were littered with broken doors, smashed cupboards and pieces of fallen walls. It was like running behind a bulldozer clearing a road.

We ran into some officers along the way, carrying some injured people.

"Where'd it happen?" Joshua asked shortly.

"In the hall again..."

"Damn stupid bastards!"

It wasn't clear who the detective meant. The bandits that dared to repeat their sabotage, or his colleagues who had failed to keep the building secure?

A police drone appeared above me. Part of its hull was crumpled, baring broken and sparking wires. The machine held itself in the air at an angle due to its damage. Nonetheless, it returned my weapons. Unfortunately, it didn't put them into my waiting hands, it just threw them out in random directions. Then it dived, crashed into the floor and fell silent.

I caught up to Joshua at the entrance to the hall.

Smoke poured out of the hall, we heard screams and shots. The detective pressed himself against a wall, clutching a silver revolver. Three cops stood nearby in dust-marred uniforms. One of them had a wound in his leg. He babbled.

"There was a hacker attack on the building control systems at the same time as the explosion. We're locked out of the armory. The security cameras aren't working, pulse interference took out all the drones."

"Bastards," Joshua spat. "Alright, we need to get these assholes out of the hall. How many are there?"

"We don't know exactly. Judging by the shots, maybe seven, armed with assault rifles."

"Any hostages?"

"Unknown, sir. I doubt any employees or visitors survived the explosion in the hall."

Joshua Culkin ordered the injured cop to give me his armored vest.

"You get to the hospital."

"But it's closed."

"Just leave, you're wounded."

*Obtained: Police Armored Vest (compatible with UniSuit)*
*+2,000 armor.*
*Durability: 44/100.*

The cop limped away. Three more officers joined us, running from the same part of the building as we did. They said the hackers locked all the doors, so we wouldn't get reinforcements for a while.

We could hear frequent bursts from automatic rifles in the hall, with rare pistol shots echoing out in response. That meant someone was resisting the attackers.

Joshua split us up into two groups and gave me an order. "Stay behind me and don't go anywhere."

Bossy guy. But I still stood behind Joshua's back.

At a silent command from the detective, we moved into the hall as two units. I stopped sticking with the boss and ran to where the registration windows should have been. A single image was spinning in my head: Heylia Grant. What happened to her cute smile and thousand braids?

The hall was full of smoke and dust. I tripped over piles of bricks and civilian corpses, slipped on spent shell casings. The figure of a man emerged from the smoke before me. He wore an armored vest over a yellow jumpsuit. Since I was in civilian clothes, the bandit didn't realize right away that I wasn't a member of the public trying to escape. He lifted his assault rifle, but the bullet aimed at his forehead from my Glock was faster. Two more yellow figures appeared in the smoke. Annoyed that I couldn't loot the assault rifle, I dropped and rolled behind a pile of bricks with part of the registration window wall sticking out of it.

I looked through the window and watched as the bandits examined their dead comrade. They quickly split up and moved toward me, approaching from the right and left. Damn, I should have listened to Joshua... I heard screams and shots from our cops, but it was all too far away. Shouting for help would mean giving away my position.

Once again, I decided if I was going to die, I'd die well.

I leaned out of the registration window and aimed at a bandit. I shot a few times and he fell down on his back, but then rose and fired a long burst from his rifle.

The other bandit crouched behind a fallen locker and joined in on the firing. I pressed myself into the floor for a while, felt shards of broken brickwork shower down around me. A bullet found its way into my left shoulder.

I rose my head and looked around. The smoke had dispersed enough for me to see that the wall had collapsed. I saw a policeman crouching behind some overturned filing cabinets,  shooting. Two bandits lay opposite him, close to the outside exit. Not far behind them I saw Joshua and two cops slowly approaching the bandits.

The assault rifle fire stopped. Both bandits were reloading. I rose slightly and started crawling away. I had time to see one of the bandits frozen in the characteristic pose of a man throwing a grenade...

It landed exactly where I'd just moved from. I stopped trying to hide, rose all the way up and ran. The grenade exploded and I felt a rush of air at my back, felt as if I was running on rails trying to outrun a train. I didn't outrun it.

I flew ten feet, fell down near the collapsed wall of the registration section. Pain overcame me, the armored vest hung off me in rags and slipped down to the floor. One of the bandits aimed an assault rifle at me, but I didn't even have the energy to crawl away, let alone lift my Glock.

At that moment, someone grabbed me by the shoulder, dragged me across the floor and roughly pulled me behind some metal columns. It turned out the surviving cop had saved me. After I collected my wits, I grabbed a medkit, injected myself with a painkiller and took a pill to recover some health. If I survived, I'd go to the police hospital and buy some stronger health boosters. Then I helped my savior and remembered to say thanks.

He nodded silently. After the injection, the cop's white face reddened slightly, his sagging body lifted. He continued firing on the bandits with renewed energy.

I crouched and joined in. The bandits were between a rock and a hard place. We took out two, and the other two ran toward the exit. But Joshua Culkin ran after them, shouting.

"Where you goin'?! Stop!"

The huge square detective took an incredible leap — the kind I could take in my upgraded UniSuit — and crashed down on the fugitives. First he pressed them down with his body, took away their guns. Then he stood up, holding them by the scruffs of their necks. One of them got the guts to pull a knife. He found himself pressed against a wall.

"You guys, get outside!" the mighty detective ordered.

The cops and I ran over and jumped through the broken doors. It was chaos at the entrance to the police department: burning cars, damaged drones colliding and clattering to the ground. And in front of the stairs... That same bright blue car belonging to the player Hasty, that almost knocked me down by the park. The license plate was covered up, but I was no police drone. I had brains. I could easily remember a car. How could he have escaped that chase?

A bandit stood guard by the car's open door, in a yellow jumpsuit with a grenade launcher held atilt. When he saw cops running out of the door instead of his brothers, he got the picture. He put away the grenade launcher and jumped into the front seat. The engines roared and Hasty's car careered away. The cops started shooting while I took out my tablet and aimed it at the departing car.

*Chrysler Turbine Car.*
*Class: Streetracer.*
*Owner: Hasty Torpedo.*
*Speed: unknown.*

And a bunch of unknown parameters that required special skills for auto enthusiasts, mechanics and who knew what else.

After the attack on the police, the traffic jam had instantly cleared up. Several abandoned cars with open doors stood on the road, but none of them could have caught up to the bright-blue car of the Swiftville player.

Only the players in Central Park were enjoying beer and sandwiches, lazily watching yet another bout of mayhem.

I returned to the hall.

A draft cleared the smoke: the doors in the building were finally unlocked. Policemen and doctors walked among the ruins. They stacked the bodies they found against the wall. Joshua Culkin barked out orders, squads of well armed cops ran around in single file, taking up positions... What for? Seemed to me like the horse had already bolted.

Death in Adam Online looked terrible... when you had the right settings for it. Unfortunately, I did, and I couldn't change them. I passed by the bodies of the dead and saw all their death grimaces.

It's one thing when you fire an awesome headshot with an Uzi and your opponent's head explodes in a shower of blood like in a cartoon. With the violence settings on maximum, it even looked funny and grotesque.

Corpses were another matter.

The knowledge that they were NPCs didn't help much. Nobody needed realism like this... But I stubbornly walked by the rows of bodies until I stopped opposite one. Even death hadn't marred Heylia Grant's beauty. She lay half covered by a white sheet, her eyes closed and her full lips pursed.

A police medic pushed me away and covered Heylia's face. Nurses took the stretcher and lifted it. Thousands of braids fell from under the sheet.

So much for our stroll in the great outdoors.

I turned away.

Of course, the dead police officers were replaced by others. Police academy graduates. But the trouble was, only players were revived in Adam Online. Dead NPCs disappeared forever. Sure, if it was Heylia Grant's appearance that I needed, I could find a prostitute that would look just like her. All I had to do was visit an expensive brothel. Those places have all the equipment required to create a perfectly match.

But Heylia had something the whore wouldn't have: a personality prototype. Heylia knew me, the CSes had already activated creative functions for her. The longer I spoke with her, the more complex her behavior would have become. She'd have become less like an NPC, emulated human behavior more and more. It would have been more fun to spend time with her.

In the great outdoors.

"Ugh," I groaned, approaching Joshua Culkin.

The tireless detective sat quietly on a heap of bricks, himself looking like a giant brick, and smoked. He lifted his gaze to me.

"What did I tell you, rookie? Is that what you call staying behind me?"

"I couldn't just hide behind your back, sir."

Joshua stretched, discarded his cigarette butt and rose.

"If I give you an order, you follow it. I won't let it slide next time."

We approached a damaged police robot. It looked somehow sad. Its machine gun arms lay along its body, and its bent knees gave it a comical appearance. The robot's entire hull was riddled with bullet holes.

Joshua pulled a panel off the hull and looked inside. "Full ammo. It didn't take a single shot."

I touched some familiar blue shards littered all around with my foot. "Pulse grenades."

Joshua Culkin lit another cigarette. "What's going on in Liberty City? Where did all these guns come from?"

I barely held back a smile. There were plenty of weapons in every kiosk. But memories of Heylia's corpse snapped me back to seriousness.

"This means our investigation is even more important."

"That's right... But I doubt that the yellow piranhas have anything to do with weapon deliveries to the Luxor District."

"Why's that?"

Joshua chewed his cigarette. "They're a powerful criminal syndicate, but they're still criminals. They control the slums. Being outside the law is more important to them than just being. You saw for yourself that they're willing to die just to avenge a single arrest of one of their own."

The detective went quiet, giving me time to voice a suggestion.

"You think the criminal syndicates aren't the ones delivering weapons to the Luxor District?"

"That's right, rookie."

"If someone from outside the criminal world is doing this, then the question is..."

"Come on, rookie, surprise me."

"Why is this respectable person..."

"Or organization."

"Or organization, why are they robbing banks? Nobody at the height of society needs stolen money."

The detective laughed. Even his smile was square. "You have too high an opinion of capitalists. They created jurors and the banking system for robbery."

It hit me. "What if the bankers are robbing themselves?"

"But why?"

"Insurance? Covering up financial machinations?"

The detective put out his cigarette on the robot, took out another one, put it in his mouth, but didn't light it.

"Well done, Leo. But we've already considered that. The bankers are clean. But how clean can their dirty consciences be? They steal more than any syndicate, but in this case the bankers are the victims. Dig more. But your train of thought impresses me."

My tablet beeped.

*See? When you talk about important things, people*

*like it.*

*Reputation with Joshua Culkin increased: +3.*

"Happy to try, sir. Will you give me a badge?"

"Don't test my patience, kid." The square smile disappeared. "I told you, you have to earn the right to wave around a license to do whatever you want."

To change the subject and maintain my reputation, I pointed at the corpses on the stretchers. The nurses were picking them up and quickly carrying them off somewhere.

"We can't leave this unpunished."

"That's not your business, rookie. Don't worry, we know how to respond and when. Actually, rookie, you should head home. I'll call you when I need you."

Joshua Culkin lit his cigarette and headed toward a fallen coffee machine. It had taken a few bullets, but it was working. The square detective picked the machine up with a mighty heave and ordered himself a coffee.

I left the police building and my tablet squawked a series of signals:

*Two Golden Piranhas gang members killed: +10 XP.*

*You have continued to battle crime in the community. Your reputation with the authorities of all Rims has increased: +1.*

*The criminal elements consider your activities somewhat damaging to their own community. Your reputation with the Yellow Piranhas gang has dropped: -*

1.

*You helped the police deal with a bandit attack. Reputation with LCPD increased: +1.*

*Your current Reputation: 8.*

Yep, negative reputation with criminals was counted into the total amount. The more you helped good people, the less happy the bad ones got. So you couldn't reach the status of Saint, which was given when reputation reached one hundred or more, just by killing bad guys. Balance will be maintained.

In addition, the generosity of Rim Zero was all gone in Rim One. In the former, you got ten points for killing a player. Now it was only five. And if the player or NPC was very low in level, then you'd take a hit to your reputation and get the Degenerate achievement for killing the weak.

*Quest True Detective updated.*

*You visited Detective Culkin. Well done, that wasn't hard enough to merit a reward.*

*Here is something a little tougher:*

*1. Take part in the operation to get information from the agent infiltrating the thieves' gang.*

*2. Get a special detective badge.*

*3. Find out who is behind the weapon deliveries to the Luxor District.*

*4. Find out the thieves' organization's hidden goal.*

*...*

*That's all for now. Or is that not enough for you?*

I tapped on the line with the dots.

*Can't do it without hints? Can't think on your own? Here's another task:*

*5. Avenge Heylia Grant's murder (optional).*

*...*

I pressed on the three dots again.

*6. Coffee... Don't forget about coffee (optional).*

I put the tablet away.

Heylia... I understood, of course, that she was never alive, was never a person. She was just a complex imitation of what I, the player, wanted to hear and see. I even understood that her affection for me and her instantaneous death were among the hooks the CSes were using to influence me.

And it worked.

I hadn't spoken to such a cute and nice... person as Heylia in a long time. The saleswoman Irene was nice too, but I'd have to go to quite some effort to get her.

That was the whole point of the game. To make us try to achieve something. In Adam Online as in the real world.

We spend our whole lives trying to achieve things, then we die. Kind of like NPCs.

But NPCs existed for us. Who do we exist for?

# Chapter 7
# Company Secret

I DIDN'T HAVE very much money left, so I could forget about the Apple store. I found the nearest All-Seeing Eye and started looking at the goods on offer. A salesman approached me.

"Need any help?"

"Just browsing."

There wasn't much to browse. All I could afford were the Oculus One virtual reality glasses. Ordinary glasses that connected to your tablet and showed some stats. They had no interactive functions, just static information. Those glasses were very unreliable in battle, they had to be adjusted constantly. There was also a primitive upgrade for sale, Glasses Elastic.

If you tried to attach a string or some elastic you found yourself to the glasses, it would fall off in a couple of seconds. Want to upgrade items? Learn the right skills. Yep, even for something as simple as attaching a string. It was probably part of some skill.

Next to the glasses were some Oculus Tactics: they were broad, covering half the face. They attached to the head with a comfortable strap or straight to the UniSuit helmet. But they cost a ridiculous amount.

I sighed and confirmed the purchase.

*Obtained Oculus One Virtual Reality Glasses.*
*+1 Perception.*
*-50% to attractiveness with NPCs of a feisty, joking or aggressive character.*
*Price: 1,999g.*

The elastic also gave minus ten percent attractiveness with all NPCs. In other words, I'd better take them off before trying to play with anyone. So what was the point of the glasses? Shit. I was getting real sick of virtual poverty. Maybe I should just give up and become a bandit? Rob a bank, work for the mafia bosses. I remembered the sophisticated armor and spells that Vildana had. And Banshee and her gang had pretty good gear. Her katana alone was worth all I had.

I left the store with those thoughts. No, unfortunately my plan contradicted the idea of becoming a rich mafioso. I had to become a detective so I could use all the power of the police department in my search for Nelly Valeeva.

Makarov would sure be surprised when he found out that I'd found her without searching through the mist of Rim Five or Six, and far quicker than if I had. That would prove that the major general hadn't made a mistake when he chose me for this mission.

True, I did have one concern: what would I do when I found Valeeva? I had no instructions for that. Nobody knew what condition her binary array would be in. What if she wasn't capable of speech? What if... Never mind. I'd have to find her first. Then I could figure it out.

With those thoughts, I walked into some store with the unassuming name 'Johnny Lane: We Buy and Sell Weapons.' It was squeezed between a jewelry store and a specialist furniture store. Johnny Lane himself stood behind the counter, a wrinkled and hunched old man wrapped up in some kind of cotton waistcoat. No doubt about it — an NPC. No player would decide to look like an old man.

His stats didn't show anything except his name and employment. All the rest required at least fifty Knowledge. In other words, he was a trading final boss.

The wall behind the old man was covered in unusual weapons. A saber combined with a machine gun. A machine gun combined with a saw. An electric chainsaw whose chain, judging by the blue shimmer, had an extra Plasmashock effect. And much more that made my martial heart swell with joy.

"Hello, young man," the grandpa wheezed. "Looking for a fun way to get even with your enemies?"

"Firearms combined with bladed weapons? Sorry, gramps, that ain't my idea of a good time."

"So the young man is, as it were, a professional?"

Johnny Lane walked out from behind the counter, touched a column with his hand. The walls parted, revealing a hidden store room. The old coot took a wide-barreled pistol off the wall. It looked like a flare gun. He passed it to me.

"Here's something new for you, an incredible weapon. It doesn't kill, but it turns enemies into obedient allies."

*Obtained knowledge: Parasite Pistol.*

*Magazine: 1 shot.*

*Ammunition: container housing a bizoid telepath larva.*

*Damage: none.*

*Optimal range: 10-160 feet.*

*Price: 50,000g.*

*When the bizoid telepath larva hits your opponent, it turns them into an ally that will fight on your side. The lifespan of the larva depends on your current Health. Each point of health adds one second to the larva's lifespan. (Current duration: 8 seconds).*

*Bonus: when active, the larva steals one enemy health every second and transfers it to you.*

*Bonus: with Knowledge at 10, the larva is capable of retrieving random items from the enemy's inventory.*

*Bonus: with level of... (requires 10 Knowledge).*

*Bonus: unknown (requires 50 Knowledge).*

*Bonus: unknown (requires 100 Knowledge).*

*Attention: the bizoid telepath larva does not affect creatures with the Bizoid Seed Protection upgrade.*

*Attention: the larva does not affect mechanodestructors or angels.*

My eyes lit up. What a gun. We didn't have guns like this in my time, like we didn't have bizoids. The combination of biocrafting and weaponcrafting was something new to me. I didn't know why I might need the gun, what I'd do with it, but I wanted to have it in my collection.

I mentally shook myself, then returned the weapon indifferently.

"Sounds fun. But I came to sell, not to buy."

Johnny Lane's mood noticeably dropped.

"Are you sure? I'll give you a discount."

Instead of answering, I laid the Lefaucheux musket that I'd found at Three Bucks's camp on the counter. Johnny Lane turned the musket in his hands, took out a magnifying glass and examined the frame.

"Ooh! One of the Three Forms of Death muskets. The gunsmith Lefaucheux gave each of these muskets an ability that could guarantee the opponent's death.

"Yeah? What ability does this one have?"

"Unfortunately, my dear man, the features of the muskets remain unknown and do not work until the owner has all the muskets of the series."

"Will you buy it?"

"On two conditions. One: you trade the musket for the parasite pistol. Two: I'll promise to buy the other muskets at the highest price when you find them and bring them to me."

Hmm, suspicious. Why did the old man want to get rid of this pistol so bad? What was wrong with it? I was confused.

"Gramps, your sign says 'We Buy and Sell Weapons', not 'We Trade Bad for Worse.' If you want it, buy it, if you don't, I'll go somewhere else."

*Trading skill learned: +10 XP.*

*You are crude, short-sighted and treacherous. Excellent characteristics for a trader. Oh, and don't forget, this skill only works on NPCs. Other players may be cruder, more short-sighted and more treacherous than you.*

Johnny Lane smiled.

"You'll be conned anywhere else. I run an honest business. As it happens, I like you, I'll give you the pistol for twenty thousand and the musket. And the offer on the other guns in the series stays."

I took the musket.

"I don't have twenty thousand. And if I did, I wouldn't buy it."

Johnny Lane grabbed the musket at the other end.

"I can do credit."

I pulled the musket back.

"Credit so I can pay money I don't have yet for a gun I don't need?"

Johnny pulled the musket toward him.

"Payment by installments then?"

"I came to your store to get money for a gun. What does that mean, gramps?"

"That you robbed and killed someone?"

"Or that I need money."

Johnny Lane released the musket.

"How about this... I'll give you the pistol and two thousand, you give me the musket and sign a contract to search for the others."

"Or better, you give me the pistol and five thousand, I'll give you the musket and no promise to search for the others."

Johnny Lane frowned.

"Now I know for sure that you're a murderer and a thief. Really think you can treat me like this when I'm being so kind to you?"

"Yep."

The old man faked a sigh.

"Deal. But remember, I'm willing to pay more for the muskets than anyone else. Bring them only to me."

*Three Types of Death.*

*Find and bring to Johnny Lane all three Lefaucheux muskets.*

*Musket #1: not found.*

*Musket #2: completed.*

*Musket #3: not found.*

The musket found a new home on the wall in the spot previously occupied by the parasite pistol, which was now in my inventory. Along with five thousand gold. I checked how much ammo I had for the pistol, but it was at zero.

Hey, gramps, what about ammo?"

"Ammo wasn't part of the deal, young man," Johnny replied calmly. "If you want to buy telepath larvae, they're one hundred gold a piece."

"Alright, how many do you have?"

Johnny placed seven glass vials on the counter. A semi-transparent creature floated in green liquid within each vial. They looked like fetuses. The creatures stirred their fins weakly. One pressed a dull eyeball against the glass and opened its mouth.

I got the vials and the old man got seven hundred gold.

*Obtained: vials of bizoid telepath larvae.*

*Ammunition for the parasite pistol.*

*Unknown property (requires 50 Knowledge).*

*Unknown property (requires Biocrafting skill).*

Another message appeared above that one:

*Eagle Eye skill increased: +5 XP.*

*These bizoid telepaths look a little the worse for wear, don't you think?*

I shook a vial in front of the old man.

"What's wrong with them?"

"They're fine."

Johnny Lane didn't even blink when the bizoid in the vial I shook floated to the top, its belly up. The interface confirmed that the ammunition was no good.

"This one... This one is dead."

"The expiry date is near," the old man answered coolly. "They'll all be dead in a week."

I took a deep breath, preparing to give him a piece of my mind, but the old man spoke calmly.

"You wanted the pistol? You have it. You can get fresh ammo at Haldane Lake, they make these vials there."

*Marker added to map: Rim Four, Haldane Lake.*

I just helplessly dropped my hands.

"Can I find them in Liberty City?"

"I doubt it, young man. I have the rarest goods in town. Nobody else has them. It's not my fault the vials are perishable, is it?"

I got a grip on myself. What could I expect from a person... um, from an NPC that looked like a conman? A crystal-clear conscience? That I had to earn by increasing my reputation.

*Trading skill increased: +5 XP.*

*No con, no sell. Learn how to sell spoiled goods to rookies like yourself.*

I put some other items on the counter: powder and bullets for the musket, AK ammo, some upgrades: Autolooter, Stabbing and Cutting Strike, the 'Activity' Bidirectional Sexual Pleasure Booster. Johnny Lane cast a hypercritical glance on each of them. He shook his head at the pleasure booster.

"Pointless. Who wants to make love in a UniSuit?"

I looked away.

"Each to their own. Some wouldn't mind doing it on a chair, or in a bus."

"Out of respect for you, I'll give you four thousand for all this garbage."

"Ten."

There must have been something in my voice. Johnny cringed and nodded.

"Sure, sure. But... Nine."

I nodded sternly. I decided I'd earn money off some side quests until Joshua Culkin called me. Although I wasn't sure that working with this crook Johnny Lane would make me much gold.

I stopped before leaving the store.

"Any ideas where I can find those muskets?"

"You're the tracker, you find 'em."

"So far the tracks only led to you. Tell me, why do you need these muskets so bad?"

Johnny Lane scratched his nose.

"Heh, trackers these days. Look around, tell me what you see. That's right, a store that trades in unusual weapons. And the muskets are unusual. But they have to be with each other to work properly. Look... I can tell you aren't much of a tracker. Might need some help.

Here, take this."

*Obtained: Old Map.*

The yellowed old piece of paper was a hand-drawn diagram of streets. At its center was a drawing reminiscent of breasts... Or did everything remind me of breasts these days? In the corner of the page was the monogram of the gunsmith Lefaucheux. And a heading:

*Evil itself hides beneath the ground.*
*But only the good can reveal the truth.*

That was clear enough; the musket was buried in some kind of treasure trove. But where? And what did 'the good' mean? Maybe only players with high reputation could find the trove? But how high?

I suddenly remembered how the landlord had bragged about his bunker, saying it was so deep under the ground you could hear the devil knocking. Kind of a creepy coincidence.

No matter how much I studied the map and span it around to look from different perspectives, I found nothing new. It looked like I just had to find the place on the map and dig up the damn musket. But there was a problem with the search; most of the city was shrouded in cloud on my map, which meant it was unexplored territory. Even if I got a complete map, I'd go crazy trying to match this paper up to it. And the boob-like squiggles didn't clarify much.

I started puzzling it out step by step.

I left the Central Park district and the police department a while back. There were lots of restaurants and bars there. The signs blinked, span and did all they could to draw in customers. Hmm, maybe I should spend the rest of the money on food? I hadn't eaten for several days. My consciousness hadn't yet adapted to the fact that I could just not eat. I kept getting hunger pangs.

I was dreaming of a well cooked steak and a glass of cold beer. In the real world, a lunch like that with real steak would have cost me a week's pay. But thanks to Adam Online, nobody in the world had to feel financially strangled. Everyone could eat virtual steak that was like the real thing.

Only someone who had tried meat in real life could tell the difference. Here Adam Online definitely matched up to the expression "Better than in the real world." Real meat, which I'd eaten plenty of in kebabs at Makarov's manor, was too sinewy, or too fatty, too bony. In other words, it had flaws. Like everything in the real world.

My glance fell on a cafe sign that read 'Star Buck.' On the sign was an astronaut who had raised his helmet visor to enjoy a cup of hot coffee. I guess the slogan 'Taste of Earth' was meant to imply that the coffee was the most natural, the tastiest, the most pure. Ironic for virtual coffee in a virtual world.

I went into the cafe and picked up a pack of the most expensive coffee at the counter. Then I went out, called a taxi.

"Police department, please."

"They say there was another explosion there today," the driver said. "The Yellow Piranhas are mighty upset. It's a war, bro."

"Uh-huh."

I took out my tablet and opened my stats. I put two points into Knowledge, taking it up to ten, and two points into Insight, increasing it to level two. I needed to improve my skills of communicating with NPCs.

*Insight skill increased to level 1.*
*Unlocked additional NPC stat: Interests.*
*Now you can find out what an NPC is looking for in life.*

*Insight skill increased to level 2.*
*Prompter. Even more hints to help you use the previous hints.*

I was missing one point of Knowledge before I could unlock the unknown property of my Max Payne leather jacket.

Concrete blocks surrounded the front entrance to the LCPD building. Central Park was similarly protected. Police mechs and armored transports guarded the entrances and exits. Three helicopters circled above the district, and countless drones swarmed at the height of the street lamps. The street had been cleared of burnt out cars, the crime scene investigators had studied the evidence, gathered up the shell casings and picked things up from the asphalt with tweezers.

The police mechs categorically refused to let me inside the building. Reminding them of my acquaintance with Joshua Culkin didn't help. If they'd been people, my Insight skill might have helped a little. But how could you influence mechanodestructors whose character line read 'Strict' and whose interests were 'Serve the interests of the LCPD.'

"Did you mishear me again, rookie?" Joshua Culkin growled, splitting off from a group of investigators. "What do you need?"

I waved the coffee packet.

"Not here for you, I want your coffee machine."

"My coffee machine doesn't give just anyone coffee," the detective frowned. "Come on, I'll make sure you don't break it."

Joshua's office had been tidied up a little. The furniture was clear of dust, the shards of glass were in a pile, and two workers stood by the windows, installing glass in the frames. Police drones watched them from outside the window.

The detective brushed away the dust caked on the coffee machine. When the coffee was ready, he poured two cups. We sat down just as we had the last time. Him in the armchair, me on the chair opposite.

"Ah, rookie..." Joshua took a sip and closed his eyes. "You know how to be an asshole and a good guy at the same time."

I took a sip too. Tasty. Some messages about coffee buffs lit up in my glasses, but I quickly cleared them. They were meaningless. What was the point of seeing that I'd gotten plus one to Agility for a few minutes? I was just sitting in a chair, not running.

*Coffee Break.*
*Well done, good job, the boss is happy.*
*Reputation with Joshua Culkin increased: +1.*

The detective leaned back in his chair and took out a cigarette.

"So why're you here without an invite?"

I took out the map and put it in front of him.

"I need to find this place in Liberty City."

The detective looked at the doodle in the center of the map.

"What's this? Tits?"

"Possibly."

"How do you plan to find this place?"

"Using the departmental database. I need access to your system so the computer can analyze the drawing and find matches with the city map."

Joshua lit his cigarette and blew out a puff of smoke.

"You gone cuckoo? Who'll give you access to our system? You don't even have a badge."

It was a good thing the detective didn't ask what I was looking for.

"Maybe you will?"

The detective took a long look at me, then sipped his coffee, stretched. More coffee, another stretch. I held his gaze, but tried to look calm and untroubled. The detective scooped up the map and rose.

"Make some more coffee, I'll be back soon."

# Chapter 8
# Two in the Dark

THE TAXI DRIVER barely waited for me to get out of the car. He shot right off. The taxi careered away, splashing through puddles until it was too far for me to hear. I stood in a gap between two old buildings. Dimpled red bricks, abyssal black windows, doors and fire escapes banging and screeching in the wind.

The LCPD computer had identified this street junction on the map. As for the drawing that looked like tits, it was the roof of an abandoned temple in the Stanton District, a slum in Liberty City where few lived except players and NPCs with a negative ranking.

The taxi driver even doubled his price to get me here.

The place was empty of people. The only signs of life I saw were unusually large rats darting along the walls of houses. One froze, rose up on its hind legs and twitched its whiskers, sniffing me.

*Liberat.*
*Level: 7.*
*Giant mutant rats that live in the sewers of Liberty City. Judging by the color of their teeth, the liberat was*

*poisonous.*

A second liberat stopped nearby, then a third. Their legs looked like muscular human arms. As I walked, a few more popped up. Then I took out my Tesla revolver. The clever creatures knew that gesture. In a blur of fur, they all disappeared into hiding.

Before I came to the slums, I went home to grab my UniSuit, Uzi and revolver. But I decided not to activate the UniSuit just yet. I doubted there would be bandits in the slums as heavily armed as those in the deserts of Rim Zero. And high-level mobs like the soldiers of the Yellow Piranhas didn't hang around here. On top of that, I brought a spade. I had treasure to dig up, after all.

I walked along the alleyway between the buildings. The rats' squeaks and clicking claws followed me all the way. Thick shade fell from the buildings. It was noticeably colder than in the more respectable parts of the city. The sun refused to shine here. The liberats would bite it. The temple was meant to be at the end of the street, after a right turn. That was if I believed the map piece that Joshua Culkin gave me.

The street was covered in garbage. Bottles, boxes, food packages and beer cans. My Eagle Eye signaled some discoveries: ammo, rusty scissors, rotting weaponry. None of it interested me. An item hung off the remains of a rusty car: Vagrant's Rags. It gave plus fifteen percent to stealth during the day, upgraded the lockpicking skill, and allowed you to tame liberats. The number of liberats you could tame was equal to your Knowledge.

God knows who would want to be a vagrant, but it still seemed a better choice than a bizoid to me.

I heard a familiar chirp from above. A police drone quickly descended on me.

"Dear citizen, the police department asks you to refrain from taking strolls in this city district. In spite of our attempts to prevent crime, we cannot currently guarantee your safety."

I nodded and kept going. The drone hovered above me for a while.

"Dear citizen, the police department warns you: this district is unsafe due to aggressive creatures and damaged infrastructure. Walking in this area may lead to injury or death. Are you sure you wish to continue?"

"I am, thanks."

The drone flew on a few moments longer, then quickly rose above the roofs and disappeared. Such a caring police force.

The farther I went down the street, the darker it got. The liberats got bolder. One ran across the road just a few feet from me. I aimed and fired. The Tesla revolver charge lit up the walls of the houses. I watched in the gloom as the blue stream of energy reached the liberat and bored a hole in its body.

The drums span, the air around the revolver shimmered again, and I shot a second creature hiding behind a garbage can. The liberats didn't stop following me, but they got more careful. Stopped running around in the open. I'd taken out seven more before I reached the turn. Each gave me one XP.

The abandoned temple stood in an empty lot. It was gloomy and cold. But a ray of light fell on the temple itself, making it stand out from the other structures. I started to cross an obstacle course of holes full of dim water swarming with worms. The liberats made themselves known again. I had to kill a couple before they left me alone. It was a good thing the Tesla revolver was quiet. I didn't want to make much noise in this abandoned place. Who knew what monsters I might wake up?

*Achievement Liberator completed: +50 XP.*
*Kill 10 liberats.*
*Completed: 10/10.*

*Achievement unlocked: Liberator II.*
*Kill 100 liberats.*
*Completed: 10/100.*

I was still around sixty feet from the temple when I saw a flash of light in the dark windows of the temple. I immediately ducked behind a pile of bricks and hid. There, the light flashed again. This time it was in another window, as if someone was walking around with a flashlight!

I took out my tablet and activated my UniSuit, swapped my Tesla revolver for the Uzi. Then I waited until the flashes of light weakened, which meant that the person with the flashlight had gone deeper into the building. I ran from my pile of bricks to another, splashing through worm-infested water.

Soon I reached the entrance. The ramshackle door barely held on its hinge. The temple wasn't Christian, it belonged to one of the made-up religions. Even in virtual reality, I didn't want to defile a church by running around it and shooting. Although it was a little annoying that the domes that everyone thought looked like tits looked a lot like the domes of Eastern Orthodox churches.

I spent a few minutes thinking about which CS algorithms were responsible for not offending religious beliefs, or not discriminating by sex or race. It must take an incredible amount of resources to calculate all that. And for what? Just to create the scenery for a quest.

The floor in the temple was wooden in places, stone in others. I felt garbage beneath my feet, but I made no sound. Silent movement was one of the class bonuses of the tracker. However, the silence didn't extend to fast walking or running.

I kept walking through the temple's rooms. Sometimes I ran into statues of deities, sometimes got tangled in drapes covering niches containing other statues. I had to walk around big holes in the floor. My Night Vision adapted to the darkness, but unfortunately, the farther I went, the less I could make out the outlines of items. My Night Vision didn't let me see in pitch black, of course. Night Vision required at least some weak light. Seeing in the dark wasn't available to people directly, they had to get it through upgrades.

I saw the outlines of a door ahead, then suddenly saw light. I hid in a niche in the wall covered by ragged drapes. I heard footsteps and saw an orb of light float out of the door. Behind the orb walked a familiar figure in armor.

Vildana didn't look from side to side, she just stared at the palm of her hand where Three Bucks's amulet lay.

The stone at the amulet's core flashed red sometimes, with long delays in between.

*Vildana, War Mage*
*Level: 24.*
*Health: 5,000/5,000.*
*Armor: 745/12,000.*
*Other types of defense: unknown (requires 15 Knowledge).*
*Childkiller, Degenerate, Enemy of Society, Poisoner, Destroyer, Thief, Anti-Social Element.*
*Warning: Vildana's Reputation is -68! The authorities will be grateful if you kill this villain or deliver her to the police.*

Vildana cast her gaze around the room. It held for a second on my hiding place. She turned and left, keeping her eyes on the amulet. The orb of light floated behind her. I waited for it to get farther away, jumped out of cover and followed. Vildana moved faster; I had to tread carefully. Soon she disappeared in the maze of corridors.

I wondered how she'd gotten there. I thought she'd have gone to a magic zone, somewhere in the worlds of Goldivar and Himmelbleu, a separate fantasy universe with several different kingdoms, continents and an ocean.

I sped up to a fast walk, listening carefully. I heard a rumble, then it sounded as if a heap of sand was falling in from somewhere. I followed the sound and reached the entrance to the prayer hall.

It was brighter here. The sunlight illuminating the temple from outside fell through a hole in the roof. At the center of the hall stood a statue of a two-headed and six-armed creature. Dust glinted in the rays of light, and multicolored butterflies darted around, alarmed by Vildana's presence. The creature was a god. It had defeated the forces of evil and driven them underground. A vanquished snake or dragon twisted between the six-armed god's feet. I recalled the message on the map: "Evil itself hides beneath the ground." It was easy to figure out where to dig.

The girl dropped the amulet, which now burned an unceasing red. She took out another of her spell scrolls, muttered something. The scroll turned to vapor in her hand. Vildana extended her hand, closed her fingers and jerked her arm up as if pulling someone out of water.

The floor began to heave and bulge under the influence of magical forces. Bricks flew to the side, a heap of earth and stones flew up and hung in the air. Vildana shook her closed fist and the clump of earth quickly crumbled, revealing a chest. Vildana drew the chest toward her in the air and unclenched her fist. The chest fell at her feet with a crash. She took out her sword and cut off the lock.

Damn. I was the one that gave her the amulet that could find treasure. And abandoned historical or religious buildings were the best places for that. But even taking that into account, the chance of us coincidentally meeting on a treasure hunt was too low to look like anything but an absurd set-up. Liberty City had dozens of abandoned places. Even just in the slums.

What was I to do? Openly talk to her? She'd cut me down without a second thought. Just like I fought for my good reputation, she'd fought for a bad one. And had far more success than me.

Dropping down to her knees, Vildana opened the

lid of the chest. No matter how I stretched my neck, I couldn't see what was inside, but Vildana soon made it clear enough.

"Shit, just garbage..." With those words, she started throwing item after item out of the chest. A joyful exclamation told me that she'd found something useful.

She took off her helmet and equipped a tiara that immediately began to gleam under the rays of sunlight. The girl rose and jabbed the chest with her foot. Adjusting her tiara, she began to walk around the hall.

# Chapter 9
# Losses

I DECIDED TO WAIT a little longer. Who knows, maybe the treasure chest with the musket inside wouldn't be visible to her amulet? But my worst fears came true: the stone stubbornly gleamed red. Vildana walked around the statue for a while, looking for the right spot.

"Alright," Vildana said. "The last scroll..."

She activated a spell. The earth bulged again and a large flat box emerged bearing the Lefaucheux crest. It floated closer to Vildana and she lowered it to the ground. She got down on her knees and sighed in happiness.

"Ooh! It's so big..!"

Okay... I took out my tablet and brought up the description of my Uzi in my glasses. It dealt fifty five damage. Plus another ten to fifteen from the upgrade. Vildana's health was five thousand in total. Her armor was almost nonexistent. With her reputation, not many would agree to fix it for her... But the line 'other forms of defense' threw me for a loop. That could mean something that my gun couldn't deal with.

On the other hand, I had the element of surprise on my side. I could get close and start shooting right away. Fire all sixty rounds into her gorgeous back. Just a shame I hadn't upgraded my reload speed. I'd have to hide after emptying my magazine... Hmm, but where? The temple hall was large and empty. Vildana moved faster than me. She only needed to catch up to me once and cut me down. Or throw fireballs, or shoot explosive arrows... In other words, after I emptied my magazine I'd be defenseless for a few seconds. I looked up. That was it. I could jump onto the statue. My UniSuit upgrade would let me jump ten feet. Enough to climb even higher and get over the top of the statue, hiding from any return fire from Vildana. A nice ivory tower for me. Then I could reload and say good bye to the pretty mage.

"Fucking bastards!" Vildana cried.

She stood up and kicked the chest with the musket. Just as I thought; only someone with a positive reputation could open the chest. I gripped the handle of my Uzi. What if I did speak to Vildana? Maybe offer a share of the reward from Joshua? Yeah, that'd be the best outcome.

I felt a sudden pain in my left foot. Short, but sharp.

*Damage taken: -32.*
*Watch your step. A liberat bit you.*
*You are poisoned by liberat venom:*
*-1 to all stats for an unknown duration (requires Military Toxicology level 2).*

The mutant rat scrabbled around my feet. Its huge body shivered odiously. I tried to kick it away with my foot. I couldn't shoot. Not only would the noise give me away, I'd also have less ammo for Vildana.

*Damage taken: -29.*

*The liberat again... Are you enjoying this, or something..?*

I managed to crouch down and hit the liberat in the face. It let out a loud whine and went quiet. I rushed to turn around... Too late. Vildana raised her hand, casting some force field spell on herself. As the force field surrounded her body, it emitted a wave. Raising a wall of rubble and dust before it, the wave hit me and threw me back several yards.

My vision blurred, my head span. The system brought up some information on my virtual reality glasses, but that was the last thing on my mind. Those logs were more of a hindrance in a fast-paced battle.

"Is that you, old buddy?!" Vildana shouted. "I remember promising to cut your head off!"

I tried to stand, but my feet and arms wouldn't go where I told them.

"Wait! I wasn't going to attack you!"

"Sure, sure. You had that gun ready just in case? And your UniSuit equipped. Don't **** with me now."

My vision cleared. Vildana moved toward me, still projecting a force field around her, pushing away dust and stones as she walked. She raised her hand and a rusty axe appeared in it.

"Afraid my sword broke. I'll have to cut you down with a shitty blunt axe."

I opened my mouth to sue for peace again, but then I felt another pain, this time in my right foot.

*You got bit again. Damage taken: -26.*

"God damn, I'm sick of you guys!" I shouted

before kicking the liberat. It squeaked and flew toward Vildana, hitting her force field and leaving a bloodstain on the invisible wall.

"You throw dead animals now? That's new."

Vildana started spinning her axe above her head. The force field reached me, constricting my movements. Raising my hand and aiming my gun was a struggle. And Vildana's rusty axe span on overhead. Up close, I saw that her armor was in a terrible state: torn, cut, covered in strange white streaks, probably the poisonous emissions of some unknown beast.

A little late, I realized that the Tesla revolver would be more useful here. Vildana didn't pay much attention to defense against energy weapons. Although mages had good skills for resisting it.

I let Vildana come a little closer, then pressed the trigger.

I had lived long enough to realize something: any endeavor required planning in advance. But I'd also figured out that any plan became worthless as soon as you put it into action. It was time to get wise and remember that after figuring out your plan, you had to figure out another one for when everything went south.

Nothing ever goes like it should.

I'd planned to be in Rim Five, but started in Zero. I'd planned to finish my first quest quick, but ate a bullet from Amy. I'd planned to empty my magazine into Vildana... Well, I'd done that at least. Her health had dropped to a thousand and change, and continued to fall. The remains of her armor fell along with her health.

Vildana was back in the dirty dress she wore when held at Three Bucks's pleasure. She was also thoroughly covered in blood. It splattered all over the floor around her. Damn those high violence settings.

My Uzi shots prevented Vildana from moving, but didn't stop her from smiling as she took another bullet strengthened with incendiary and explosive effects.

When a series of empty clicks replaced the hail of bullets, Vildana even got upset.

"Is that all? That was quick... A one pump man, huh?

It was time for me to jump onto the statue as I'd planned... but the force field pressed me to the floor, I couldn't jump over so much as a brick. Vildana herself moved quickly and deftly. I'd just thrust my hand into the chest compartment of my UniSuit when her axe fell. She cut off my hand. I felt that horrible feeling again, seeing my hand at my feet, still clutching an Uzi magazine.

"Oops. I hope that wasn't your favorite hand." Vildana laughed.

The blood from my stump sprayed my face, and the system squawked out a notification:

*Damage taken: -1,000. Left hand lost.*
*Heavy blood loss: -10 health per minute.*
*Damage taken: -27, liberat bite.*
*Damage taken: -32, liberat bite.*
*Damage taken: -21, liberat bite.*

It was as if those little bastards had made a deal with Vildana. Why didn't they go for her? Did the force field save her, or the aura of her negative reputation?

Half blinded, I trampled on the creatures haphazardly. Sometimes I hit one. Mostly I just took more bites. Vildana walked around me, lazily waving her axe.

"How did you end up here?"

"I wanted to see you."

"Happy now?"

"No. I was hoping for a hug. Please don't cut off any more hands..."

Another wave of that axe. My knee suddenly felt cold, as if my leg had been plunged into cold water. Pain followed the chill. I couldn't help but scream.

*Damage taken: -1,000. Left leg lost.*

Naturally, I couldn't keep upright. I fell down, to the gratitude of the liberats.

*Damage taken: -22, liberat bite.*
*Damage taken: -19, liberat bite.*
*Damage taken: -20, liberat bite.*

*You've been bitten so many times that you just couldn't help but learn a useful lifehack for this new way of life.*
*Poison Resistance skill learned: +10 XP.*
*Duration of poison debuffs reduced by 15%.*

I didn't know what Vildana's plan was. Nothing ever goes like it should. That was all that gave me hope. If you plan something and it goes wrong, then the same thing has to happen to everyone else sometimes.

Of course, I didn't think of any of that while I was lying on the floor bleeding and watching as the axe fell and cut off my right leg. I completely lost any interest in what was happening. I wanted it to just end, wanted to rematerialize at the respawn point or the Projectoria station. It didn't matter.

My augmented reality glasses stubbornly showered me with useless data.

*Damage taken: -19, liberat bite.*
*Damage taken: -22, liberat bite.*

Then, as if for variety:

*Damage taken: -1,000. Right leg lost.*

I moved my gaze to the six-armed god. It was beautiful work. The god had a human face, and pointed ears like an elf. Vildana said something then, probably a witty remark. I wasn't listening anymore.

Nothing ever goes like it should.

For example, through the system messages and drops of blood on my glasses, I watched as the temple roof, those same breast-like domes, suddenly collapsed. Sunlight chased away the liberats. The sun blinded me too, so I didn't notice the police drones flooding through the breach right away. Six in all. They flew at Vildana. She managed to cut one down with her axe. The rest, after reading her her rights and inviting her to surrender, opened fire. Vildana waved her axe in response and swore so badly that even Amy would have blushed. Shards of drones littered the floor. It even seemed like Vildana had won. But then the temple wall collapsed. Several police mechs leapt into the hall, emitting their strange ethereal cries.

"Fuck," Vildana said.

The robots asked her to surrender, but Vildana raised her axe and took a step forward. Then they opened fire with all their machine guns. No force field would have saved her from that kind of firepower. Vildana was thrown back to the wall, and the mechs kept shooting until her body stopped moving.

A police drone hovered above me.

"Detective Culkin conveys his salutations and the following message: 'I knew you'd get into trouble in those slums.'"

"Shame I can't wave at him right now."

The drone flew off and was replaced by an ambulance drone.

"You have been seriously wounded. Which hospital would you like to be delivered to? Liberty City Civil Clinic, Veterinary Clinic, the Freedom Hospital for the Disabled..."

"Doctor Cid's clinic."

"Understood."

"Grab all my limbs and gear. And that box over there too."

"Of course, sir."

A drone with a damaged hull grabbed the box with the musket and lifted it. I was put into an ambulance drone. After which, thank God, the game saved me from the need to lie down waving my stumps around until I arrived. One of the world's conditions came into force: I was supposedly injected with something. I closed my eyes.

There's no bad without good: thanks to Vildana's butchering tendencies, I'd completed that crazy Invalid quest from Dr. Cid; I'd lost all my limbs. The pain? The pain was just as hellish. But... I seemed to be getting used to it.

# Chapter 10
# Minimum Information

IT'S SAFE TO SAY that I left Dr. Cid's clinic thoroughly relaxed. It was a purely psychological sensation. You could only get tired in Adam Online for a short time, depending on your Health level.

The doctor sewed all my limbs back on, rewarded me with everything he'd promised, and offered me a new quest: to collect and bring him other people's amputated limbs. Cid didn't have enough materials to work with. But I decided I wouldn't do that. Cut off other people's arms and legs and take them to a clinic? Fuck that. I had more interesting matters to attend to. I still hadn't used the Sexodrome bed for what it was designed for.

I'd gone up two levels, and with them I had two spare stat and skill points. I invested in more Knowledge, raising it up to nine, and Luck too, to five.

I opened my tablet and checked my inventory. The items with additional skills revealed were highlighted green. The first thing I checked was what hid behind the previously unknown property of the leather Max Payne jacket.

*Unlocked skill Time Slow: 3 seconds.*

*Attention: this skill works only when the item is equipped. It disables when the UniSuit is activated.*

*Cooldown: 16 minutes (increase Agility to reduce cooldown time).*

*Attention: this skill is useless against an enemy with an identical or similar skill.*

Not bad, although it wasn't much.

What else had my increased Knowledge unlocked? The telepathic bizoid larva in my parasite pistol would now give me random items from the enemy's inventory.

In addition:

*Bonus: when the Biocrafting skill is increased to level 2, you can use larvae to restore 100% health (either to yourself or to an ally). This destroys the larva.*

Eh. A little too complicated. Biocrafting didn't interest me much. And shooting myself with gross larvae interested me even less.

Next:

*Doc Martens Boots.*
*Unlocked skill Sprint.*
*You can run 300 feet in five seconds. Be careful when turning, don't fall on your face.*
*Cooldown: 24 hours.*

Incidentally, it's worth noting that the cooldowns in the item descriptions were shown in game time, not real time.

I had to spend my skill points on... Hmm, that was a mystery. I couldn't figure out what was important and

THE CITY OF FREEDOM

what wasn't. After all, nothing ever goes like it should. I thought I'd quickly level up by sticking to firearms, preferably rifles and shotguns. Instead, I was using an automatic Uzi and a Tesla energy gun. I thought I'd track down Nelly using Tracker skills. Instead, I was getting into fights at short ranges in which Trackers had no advantages. Should I change my class?

I opened my skill list:

*Pistols and Revolvers (Default), level 1. (Max Payne Leather Overcoat +1).*
*Rifles and Shotguns (Tracker).*
*Eagle Eye (Tracker), level 3.*

*Automatic Weapons, level 2.*
*Battlefield Surgery, level 2.*
*Radiation Resistance, level 1.*
*Night Vision.*
*Energy Weapons.*
*Military Toxicology.*
*Explosives.*
*High Climber.*
*Decorator.*
*Knife Combat.*
*Insight, level 2.*
*Seducer.*
*Poison Resistance.*

*Time Slow (Max Payne Leather Overcoat).*
*Sprint (Doc Martens Boots)*

On the other hand, I liked what I had. Eagle Eye had helped me out a lot, along with Night Vision, Silent Movement and Stealth. Overall, the Tracker class seemed promising. I opened the class sheet:

*Tracker class bonuses:*

*Class skills Eagle Eye and Rifles and Shotguns available, along with accelerated leveling for these skills.*

*Accelerated leveling for Night Vision and High Climber.*

*Improved hearing. The higher your Perception, the farther away you can hear things.*

*Additional stat unlockable at level 30: Accuracy.*
*A Tracker's Accuracy is always two percent higher than hostile NPCs or players, apart from those who are also Trackers or have other accuracy upgrades.*

*Silent movement. The Tracker's steps are silent for NPCs or other players apart from those with improved hearing. When using ground vehicles, engine noise is 20% quieter.*

*Improved stealth in darkness. NPCs or players with lower Perception than the Tracker cannot see them at night time or in dark buildings.*
*At Perception 10, tracks become visible on soft surfaces (grass, sand, etc.) more clearly than to other people. At Perception 30, the Tracker can see tracks on hard surfaces. At Perception 100, the Tracker gains the ability to see a transparent representation of whatever left the tracks, i.e. recreate an image of what happened (requires a special UniSuit upgrade or the Circumstantial Simulation skill).*

*At Knowledge 200, the Tracker can see through walls and items, and also gains other skills.*

I decided that even if my plans all went awry in the first second, that was no reason not to follow them. I had to put effort into staying the course, otherwise I'd confuse my ideas and plans and screw up.

I saved my skill points. Necessity could tell me where to invest them later.

The Dr. Cid's Clinic that I'd been delivered to was in an unknown district, so I decided to get to the Johnny Lane store via the subway. Helpfully, every subway station was near a Projectoria station. More and more green points appeared on my map.

It was empty in my subway car, save for some homeless person sitting in a corner, drinking from a bottle. My augmented reality glasses showed an exclamation mark above his head, but I had enough quests as it was.

I opened the Adam Online social network page on my tablet.

Two people had sent me friend requests. Banshee, the bandit that I'd successfully killed at the bus stop. Banshee was just as bald and angry-looking in her avatar as in the game. I could see the pommels of her twin katanas behind her back. She'd changed her clothes for Samurai garb, which probably gave her crazy bonuses to Agility. Banshee had attached an audio recording to the friend request: "Still alive, asshole? I'll fix that soon."

The second friend request was from Offo. He had a mohawk instead of a clean shaven head, and he wore a black leather jacket covered in studs. Offo sent me a video message of him and Ghost standing with arms around each other's shoulders in front of some bar in the slums. Ghost had already leveled up into a muscular boxer in gold gloves.

"You really played us, dude," Offo said. "We believed your tales about rich drivers like chumps. Anyway, Leo, join my guild and you can be our top lieutenant."

Ghost elbowed Offo in the side. "I'm your top lieutenant," he whispered.

"I'm planning to take over the criminal underworld in Liberty City, I'll need lots of lieutenants."

Offo's page was full of videos, achievement badges and other signs of bravado like incredibly rare weaponry and gear. He had placed his minus reputation number at the center, along with his detailed stats and all his skills and achievements. He was proud of his negative reputation, although he was a long way off Vildana still.

I added them all to my friends list. I realized something amusing: all the female players I'd met seemed to want to kill me. Amy would attack me because she knew I'd want vengeance. Banshee wanted to avenge herself. And Vildana... she'd already tried to kill me just because. For fun.

Unfortunately, I couldn't find Vildana on the social network. There were around five thousand users with that name. I'd hoped to be able to add her. I wanted to make sure she wasn't holding a grudge against me. After all, it was the police robots that had killed her, not me.

The girl knew magic and magic characters. That meant she could help me with the mysterious sword I found in the secret cache in the apartment. On the other hand, her character had died, which meant that right now, she'd be hard at work in Rim Zero, leveling up a new one. There was no guarantee that she hadn't returned to a negative rating.

After this, I started searching for the person I'd opened the social network for in the first place. I entered into the search bar: "Hasty, Swiftville, Chrysler Turbine Car."

One result appeared: a standard page with the minimum information. It mentioned that Hasty competed in the yearly Big Race, one of the most noteworthy events in Rim One.

The Big Race took place on the outskirts of Swiftville and it lasted twenty four hours. All types of wheeled ground vehicles equipped with internal combustion engines took part. The Big Race was an exhibition of the incredible cars that players assembled themselves or bought in corporate car showrooms or from other players. The rules of the Big Race allowed aggression. You could knock out enemy cars any way you liked, as long as you didn't use magic, firearms or energy weapons. The cars were fitted with saws, spears, spinning discs and other devices. There was a myriad of options for tactics on the track.

The popularity of the Big Race and cars in general was easily explained. In real life, people had no access to private transport. Only the well-heeled could afford their own electromobile. Or middle-class people like me who weren't paying off loans for a pod or dissociative electrolyte.

I sent a friend request to Hasty. I hoped to learn

more about him or to ask about his involvement in the raid on the police department. Crossover quests like that, where players encountered other players, weren't rare.

The subway train stopped at the station I needed, and I got out not far from the street that was home to the 'Johnny Lane: We Buy and Sell Weapons' store.

Johnny Lane, the old rogue, cheat and all-round bastard, had a pleasant surprise for me. Without haggling or prevaricating, he transferred fifty thousand gold for the musket.

"I'll give you a hundred for the third gun."

I scratched the back of my neck. Did I have this wrong? What if the muskets were a super-class weapon? But I imagined the process of loading a musket and grimaced. No matter what incredible abilities they possessed, the long reload time was a serious flaw.

With those thoughts, I walked out of the store.

Life was finally starting to look up. I had sixty five thousand gold, free time and a desire to test out my Sexodrome bed. I reached the nearest Projectoria station and teleported to the street with the Middle Class store.

Why was it so important to me to get Irene in particular into bed, or another advanced NPC? Sure, I could go to prostitutes, but they were boring. Their entire purpose was to satisfy lust. I wasn't interested in satisfaction alone.

I wanted connection.

I missed the strange feeling that came when an empty NPC, who initially only parroted pre-scripted phrases from the CSes, came alive and grew before your eyes. With each sentence, the character's speech became more complex. They literally fed on your ideas. They weren't just reacting to words by selecting suitable answers from a database. They were thinking. Identifying meaning through analysis and synthesis. Generalizing, classifying, abstracting. Hell, some of them had a better sense of humor than I did. Of course, NPCs thought within the limits of their algorithms, but all the same, it was a miracle to watch.

Long conversations with NPCs were a game that I'd missed.

Sure, prostitute NPCs could be as complex as Irene or Heylia, but their fixation on sex limited their character development. And their quests were idiotic: taking vengeance on a pimp, or a client who didn't pay, or solving some other problem of the streets.

I remembered a conversation with Olga.

We'd just built our house on the flying island, and we were happy that we didn't have NPCs appearing out of nowhere and offering us quests all the time. We sailed out into the middle of the lake on a big raft and laid on our backs, staring into the blue sky and looking for shapes in the clouds that so rarely appeared above the magnificent floating isles.

"I wonder how NPCs see the world?" I asked Olga.

"They're generated with a full set of characteristics, memories and other attributes," Olga explained. "They see the world the same way a player does. After all, they not only have to interact with players, but with the world too."

She was always smarter than me, which meant she often missed the point of my questions. I corrected myself.

"Damn, that's not what I mean. I mean, do they see the same interface as us? Item descriptions, stats, hints? Do they see any of that stuff?"

Olga turned toward me. The wind cast her hair onto her face.

"Anton, you're better off not knowing how the virtual world of Adam Online works."

"Why's that?"

"The fascination of the unknown will be gone. You'll stop just perceiving the game and start doubting it. In the end, you'll ask why you're playing at all."

"So I'll be like you, then?"

"Worse."

"How?"

Olga turned away, took out a slender cigarette and lit it.

"Why don't I just tell you about the interface? As far as I know, complex NPCs use a special interface that differs from the standard game interface. It's not even an interface exactly, it's a kind of gameplay administration console."

"What can the console do?"

"Everything. It can get any skill, level, item, building. Move the character to any location in any Rim. It can quickly change a character's race, give it any stats or skills. Any amount of money."

"The ultimate cheat code."

"Yeah, in the first versions of Adam Online, players hacked NPCs and got access to the console. That was before the world found out about informational entropy. Then a hard divide was introduced between players and NPCs."

"No way! So the limitation didn't exist to begin with? We're people, but NPCs aren't anybody at all..."

"You see, when players entered the game world through gyrospheres or a virtual reality capsule, they connected to the game for a short time. The difference between players and NPCs was obvious. They were pieces of code, and we were the ones playing with that code. But taharration transfers the consciousness from the body. You lose your connection with reality. For the control systems, both you and the barman in the tavern giving you a quest are binary arrays. Of course, human arrays are more complex than an a non-playing character, but all the same, we look pretty much the same as NPCs. All our differences are in the code block and the data type determination."

"Can we still get access to that console?"

"No, ever since the limitation, we can't."

We fell silent, gazing at the clouds. I got scared for a second. It turned out that I was just as empty an entity as an NPC. Only I follow the game rules, while NPCs had their almighty console, but at the same time were forced to adapt to suit me.

Olga threw her cigarette butt in the water.

"That's why I warned you that you're better off not knowing how it all works. Living in the game becomes frightening. And living in..."

Olga didn't continue her phrase, but I recalled that conversation a thousand times after her suicide. I guessed how that sentence ended: living in Adam Online is frightening, and living in the real world is intolerable. Olga had no choice left to her. She just stopped living.

# Chapter 11
# An Interesting Place

IRENE SAT BY A DISPLAY case and watched the street in boredom. Occasionally she adjusted her hair or took a sip from a glass of juice. She looked mysterious and beautiful.

In moments like that, it was easy to forget that Adam Online was a game that we were playing not of our own will, but due to 'human necessity,' as it said in the Glocon statute. In moments like that, it was easy to believe that Irene was just a beautiful, bored girl. I could believe that my heartbeat really was quickening, that it wasn't just in my digitized imagination. That I wasn't a corpse lying in a bath of dissociative electrolyte somewhere in a bunker in Chinese Kazakhstan, but alive, awesome, almighty...

"Oh! Hi, Leo," Irene rose to greet me. "How can I help you?"

"Just browsing," I answered.

"Browse away."

"I want to dress up to make a good impression. Got a date."

"You know, it isn't your outfit that makes an impression, it's your personality."

Hmm, a naive soul. What about the bonuses and properties of items? They sure help.

I stepped toward a clothes rack. "You say clothes don't help make an impression?"

I chose the velvet jacket that Irene herself recommended to me last time. I now saw a previously locked property that had required the Seducer skill to unlock.

*Deadly Compliment.*
*You can give an NPC a compliment that will seduce them up to 90%. This percentage may significantly decrease due to certain properties of target NPCs.*
*Skill cooldown: 48 hours.*

I quickly put the jacket on. I read the salesgirl's stats at the same time:

*Irene Laggan.*
*Level: 32.*
*Class: unknown (requires 12 Knowledge).*
*Occupation: saleswoman in a Middle Class store.*
*Interests: Swiftville, The Big Race, Motorcycles, Flowers, Cars, Speed, Adventures and five more interests (requires Knowledge 50).*
*Character: Feisty, Adventurous.*
*Mood: waiting for something interesting.*
*Seduction probability: 67% (Furr Velvet Jacket +37%).*

Strange. Why was the seduction chance so low? Oh, right, it was probably her class. And my dumb glasses with their elastic strap. Well, to hell with those thoughts. Irene was waiting for something interesting...

I approached her and took her by the chin.

"What do you think of this jacket?"

"You'd look like an arrogant asshole if it weren't for the glasses."

"Do you like arrogant assholes?"

Irene fell silent and walked away, removing my hands. Oops, I said something wrong. Eh, no guts, no glory. I took out my tablet and put both skill points into Seducer.

*Seducer skill upgraded to level 1.*

*Now you'll get some hints about what to say at any given moment. This only applies if your Seduction Probability is above 50%.*

*Seducer skill upgraded to level 2.*

*NPC resistance to seduction reduced by 25%. The important thing is not to talk about things that are unpleasant to the NPC you're seducing.*

The words 'Flowers' and 'Motorcycles' in Irene's stats were highlighted an inviting green. 'Big Race' and 'Swiftville' were a threatening red. I didn't know much about motorcycles, and even less about flowers. What was I supposed to do? Compare Irene's beauty with a motorcycle? Or stick with flowers? Or with a flower on a motorcycle? A motorcycle in a flower meadow?

No matter how strange it seemed, the game was exciting. I didn't want to just have sex with Irene anymore, I wanted to solve the puzzle of seducing her.

Then I noticed that the seduction probability had fallen by a few points. Alright, so I couldn't let time drag on too much. I guess it made sense. She had a 'feisty' character, after all. Time was an important factor in talking to Irene.

I approached decisively and put an arm around her waist.

"You know, when I see you, I nearly crash my bike..."

I didn't know what to add about flowers. But I didn't need to. I got a notification that the seduction probability had reached one hundred percent. We kissed for a while. Irene retreated slightly to some clothes racks. I pulled her to me, not letting her leave. She sighed.

"Arrogant asshole. You..."

But I covered her mouth with another kiss.

Irene didn't resist for long, but then she pushed me away.

"Not here."

"My place. I have a comfortable..."

But Irene didn't let me brag about the sexodrome. She took me by the hand and led me to the part of the store with the fitting rooms.

"Here," she said, pushing me into one of them and closing the door behind us.

She turned and leapt on me, wrapping her legs around me. Her arms snaked around my neck.

"Feisty adventurer..."

"You wanna talk?"

"Yeah."

I took off her uniform jacket. Then I started to unbutton her blouse. Irene hung off me, pressing her nails into my neck and aggressively biting my lips as she kissed me. My augmented reality glasses diligently reported the damage.

*Damage taken: -1.*

*Damage taken: -2.*
*Damage taken: -1.*

I pulled the glasses off my face, threw them into the corner.

The girl's blouse quickly followed, but for some reason landed safely on a hanger in the fitting room. Of course, the salesgirl wasn't wearing a bra. Mirrors hung on three walls. I had three perspectives of Irene's thighs, covered in fishnet stockings. I put my hand under her skirt, found the elastic of her stockings and pulled them down.

Then I raised my hand higher and felt her panties, grabbed the hemline, started slowly tugging...

"Mr. Leonarm, sir!" a robot's voice squawked above my ear.

Irene froze and tore herself away from my mauled mouth. I raised my head and saw a police drone floating above the fitting room. It looked to me as if the camera-equipped frontal section was smirking and blinking with a green light.

"Joshua Culkin sends his regards. He urgently requires your presence."

"I'm busy."

Something clicked in the drone and I heard the detective's voice.

"You working or not, rookie?"

I released Irene's panties.

"I'm doing my best."

The drone flew straight to me.

"Listen, if you want to get a badge, I'll see you in the Luxor District in five minutes."

"But I..."

"Fasten your belt and get over here."

The drone rose to the ceiling and flew off. Irene unclenched her legs and climbed off me.

"Go play with the boys."

She picked up my glasses and handed them to me. She gently pushed me out of the cabin, along the racks of clothing and escorted me out onto the street.

I put the glasses back on. A mark appeared on my minimap from Joshua. At the same time, the nearest Projectoria station to the mark was unlocked, so I didn't have to work my way through the whole city.

"Let's continue this at my place?"

I looked for my apartment on the map, marked the address and sent it to Irene. Irene showed no reaction, but my interface showed that she'd accepted the marker. A confirmation appeared a second later.

*Irene Laggan offers a partner agreement:*

*Agreement: Irene — Leonarm.*

*1. Good Bye Weapons. You cannot kill each other.*
*This is a mandatory clause of the contract and it cannot be changed.*

*2. Shared Transport and Housing Inventory. You can see and use the inventory of Irene's motorcycles as if it was your own. Attention: this does not extend to personal inventories.*
*Add personal inventory exchange >*
*Invite Irene to stay at your apartment at Lakeview Estates >*

I immediately confirmed that action. Irene Laggan reacted.

"I always wanted to live by a lake!"

*3. Skill Exchange. Irene Laggan shares no skills with you. She cannot teach you anything.*

*4. Pleasurable Pain. You can deal each other no more than 10 damage per hit.*
*Suggest change to damage amount >*

*5. Availability. You will see each other on the map. Excludes locations where accessibility is limited (Kuznetsov portals, dungeons, private player locations etc.).*

*6. Fairness. Experience points and material valuables gained will be split 50/50.*
*Suggest another rate >*

*7. Openness. You can invite three more players or NPCs to the agreement. The experience split will change accordingly.*
*Attention: the amount of participants of this partner agreement is limited to five. If you wish to conclude an agreement with more participants, use a guild contract. To do this, you must create a guild.*
*More about creating guilds >*

*8. Allied Obligations. Attacking another participant of the contract is viewed as an attack on all participants. If you do not have time to help a partner or do not want to, and they die, you will receive the Traitor mark and will lose 10 Reputation.*
*Refuse or change terms >*

*9. Contract duration: until either party decides to break the contract. In this case, the 'Good Bye Weapons' clause will remain in effect for one hour after the contract ends.*

*Set duration >*

It was a standard contract that players mostly used to share experience. I'd done it before. What was the point of sharing loot with an NPC?

On the other hand, this kind of collaboration helped you level up a little faster. NPCs supposedly did things too, got experience that they could share with the player. But the advantages weren't worth the trouble; the player had to share too. If I had skills for influencing NPCs, like that Communicative skill, I could convince Irene to share her experience with me and not expect anything in return. But again, that would take time.

Even thinking about it took time.

Most players changed the Allied Obligations clause. Those damned NPCs regularly got into trouble. Who wanted to have to trawl through all the zones and rims to save an NPC from some spiderbot attack?

I changed that clause to only require help when we're within each other's sight. Naturally, that also limited the NPC in helping me.

"Hmm, I thought you were more caring than that," Irene noted, accepting the changes.

I left the store, turned and looked through the window. Irene stuck her tongue out at me in response.

The Luxor District took up its own island, surrounded by

the waters of the Conlin River. The district was famed for its high property prices, second only to Londinium. All the financial institutions of Liberty City were concentrated here. A system of outposts surrounded the island. Their purpose was to confiscate all incoming weaponry, even knives, and to block magic skills with counterspells. In short, it was a true island of safety.

In less than five minutes, I was where I needed to be at the Projectoria station by Memorial Bridge. The main checkpoint into Luxor District was there. The station blinked green.

"Transfer paid for by Liberty City Police Department. Thank you for maintaining a good reputation with the authorities."

Joshua Culkin met me at an armored police car. He cast a critical glance over my velvet jacket.

"Why the hell you all gussied up, rookie? You look like an unemployed pimp."

I changed the jacket to the leather Max Payne overcoat.

"That's better."

A police drone flew over to me. I handed it my weapons and my UniSuit. We walked through the frame of the checkpoint. The cops still had guns, so I didn't have to worry about getting killed if it all went south.

While we walked to the Liberty City Exchequer bank, Joshua Culkin gave me a sermon.

"Remember, rookie, no amateur dramatics. Don't get into any fights, don't try to arrest anyone or save anyone. All we need you to do is wait for the agent to transfer the info. Got it?"

"Got it, sir."

Joshua Culkin looked at me with suspicion.

"Don't even think about violating that order. I'll

get mad."

We stopped by a black wagon. Joshua climbed into it. He pulled out an earpiece and handed it to me.

"Put it in your ear."

I did as he asked. I nodded, confirming that I heard Joshua through the earpiece, and walked toward the bank. Joshua shut the cabin door and I moved further toward the entrance to Liberty City Exchequer. Once inside the bank, I stood at the end of a short queue.

"Don't rush," Joshua said. "Try to end up at the counter when the robbery starts. It'll be soon. We can see their transport already, they're parked opposite the entrance."

I cast a glance over the others in the room. I wondered how many of them were players who had just come to open an account, with no idea that they were about to be part of someone else's mission. I didn't have to worry about any heroics from them. Even a player would be powerless against armed bandits.

"They're approaching the bank," Joshua reported. "Yep... They have a hacker with them. He's substituted the feed from our drones. Great, that means we'll find out how do they do that."

My turn at the desk came around before I had time to get annoyed at this in-game bureaucracy simulation. An android clerk sat on the other sound of the window. He received all my data automatically. I worried that the error with my username would prevent me from opening an account. But it seemed to work. The standard error popped up in my glasses.

*Attention: username cannot be %Username% (Error! Check taharration system settings).*

*You cannot currently withdraw funds to a bank account.*

*Obtained: 10,000g.*

That meant that when I left the pod, I wouldn't be able to use any of the money I'd earned. But that problem was solved by transferring all my funds to my old account. It was linked to my account in the real Bryansk Capital bank. So I would be able to...

*Hold on, rookie, it's starting.*

"Nobody move, this is a robbery!" someone shouted. "Get on the floor, on the floor, now!"

Armed bandits spread out around the hall. They all wore masks. Some were simple black balaclavas with holes for the eyes and mouth, others were animal masks. One in a monkey mask barred the doors, and a chicken and elephant ran to the basement to empty the bank's vault.

A few shots rang out. The robbers were killing the bank's guards. The people around me fell to the floor and covered their heads with their arms. I slowly crouched down on my heels, then wanted to lie down carefully, but someone hit me in the back with a gun stock. I looked around. Above me stood a robber in a tiger mask, aiming a pump-action shotgun at my face.

"Hurry it up, bitch."

*Hey, rookie, what's happening?*

Hilarious... I thought other players might become a part of my game, but it turned out I'd become a character in a quest belonging to Amy McDonald. When players got involved in each other's missions, it was always unclear who was playing in whose. Or, as one game philosopher said: "Adam Online plays the players, who think they're playing Adam Online."

Amy pulled her tiger mask back.

"Missed me?" With those words, she gripped the shotgun's forestock and shot me right in the face.

*Hey, what's going on? Rookie? You really are an ass.*

# Chapter 12
# New Levels

GRISHA DIDN'T TELL anyone that he'd defeated an NPC over level four hundred. The trouble was, level four hundred was the limit. There was no higher level. What did this mean? Probably that the CSes were creating additions and expansions to the Adam Online universe. That meant that the level cap had been raised to five or six hundred. And to get there, you'd have to go to Rim Six.

But later, while visiting Nika for a new batch of CN, he told her of the battle with the dragon Ozerg. She reacted enthusiastically and thoughtfully.

"New levels? That means new skill levels too. And totally new skills and achievements."

"That's what I'm saying," the black cube answered sadly. "But I'm bound by my contract with the Black Wave and that freaking Mariam."

"New components, new processes, new crafting possibilities..." Nika continued.

"Whoever gets there first gets the worm."

Nika shook out her fine black hair and looked at the cube.

"You understand what we have to do, right?"

The black cube span from right to left, which meant confusion.

"What?"

"Go there. But just you and me. The two of us will get more together, you know that."

"What about three of us?" Grisha asked carefully.

"Hell, seven of us could go... But big parties bother me. Just you and me."

"But the war..."

"The war is doing a great job of distracting Fortunado. Let him play around with his silly guild and guild wars."

Grisha even transformed into a humanoid mech with a screen on his chest to display his human avatar.

"You want me to betray the guild, betray my brother and violate all our agreements with Mariam!"

Nika shrugged her thin sharp shoulders.

"A hundred or two hundred new levels. New gear. Loot. Perks. Zones. You'll be so high on the leaderboard that nobody will come close to you for years."

"I'd fall out with my brother, with the guild members," Grisha parried. "On top of that, Mariam would be furious. I don't know who she is, but she's as powerful as, as..."

"As an NPC over level four hundred?" Nika laughed.

Grisha's animated avatar froze in amazement.

"That's right. Ha-ha, I'm right after all. Mariam is just a quest for high-level players. That's why she approached us, the people at the top of the leaderboard. Haha, and Fortunado still thinks it's all a plot of some secret service, some mysterious spies. That idiot."

But Nika shook her head.

"No, no, you're the idiot. The conversations with

Mariam that you showed me make it clear that she knows about the real world."

"So what?"

"NPCs can't know that Adam Online is a virtual world. They can't know about the real world."

"Why not?" Grisha asked in confusion. "Where'd you get that idea? You just know?"

"Sorry, but you're being a fool. NPCs consist of a million algorithms that imitate human behavior. Imagine if one found out that his entire life was imaginary. If he learned and got proof that his entire world was an amusement park for humans that just visit it from somewhere outside. Learned that even he himself was part of that circus. How could that knowledge fit with the in-game behavior of a non-player character?"

"I don't know."

"It couldn't. It's simpler to just cut the subject of reality out than to fix the behavioral bugs the knowledge would bring. If you tell a non-player character that their entire world is a fake, he'll laugh at you, insult you or hit you. Or just ignore you. Anything except talk about it. Just like atheists that don't want to believe in God."

"Hmm. I've never tried it."

"Non-player characters in Adam Online are capable of conversing on any subject and planning and carrying out tasks that exceed the difficulty that humans are capable of. But they'll never talk about reality."

Grisha drooped.

"Ugh, so Fortunado is right again, and I'm wrong?"

"Most likely."

"Fuck it. My ranking is higher. I'll just level up to four hundred and one and everyone will find out that there's a new expansion."

"No, you won't. In Rim Five, level four hundred is the limit. Until you get to Rim Six and start earning experience there, nothing will happen."

"How do you know?"

"History, Grisha, history. You should read more. It was exactly the same when Rim Three opened."

"We-e-ell, when was that? Our parents were still young then."

Nika gave Grisha plenty of time to think. She planned to level up to four hundred, and then go to Rim Six.

With Grisha or without him.

Nika distanced herself completely from direct participation in the guild war against the Black Wave. She stated that she'd sell weapons and gear to all sides of the conflict without prejudice. And so she did. Grisha got his component nanomass, the coalition got nifty mechanodestructor frames or advanced plasmaguns. Nika couldn't equip everyone, so she focused only on the main buyers, the time-tested: the Black Wave and the Golden Horde.

"Did you choose your customers by color, or something?" Grisha laughed.

"By degree of threat to my prosperity," Nika answered. "I'm better off not angering you."

The coalition didn't attack in Rim Four, where Fortunado had been feverishly upgrading his base's defenses, but in Rim Three, where the Black Wave had captured the Langoliers' base. It was unknown whether the Langoliers had convinced their allies to try and win back the base, or whether some of them somehow sensed that the base's proximity to Dimension X was strategically important to the Black Wave.

Fortunado would have been a bad guild leader if he couldn't adapt to changing situations. When a horde of flying machines advanced on the Langoliers' base, he contacted Grisha with an idea.

"Draw them off somewhere far away. Then we'll be able to burn all the ground troops with bizoid acid."

"Me, alone, against a whole armada?"

"Weren't you bragging about being the strongest player in the game? So whip 'em all into line."

"But there are over a hundred of them... It's unrealistic. I'm tired of bowing."

"Are you hearing me right, bro? I said draw them away, not heroically kill yourself against an excessive enemy force."

"Draw them away, you say?"

"Far away."

"Is a near-earth orbit far enough?"

"Woah, LeCube can go out that far?"

"Not yet."

While Grisha fought with Camper in space, an entire war unfolded beneath them.

Although Fortunado bragged about his ability to predict the enemy plans, the coalition managed to deal an unexpected and rapid blow. This angered Fortunado. He thought himself a strategic genius and saw that the enemy would attack in several directions at once, but didn't guess that it would happen so quickly and with so little warning.

The brother was certain that he had calculated everything, that the enemy wouldn't concentrate on any captured bases in particular. Especially considering that the allied guilds were still feuding. The loss of their home base weakened the once mighty Langoliers, which was advantageous to all the others.

In addition, Fortunado realized that his spies were useless. Several Black Wavers left the guild specially to join the Free Adamites with the aim of reporting troop movements and other observations.

None of them even hinted that the coalition troops were deploying all across the nearest zones in Rim Three. All the enemy forces had moved to the former base of the Langoliers at once, with none left behind, no latecomers. This was in spite of the fact that the respawn towers were different distances from each other, some even a couple of days away from the zone of the Langoliers' base. Whoever calculated all this was certainly a better strategist than Fortunado...

When it became apparent that the base couldn't be reclaimed, the coalition hurried to retreat. It wasn't exactly crushed, but an unsuccessful attack is almost a defeat. The Black Wave was able to prove that it was rightly considered the strongest guild in Adam Online.

Nonetheless, Fortunado was not overjoyed.

"Yes, we won a fleeting battle. But we won't be able to withstand a long-term conflict."

Crusher and Most Ancient Evil were proud of their epic victory and argued accordingly.

"What do you mean? We beat 'em once, we'll beat em again!"

"Who's this clever strategist of theirs?" Grisha wondered aloud.

"I'm wondering the same," Fortunado answered. "Han is an idiot. The Viatichi prince is an even bigger idiot. The Free Adamites are all idiots."

"But," Grisha laughed. "Those idiots attacked, and

you didn't foresee it..."

"If they have anyone worth anything, it's the Langolier leader, but the coalition wouldn't have agreed to follow orders from someone who lost half his guild in a battle against LeCube alone."

"I'm just the strongest player in Adam Online." Grisha proudly lifted a corner of the black cube.

It was the truth, and Fortunado didn't argue. Even if he did feel envy.

After wiping out the top players and defeating the dragon Ozerg, Grisha had leveled up so much that he wasn't just in the top ten, he was at the top of the leaderboard by an imposing margin.

*Adam Online Ranking Leaderboard (Asian Cluster)*

*1. Grisha — 392 (Mechanodestructor, Guild: Black Wave)*

*2. Nika — 353 (Android)*

*3. Saidullaev Henrich Vasilyevich — 301 (Mechanodestructor, Guild: Black Wave)*

*4. Fortunado — 257 (Mechanodestructor, Guild: Black Wave)*

*5. Knight_Ivan — 255 (Human, Guild: Viatichi)*

*6. Blondie Lee — 251 (Fallen Angel, Guild: Black Wave)*

*7. Crusher — 249 (Fallen Angel, Guild: Black Wave)*

*8. Most Ancient Evil — 239 (Bizoid, Guild: Black Wave)*

*9. Slippery Joe — 222 (Bizoid, Guild: Golden Horde)*

*10. Alan Kachmazov — 219 (Super, Guild: Langoliers)*

Before, Fortunado had always walked ahead of his brother.

# Chapter 13
# The Taste of Peaches

GRISHA FOUND HIMSELF in a contradictory position. He didn't want to fall out with his brother, or the Black Wave. But on the other hand, Fortunado's stubbornness angered him. Any moron could see that the advantages of exploring Rim Six far outweighed what Mariam could offer.

Moreover, in spite of Nika's insistence, Grisha remained convinced that Mariam was an NPC involved in a hidden quest for high-level players. The fact that she knew about reality... Did Nika really not understand that you could make an NPC say whatever you liked? NPCs didn't have to know something to discuss it. Maybe the clever programmers from the Global Consortium of Standardization in Adam Online had come up with an NPC that could talk about reality without attaching any importance to it?

The hot phase of the guild war was over. The coalition no longer mounted large-scale attacks. They made do with isolated raids. The Black Wave also stayed on the defense, not giving in to the coalition's attempts to provoke them.

"They're trying to lure us out," Fortunado said.

"They're making as if they're vulnerable. They plan to draw us out from behind our defenses into an attack."

"Why not attack, boss?" Most Ancient Evil asked. "We could just gather our strength and crush the coalition."

"We wouldn't crush them. Our strength is in the fact that we're defending. That's easier than attacking."

"Well, you know better, you're the boss," Most Ancient Evil agreed amiably. "I'd fuck 'em up."

Grisha spoke up more and more rarely in those meetings. He silently watched his brother. His annoyance grew: why should he obey his brother just because he was supposedly smarter? Fortunado failed to see what Grisha had already seen: the hidden quest to conquer Rim Six. How could he consider himself a great strategist, but fail to see such an obvious gap in his logic?

Grisha went to visit Nika more often than their business arrangement demanded. She was the only person to which he could speak his mind openly.

"Come to cry on my shoulder again?" Nika laughed. "I'm using it right now, but there's a spare shoulder in the corner over there, go cry on that."

Grisha silently took his base form and watched as Nika worked on another configuration for LeCube. She stood in the hangar opposite a three-dimensional projector panel. Its entire surface was full of numerous tiny icons, each of which represented a component, substance or process. Thousands of interconnecting lines stretched between the icons, as if a cat had unrolled a ball of wool until it got stuck in it. Nika swapped component icons, moved the connecting lines.

Sometimes she had to drag an icon from one corner of the projector panel to the other, but the mosaic of icons wasn't finished. When she dragged an icon to the edge of the projector panel, it scrolled to reveal an even greater number of icons. When the connections suddenly broke due to an error in a component link, Nika swore and went back to where she started.

Grisha didn't like crafting in any form.

"I don't get what's so fun about dragging icons back and forth."

"And I don't get what's so fun about being a robot and killing other robots in duels," Nika answered calmly. "Each to their own. Crafting is a puzzle, and solving it gives me the same pleasure and progress as your little battles and wars."

"But it takes you tons of time to pick the right component connections and make all these processes work in tandem."

"Sometimes it takes forty to sixty hours of constant crafting just to fix bugs in the Second Skin program configuration. Now do you understand why they're so expensive?"

"I understand that, I just don't get how these tortuous puzzles can be fun."

"Apart from the process, the result itself interests me. I have a special interest in crafting, remember?"

"I remember. You also promised to show me what you've achieved. Were you able to create a version of reality within this virtual world?"

"Don't lie. I promised that I might show you."

All the icons on the projector panel started flashing, then melded into one. There were so many rows of icons that it took nearly half a minute. Nika stepped back from the projector panel.

"Done. I've updated the Second Skin

configuration. Now it'll use fifty percent less component nanomass than before."

Grisha transformed into the humanoid mech with the screen on its chest.

"By the way, can you upgrade LeCube itself?"

Nika brushed a straight black lock of hair from her forehead.

"That frame is already the most complex and advanced production in all of Adam Online. That not enough for you?"

"It's as if LeCube is always working at the edge of its capabilities. I've nearly died more than once."

"But you haven't died, right?"

"You promised that LeCube would be invincible. That it would have no weaknesses."

"I promised that LeCube would be strong and unusual. So I lied a little about the weaknesses... What did you expect? I needed to sell it to you. There's nothing invincible in this game but the game itself. Your immaturity amazes me, Grisha."

"Imma... what?"

"Immaturity and ignorance."

A sad emoji appeared on the mech's screen.

"You and Fortunado are so alike. You think you're so smart."

"Because we are smart. And?"

"And you're avoiding my question, insulting me. But I'm the one at the top of the leaderboard, not you."

Nika suddenly softened, as much as an emotionless android could.

"Grisha, don't get me wrong... It isn't LeCube working at the limit of its capabilities, it's you. You decided that LeCube is an invincible frame, so you rush into every fight. But LeCube isn't a magic box that I created by waving some magic technology wand. It's an extension of the possibilities of crafting in Adam Online. No matter how many magic wands you wave, everything you do is within the limits of the game algorithms. And since almost anything is within their limits, you got the impression that LeCube is a cheat. So you act rashly and get yourself into trouble."

"You mean I'm just less afraid now?"

"Exactly. If you think you're subjecting yourself to a particular risk in LeCube, then leave it. Go back to your trusty old frames."

"No way."

"Then keep on." Nika tapped the lone icon on the projector panel that had formed from all the others, and tossed it to Grisha. "This one's free."

Grisha accepted the config.

"I thought about your offer. I'm not going to Rim Six. While the Black Wave exists, I just can't. I'd be a traitor."

"As you wish," Nika answered. "I'll go alone."

"You know that I'll meet you at Jamilla's Tomb and kill you, right?"

"We'll see who kills who. Without my CN, LeCube is just a cube."

"All the crafters are trying to recreate this frame as we speak."

"Let them try."

"I can share information about LeCube. That will help them create the component nanomass. That would put an end to your monopoly."

"No, fool, it would put an end to yours. You'd stop being unique. The coalition would have their own LeCubes. You know perfectly well how that would end for your silly guild."

Grisha hesitated... then showed a happy emoji on his chest.

"Maybe that'd be for the best? No guild, no obligations."

The friendship between Grisha and Nika was too strong for them to sulk with each other. They just took it as a given that Grisha would respond to any attempt by Nika to get into Rim Six the same as he would to any other player; with all his strength. They spoke of it no more.

Nika slowly leveled up with her crafting.

Grisha fought.

An unsuccessful attack dampened the coalition's enthusiasm: they no longer attacked the Black Wave's home base, instead concentrating their strikes on smaller bases and the guild property of Grisha and Fortunado. The guild had many resource mines, all in different locations, different Rims. It was impossible to mount a strong defense at each resource point like they did with Shoreline. The coalition methodically attacked the guild's resource centers with overwhelming force. With each coalition victory, the Black Wave had fewer and fewer resources, which affected the guild's defensive capabilities.

Grisha and his squad of high-level guild members flitted from one base to another, deflecting attacks. But they couldn't make it to every attack in time. They took back some bases, but others became closed to them forever. The coalition split the captured bases between themselves and steadfastly defended each one.

Fortunado's prediction was true: if the Black Wave

didn't think of a way to turn the situation to their advantage soon, the coalition would simply devour the guild piece by piece.

Fortunado was far from happy. The assistance from Mariam no longer covered the losses from the captured mines. For days in a row, the guild leader sat in his Octopus frame before a projector panel, moving structures, counting resources, trying to compensate for the losses.

But Grisha, after returning from another skirmish, seemed strangely happy. He even joked.

"We should sue for peace, bro. We can't resist them, you know that."

"We can as long as we want to."

"But do we?"

"You talk as if you want to abandon the guild."

"I don't. It's just that I see it every day on the front lines. We're being bled dry. We're running out of energy units, nutrient sets for the bizoids. The angels and mages are running out of mana. We lost our oil, and with it our tanks and jets. What else is there to say? Soon we'll run out of water for raising acid bizoids, and without them our base defenses will be crippled."

Fortunado slumped.

"I know that better than you. And I knew it before."

"So what are you planning to do, strategist? Soon we'll lose our base at Jamilla's Tomb."

Fortunado waved all his octopus tentacles.

"Maybe that's for the best."

"How's that?"

"Mariam will see that she needs to help us more if she wants us to protect the passage to Rim Six."

"Are you sure she really doesn't want anyone to

get there?"

"Who knows what she wants. She hasn't contacted us in a long time."

And so the days passed in constant defense at the brink of defeat. Fortunado performed miracles, managed to distribute his scarce resources to maintain the defenses. Grisha went back and forth between combat missions and Dimension X to stock up on component nanomass.

During one of those visits, Nika surprised him.

"I want to show you something."

"I hope it's an atomic bomb, a second LeCube or at least some never-before-seen program config that will kill all my enemies?"

"I can't make you an a-bomb, a second LeCube would take too long, and no program configuration with those parameters exists."

They walked toward the hangar that was previously inaccessible.

*World 0.4+, Alpha Test.*

Nika waved her hand and a lock clicked, motors whirred into life. The panels of the gate began to open.

"I've been working a lot and running a lot of experiments. All unsuccessful... Unfortunately, I'm getting closer and closer to accepting that a constructor that imitates the real world can't be used to build a true imitation of the real world."

"Even I know that," grumbled Grisha. "You especially can't use phrases like 'true imitation.' Don't you hear how that sounds?"

To his surprise, Nika looked offended.

"Tell me, have you eaten peaches?"

"Peaches... What? Sure, I ate them a thousand

times when I played as a human. I tried all the fruits, all the food I could. I even had the Garfield achievement..."

"Do you remember the taste of peaches?"

"Yep."

"Have you tried real peaches? Not in Adam Online, but in real life?"

"I don't remember. Probably not. Where would I have gotten them? I ate Peach Flavored Fruit Mix vitamin rations, like everyone."

"I ate real peaches," Nika said. "When I was sent to the special school. Everything there is real. Milk, bread, chicken. No synthetic soy replacements. No virtual emulations."

"So what? You just bragging?"

Nika waved that away. "Unlike you, I compared real peaches with the ones in Adam Online. Virtual peaches are like real ones, only better. The texture is like it is in real life, only nicer. And the juice of virtual peaches flows along the lips just the same as the real stuff. Only it doesn't make your fingers sticky."

"What're you getting at?"

"Since the constructor reproduces reality, why can't it reproduce it completely? Do you know what real peaches have?"

"What?"

"Flaws. Bruised sides, growths on the skin. Some had stems that made them harder to eat."

"Think about it, virtual peaches are full of flaws too. The game has rotten meat and sour apples. They give you debuffs..."

"That's the whole point, virtual reality can imitate flaws. But it doesn't, because nobody wants them. Nobody wants to eat bruised peaches if there are perfect ones. Adam Online is capable of reproducing reality in all its details, but the CSes are limited. They reproduce the world that the player wants. Because the players come here from a world they don't like. Even the flaws are such that they don't stop you enjoying and eating a peach."

Grisha transformed from his base configuration into the humanoid mech config.

"Enough foreplay. What is it you have?"

"The final experiment. Today I want to create a reality within our virtual world."

Grisha showed a surprised emoji on his screen.

"So what am I doing here?"

"I'm afraid."

"What is there to fear?"

"That it works. Or that it doesn't. Both are scary. I want you to be here with me."

Grisha cleared the emojis from the screen and spoke briefly.

"Let's go. Don't be afraid."

# Chapter 14
# Cunning Rat

AFTER CROSSING the threshold of the World 0.4+ hangar, Grisha expected to see something miraculous, something to astound the imagination. He didn't know what exactly, but he'd caught the contagion of Nika's worries. That was why he looked around the empty building twice and read its stats three times. He found nothing unusual within it except an extremely high energy drain.

He showed a perplexed emoji on his screen. "Where is everything?"

"It'll be here soon," Nika promised.

She walked to a projector panel and called up the crafting interface. Icons and threads covered the panel's surface. Grisha slumped.

"I thought you were ready to show it all to me, but you're up to your same old tricks."

"Have a little patience, the experiment requires a lot of resources, I can't maintain it for long. In the meantime, listen to a story about game balance."

Nika spoke unhurriedly, shifting around her icons and threads.

In the beginning, game balance in Adam Online Beta gave rise to many surprising questions. For example, the CSes generated level two venomous mosquitoes in the Firefly Swamp zone. Those attacked a level eight mechanodestructor of the LG Humanoid Mech class... and bit him to death.

So mosquitoes killed a robot.

A review of this incident showed no errors. Adam Online is a living world, one that evolved according to its own laws. Even violations of that evolution seemed to be part of it. The control systems built the world according to their base algorithms. They couldn't do anything 'wrong.' Something that seemed like a bug to the beta testers was a product of the world's foundational evolutionary processes. As were the mosquitoes that could kill humanoid battle mechs.

The beta testers caught those mosquitoes and split them into their components. It turned out that the venom that was supposed to do minor damage (and exclusively to living creatures) contained the 'alkali' element. That element was used to create ammunition mixtures with alkaline acid, which instantly ate through many metals and dealt bonus damage to mechanodestructors and armored vehicles.

Further study of the test zone made it clear that a huge layer of this element had been generated not far beneath the Firefly Swamp. The swamp water was rich with it. The world of Adam Online was alive, imitating reproduction. The mosquitoes laid their eggs in that very water. Accordingly, the ones that hatched in the swamp already carried a small dose of alkali. Their bodies stored it, processed it, turned it into a deadly concentration of alkaline acid. The mechanodestructor's death then seemed logical. Mosquitoes had bitten a robot to death.

And it made sense. It meant that the same types of NPCs, the same mosquitoes, would differ from zone to zone. Each swamp had its own mosquitoes, each scrapheap its own spiderbots, each forest its own werewolves.

In general, the more the beta testers looked for bugs, the more they were convinced that there were none to be found. There were only unstudied phenomena of the virtual world. To fix them would mean to introduce crutches, which would be a serious intervention in the world's logic, which would, in turn, lead to truly unpredictable bugs.

Adam Mickiewicz, the creator of Adam Online, analyzed all those cases and decided that there would be no crutches. The control systems had a clear task, and they performed it: they genereated worlds, taking into account interactions so complex that the people studying those generated worlds couldn't even understand them.

"Mr. Mickiewicz, have you gone insane?" one of the project investors said to him when Adam presented his results. "You not only claim that there are no bugs in the worlds of Adam Online, you also tell us that every single mosquito larva in a swamp will be important?"

"Exactly right. In the virtual world, everything will be as it is in reality. Material will not come appear out of nowhere and disappear into thin air."

"Yes, but at the start of that process of 'creation,' it must come from somewhere."

"At first, the control systems will create it out of nowhere," the Pole agreed stolidly. "But then, everything in the world will live and interact on its own."

"Every shitty little larva?"

"Every larva, every blade of grass, every pebble and mote of dust, sir. Just like the fish that will control the population of mosquitoes in zones by eating the larvae."

"Can you imagine the computing power required to maintain the operation of just one of these smelly swamps?"

"It is unimaginable, sir. Incidentally, smells are also components of the world."

"And where do you think we're going to get the computing power required to create an entire game universe? From the future? From fantasy novels set in virtual worlds? From our asses?"

"You can only pull your wit out of your ass, sir."

"Where will we get it from? Answer me."

Adam Mickiewicz approached the investor and tapped him on the forehead.

"From up here, sir. Right from where we get the real world. Our consciousness."

Nika fell silent, still moving the icons on the panel. The screen on Grisha's chest flashed with a surprised emoji.

"I don't get it. Why are you telling me this?"

Nika stepped back form the panel. All the icons shook as if they wanted to jump out of the screen.

"Firstly, to keep you quiet so I could concentrate. Secondly, to help you imagine that this hangar is about to undergo the same process that happens when new

Rims are generated. What I'm about to do will be a kind of imitation of the control systems within the very virtual world that they generate."

"Ahem. You're going to be, like, a CS within the CSes?"

Nika thought for a moment, pushed a lock of black hair away from her brow.

"An interesting thought. But it isn't quite like that. You often ask me whether I use cheats. This here — the CSes will perceive this as a cheat. Although it's intended to cheat us, not them."

Grisha showed a thoughtful emoji on his screen and, then gasped.

"You cunning rat, you! And I believed you when you said you were scared, that you needed encouraging words of support. You just brought me here to protect you against the tech support bots, didn't you?"

Nika shrugged.

"Like I said, you're immature. But don't be offended. Your immaturity is very sweet."

"You understand," Grisha said, with an angry emoji, "that the controllers will follow the support bots? There's no way to fight them off. They'll just kick us off Adam. Give us penalties."

"There's a risk of that. But I hope to be in time before the controllers arrive."

Grisha took a step back.

"This venture of yours is going to get me banned from Adam Online... You realize my life would be over, right?"

Nika tried to display concern on her emotionless android face.

"If I don't perform this experiment, I won't get the data I need to transfer my consciousness into another body. And that means my life will be over. In the truest sense."

"I'm sick of you using me all the time," Grisha snarled. "You never explain anything properly, you're always pretending. Hell, you just lie to me. Why should I help you?"

"Because you're my only friend. The only one I've told everything."

"Everything, sure. I bet you're still hiding something."

"I hid what you didn't need to know. You just wouldn't understand. Does that anger you?"

"It sure does."

"Then your cowardliness angers me. In Adam Online, you're a fearless hero ready to risk all your unlimited respawns. The biggest bully on the leaderboard. But as soon as the risk becomes real, you wuss out."

"Bullshit."

"You remember our childhood? That time when you and Fortunado ran off and got into that illegal taharration pod in the underground landing? You were scared then. Fortunado is braver than you."

"I was right! If we hadn't have done that, we wouldn't have had the problems we ended up with."

"You fear problems from the past. I'm solving problems of the present. Enough. You're free to go. But if you do, then I was wrong about you, fake hero."

The emojis on Grisha's screen changed rapidly: anger, rage, pity, confusion, thoughtfulness.

"How much time do you need?"

"No clue."

"When will the tech support bots get here?"

"Five minutes."

"Woah. Why so long?"

"Their procedure for analyzing cheating is complex. What I'm about to do in this hangar will be an anomaly that doesn't exist in their database. The CSes need to decide what it is in the first place, how to deal with it and whether they have the authority to remove it. There are a bunch of procedures and protocols they have to go through. And most of all, human beings will be involved in that chain. All my calculations rely on their laziness and stupidity."

"Humans? From where, the real world?"

"Yep. All suspicious incidents of undeclared activity in Adam Online have to be assessed by Glocon officials. They're the ones that decide whether a hacking attempt is taking place."

"Wow. I thought the CSes and QCPs acted autonomously."

"Contacting a human administrator for confirmation is a formality. Human beings aren't capable of understanding the data the CSes present. The paradox is that usually, admins hand over the responsibility to decide whether something is a cheat or not to the CSes. Meaning they only contact humans to get the authority to act at their own discretion. It's like the CS says "There's some weird shit going on in such-and-such cluster in such-and-such Rim, can we figure out for ourselves what it is and take the right measures?" In short, we have enough time before the controllers get here."

"So it's my job to deal with the bots?"

"Uh-huh."

"I'll lose my reputation."

"Everything has a cost."

A joyful emoji appeared on Grisha's screen.

"Yep. So are you ready to pay it? Remember how you told me about monetization and how corporations used to get cash out of gamers for every little thing?"

"They still do... But I get what you're hinting at. I'll give you five hundred thousand CN."

"A million."

"I don't have that much."

"You can pay in installments."

Nika immediately sent Grisha a contract to sign. He was surprised.

"Did you write that up in advance?"

"Grisha, you wouldn't believe how predictable some people can be. Worse than NPCs."

Nika took up a position opposite the projector panel. Grisha switched to his spiderbot config, replacing all his missile launchers, plasma guns and cannons for ordinary machine guns. He took up a position at the hangar entrance, but Nika corrected him.

"Stand by me."

"That's a bad decision, I should guard the approaches..."

"No. All objects, bots or NPCs appear outside the player's field of vision."

"Why?"

"So as not to ruin the illusion of reality. Items can only appear out of thin air when they have that property, like magical crap or teleportation."

Grisha looked around the hangar.

"Some realism that is. But I get it. If we both keep the surroundings in our view, the bots will be forced to appear outside the hangar, right?"

"Exactly," Nika nodded. "Although I can't guarantee everything will go according to plan."

Grisha waved his machine gun legs.

"Don't worry. While I'm here, everything will go fine."

Nika gratefully shook his leg.

"That's what I love you for."

Nika turned back to the projector panel, while Grisha clanked and rattled onto two hind legs, aiming his remaining three pairs of machine guns at the hangar entrance.

"By the way, what if we shut the doors? Maybe then the bots won't get in."

"No, no, we can't do that. We need to leave them an entry point, otherwise they'll appear right in front us, ignoring the maximum reality conditions."

"Then let's begin."

Nika hesitated, then stretched her hand out to the projector panel.

"Yes... Let's."

# Chapter 15
# No Blood, No Bodies,
# No Bullet Holes

A MILLION ICONS shot across the panel's surface. Nika was in her element, working her long fine fingers, gathering icons into clusters, tying up threads, grouping, uniting.

It was a sight like nothing else. If a robot had breath, Grisha would have been holding his. With one pair of eyes, he kept an eye on the hangar entrance, and with another — on Nika and the empty space behind the projector panel. Something incredible was sure to happen at any moment.

But nothing happened. Grisha unhurriedly moved his mechanical legs.

"Has it started? Anything happening?"

Nika waved in annoyance.

"It all started a while ago."

Grisha turned all his sets of eyes to the empty hangar space, trying to make something out in the darkness. All he noticed was a strange shimmer, a slight distortion in the space behind him. Like the heat over hot asphalt.

"So this is reality?"

Nika waved him off again.

"If I wanted to chat, I'd have called Fortunado. Please be quiet."

"Fine, fine," Grisha agreed, before immediately asking another question. "When your reality appears, will you transfer your consciousness there?"

"Gregory, you dickhead, this is just an experiment that I'm using to collect statistical data. I'm not modeling reality to live in it, but to test the process of transferring consciousness to another carrier."

"Ahh, so that's it. Got it."

Grisha didn't really get it, and wanted to ask more questions, but a loud and friendly voice stopped him.

"Good time of day, players."

A standard blue-eyed, broad-shouldered Arild lumbered into the hangar.

"The dispatch station received a notice that there have been bugs in this zone. Are you ready for me to perform a scan? Yes-No?"

"No," Grisha answered, punctuating the word with a volley from a machine gun.

The bullets split the Arild's body in half. One half flew through the doors, the other stayed where it was. A gleaming smiled remained frozen on the bot's dead and bloody face. Several new bots immediately took its place, all repeating that idiotic greeting. They got the same welcome.

Grisha brought up his Reputation on his neurointerface. He'd had fifty three. After killing the bots, it was down to forty six. So each lost him a whole point? That was huge... Grisha turned to Nika, wanting to ask her how long the experiment would go on, but he stayed silent.

That strange shimmer was gone from the center of the hangar now, and in its place was... an ordinary room. A soft gray carpet on the floor, plastic tables and chairs, an old sagging sofa. An old projector sat on a crooked plastic table. The surface of a holographic screen stuck out from it. The room was limited to three walls, one of which had a window covered in dirty plastic shutters.

"This is... I've seen this room somewhere before."

Nika didn't answer. She just kept working her magic on the projector panel icons. The room twitched from time to time as if convulsing. The items started to distort: first a chair stretched out into an infinite perspective, violating all laws of space, then the sofa began to flicker, shrinking and growing.

Several Arilds appeared at once.

"Good time of day, players."

"Good time of day..."

"Good time..."

The voices melded into a single choir.

"The dispatch station received..."

"Notice that there have been..."

Grisha answered with a long volley, cutting down the crowd of bots. Along with them, he cut his own Reputation down to twenty nine. But the bots kept coming through the door in an endless stream. Some only had time to greet the players, others got to their statement about starting a scan, but they all fell to Grisha's bullets. The opening in the hangar gates was red with blood, and the entrance was full of body parts and corpses. Some of them twitched weakly.

*Your reputation with the authorities of all Rims has decreased: -2.*

*What's going on with you? Are you in a bad mood? Problems in your work or personal life?*

*Achievement unlocked: Social Suicide.*

*Lower your reputation from 50 to -50 in 2 minutes. Drop 48 more reputation points within 1 minute 02 seconds.*

Taking advantage of the fact that the Arild bots were now somewhat slowed at the entrance while they climbed over corpses of their copies, Grisha asked another question.

"What is this room? It's vaguely familiar."

Nika stopped waving her fingers across the projector panel. Turning her back to the bots, she read some lines that quickly flashed up on the screen. From time to time, she corrected the position of a few icons or returned a connecting thread that split off as her arcane processes continued.

"You don't recognize it? It's the common room in the boarding school we lived in when our parents went on their taharration rotation."

"That's it! You've restored it from memory? Awesome. I remember now... We used to watch archive pornography from the twentieth century on that projector. Couldn't get our hands on anything newer."

"I have a photographic memory," Nika replied.

"Is that why you're so good at crafting?"

"Of course. If I can remember any room down to the smallest details, then no icon or interconnected process can escape my attention."

Grisha went back to shooting the bots, falling

deeper into nostalgia.

"And behind that wall over there, with the closed door, there was a corridor that led to the room with the gyrorbs. We crept in there at night when the teachers were asleep and played DotA 5... And on the left is the entrance to our room. Ah, childhood..."

*Your reputation with the authorities of all Rims has decreased: -30, disgust.*

*Good NPCs will try to avoid conversing with you, will ignore you, and if you are persistent — will call the police. High chance of refusal of service.*

"Good time of day, players."

"Shut up, dammit," Grisha answered, releasing another rain of fire on the hangar. He turned to Nika. "Alright, you've made this room, but what does it have to do with transferring consciousness? You planning to move into that sofa?"

Nika didn't answer. She was anxiously reading logs.

"Good ti..."

Another volley from all Grisha's machine guns destroyed yet another batch of bots. There were so many corpses that they were half blocking the hangar entrance. The new Arilds had to climb over a pile of their brethren. Most of them died at the top, increasing the obstacle's height. Experience points fell from the killed bots, but the value of their lives was too low to noticeably increase Grisha's experience bar.

*Your reputation with the authorities of all Rims has decreased: -40, strong disgust.*

*Only bandit NPCs will talk to you, or police during an arrest. Most legal merchants will refuse you service. No access to services of Projectoria and Respec-T stations. You will be automatically blacklisted.*

Grisha started to panic.

"Hey, I'm going to have a rough time with this reputation. This experiment over soon?"

"A couple of minutes... Don't worry, we'll be done before the controllers get here."

The android's face poorly expressed emotion, but Grisha could read worry and annoyance in it. Something was obviously going wrong for Nika. She furiously moved icons, making the room distort in surreal proportions. The items of the interior interwove between themselves in miraculous fashion. The table flowed into the sofa, the sofa suddenly looked like a writing desk while still somehow looking like a sofa. The window with its shutters melded into it, twisted like a bundle of wires.

"Damn, even the strangest drugs don't do this," Grisha said. "Your reality doesn't look much like one."

Nika ran her fingers through her hair.

"Strange... It can't be... This means..."

Grisha didn't hear the rest. He was forced to cut down another squad of smiling Arilds.

"What was that?"

Nika ignored his question again, moving around her icons and threads. In the meantime, Grisha's neurointerface squawked out a new notification.

*Your reputation with the authorities of all Rims has decreased: -50, rage.*

*Positive NPCs will entirely refuse to talk to you or offer you services. The police have begun to hunt you. The price on your head in the Blacklist has increased. A reward of 500,000g or higher has been placed on your head.*

*Social Suicide achievement complete: +100 XP.*

*Achievement unlocked: Social Suicide Again.*
*Lower your reputation from -50 to -100 in 2 minutes.*

"Damn it, I didn't sign up for this!" Grisha shouted.

Although Nika was busy, she still didn't miss the chance to taunt him.

"Yes, you did. Read the contract."

"Cunning rat."

A new wave of bots arrived. They needed more time to climb over the pile of corpses. In addition, it turned out that one of the bots had survived under the heap of bodies. Firing off his introductory phrase, he started scanning the area for errors.

At that moment, Grisha felt the ground under his feet shake, but it was somehow strange. It seemed as if the entire image of the world shifted, blurred, like static on a video signal. Grisha had never seen anything like it.

"What's this?

"I... I don't know. This is all wrong..."

"Should I keep killing the bots?"

Since Nika didn't answer, Grisha mowed down another wave.

*Your reputation %Username% with the authorities*

*of all Rims has decreased: -60 {show_log}, hatred.*

*NPCs higher than you in level will attack you without warning. The rest will call the police and tech support. Weak NPCs will run away or might attack you from behind if ?????. {Range_unit_class} ??? will take a warning shot to avoid having to approach. All representatives of legal authorities have begun to search for you and will shoot to kill. Apart from tttttttttt%%%% {CS%system%message#00000001??}*

"What the hell is going on with my neurointerface? Huh? Nika?"

The world blurred even more, and Grisha's machine guns stopped firing. He felt his control over the spiderbot weakening. He could no longer take on his base form. The neurointerface stopped accepting commands. Turning toward Nika took an enormous effort, as if his base stats had suddenly fallen and his control over LeCube was gone.

Nika stood opposite the projector panel and watched with fascination as a single icon blinked in the center. She brushed a lock of hair out of her face and repeated over and over:

"Damn, who would have thought..."

"Nika... What's happening?"

The android turned her blurry face toward him. The world was no longer doubled, it was tripled. More than that, it was turning into a multitude of transparent duplicates, overlaid on top of one another, repeating each other to infinity. Nika's voice was distorted, as if playing from a corrupted recording.

"It was always here. I didn't do anything."

Then Grisha felt as if he was falling, as when he

entered taharration. The moment when the consciousness could pinpoint the immersion in dissociative electrolyte, when the waves of blue joined above the face... Grisha even felt the presence of his human arms and legs, a feeling that was quickly forgotten in a mechanodestructor frame.

For a second, Grisha was in darkness, with Nika floating before him. She couldn't move either, she just floated there, her arms and legs out to the sides. It lasted a single instant, and then a tunnel appeared that dragged Nika and Grisha to the nearest respawn point.

There they resurrected.

The tower, however, was within the territory of Dimension X. They resurrected not far from the 'World 0.4+, Alpha Test' hangar. They stood in silence for a few seconds. Nika looked at Grisha, stunned. He was stunned too, although LeCube's black sides didn't show it.

The interface took on its usual appearance, with no more errors. Grisha switched to the config of the humanoid mech with the screen on its chest. Now he could express emojis of surprise and exclamation to his heart's content.

"Is it the same for you?" Nika asked.

"What exactly?"

"No system messages? That we died, that we respawned. No penalty?"

"That's right," Grisha said in amazement. "Just silence. And my reputation is back at fifty three."

"Check your log."

Grisha opened the least used part of his neurointerface: the text event log.

*[52-1454] — revival at respawn point 3450-1905*
*[52-1442] — program configuration activated*
*(...)*

"It's like none of it happened," Grisha said. "No achievements, no kills. Nothing from during your experiment."

"Same for me... But I still have knowledge that doesn't depend on game achievements." Nika tapped her forehead. "They can't take that away from me."

She quickly walked toward World 0.4+, Alpha Test. Grisha followed.

"What sort of knowledge? What the hell even happened? A glitch?"

"I'm not even sure I know yet. Not a glitch. More like an unexpected player scenario."

"Did you get the data you needed? Did you find out if you can transfer your consciousness from Adam Online to another carrier?"

Nika ignored his question. Grisha didn't push it. He knew Nika would answer sooner or later. As they approached the hangar, they saw it was closed. No blood, no bodies, no bullet holes.

"Everything is just like it was before..."

Nika placed her palm on the lock.

"Looks that way."

The door rose, revealing the empty hangar and the large projector panel. Nika rushed toward it and activated it.

"It didn't happen like I planned it at all. Everything went wrong... beautifully wrong."

"What happened exactly?"

"It is possible to transfer consciousness from Adam Online into another body. But I'm not the one who came up with it."

"Who did?"

Nika shrugged her slender shoulders.

"I don't know. Adam Mickiewicz? The CSes? Someone from Glocon? In my attempt to recreate a copy of reality, I called up the interface for the exit protocol from Adam Online."

"Not through the quit command, but through some crazy thing you crafted? Are you sure it was the exit protocol?"

"There wasn't enough time to get deep into it, but..." Nika slowed as if she was having trouble expressing her thoughts. "I might be wrong, but... it looks like you can set any taharration pod as an exit point from Adam Online."

Grisha scratched his head. "Meaning..?"

"If I'd launched the exit protocol, I could have woken up in any available body. Any of the millions of bodies currently in a taharration pod connected to Adam Online."

"Oh..."

"Oh is right."

"Oh, fuck."

"Also right."

# Chapter 16
# Tricks without a Pistol

I'VE SAID IT before. Nothing ever goes like it should. There's no point in plans. Chaos always has its say. On the other hand, if nothing ever goes like it should, then that's a predictable event too, right? Maybe it's worth planning carefully, but being ready for things to go wrong. Of course, there was always the risk that things would go wrong in your preparations for things to go wrong... But it was better to stop that train of thought there, or it would chug on forever.

Suffice it to say that from the first cry of "This is a robbery!" I activated the time slow ability from my Max Payne overcoat. And kept it at the ready. When Amy pulled the trigger on her shotgun, I used the skill.

Three seconds was enough to dodge the shower of sparks and shot fanning out from the barrel. As if moving in jelly, Amy reloaded her shotgun, the shell spinning in the air and leaving a smoking trail behind it. There was enough time to sweep my leg around and knock Amy off her feet.

When it was all over, Amy was lying on the floor. I grabbed her shotgun.

"My turn," I said, aiming the barrel at Amy.

"Hey, don't shoot me in the face, that's rude," she whined.

"Yeah?" I shouted. "I should know, right?"

The robbers noticed me and opened fire. I had to jump behind the cashier's counter. Bullets tore through the partition, showering me in splinters and broken glass. An android cashier with a split skull lay beneath the counter. I saw the remains of a human brain full of implants and chips inside.

Detective Culkin sounded off in my earpiece.

*Don't catch a bullet, rookie. The bandits can't find out that you're our guy. You hear me? God dammit, why does everything always go wrong with you?*

The bandits also seemed worried that things were going wrong. They started to make a fuss. Before they'd even filled all their bags with money, they rushed to the exit. The bandit in the monkey mask lagged behind the others. That made it clear; he was the undercover agent. I turned to Amy. She ran to the opposite side, into the labyrinth of the bank's offices. She clearly realized that I'd shoot her if she joined her comrades.

Two feelings fought within me. I had to get the agent's intel... but I wanted to take vengeance against Amy even more. Player versus player was sacred. Damn the quests. I rose behind the bullet-peppered counter and aimed at Amy's back. I shot, but she ducked around a turn in the corridor.

*Hey, asshole... I order you to...*

I pulled out my earpiece and tossed it over the counter. Jumping over the prostrate bodies of the bank's customers, I rushed after Amy. It looked like she'd put lots of points into Agility. She ran quickly, constantly turning into new corridors. I kept knocking my shotgun against the walls and fell farther and farther behind. If it weren't for my improved hearing, I'd have lost her. I had to throw the shotgun away to run faster.

We ended up outside the bank, at the back of the building. The gates were wide open. The dead bodies of guards lay here and there, with hacked police drones circling endlessly above them. To them, nothing untoward had happened.

I ran through the gates and found myself in an empty street bordered with high fences at either side. Amy was already far away, toward the end of the street. There was a motorcycle there. The bandits' truck stopped next to it. The driver waved to Amy. She waved in answer and jumped onto the bike. The driver sped off and Amy started the bike's engine, turning to follow them. She even waved me good-bye.

Watch yourself, slick. I got some tricks of my own. Amy was already gaining speed. She leaned down to the handlebars and flew toward the junction onto the main street. That was when I activated the Sprint skill from my boots.

The wind rushed in my ears. The fence and asphalt merged into a solid line, as if I was flying through a blurry tunnel. It reminded me of resurrecting at a respawn tower. In a few seconds I'd caught up to Amy, drawn level with her... The girl turned her head toward me with no idea what had happened. I jumped and knocked her off the bike. It kept going to the end of the street, fell on its side and span in place like a top.

Amy and I flew to the fence, catching a few cuts. Her health and strength weren't as high as mine. I leapt to my feet. All she could do was sit and take out her energy pistol, but I kicked it out of her hands. We both rushed for the weapon at the same time, but I stopped Amy with a swift kick to the stomach.

"Fuck," she cried, flying off to the side.

My augmented reality glasses were a little askew, so part of my neurointerface was hidden. I could only read half of each phrase:

*Close-Quarters Combat skill learned: +10*
*Wave your arms and legs about! Hit mo*
*Congratulations, Leonarm, you levele*
*Attention: you have unused stat poin*

I couldn't see the rest. I raised the energy pistol and aimed it at Amy. I adjusted my glasses.

"It's done, it's over, I've won."

Amy kept hold of her stomach. She sat on her heels and leaned her back against the fence.

"So what are you going to do now?"

"Depends what you say to me."

"Go to hell. You can shoot me, I'm sick of living with this reputation anyway."

I read her stats:

*Amy McDonald, Human.*
*Class: Bandit.*
*Level: 18.*
*Health: 2,345/5,000.*
*Armor: 0/12,000.*
*Warning: Amy McDonald's Reputation is -33! The authorities will be grateful if this villain is killed or delivered to the police.*

Did falling off that motorcycle really take out all her armor? Or did she lose it before, in the crossfire with the guards?

"I could shoot you," I said. "But I could do

something worse, too."

"I'd forgotten how much of a buzzkill you are."

"I'm working with a detective. I have the authority to arrest you and put you in jail."

I was lying, of course. Without a badge, all I could do was get coffee for the boss.

Prison was less pleasant than death. Rare was the player who wanted to spend their taharration rotation sitting out a simulated prison sentence.

Amy tensed and tried to stand.

"Listen, Leo, I was in the wrong. But I didn't want to kill you."

I pushed her back to the ground.

"You did kill me, though."

"I had my reasons, dickhead. Though they might sound strange to you."

"Speak."

Amy spoke, and I noticed how difficult it was for her to get the words out. And it wasn't the contrived hesitation so common to women wanting to make the impression that they were sharing something intimate.

She really was sharing.

"You've heard about the neohikki, right?"

"Hikki... That's what they called people in the past that left society and lived in isolation. Didn't come out of their apartments and all that. They were usually the main consumers of games and video content. They disappeared into virtual worlds. These days, we call people neohikki when they leave society even in the virtual world."

Amy nodded.

"The neohikki don't just avoid contact, they avoid contact with real people. Both in life and in Adam Online. But they're happy to talk to NPCs."

"I didn't know that. I don't know much about mental illness."

Amy faltered again.

"They... deliberately search for advanced NPCs in Adam Online, and speak only to them. Some of them live with those NPCs as if they're a real family."

"I can imagine that. It's not hard in Adam Online. What are you driving at?"

Amy ran her fingers through her hair, nervously scratched her nose, ran a palm over her lips.

"I'm one of them. A neohikki."

As soon as she said that, she pulled her head down into her shoulders as if expecting me to hit her. I could have done, of course, considering what she'd done to me. Would have leveled up Close-Quarters Combat a bit too, but all the same...

"You? You don't seem the type. The neohikki are idiots. You can talk like a normal person."

Amy ran her palm over her lips again.

"I thought... I thought you were an NPC sent to me in place of... Well, to compensate for my losses. Like a quest."

I must have had a fearsome expression on my face. Amy's head withdrew into her shoulders again.

"Me? An NPC?"

"Yeah, so what, god dammit?"

Amy's answer was so naive that I had no idea how to react to it. I kept forgetting that ninety nine percent of Adam Online's players had no idea how this world was built. For them, it was a miraculous space in which they could do anything.

"Don't you think the way I talk, the way I act, makes it obvious that I'm a person?"

Amy responded in a barely audible whisper.

"The one I lived with for years was even smarter than you."

"A buzzkill like me? What if he was a player too?"

"No. He was... How can I explain it..? I... cultivated him myself."

I stopped understanding.

"How's that?"

"Well, you meet an NPC and start talking to them. The longer you talk, the more they understand you. It's called 'nurturing.' Over years of communication, NPCs become the same as people. You can't tell them apart."

"I didn't know that happened. I talk more with real people."

Amy shrugged timidly.

"We have a hard time with people."

"Is it hard for you to talk to me?"

"Very."

"So you killed me when you found out I was a person?"

"Yeah, when you told me about the real world."

I chuckled. "Yeah, NPCs can't know anything about the real world. For them, Adam Online is all there is."

She sighed. "No... After enough nurturing, they start to understand it all. The companion becomes a fully fledged person."

I didn't try to convince her that a set of algorithms supported by hundreds of CS creative functions was far from a person.

"What happens then?"

Amy grimaced pathetically.

"They die."

"Why? How?"

"They kill themselves."

I exhaled.

"From bad to worse. Are you sure you're not confused about any of this?"

"After everything you said about the CSes, I'm not sure about anything any more. Maybe I am confused. Maybe my companion was a part of the game, a creation of the CSes? We neohikki are proud of our differences from the other players in Adam Online. We believe we have special goals... Now I'm not sure of any of it."

"So why the hell did you take me out, fool? Because you weren't sure?"

"That too. Plus, I wanted all the loot. And the reward for the core. I just needed to level up. I want to be a super, you understand..."

"No, I don't understand."

I aimed at Amy's head. She drew it down into her shoulders and shut her eyes. She covered her face with her hands as if wanting to hide her embarrassment.

"Alright. Why do you want to become a super?"

"To take vengeance against a certain player. Supers are the strongest characters, and they're not as gross as bizoids or as weird as mechanodestructors."

"Your enemy is a player? Or an NPC too? I'm not sure which you mean any more."

"He's a player. He was the one who convinced my lov... my companion that the world is a fiction and he had to die to be free."

"He convinced an NPC to kill itself? His Eloquence skill must be pretty high."

"It was sport to him. But to me..."

Amy suddenly burst into tears. It took a lot to cry in Adam Online. She must have been really upset. I even felt a little ashamed that I'd made fun of the girl. I lowered my pistol.

"Stop crying."

"My companion was my entire life..." Amy sobbed. "The only creature I could live with in peace. I can only really live in Adam Online. For me, the end of my taharration rotation means living in a prison. A prison of the real world."

"That's true for many."

"I didn't know what to do."

"Get a new companion?"

Amy stopped crying and looked at me with the hatred I was used to.

"You're such an asshole. I spent my whole life nurturing my companion. We're not talking about using some skill to tame a spiderbot."

I holstered my pistol and sat next to Amy.

"I don't know if this will make it easier for you, but everything you said about companions is true, that's roughly how it all works. They're your pets. Although considering the madness of the neohikki, it's more like you're their pets."

"No, no, you don't understand," Amy threw up her hands. "Until you try it yourself, you'll never understand."

I suddenly remembered Heylia. I'd taken her for a person so easily. Actually, no. I'd *agreed* to take her for a person. Irene, too...

Amy was right about something. Can't NPCs just keep getting more and more complex, to infinity? That would mean they'd start to surpass humans. Or, on a more pragmatic level, they'd start to take up too many of the control systems' resources in supporting their creative functions.

I laughed.

"If you peel away the mystical layers you neohikki have put on your relationships with NPCs, you could say they just have an in-built self-destruct mechanism."

"What do you mean?" Amy's tears dried up. She was back to that somewhat gentle and trusting mode with which she listened to my stories of Adam Online.

"As soon as an NPC reaches a certain threshold of complexity and begins to think about the existence of a world beyond Adam Online, that's a signal that it has to be wiped. Even if your enemy really does enjoy destroying other people's companions, there's no point in taking vengeance against him. Your companion would still have died. It isn't a bad player that you have to take vengeance against. It's the rules of the game."

"I don't believe you."

"I don't care. I'm right — he would have died. He wouldn't have withstood the weight of existence."

Amy rose to her feet. I jumped up too, pulling my pistol back out.

"Where are you going?"

"But I thought..."

"You wasted me and thought you'd get away with some tears and a tale about a 'living' NPC? Before you go back to your prison of reality, you're going to have to sit in a virtual one."

"Don't mock my feelings, asshole," Amy whispered. "What do you want from me?"

I gravely span my pistol in front of her face.

"I want to arrest you, gain some reputation with my boss, finish a bunch of quests. Get experience, level up. What else do you think people need in this game?"

"Please..." It was hard for Amy to talk. "Don't

arrest me. I don't want to lose time. I can pay you."

"Then tell me everything you know about the gang that organized the bank raid. Who hired you? Who led the operation? Who gave you the guns? Where did you get them? The Luxor District has strict gun control. And yeah, how much money do you have?"

Amy could barely hide her joy that all I wanted was money and intel. She froze for a second, staring into space. I envied her again. She'd already got herself a neurointerface. I was still walking around like an idiot with glasses on a string. Hanging around on the dark side sure was profitable.

"Ugh, I failed the mission," Amy sighed. "Fine, dammit, I'll tell you everything. I'll give you all my map markers and some game logs too, so you know which NPCs are involved."

# Chapter 17
# Actors and Scenery

AFTER HEARING AMY out, I let her go. But first I got what she promised, along with fifty thousand gold to sweeten the deal.

"I was going to take your laser pistol too," I said. "But I feel bad for you, and there's an art to saying good-bye. Especially to freak neohikkis like you."

"You're a true servant of the law," Amy said. "Arrogant and corrupt."

Although she was trying to look brave, it was clear that she had no idea what she should do next.

She slowly approached the motorcycle and picked it up.

"Hey," I shouted. "Want to increase your rep? Kill the Yellow Piranhas. They're a gang that declared war against the police department. You get bonus reputation for them right now."

"Thanks," Amy nodded.

"And come visit me sometime. We don't have to be enemies. I can give you some tips on leveling up as a super."

I immediately started fantasizing about Amy

standing by my Sexodrome, me approaching and kissing her. This time she didn't push me away and reject me like she did on the alien spaceship, stuck to the walls by Bully's claws...

"Huh? Are you frozen, dickhead?" Amy's voice shook me from my reverie. "What makes you think I'm leveling up wrong for a super? You know how high my Agility is?"

"Yeah, I do," I nodded. "But it's not about Agility. Your class is Bandit. You can't even become a Joker. You can't be a Catwoman either, even if you go up to three hundred Agility. Class skills are no less important than your Knowledge and Agility stats. Apart from that, to become a super, you'll need to create a multi-class character, and that means you have to level up the classes carefully. The Bandit class has a different set of skills, and..."

"Ugh, enough!" Amy shouted. "I'd rather you shoot me than bore me to death."

Amy McDonald jumped up and mounted the motorcycle. I admired the curves of her fine figure. Naturally, I compared her to Vildana. The girls were complete opposites of each other, but they had one thing in common: neither had any intention of sleeping with me. And both thought I was a killjoy.

"I'm not a killjoy, you know. I just want to help."

Amy looked back over her shoulder.

"I don't remember asking for help."

"All the same, remember: 1884 Lakeview Estates, 119th Street."

Amy started the bike and rode away without a word. I still didn't quite know whether we were friends or still enemies.

I wandered into the bank building, still thinking about why everything always went wrong both in life and in this game. I came to an unexpected conclusion: nothing could possibly go wrong in Adam Online.

Of course, there was a certain amount of randomness, especially in player-vs-player scenarios. Human behavior was unpredictable, but controllable. The control systems managed us, predicted our motives. You didn't have to be a mighty artificial intelligence to know it: if one player killed another player, the victim would always want to take vengeance.

Cops swarmed the bank's corridors, drones flew beneath the ceiling. I heard the booming voice of Detective Culkin from afar. He was not best pleased.

That reminded me of the points I'd got, and my level-up to sixteen. I stopped and put the point in Health, raising it to nine. Also:

*Energy Weapons skill upgraded to level 1.*
*Now all energy weapons will fire more accurately and do more damage.*

That's better. I moved on, still deep in thought.

Human behavior was unpredictable in everyday life. No artificial intelligence could predict what mood you might be in at any given moment, but it could arrange the conditions to encourage the correct mood. If you can control a person's emotions, you control the person. (Sure, not really a person, but their binary array.) Vengeance was a simple motive. The control systems had created conditions in which Amy and I meeting again would be more probable. They'd built the scenery, handed out the roles and ensured that random onlookers wouldn't interfere with the actors, but would just do their thing in their own scenario.

I exited a corridor into the bank's main hall. There were even more cops there. A police mech hopped around on its mechanical legs. The light on its head doused the walls in blue and red flashes.

I still couldn't stop thinking.

We're unpredictable in everyday life, but in the game, we're rats in a maze. We race each other to the goal, make wrong turns, end up in dead ends. Still we keep moving. Only the maze's architect can see all its twists and turns. Our choice is limited to direction: forward, right, left or back. It didn't take much effort to make the rat run along the turns in the storyline that agreed with the rules of the game world, with the current state of the zone and with the actions of other players running in their own maze.

Players liked unexpected twists in the story, they liked that every turn hid a surprise. And only the labyrinth's creator knew that there was nothing unexpected about it. For the CSes, everything was going according to plan...

"ROOKIE!" Joshua Culkin shouted. "What the hell have you done? Are you stupid? I explained the plan of action pretty clearly. Why didn't it go to plan?"

"Detective, it all went a lot better than the plan."

"Better? Better?" The detective's square head rushed me, shaking a square fist. "Our agent didn't manage to pass on the intel, you ran off somewhere and got the whole place shot up. People have died for nothing. That's it, you're done, asshole, I ain't working with you any more..."

"Simmer down, Josh. I know who gave them the guns and where they are. If we hurry, we'll catch them there."

The detective fell silent, looked at me. He called over a police drone and ordered it to return my gun.

"You better not mess this one up, rookie. Where are we going and how many bodies do we need? I only have two or three commandos to spare, and a couple of drones. We can't take too many anyway, we can't turn the Luxor District into a warzone."

I chuckled, gesturing at the ruined bank and the corpses covered in sheets.

"A little late for that, don't you think?"

Joshua Culkin, myself and two police commandos piled into an armored car and careered along the peaceful streets of the Luxor District. The detective's square figure was a perfect match for the armored car's boxy compartment. Next to him, the commandos looked small even clad in their UniSuits and exoskeletons. I saw the tops of palm trees and skyscrapers float by through the car's open hatch. Two drones flew escort alongside us, adding their own voices to the armored car's sirens.

"Dear citizens, this is a police transport, please clear the way. Thank you. The police department apologizes for any inconvenience caused."

Joshua Culkin sat behind the wheel, making it look like a toy in his square hands.

"Is your source reliable?" he said. "What if he lied? What if there aren't any weapons there?"

"If she lied," I answered. "Then she knows I'll find

her and kill her."

"A chick?" Joshua snorted. "I got no faith in them."

"Kind of sexist, detective."

"I just know life, rookie. I've been married four times."

"And all your wives lied to you?"

Joshua Culkin fell silent, making as if he was watching the road. One of the spec ops guys answered for him.

"Haha, it's old Josh who cheated on 'em with every whore he locked eyes with."

"Still don't trust dames," the detective muttered.

I remembered Amy's story about how some NPCs could become complex enough to understand their own false nature. Even if that was true, Detective Culkin certainly wasn't one of them. He was a blocky, obstinate, overconfident iceberg, was what he was. I imagined Amy trying to 'nurture' him and increase his complexity. It was more likely the detective would have changed and simplified her.

We left the center of the Luxor District, crossed the residential areas where the most expensive apartments in Rim One were sold, and drove out onto the riverside.

We drove along it for some time. I admired the view of the Conlin River. I could see the section of Liberty City on the other side of the river through the mist. Airships gently floated above the skyscrapers, which stood like blades of grass. Even the peak of the respawn point was lost in those majestic heights. Patrol boats floated along the smooth river, leaving a foamy wake. Police drones patrolled other sections of the watery expanse. From afar, they looked like swarms of gnats over a swamp.

"We're here," Joshua said simply, stopping the armored car. "We go from here on foot."

We left the vehicle. I enjoyed a deep breath of river air faintly tinged with silt. Joshua Culkin offered me a police exoskeleton, but I regretfully refused; it required over fifteen Strength to equip.

I decided to keep my overcoat equipped. The ability to slow time seemed far more valuable than being able to jump three meters and soften gravity, which was what my UniSuit allowed.

Joshua Culkin himself didn't even take any body armor. He stayed in his white shirt and suspenders. He took out some binoculars and surveyed the area.

I looked around too. We were a great distance from the moorings on the riverside, above which rose the dock building, with huge yellow lettering on its wall:

*Liberty City River Infrastructure Department.*
*URI No. 395-A.*

Several boats bobbed at the moorings, and a pair of trucks bearing the emblem 'Gourmet, Restaurant Chain' were parked at the dock gates. The zone was surrounded by an electric fence, and three armed guards stood at the gates. A few more patrolled the fence perimeter. I saw those details thanks to my Eagle Eye skill.

"Hmm..." said the detective, putting his binoculars away. "Why guard a building that cleans the river bed? And why are there Gourmet trucks there? This is suspicious."

"And why are they armed?" I added. "Only the police are supposed to have guns in the Luxor District..."

"Or those authorized by the police. You, for example. I suspect, rookie, that your informer told the truth."

For some reason, he didn't sound too pleased about that. Could he be jealous that someone was cleverer than him when it came to solving this crime?

The detective ordered a drone to hover above the dock zone. He took out a tablet to look at the position of the buildings and the alleyways between them. I watched over his square shoulder. The zone was blurred on the drone's video feed.

"The bastards are scrambling the signal. They know the access codes to the drones," Joshua explained.

"That means one of them is a cop from the department?"

"Could be. And it's a clever idea. The river infrastructure department is a municipal building. The last place we'd look."

"The informant told me that the bandits spoof the feed from the river drones in the same way. They deliver containers of weapons with helicopters to the middle of the river, to the edge of the radar zone. They dump the shipments in the water, then deliver them to the dock with boats and take them in trucks from there to drop points for the bandits."

"She's pretty well informed."

I didn't bother telling him that Amy had completed a mission to deliver those containers.

*That mission with the helicopters was so dumb,* she'd complained. *I'm not a good pilot, the thing didn't do what I wanted it to do, the controls were stupid. And I had to drop the container in this tiny square so the bandit boats could pick it up before the river patrol got it. And there was only a few minutes before the anti-air system would have knocked out my chopper. I got shot down twice, I barely managed to jump out in time.*

Joshua signaled the commandos to walk around the zone and sneak through the fence from the other side. He ordered me to stick close to them again. This time I decided to listen.

We waited for them to get into position. Joshua and I crept toward the entrance to the dock zone, running from building to building.

"Hey, Josh," I whispered. "Why don't we just ram through the gates with the armored car?"

"Too noisy. I want to stay undetected as long as possible, so they don't have time to cover their tracks."

"Strange argument, detective, but you're the boss."

"I sure am, rookie. Now listen to my orders: shut up and follow me."

# Chapter 18
# Pack of Cigarettes

THE COMMANDOS cut through the fence. They waited for a guard to walk by and took him down, then crept into the zone and neutralized a second guard. Joshua and I crept toward the gates and hid behind the trucks. As I understood it, the two guys at the gates were our job. The commandos waved to us and crouched behind some barrels by the entrance to the building.

Joshua's square body moved incredibly quickly and quietly. He leapt out from behind the truck and was between the two guards in a second. He grabbed them by the collars and smashed their heads together. I barely held back a smile: that move would never have worked in real life.

The detective carefully laid the guards under the truck and waved me over. We crossed the yard and joined the commandos. Joshua gave orders.

"You keep watch here, me and the Rookie will go inside. Don't get involved, whatever happens. Your task is to guard the entrances and exits."

The commandos split up and took up positions at the edge of the yard. Drones hovered above them: they were useless after the hacking block. They just followed us as if on a leash.

The detective opened the door and slipped inside. It looked like magic; with his size and shape, Joshua was practically a doorway himself.

We found ourselves in a large room. River water splashed in its center. Containers bearing the logo of the Tenshot store chain towered over the mooring. To dispel all doubt that they contained weapons, the containers were marked '10mm Ammunition', 'Uzi', 'F-40 Pulse Grenade' and so on.

"Damn, there's enough firepower here for a whole army," I breathed.

"And here are the soldiers," Joshua whispered.

We hid behind some columns supporting the building's ceiling. A boat floated to the mooring, its engine humming quietly.

The same bandits that robbed the bank got off it. I recognized them by the animal masks hanging on their necks. I looked over each of them and relaxed. Amy wasn't among them. That meant she'd come to her senses.

There were two things I still didn't understand: why did Joshua decide that we had to get in here unnoticed, and why didn't he even bring a gun with him? Did he plan to knock them all out hand-to-hand?

As if to make my doubts worse, two mechs appeared by the mooring. They were the same model as the police mechs, with machine guns instead of arms, but with no lights or police markings. Between the robots stood a middle-aged bald man in a business suit. A comically large red nose stood out on his slightly swollen face.

When he saw him, Joshua chuckled wryly and glanced at me.

"Do you know him?" I asked.

"Everyone knows him. It's Weinhardt."

"What's he famous for, his big nose?"

"He's the mayor of Liberty City."

Joshua stood and walked out from our cover.

"Mr. Weinhardt, like I said last time, you're a greedy bastard. But I didn't think you were a stupid one too."

I took out my Uzi and jumped out from behind the column, intending to support the brave detective. To my surprise, nobody reacted much at all at the sight of Joshua. I switched my crosshair between the robbers and the mechs. I knew that if they started firing, we wouldn't survive.

"What are you doing, boss?" I whispered.

He waved me away and walked along the mooring. The mayor walked toward him.

"I see you're as rude and incompetent as ever, detective."

"I'm about to be even more rude and incompetent, jackass. Why did you come here?"

It was as if they were in a duel of words, only Joshua's position was the weaker. After all, the mayor had two heavily armed mechs behind him.

"I have a couple of questions for you too, detective." The mayor showed no fear whatsoever of Joshua or myself. "Firstly, how are things? And secondly, why were your people present during the raid on the bank?"

Joshua shrugged his square shoulders.

"Listen, Weinhardt, I haven't replaced the whole police department. I have bosses too, and they're worried about the robberies. I held up my end of the deal: you got the access codes to the drones."

With those words, I finally realized what was wrong. While Joshua approached the mayor, I slowly stepped back.

Joshua spread his arms as if he wanted to grab the mayor.

"I even arrested an innocent gangster from the Yellow Piranhas to confuse the investigation, but the game's up thanks to your idiocy."

The mayor and the detective reached each other... and embraced like old friends. Joshua turned toward me.

"Sorry, rookie, but your clever investigating hasn't helped you. If our mayor hadn't showed up here in person, then I'd have let all this slide. But you did your job too well."

The raiders aimed their guns at me and arranged themselves in a semicircle behind Weinhardt and the robots. Both the bots aimed their machine gun barrels at me.

To win time, I feigned surprise.

"So it turns out the mayor has been organizing armed raids, and the chief detective is in on it?"

Joshua laughed.

"In on it? I came up with the whole idea, rookie."

"Why?"

"Because..."

The mayor grabbed the detective by the arm.

"Why are you yapping? Take care of him and throw him in the river."

The detective shook his square head.

"It's you politicians who solve everything by killing

your enemies. Leonarm is a smart guy. Let him make his choice."

I took another step back. The detective continued.

"You see, rookie, the Luxor District is getting crowded. The island has no room to grow. So the only thing growing is its property prices."

"They're exorbitant," the mayor interjected. "It's impossible to open new businesses here. The cost of land or property exceeds all potential profit from a future business."

"So you decided to rob banks to make enough money to buy land?"

Joshua Culkin smirked.

"Hey, rookie, don't play dumb. You can't count on winning time here."

Maybe I couldn't win time, but I could definitely slow it down.

"Alright," I agreed. "Sure, increasing crime in the district would lower the property prices. Decent plan, predictable. But what's unpredictable, boss, is you betraying your colleagues. How many of them died for your cunning plan? You dragged corpses out of the police department yourself after the explosion in the hall. Were you really just acting?"

I remembered that it was all just a game, but my anger was real. I remembered Heylia's face, her thousand braids, and got even more angry at this bent cop. He messed up my date! So I finished up my speech with a trite phrase.

"How can you live with yourself after such a betrayal?"

Joshua took out a pack of cigarettes with a habitual movement, lit one.

"Rookie, you can't imagine how easy it is to live

with seven figures in your bank account. As for the corpses... police work is dangerous."

Mayor Weinhardt stepped forward a little.

"Alright, Josh, your rookie's made his choice."

"Seems so. Shame. Sorry, Leo. Now it's time to die-e-e-e-e..."

The detective's voice stretched out into a slow howl; I'd activated Time Slow. But both the robots and the bandits followed my smallest movements. As soon as I jumped behind the column, they all started shooting.

*Damage taken: -150, injury to left leg.*

Taking cover behind the column, I swapped my overcoat for my UniSuit and my Uzi for the Parasite Pistol. After making sure that the bizoid telepath larva was still alive, I loaded the charge into the pistol. Then I waited for a break in the shots and stuck my head out.

Since the detective had become a hostile NPC, the lines about his mood and character had disappeared from his stats. But I could see his health: two hundred and fifty thousand. The blocky Joshua would have withstood a hit from a grenade launcher... maybe more than one.

The mechs each had ten thousand health. The rest were ordinary bandits with standard stats around my own level. They all calmly moved toward me. Apart from Mayor Weinhardt. He wasn't a combat NPC, he was more likely a Politician class, so he stood to the side.

I was alone against a small army. Retreat? No way. That wasn't what I'd gone there for.

"Hey, detective!" I shouted. "I worked for you, now you're going to work for me."

I couldn't hold that statement back. The storyline

itself pushed you to clichés like that. I aimed and fired. The empty parasite container automatically ejected from my gun, spraying out liquid, while the larva itself screeched toward Joshua. With a smacking sound like a kiss, it pierced the detective's neck. The number eight lit up in my glasses. But the countdown hadn't started yet. The larva probably needed a little time to take control.

I loaded a second capsule and shot a bandit armed with a machine gun. A second number eight appeared in my glasses. The larva in the third capsule had died. The fourth lay on the bottom, strangely immobile. I decided not to use it for now. I loaded the fifth...

The larva in Joshua Culkin came alive.

The detective stopped, turned and rushed the nearest robot. He jumped onto it, tore off its head and pulled out a handful of wires. The mech waved its arms, fired randomly into the ceiling, tried to throw off the gigantic boxy detective.

"Don't you dare touch my best friend!" the detective cried fiercely, pulling wires and cables out of the mechanodestructor. "I'll kill you all!"

The immobilized robot sprayed out fountains of sparks, swayed and fell on its side. Joshua jumped off it and headed toward the remaining enemies, spreading his arms as if he wanted to hug them all.

The raiders and the second robot hesitated for a moment, then identified Joshua as a hostile character and opened fire on him. I watched with pleasure as the detective's health fell rapidly.

By that time, the second larva had activated. The bandit with the machine gun stopped firing at Joshua, turned and blew the head off his nearest comrade. Then a second. The remaining three raiders switched targets and returned fire on the machine gunner.

Another enemy gone.

I shot at another bandit, but missed. I reloaded the parasite pistol with my last capsule and aimed, choosing my victim.

*Obtained: Freshly Opened Pack of Camels.*

*You have a pack of cigarettes in your pocket. Today is a good day.*

Hmm. The bizoid telepath hadn't chosen the most valuable item from the detective's inventory.

Joshua looked terrifying: covered in blood, with open wounds, clothing ripped to shreds, but just as large and angry as ever. He came crashing down on the second robot, covering its machine guns with his body. The man and the robot fell to the floor. Joshua strained his powerful muscles and... tore off the mechanodestructor's machine gun arm. He took hold of it like a club and began to beat the mech around the head with it.

"I warned ya! Don't you dare touch my friend, fucking rustbucket."

I had three seconds left of this unprecedented caring from the detective. Over that time, he managed to pierce the robot's head with its own torn-off arm. The robot jerked its legs, shook and sprayed out sparks. Joshua jumped off it and walked toward the bandits. They shot him without pause. They switched magazines and shot him again, covering the floor with empty shell casings. Joshua's health was around sixty thousand. Still a lot.

Joshua almost reached them, intending to grab them in his deadly embrace, but then stopped, shook his head and shouted.

"Stop shooting me, idiots!"

Before the bandits could switch fire to me, I shot a parasite at one with a Kalashnikov rifle. But I didn't have time to get behind the column. Bullets ricocheted off my UniSuit.

*Damage taken: -1,356, various bullet wounds.*
*Upgrade slot #1 destroyed. Light Gravity skill lost.*
*Upgrade slot #4 destroyed. Jump skill lost.*

Another hit and my UniSuit would be gone.

I reached the cover of the column, equipped my Uzi, used some anesthetic and stopped the bleeding.

*Battlefield Surgery skill increased: +10 XP.*

I didn't see what was going on with my enemies. By the sounds of it, I guessed that my temporary ally with the AK-47 had taken care of his comrades, but wasn't holding up well against Joshua. First I heard his assault rifle firing, and Joshua swearing. Then the sound of a punch and... The rifle fire cut off with the sound of a splash into the water.

I glanced out from behind the corner and was immediately pulled out into the open. Joshua had grabbed me with his square arms.

"Gotcha, rookie."

# Chapter 19
# Too Much Stress

JOSHUA CULKIN shook me so hard that my UniSuit durability dropped to zero and the whole thing fell off me.

*Apple Sierra C UniSuit destroyed beyond repair.*

My Furr jacket automatically took its place. By default, lost equipment or items were automatically replaced by something similar. If there were several similar items, then the most expensive one was used. That setting could be changed, which, naturally, I'd forgotten until that moment.

"I'm going to wipe the floor with you, you fucker," Joshua Culkin roared.

Shrouded in a handsome velvet jacket, I hung from the detective's arms. I somehow doubted the Deadly Compliment bonus would help me in this situation.

"You have... S-such s-strong hands," I ventured.

"Thanks, rookie."

Could the compliment really have worked? Joshua Culkin stopped shaking me, but then got a grip on himself.

"Fucking bastard!"

I tried to aim my Uzi at Joshua's face, but it was impossible. He was shaking me like a rag doll. The detective's fearsome bloody face flashed before my eyes, then the ceiling, then a slice of the river, then the laughing Mayor Weinhardt.

Each shake took away a little of my health. If this kept going, then Joshua would just shake me to death.

As if reading my thoughts, he swung around and threw me into the wall as if I weighed nothing. My back and the back of my head took the brunt of it. Even my glasses on their string flew off my nose. But I could still read the system messages.

*Damage taken: -1,567, numerous bruises and contusions.*
*Apple 'Sierra Zed' Helmet destroyed beyond repair.*

Taking advantage of the pause while Joshua ran toward me, I emptied my entire Uzi magazine into him. The explosive force threw other enemies back slightly, but not Joshua. I don't even know what would push him back... a nuclear explosion?

The fierce detective grabbed me in his arms again, raised me into the air, shook me hard and threw me into another wall.

*Damage taken: -1,560, numerous bruises and contusions.*
*You're more a bag of loose bones than a warrior right now.*

"You like that?" shouted Joshua, advancing on

me. "That's my strong arms in action."

Instead of picking me up and shaking me again, Joshua clenched his fist and punched my Uzi. My favorite machine pistol broke into tiny pieces. I didn't even bother reading the obvious message that it was broken beyond repair. Pain shot through my hand. I worried that it had been torn off again...

*Damage taken: -1,002, right hand mutilated and broken.*

*Restoration will require a doctor or a Battlefield Surgery skill of level 10 or above.*

"You made the wrong choice, rookie," Joshua barked, picking me up in his arms. "You ain't cut out for detective work. Too much pressure."

Joshua roared and threw me into yet another wall. This time I knocked down a carefully stacked pile of boxes. A bunch of perfect peaches spilled out of them. I was surrounded by the aroma of crushed fruit.

*Damage taken: -666. You fell and hit something again.*

*You shouldn't be alive right now. Run while you can.*

What an interesting number... I sighed and took out my parasite pistol. Joshua Culkin stretched his arms toward me. I loaded the last capsule, with the half-dead larva. Square fingers dug into my body. I felt like a baby whose father had decided to throw him up into the air as a game. Only Joshua wasn't planning on catching me.

"Fucking bast..."

I shot the parasite larva right into his mouth.

Joshua dropped me in surprise, backed up, coughed and spluttered.

"Ugh... What the... You..."

I received a message in my augmented reality glasses.

*You have made a scientific discovery.*

*Knowledge received: bizoid telepath female. Instead of one larva, this capsule contained a pregnant female. This larva has a longer duration of 32 seconds.*

*Natural Scientist skill learned: +10 XP.*

*Keep a close eye on nature. A whole world of wonderful discoveries awaits you.*

I adjusted my glasses. The number thirty two began to count down.

"Hey, buddy," Joshua babbled. "What happened? Did someone hurt you?"

"Afraid so."

"Just show me who and I'll kick the shit out of 'em. Those fuckers."

Mayor Weinhardt had hidden somewhere. There were no other enemies left alive. Joshua walked around me like a guard dog, clenching his fists.

Loyally protecting me against attack...

Limping slightly, I walked over to a machine gun, picked it up in one hand and aimed it at the detective. There was something a little shameful in it. Like I was killing a disabled person.

I remembered Heylia, our lost date, her corpse and lifeless thousand braids. Sure, it was all just a game and not real. I knew that. But rage was always real. And it didn't matter where it came from, whether from a real death or an imagined one.

"What are you doing, buddy?" Joshua asked, looking at the gun in my hand. "Looks calm, nobody here to hurt ya."

The detective patted his pockets, looking for the pack of cigarettes I'd taken from him.

"This is for Heylia," I said, pulling the trigger.

"What?"

The machine gun shook in my hand as if it wanted to jump away and escape. I shot with one arm. Most of the bullets flew off who knows where, anywhere but Joshua. But their destructive power was huge: they shot holes clean through the walls, letting in rays of light. When they hit Joshua, they did massive damage. I was hitting rarely, most of my shots were wasted.

But it was enough to silence the invincible detective. I shot and shot, with small breaks to correct the gun's position. I was afraid I wouldn't be able to kill Joshua before the parasite stopped working. When the machine gun fell silent, the detective's health was down to seven thousand.

*Handheld and Mounted Machine Guns skill learned: +5 XP.*

*A strong weapon in weak hands? Increase your Strength to avoid embarrassing yourself when you fire big guns.*

I threw away the machine gun and picked up a Kalashnikov. I shot the rest of the magazine, taking

Joshua's health down to five thousand. The detective watched my actions in pain. Subject to the larva's will, he didn't understand why his best friend was shooting at him.

His confusion wouldn't last long. Just another twelve seconds.

What could I do? Fire my Tesla gun? But the revolver was too slow, its damage poor. Should I just run away? But I'd almost won. And anyway, those commandos were guarding the doors. I wasn't sure whether they'd side with the law or with their boss.

I didn't waste any time. I picked up another gun and shot Joshua. I couldn't reload with one hand, so I just threw away one rifle and picked up another.

*Automatic Weapons skill increased: +10 XP.*

I knocked the detective's health down to three thousand. The larva timer was at five seconds.

My Eagle Eye skill activated again. I noticed that my skewed machine gun fire had broken open one of the containers of weapons. Inside it, something pulsed with a soft white light. I rushed to the container, straining every sinew to break open the wall and take out the grenades. I didn't have time to read what kind they were exactly. They weren't the color of pulse grenades.

"Hey bud, I really want a smoke," the bleeding Joshua said. "You know where my cigarettes are?"

"Just a sec, I'll give you a light," I replied.

Three seconds — I flipped the safety on one of the grenades.

Two seconds — I approached Joshua and stuffed the grenade under his shirt. I took out another one and did the same.

"Ha-ha! That tickles!" the detective laughed.

One second.

The kindhearted look on Joshua's face disappeared. From what I understood, people who were subject to the bizoid telepath's influence had no memory of what they'd done. Joshua watched in confusion as I ran off, jumped behind some crates and peeked out.

The detective felt his shirt, tugged at his collar and looked down... then lifted his head and said something. Probably his classic line: "Fucking bastard."

The delay between the two explosions was short. Joshua's square body warped, then burst like a huge abscess in an explosion of blood and meat. Scraps of flesh, weapons, broken planks, chunks of robots and corpses flew in all directions. The shockwave knocked over the crates I was hiding behind. Even the boat at the mooring rocked and floated back a little.

Shrapnel hit the crates, smashing them into pieces. It was a good thing they just had peaches inside, and not more grenades. Otherwise I'd have been blown into even smaller pieces than the corrupt detective.

I left my cover, expecting my glasses to be flooded with rewards and quest completion messages. But a humble couple of lines is all I saw:

*Damage taken: -321, shrapnel injuries.*
*Explosives skill increased: +10 XP.*

Oh, that's right. I still had Mayor Weinhardt to deal with. The quest couldn't complete without him.

# Chapter 20
# Just Eddie

MR. WEINHARDT scurried around near the mooring, approached the river's edge, sat down as if he wanted to hide, walked back again to take a run at it, then hesitatingly approached the edge again. But after the explosion, the boat had floated too far away to jump to.

I took out my Tesla revolver.

"Game over, Weinhardt."

Sure, it sounded dumb, but I wanted to hurry up and finish the quest. The mayor looked over his shoulder in fear, then gathered himself.

"Who do you think you are? You're not even a detective. You have no right to make an arrest."

"You're right."

Keeping my gun on the mayor, I approached the pile of meat that was left of Joshua. Loot was all over the ground. There was plenty, but I chose the only thing I wanted.

*Obtained: LCPD Detective Badge.*

*Obtained: Yossie Classic Handcuffs Set (x10).*

*These handcuffs allow you to limit the freedom of movement of any NPC or player observed in performing illegal actions. But be careful: those who have the Lockpicking skill of the correct level can easily take them off.*

*Congratulations, Leonarm, now you can arrest criminals or use the handcuffs for other things.*

*You do like experimenting in bed, right?*

Next came a list of the bonuses from the detective's badge, like the Communicative skill.

But there were no updates to the quest progress.

I placed the badge on my left breast. It stuck there on its own. Now it would always be visible, whatever I wore: an exoskeleton, a UniSuit or even if I decided to walk around naked (which I really hoped to do when Irene came to visit me).

I approached the mayor. The expression on his face had changed:

"Listen, I apologize for Joshua's behavior. He was a fool. But I'm an influential man. Do you want to take his place? You'll be the chief of the detective department."

"My last boss said I wasn't cut out for detective work."

"Five percent of my business and a million in cash?"

That gave me pause for thought. Pretty tempting offer...

"How much is five percent?"

"Five hundred thousand a month."

Even more tempting. And a million... seriously? I could buy everything I needed. A passive income of five hundred thousand would completely solve my money problems. Of course, when converting a million gold into dollars, it turned into an amount only a little higher than my monthly paycheck. But all the same, it was very generous.

Noticing my hesitation, Mayor Weinhardt began to gabble about how we'd develop the business together, buy up property, open factories.

"We'll run the whole city like our own farm. Of course, sometimes I'll need you to complete certain assignments, but I'll pay you handsomely. Apart from that, don't forget that being a detective has its advantages."

Those words brought me to my senses. I wasn't here to rule the city. I wasn't here to work for a corrupt mayor. I had let NPCs work their way into my head. All I needed from this mission was access to the LCPD computer system.

Real people were expecting results from my work. They awaited those results so that we could overcome informational entropy and live in virtual reality for as long as we wanted... But that was above my pay grade. All that mattered to me was that after long years of soul-destroying work at the Moscow Security Bureau, someone finally needed me again. People had placed their hopes on me.

"Well, Leonarm? Do we have a deal?" The mayor smiled, stretched out his hand.

I tapped my badge.

"Mayor Weinhardt, you are arrested on suspicion of... uhm..." Police slang didn't come easy to me. I broke character. "You're just arrested for all the shitty things you've done."

I threw a cuff on his outstretched wrist and locked it.

I roughly turned him around so his back was to me and slapped the other end of the handcuffs on his other wrist. It wasn't easy with one hand. I had some help from a game condition: since I'd arrested him, the suspect should be in handcuffs, even if I didn't have both hands to work with.

"You'll be sorry, you son of a bitch. The people behind me..."

"I'm the only person behind you right now. You have the right to remain silent, so shut up before you catch a bullet for resisting arrest."

I couldn't help but admit to myself that if the mayor continued his attempts to bribe me, I might well give in and agree.

With the click of the cuffs, the system notified me that I'd unlocked the Beat Cop achievement; arrest five bandits and so on.

I took advantage of my new capabilities and called for police reinforcements. A two-minute timer showed up. The expected arrival time, apparently. I left the mayor alone and looked over the battlefield. Time to gather the loot and level up.

*Quest True Detective updated:*

*1. You took part in an operation to get intel from an agent infiltrating a bandit gang. You didn't get his intel, but thanks to your initiative, you uncovered the plot yourself.*

*You earned: +50 XP.*

*Reputation with LCPD increased: +1.*

*2. You got a special detective badge. Well done, my compliments.*

*Your reputation with the authorities of all Rims has increased: +1.*

*3. You not only found out who was behind the weapon deliveries to the Luxor District, you also arrested the ringleader, Mayor Weinhardt.*

*Take your well earned +50 XP.*

*And another +50 XP for resisting bribes. Liberty City needs honest people like you.*

*Reputation with the authorities of all Rims increased: +1.*

*Reputation with the authorities of Liberty City increased: +1.*

*4. You uncovered the secret goal of the bandit organization. A corrupt mayor was trying to lower the property prices. Take advantage and buy yourself a cheap skyscraper.*

*Catch: +50 XP.*

*Reputation with the Liberty City Real Estate Association increased: +1.*

*Reputation with the Liberty City Exchequer bank increased: +1.*

*Obtained: 20,000g.*

*5. You still haven't avenged Heylia Grant's murder.*

*Your deeds have not remained unnoticed by the dark side.*

*Reputation with the criminal world decreased: -3.*

*The reward on your head in the Whitelist has been*

*increased by 30%.*

I combed through all the items dropped by Joshua and the raiders while I read all this. The detective had:

*Corrupt Detective Suit.*
*You're in luck, Leonarm, this is a unique item.*
*Durability: infinite.*

*+50 Health.*
*+1 Reputation with the criminal world.*
*+2 to Insight and Communicative skills.*
*+1 to Pistols and Revolvers and Close-Quarters Combat skills.*
*Pistol Tricks skill unlocked.*
*Improves relationships with law-abiding NPCs by 25%.*
*Improves relationships with military-type NPCs by 50%.*
*Improves relationships with criminal-type NPCs by 25%.*
*Worsens relationships with Angel NPCs by 100%. They see only your corrupt core.*
*Unknown property (requires 20 Knowledge).*

Unfortunately, the suit was incompatible with my UniSuit and even with regular body armor. But with that amount of health, I wouldn't have to worry about people killing me quickly. The suit was perfect for city conditions. And that wasn't all:

*Health regeneration: 9 per minute.*

Not too bad. The amount of health restored

depended on my total health. If I raised my health, I could go without any body armor.

*Access to the Blacklist and Whitelist.*
*Ability to publish notices for the search and capture of criminals on behalf of the LCPD. But that doesn't mean you can declare just anyone a wanted person. Only players or NPCs with a low reputation.*

*You can call reinforcements from the police commandos.*
*You can call reinforcements from criminal groups loyal to you.*

*You can demand bribes from merchants in illegal goods or prostitutes. You can intimidate some prostitutes into giving you free services. Don't forget that this will upset the gangs that protect illegal businesses.*

I changed into the corrupt detective suit. In combination with the badge, I'd be unstoppable to NPCs.

None of the other loot was interesting: plenty of weapons with varying degrees of damage, fifteen thousand gold and equipment like "Bandit's Jacket", which gave bonuses when talking to other bandits.

On one bandit, I found:

*Keys to the Riding Raider boat.*

They granted ownership over the boat the bandits had come in on. But I had none of the skills for steering the boat, and no property on the water to store it. I didn't even have enough Knowledge to read its stats.

I returned the keys to the dead man.

I managed to grab a few grenades from the container before the room filled up with cops. The cavalry had arrived. The officers slapped me on the shoulder and congratulated me on a case well closed. Many grieved.

"Who would have thought that Joshua Culkin would turn out to be such an asshole?"

"Yeah, a real piece of work."

Metal toes clanged and a police robot walked into the dock. Its blue light span maddeningly, annoying me with its changing colors. Judging by the fresh patches on its hull, it was the same robot that met me when I first visited the police department. Stooping beneath the ceiling beams, it approached me, its machine guns still threateningly aimed forward. It spoke in a mechanical voice.

"Congratulations, detective. It is pleasing to work with honest people. I will be glad to see you in my office. I believe that together, we can bring order to this city."

I read in surprise:

*ED-909-1200054, Mechanodestructor.*
*Level: 89.*
*Class: Defender.*
*Occupation: Chief at LCPD Third Detective Department.*

Wow. So my new boss was a rustbucket with a flashlight on its head. Well, at least the mafia couldn't bribe him, and I wouldn't need to suck up to him by finding the best kinds of engine oil.

"And congratulations to you on your... promotion. Uhm... nine-oh-nine..."

"You can just call me Eddie."

The robot straightened its legs and dropped its machine gun arms to its sides. One of the machine guns transformed into a four-fingered hand. A small box opened in Eddie's chest and he took out a medal.

"For courage and bravery in investigating this crime, Detective Leonarm is awarded this medal."

His mechanical arm extended toward me and pinned the medal next to my badge. The officers around us applauded. The robot saluted and left.

*Obtained: LCPD Medal.*

*Includes a pension: 5,000g every week.*

*Keep the reward in your inventory to get the money.*

*Next payment in: 6 days and 23 hours.*

Not bad. The amount of the pension was my Luck multiplied by a thousand. Another reason to increase it.

The cops lost interest in me and started combing through the crime scene. It was a good thing that realism didn't extend to paperwork. I knew from my MSB days how depressing that could be. Our officers had to account for every round.

Another section of achievement text lit up in my glasses. I decided to distribute my points later. The first thing I needed to do was restore my health, heal my hand, and, most importantly, visit the LCPD archive to start doing what I came to Adam Online to do: search for Nelly Valeeva.

I left the dock and headed to the nearest Projectoria station. While I selected my travel point, my finger hovered over the Middle Class store, workplace of Irene, whom I really hadn't kissed enough. It looked like I was going for a new anti-record for days spent in the game without having any sex.

# Chapter 21
# Two Recollections

THE LCPD HOSPITAL restored my health and my broken hand, and was cheaper than Doctor Cid's Clinic. The surroundings there were more like a hospital than the absurd bloody decor in the clinic. Slamming doors, squawks over the radio, corridors, smells, the whisper of stretcher wheels. There were even nervous relatives awaiting a doctor's verdict.

Damn, that hospital was too realistic.

I recalled the time when I was called in to identify Olga's body.

That was over ten years ago.

*Recollection No. 1*

I stood before a corpse covered in a sheet. I could already tell by the outlines of the body — it was Olga. *Don't lift the sheet*, I begged in my mind. *I already know...*

The medic lifted the sheet.

I looked at the naked blue body, at the strange face covered in stains from the dried dissociative electrolyte. The left eye was slightly open, as if her body slyly watched for my reaction.

Why did they show me this? It was already obvious that it was her.

I came round in the waiting room, without the faintest idea of who had taken me there and when. I sat on a cold chair. A police investigator stood opposite, a middle-aged graying black man in a white gown thrown on over his jacket.

A son of the first wave of refugees, the first Africans to realize that their continent was doomed. As a rule, the best educated of them. The refugees had built their own little town on the outskirts of Bryansk. The first generation lived a crowded life there, maintaining their traditions and beliefs. But the second generation assimilated and spread throughout Rus. They spoke perfect Russian, loved to quote Pushkin and considered him 'theirs.'

"Anton," the investigator said. "I understand how you must feel, but we need to establish your wife's cause of death."

"Death?" I said in surprise. The fact still hadn't made its way into my head.

The investigator offered me a cup of coffee.

"Were there any modifications made to her taharration pod? As far as I know, you're somehow professionally involved with the technology, yes?"

I put the cup on the table.

"No. I work with quantum computing platforms."

"Aren't they the same thing?"

"QCPs are used to convert the human consciousness into a binary array, but that isn't their sole purpose. This hospital has a quantum platform too, which performs patient diagnostics and surgeries. The power plant has one, and the sewage system. They're everywhere."

The investigator picked up the coffee and handed it to me, brooking no argument.

"Drink it... So you don't know anything about taharration pods?"

"No, that's a separate profession."

"I see. Did Olga know about them? She studied for a career somehow related to taharration, right?"

I laughed.

"Listen, bro, 'somehow related to taharration' is a pretty vast category. Like how you're somehow related to treating patients because you're wearing a white gown right now. Olga studied in the same university as me, but she studied CS analysis. They're different fields."

"Could she have modified a taharration system?"

I took a swallow and burned myself.

"Do you mean to say that the reason for her death wasn't a technical flaw, but deliberate damage to the pod?"

The detective handed me a tablet showing diagrams and three-dimensional projections that I didn't understand.

"Our experts discovered that the pod's timer, the one responsible for ensuring a forced exit from Adam Online, was replaced with a duplicate module."

"What did it do?" I said, not understanding.

"It tricked the system. When the system initiated the transfer of Olga Brulevaya's binary array back into her body, the module kicked in. It gave the system a false confirmation of the transfer. The system accepted it and disconnected from Adam Online. But Olga's consciousness didn't return to her body. Some digital garbage full of zeroes arrived instead. That was the reason for her death after her stasis ended."

I tossed the tablet and the cup onto the table.

"Do you understand what that means?"

"The first post-taharration death in many years?" the cop suggested. "It's going to damage trust in the safety of the taharration process. If people give in to panic, there'll be a mass refusal to log onto Adam Online. That will have serious economic and social consequences..."

"Fuck the consequences. Olga is still there."

"Where?" the cop said in confusion.

"In Adam Online! I have to go back."

The investigator held me back.

"Hey, you only just came out of a pod yourself. You can't go back."

"I have to..."

Then it all went dark again. I remember pushing my way out of the investigator's grasp, waving my fists and demanding that I be returned to a pod. Doctors arrived to help the investigator. They gave me some anesthetic. I fell back into the chair, couldn't move. I stared at the wall. I think I pissed myself.

The investigator appeared in my field of view from time to time.

"Anton, forget about going back. You know that nobody will let you. There's a reason for the recovery period after leaving a taharration pod. Your body won't withstand another immersion. We don't need another taharration death right now."

He spoke the obvious truth. Everyone took exams for a license to use taharration pods.

All I could do was blink. It was like the shrewd

cop could read my thoughts.

"And don't even think about using an underground landing. I have the authority to keep you in custody. If I have to, I'll arrest you and put you in solitary."

I sat immobile, blinking. I pissed myself again, and I felt tears roll down my cheeks. A nurse appeared and gently washed my face with a cloth, called over a cleaner robot to take care of the puddle under my chair.

"Death in taharration is nonsense. It hasn't happened for many years," the investigator continued. "The internal service at Labsetek is involved in the investigation now too. Expect a visit from them. They still believe that taharration technology belongs to them, not to the world..."

I stopped listening to the investigator. His voice blended in with the background noise of the hospital and the buzzing of the cleaner robot. Over time, I came to a realization; Olga was dead, but her consciousness was still there, in Adam Online. By the time my next taharration rotation came around, informational entropy would have dissolved her binary array in the virtual world.

*Recollection No. 2*

After a few months, I took my vacation time and logged into Adam Online. I walked through all the lands Olga and I had owned. In some places, I saw signs of her activity. Or more precisely, evidence of her insanity. For example, our flying island had been transformed into a fortress. There was even an airfield and ten military Eurofighter replicators. Who knew what epic battles Olga's dying consciousness had waged.

Aside from the house at the lake, several whimsical structures had appeared with a bizarre architectural style; not one of them had an entrance. My weapon crafting station had been transformed into a brothel, with strippers clad in qualia armor endlessly dancing around poles. Olga had spent all our in-game savings on it all.

I wandered the zones, seeing more and more details. All the rooms of our apartment in Liberty City were full to the ceiling with identical horned helmets, enchanted to 'reduce damage from two-handed swords when held by an orc at midday.' The specificity and senselessness of the enchantment was a mark of how Olga's loss of personality had progressed.

In the garage stood a cart hitched to a robot horse without hind legs. In the cart was a pile of the idiotic horned helmets. How many had she crafted?

I decided not to check what was in our garages in Swiftville and Londinium. I just closed my eyes and said: "CS. Exit." I didn't even bother selling our property, land or possessions.

I climbed out of the blue mist of dissociative electrolyte and locked my account before I'd even taken my injections and vitamins. I took out my tablet and put up for sale our two taharration pods, which stood side by side in our now empty apartment in Bryansk.

She was gone forever.

What did I hope for, in that moment? I guess I just hoped that informational entropy was a painless death.

# Chapter 22
# A Shot in the Dark

I GOT MY BEARINGS from the police department map which I could now access thanks to the badge.

The LCPD archive was in a huge underground complex, a large hall full of information storage units: ten-foot boxes covered in blinking lights and data screens.

I headed for the center of the hall. From time to time I had to squeeze sideways between the boxes to get through. That's what I call 'high information density.' At the center of the hall were several dusty chairs and an ancient transparent screen on a pedestal. There were empty beer cans strewn around the floor by the chairs, also covered in dust and full of cigarette ash. Nobody had come here for a long time.

I placed my palm on the screen. A handprint remained on the dusty panel. The hologram of a young woman in glasses and a business suit appeared before me.

"Greetings, detective. My name is Sky. I am an artificial intelligence avatar. I service the archive of the police depart..."

"Pleased to meet you, Sky," I interrupted her. "I

need to find a person. Or perhaps not a person, but a phenomenon."

The holographic woman adjusted her glasses.

"Please be more precise, detective."

I thought for a moment. Was there any point in searching for 'Nelly Valeeva' directly? Who knows how many people or places had that name. But I guessed it was a start.

"Find all matches to the phrase 'Nelly Valeeva', both precise and near matches. Put the search depth at, say... ten transitions."

Sky thought for a moment, then said:

"I have found two hundred and forty four residents with that name. Eighteen geographical locations. Two hundred and two monuments. Three hundred and eight non-fictional game simulations. A hundred and sixteen audio recordings. And twenty thousand four hundred and three pornographic videos."

I was really curious to see what kind of pornography had been made based on this historical figure, but I stayed focused.

"Show all the results with links to the LCPD archive of events and investigations."

"Over what time period?"

"All the archive data."

"With your selected search depth, that will take a lot of time. The references must be compared with the archive records, plus cross references, variable references for..."

"I'll wait."

"Do you mind if I disappear to save resources?"

"Not at all."

The woman immediately vanished into thin air. I sat on a dusty chair. I'd have to wait. It was amusing to think that the control systems that were themselves a form of artificial intelligence were now emulating another artificial intelligence, Sky the police archivist. It was like a hall of mirrors, with all the walls reflecting each other.

Alright then. If I had to wait, I'd use the time to distribute my points. I took out my tablet. All in all, I'd gained three experience points and as many skill points. I put them into Strength, Perception and Luck. Although I was tempted to put it all into Knowledge.

*Leonarm, Human.*
*Class: Tracker.*
*Occupation: Detective at PCPD Third Detective Department.*
*Level: 19.*
*Reputation: 12.*
*Funds: 160,516g.*

*Strength: 6.*
*Perception: 6.*
*Agility: 7.*
*Knowledge: 10.*
*Health: 59 (Corrupt Detective Suit +50).*
*Luck: 6.*

I assigned my skill points like so:
*Eagle Eye skill increased to level 4.*
*Effect range increased. Now your Eagle Eye is even clearer, with even more details.*
*All optical sights zoom in to at least 4x.*

Unfortunately, I had to take the system at its word. I saw no noticeable changes in my vision. Perhaps because I was surrounded by archive computers. There wasn't much to see. Or the skill level might have been transitional, meaning it wouldn't give noticeable changes except for weaponry, but brought me closer to a level when the improvements to the skill would be obvious.

*Battlefield Surgery skill upgraded to level 2.*
*You can now treat broken bones.*
*Painkiller expenditure reduced by 50%, with the exception of healing potions and spells.*

My skirmish with the bandits in the dock showed me that I had to be able to heal faster and better.

*Energy Weapons skill upgraded to level 2.*
*Damage from all types of energy weapons increased by 10%.*

I looked away from the tablet. Sky gave no signs of life. Fine, I could wait some more.

I opened my private messages, where I sometimes got promotional offers from stores. I needed to buy a UniSuit upgrade and a tablet upgrade. With my funds, I could get either an average UniSuit at Tenshot and a crappy upgrade for my tablet, or I could just get a single advanced UniSuit at the Divine Armor store.

I spent a long time looking through the offers, but didn't buy anything. I decided it would be better to go to the stores in person. That was the only way to find anything out of the ordinary.

Or even better, I could buy equipment in the

LCPD arsenal. I might as well use that badge I'd worked so hard to get.

Time flew by unnoticed. I looked up and saw I'd been messing around with my stats and trawling through ads for almost an hour. I switched off the tablet and stood up.

"Sky?"

Silence.

"Why is this taking so long?"

The archivist hologram appeared falteringly, as if emerging from the bottom of a swamp. She spoke with breaks, her words lagging.

"I t-told you, the s-search would take time."

"How much longer?"

The hologram waved her arm haltingly, throwing a timer from the screen onto my glasses.

*5 days 8 hours.*

"Didn't think to tell me that?"

"You did not ask."

"But why so much time?"

"The computing powers of the LCPD central computer are primarily focused on managing the drone drone network, mechs and other critical systems. Nobody needs the archive. To save funds, I was moved to archaic server technologies from the first half of the twenty-first century.

Damn it. Five days to wait for who knows what results.

"Is there a way to speed up the process?"

"Yes, if you find at least one cyberclerk."

My glasses notified me that I'd received knowledge on 'Cyberclerk.' It was an android class available only to NPCs. Cyberclerks could connect to computer systems and speed up or manage their operations.

A few cyberclerks could be found in the city of Nexus, the android city in Rim Two. I got a corresponding marker on my map, unlocking a Projectoria station that was previously inactive.

As usual, the game was luring me deeper into the web of stories. To get into Rim Two, I'd have to get up to level two hundred. When I found the cyberclerks, they'd doubtlessly ask me to complete some quest for them.

Find something, bring something, help in some way... One quest would turn into another, and then a third. Storylines could keep branching out forever. It was easy to lose track of time and spend your whole taharration rotation on that maze of quests and achievements.

The game had given me a quest and an undetermined number of ways to complete it. Selecting a method turned into a quest of its own.

I could study the Hacking skill and redirect the LCPD central computers to the archive. I could learn the right crafting skills to create the modules required to speed up Sky. Or I could assemble a whole new computing network and transfer a copy of the archive to it along with Sky.

I could use brute force, get into the office of the chief of the entire police department and threaten him with a gun, force him to redirect the computing resources. I could get into politics, campaign for an increase in the LCPD budget. That would increase my reputation with the cops, but lower it with the authorities of the Rims.

And with all the residents of Liberty City. They were the ones that would have to pay the taxes for it, after all.

Even if I discarded those options, there was still a tried-and-tested way to solve any problem: buy what you need or hire an expert with the right skills. But to do that, I'd need more funds than I had.

Sky the archivist patiently flickered, awaiting my response.

What would be easier? Waiting five days to get the result, or completing all the missions that Sky would give me to speed up the process?

Using the LCPD archive was a shot in the dark. It might not hit the target, might not give any results at all.

And Sky's missions would take even more time. To level up, to get to Nexus. It was a month's work.

"Alright, continue the search."

I could let Sky search in the background, and in the meantime I could complete the quests I already had. The archivist flickered, soundlessly moved her lips and disappeared. Her voice resounded haltingly from the ether.

"...eep you up to date, ...ective."

So, where first? Should I get a UniSuit, an upgrade, or go see Irene? A squawk from the tablet distracted me from my thoughts. A video call from an unknown caller. After a moment of doubt, I switched on the screen.

I saw the figure of a girl in blinding white clothes richly adorned in patterns and magic stones. On her head was an exotic helmet with two branching horns. Her plump white arms elegantly held a serpentine staff with a gigantic gemstone at its peak.

"I have a debt to repay, my friend."

"Listen, girl, I'm getting a little tired of you. I killed your Three Bucks, you cut off my limbs. We're quits."

Vildana laughed.

"Afraid of me now? Don't worry, I have a new character."

"But no new habits, right?"

"I'm a good witch now. I help everyone who gets into trouble, and I don't make trouble for anyone."

"What about all that pain and suffering you love so much?"

"Oh, you know very well that you can get enough pain and suffering even with a positive reputation."

"Then what do you want from me? What debt..."

I broke off then, staring at the deep valley between her huge breasts. Could it be... I faked a cough, opened the map and sent her a marker. A golden scroll appeared before Vildana. She read it and nodded.

"I'll arrive at the respawn point soon, then come to you on foot."

"Why on foot? I can send a police van for you."

"No way, I've had enough of the police."

Vildana waved her hand before her, ending the call.

# Chapter 23
# Good Witch

I EMERGED FROM the basement of the LCPD and used the Projectoria station to go to my apartment. I threw my guns into the cupboards to regenerate, then got changed into my Furr velvet jacket. I didn't expect the NPC seduction effects to work on a player, but the jacket looked better than anything else I had.

I opened the Sensuality advertisement catalog and chose the Dinner for Two interior set, spending a whole twenty thousand. The kitchen transformed into a cozy dining room: handsome, but humble furniture, a table with a tablecloth and candles, at its center a bouquet of flowers and a basket of fruit. There was cutlery, a bottle of wine and some food on plates. I thought a little and added some champagne to the bottle of wine.

I switched on the background music. Before the music started playing, I got a system message with a license agreement. I confirmed that I wouldn't copy or distribute the background music playing in the room. I agreed to take legal responsibility for unsanctioned copying or commercial use of the music from the Dinner for Two set. And I confirmed that I was willing to pay 'royalties to the copyright holder equal to 12.5g per hour.'

It occurred to me too late that I could just pirate all the music I wanted. I was logged into Adam Online from an unregistered entry point, after all. The faceless %Username% would take all legal responsibility.

One last touch. I wanted to believe that Vildana came to continue what we'd started on the bus. But it wouldn't hurt to prepare for things going wrong. I opened the Home Security section and searched for methods of protecting buildings against magic.

*Saberwhip Flower.*

*Reduces the strength of all hostile magic actions by 15%. (Increase knowledge of magic to increase effect).*

*Range: 20 feet. (Increase Perception to increase the range of items like this).*

*Plant lasts 4 days.*

*Price: 9,999g.*

There was also a scientific device:

*'Ghost Busters' Magic Interceptor.*

*Intercepts or weakens hostile magic attacks aimed at the building's owner.*

*Bonus: the first magic attack is reflected back on the attacker.*

*Range: within the building in which the device is installed.*

*Operation requires: 100 energy units per hour.*

*Price: 11,999g.*

There was also a statue of some invented god that gave one hundred percent defense against magic, but cost three hundred thousand. It was cheaper to die. I bought the plant and the interceptor.

*Decorator skill increased: +10 XP.*

I heard footsteps beyond the door. I sat on the couch and made as if I was reading my tablet. I liked the fact that I was a little nervous about this visit.

The virtual world was even better at provoking real feelings than reality. In the game, human relationships were a game too. In Adam Online, you played as yourself in the first person, as your own virtual protagonist. Which meant...

"Open up, my friend!" Vildana shouted, knocking her staff on the door.

"It's open," I called back.

*Vildana, Human.*
*Class: Mage.*
*Subclass: unknown (requires 20 Knowledge).*
*Level: 13.*
*Reputation: 24.*

Huh? How did she do it? She'd started from nothing and already had such a high reputation? She'd even gotten herself a subclass. What was I doing wrong?

The good witch was dressed like an expensive whore from an expensive brothel. There were girls who, no matter how revealing their clothes, were still obviously modest. Girls who you just wanted to wrap in a blanket and tell "Please, don't try to look sexy any more." My Olga was like that.

Vildana wore that ridiculously erotic outfit with pleasure. She looked at me with laughter in her eyes, knowing the effect she had on me. As if her clothing had an attractiveness bonus and I was an NPC subject to it.

Damn.. What if Amy was right? What if I was just some highly advanced NPC? That might explain my propensity for dying.

"You look beautiful!" I said.

"I sure do. But what are you wearing? That jacket is hilarious. You look like... like..." Vildana banged her staff on the floor, trying to remember the word.

"Like an unemployed pimp?"

"Haha, that's not what I wanted to say. But yes, as a matter of fact. Where are your leather pants? You promised to seduce me with leather pants."

"I'm working on it."

She noticed my badge and continued respectfully.

"Cool thing. Well done."

"Yeah, I've been making progress too."

Vildana looked around.

"And your apartment is awesome." She looked at the table and the candles. "You expecting someone?"

I approached her and took her by the hand.

"Only you."

"How romantic."

Vildana walked over to the table and looked at the bottles.

"I don't like wine."

I took out a bottle of the whiskey inherited from that driver and put it on the table. Vildana leaned her staff against the table and sat on a chair.

"Alright, let's start our business meeting."

Vildana downed a shot of whiskey and started talking.

"After those robocops shot me in the temple, my

character died. I created a new one, a good witch. Within ten minutes, I completed the first grade in the magical academy and got some new spells. I'm used to doing that, it wasn't my first rodeo. After that, I went to visit Three Bucks's base."

"He respawned?"

"Yes and no. He didn't remember me. Even though I'd... spent time with him."

"A friend of mine, a crazy neohikki, told me that if you spend a long time talking to an NPC, they can evolve into an almost human creature."

"Three Bucks hasn't evolved. He's still a rude asshole with an idiot's vocabulary. That's why I liked him."

"So why didn't you stay with him again?"

Vildana poured some more whiskey into our glasses.

"You can't bring back the past. Anyway, that dumbass took me for an enemy and tried to kill me. I killed the whole gang. Raised my reputation."

"How long did it take you to level up enough to leave Rim Zero?" I asked.

Vildana checked her tome.

"Thirty nine minutes. Why?"

"Uhm, nice..." I didn't admit that she'd beaten my personal record for the fastest time to leave Rim Zero.

The thought occurred to me that a simple player like Vildana, who wandered Adam Online purely for pleasure, could have achieved more success in searching for Nelly than me.

We clinked our shot glasses together and downed them. I figured it was time. I sat next to Vildana and put my hand between her knees.

"I didn't come to you for that," Vildana continued,

moving my hand away. "Some punk looted an electric pistol identical to the first one. Want to buy it? I'm on the light side now, and that means I'm having money troubles."

Vildana placed a Tesla revolver on the table. My Pistol Tricks skill gave me the ability to shoot with both hands at once. It'd be a good purchase. But right then I wanted something else... I tried to put my hand under her magic clothes again, but Vildana reached for her staff.

"I can turn you into whatever animal I want in two seconds. A frog might be a good choice."

I moved away from her.

"I need money myself. How about a trade? Let's go to the bedroom."

Vildana grabbed her staff.

"Don't you get it? Have fun being a frog."

"I don't mean that," I sighed.

To my surprise, Vildana mellowed in the bedroom.

"Nice decor. Bed looks fun. Hilarious lamp. I'm just renting a smelly room in a tavern."

"The bed is called Sexodrome."

"Yeah, it says it on the side."

"What if you and I..."

"Don't forget, Leo, I'll turn you into a frog."

I sat on the bed and took the sword I found in the hiding place off the wall. Vildana couldn't hide her feelings. She reached for the sword right away.

"Agreed!"

"Wait, friend, I'm not a frog yet. The sword is worth a lot more than the revolver."

"How do you know?"

"I guessed," I answered sarcastically. "This isn't my first rotation. There was a note with the sword in an unknown language. Here it is."

Vildana unfolded the paper.

"It's the Yenav language from the world of Goldivar."

"That magic universe in Rim Two?"

Vildana didn't answer, just opened her bag and took out a scroll.

"This is a Language Scroll, it lets you temporarily understand any language."

She crumpled up the scroll, clenched it in her fist and opened it. The paper evaporated into golden smoke. The smoke flew into the note, changing the letters. We read it.

*My name... does not matter. I was a servant of a rich master in the Princedom of Yenav.*

*My master was a bastard and a low-life. He tortured me. He forced me to perform obscene acts: to dress in women's clothing and lie with him in his bed. That is why, when my master received the sword of Governor Stükke the Great, I stole it and left the Princedom of Yenav.*

*I roamed for a long time before I found a mage that could open a portal from our world to another. That is how I reached Liberty City. The people here do not know magic well, but they live better lives than us. They have no kings or masters. Here is freedom, democracy, equal rights for all. That is why I am writing this heartfelt confession.*

*Anyone who returns this sword to my former master will receive an enormous reward. I don't need it. I am becoming a thief and joining a gang. I do not regret my deeds. Curse me if you wish.*

*Obtained knowledge: the beautiful sword of unknown design turned out to be the sword of Stükke the Great.*

Vildana and I looked at each other. The good witch's eyes shone treacherously. I hid the sword away in my inventory and looked her in the eye.

"How much? And don't you dare lie to me. You know the sword's properties better than me thanks to your magic skills."

"Two million," the good witch answered.

"Good number."

"Yep. How about I turn you into a frog, take the sword and run?"

"Let me grab a weapon to make the fight at least a little fair."

I ran to the armory, grabbed my Tesla revolver and the machine gun I used to kill Joshua. I equipped my Max Payne jacket and returned to the bedroom.

"You know, Vildana, I didn't imagine our meeting like this. Why aren't we enjoying the pleasures of sex on this huge bed? A drunken fight doesn't seem as much fun."

"We've fought ever since we first met. We're not a good match."

"Shame." I raised the machine gun. "I like you."

"Likewise. A little. But now you'll be a frog. And you'll never turn into a prince. Even if I kiss you."

Vildana struck her staff on the floor. The stone at its peak shone and a beam of magic rushed toward me. Halfway toward me, it sharply banked, turned around and struck Vildana. Just like the Ghost Busters magic interceptor had promised, the first magic attack had been reflected to the attacker.

"What the..." Vildana said, before her staff fell along with her clothes, her bag, her tome and the other trinkets in the good witch's possession. Within two seconds, the beautiful girl had turned into a huge frog. I picked up all her gear.

Vildana turned back into a person again.

"...hell was that?"

"Safety measures," I answered. "No smoking or spellcasting in my house. Just drinking and lovemaking."

Now Vildana was dressed in the gray toga of a magic academy student. She had a rusty dagger at her belt. The rest was in my possession. The system flooded me with messages that I'd received magical items whose purpose I didn't know.

Among them, of course, was the Tesla revolver. In addition, my interface sent me another notification.

*Exorcist skill learned: +10 XP.*

*Technology against magic? Which will win? Upgrade this skill to fight against all kinds of magic tricks. No mage, no problem.*

Vildana grabbed the handle of the dagger. I rattled the machine gun belt.

"You sure you want to keep going?"

"Alright, you win."

She walked past me, shouldering me out of the way, sat at the table and downed another shot of whiskey.

"What now? Are you taking all my stuff?"

I sat down opposite.

"I don't have any need for magic items. I'll keep the revolver. Gotta punish you somehow for attacking me in my own home."

"Fair enough."

We clinked our shot glasses together and downed them. Vildana bit into a peach she found in the fruit basket on the table.

"What do you want for Stükke the Great's sword? Just don't ask for sex."

"Two million for sex? I'm not that desperate. What can you offer me?"

"A partner agreement."

I returned her bag, staff and other magic things. Vildana took a scroll out of her bag, cast a spell on it and handed it to me.

A standard partner agreement for players to divide rewards after completing a quest given to one of them. Vildana would complete the quest to return the sword instead of me. I'd get fifty percent of what I would have gotten if I'd done the quest on my own. At the same time, the agreement forbade the partners from dealing damage to each other.

I'd nearly put my hand on the scroll to sign before I noticed a discrepancy and pulled my hand back.

"Hey, I don't get it, why did you write that you'd get seventy percent and the right to distribute the loot? No good for a good witch to cheat her partner."

"I'm good, but not stupid." Vildana waved her staff as if planning to hit me. "I know what this sword is. It's a difficult and dangerous quest, I might die many times. I'll need to go through all the kingdoms of Goldivar. They're constantly at war and full of dragons and magic."

"So go for it. You like magic, right?"

"God, you're a moron!" Vildana took the scroll back and changed the numbers. "Happy now? Fifty-fifty."

I confirmed the agreement and gave Vildana the sword. She called me a moron again and left without a good-bye. I took out both Tesla revolvers and spun them on my fingers like a cowboy.

What a good champion I was. I'd robbed two girls in one day. And I wondered why they didn't like me.

# Chapter 24
# House of Humanity

NIKA CONFIRMED that it wouldn't be hard for her to restore the functionality of the hangar and the associated components for repeating the experiment, but...

"I won't do it. Not now."

"Why not?" Grisha asked, surprised. "Isn't this what you've been dreaming of? And you don't have to invent anything, it's all been done before us."

"Before us, but not for us."

Grisha activated the LeCube configuration that Nika had christened with numbers, but Grisha called "most human-like robot." He turned into a humanoid figure. It was very primitive. The head had only a semblance of a face, with bulbous hints of eyes, nose and a mouth. He looked more like an unfinished statue of gleaming obsidian. And he was taller than an android. LeCube had too much nanomass inside it to press it into a smaller shape.

But even that was enough for him and Nika: they lay on the floor of one of the hangars, held each other and... talked. Nika herself had long since removed the humanity chip from her head, so as not to waste resources on feelings. But no racial incompatibilities or differences could prevent Grisha and Nika from loving each other on the inside.

After all, sometimes love is just the highest level of friendship.

"Someone else created the ability to transfer consciousness, and they didn't make it for us," Nika repeated.

"Who made it?"

Nika gazed at the sky where the anomaly covering Dimension X rippled from aerial attacks.

"I know everything about Adam Online that is available to the public. Back in the real world, I even bought some secret information. You know, I have the access codes to the UN buildings. I even have access to hidden Projectoria stations. But there was nothing anywhere about exiting to reality into someone else's body. And that's precisely what that interface that we unlocked during the experiment was offering. I'm sure that option didn't exist before."

It dawned on Grisha.

"It appeared recently? Does it match the time when Rim Six opened?"

"It coincides. But I don't think that explains anything."

"So how do we get an explanation?"

"I think the Mentors are somehow involved in this."

Grisha raised himself on an elbow.

"They exist?"

"Of course."

"Have you spoken to them, seen them?"

Nika raised herself too.

"Don't be dumb, Grisha. Nobody has seen them or

spoken to them. Or if they have, then they didn't know it was the Mentors they were seeing. It's time you stopped seeing Adam Online as a world of swords and magic. There's no magic here. Nothing here happens by chance."

"Even the Mentors?"

"Everything has a reason, a cause."

"Like those mosquitoes that bit the robots to death?"

"Exactly. The Mentors are a predictable result of an infinitely complex artificial intelligence. Adam Mickiewicz warned us about that before he died."

"You know it all," Grisha muttered.

"I don't know anything, I'm suggesting a theory. The Mentors are an artificial intelligence that was created by another artificial intelligence to complete one of its tasks. I think the CSes created them to help when they couldn't control Adam Online's evolution on their own."

"You're talking so passionately, as if I'm arguing. I'm not. Are you sure of your theory?"

"Yes. Since the control systems could create anything they needed to in Adam Online, they created something similar to them, which didn't have the limitations placed on the CSes themselves."

"You talk as if the CSes are alive."

"They're not alive at all. We're alive. The CSes create and maintain the operation of the NPCs that dumb players confuse with people. Confuse with living people."

Grisha laid back down again and hugged Nika.

"I still don't understand why you don't want to repeat the experiment. Call up that interface again and try to..."

"It's impossible. Using the interface requires level

four hundred."

Grisha frowned, although his face couldn't move. He could express his feelings only through his voice.

"I don't get it. Why is the interface subject to the game rules? Might as well need a special skill for it."

"Of course," Nika answered seriously. "The game rules are the rules of this world. If you consider that this interface was created for the Mentors, it all makes sense. The Mentors know no other world. That is, unless..."

"Unless they go into the real world using other people's bodies?" Grisha finished for her. "That's messed up. You sure you haven't gone nuts?"

Instead of the usual mocking answer, Nika sighed.

"Sometimes it feels like I have. The fact that you're here is all that keeps me from it. You can't imagine how much I envy your innocence and simplicity."

"Stop, I'm blushing."

"Sorry, I didn't mean to offend you."

"Nika, how about... I have a suggestion..."

Grisha suddenly broke off, extricated himself from Nika's hug, stood up and took on his base form. Fortunado came up in his neurointerface.

"Bro, where are you? It's started. The coalition is launching a massive attack. Hurry and get to Shoreline."

Grisha turned to Nika.

"I have to go. Do I understand correctly that now you need to get into Rim Six to level up to four hundred and gain access to the consciousness transfer interface?"

"Uh-huh."

"Alright, fine. I won't stop you."

"Thank you, but no. I won't go without you."

Grisha flared up.

"But the guild is having its final battle! Whoever gets through it will be the winner."

"Oh, believe me, that battle will finish quicker than you think."

Nika even let Grisha use her respawn tower to travel to the Black Wave base. She'd never let anyone go through her tower before. She didn't want it marked on their maps.

She gave Grisha five million CN as a parting gift.

"I don't need it anymore anyway. But I do need you and LeCube."

"Cunning and calculating rat. You said you didn't have that much component nanomass."

"Ignorant dumbass."

"We're a great couple."

"Just perfect."

"I'm not kidding."

"Me neither."

Grisha joined a battle in full swing. He arrived at the respawn tower next to Shoreline, not in the Black Wave base.

His appearance in battle had always been a decisive factor in the defeat of the coalition's squads. Now Grisha was practically unstoppable: he didn't need to conserve component nanomass. Perhaps for the first time since he started using LeCube, he didn't care how much CN he had left.

He generously used Second Skin and all the configurations whose usage had been limited by a lack of CN.

At a certain point, the entire battle became a sequence of routine actions: choosing an enemy, choosing a program config, attacking, destroying the enemy, automatically picking up valuable loot and experience.

Grisha crushed his enemies one by one and in entire groups. LeCube was constantly active. He switched configurations at a lightning pace, flew from one end of the battlefield to the other. He transformed into a flying machine and joined the aerial battle, or attacked ground targets. Then in flight he transformed into the Earthworm config (another naming attempt from Nika) and burrowed into the ground to fight the coalition's bizoids, who were rushing to dig into the Black Wave base.

Of course, he achieved such success with the support of his guildmates. They prevented the enemy from gathering their strength to strike back against LeCube. They sacrificed themselves to disperse the opponent's strength.

Grisha's private messages filled up with excited shouts from his guildmates and curses from the coalition troops. Although, LeCube was so impressive in the battle that even his enemies sent him approving emojis or audio notes.

Some members of the coalition asked him for the hundredth time to tell him where they could buy a frame like that. Others threatened to report him for the obvious cheat that was LeCube. Still others offered to pay huge sums for it. The highest offer reached a couple of billion. The coalition might have decided to combine funds for it. Others threatened that their crafting masters would soon create the same frame, and then Grisha's day would be done.

All this broke Grisha's concentration, so he switched off his chat notifications. All he could see now were priority calls from Fortunado, Nika and the guild's top players.

His conversation with Nika stayed on his mind.

Grisha wasn't interested in the workings of Adam Online. He hadn't known exactly what the Global Consortium of Standardization in Adam Online did. He hadn't known that there were officials sitting at Glocon who were answered queries from the CSes in real time. He hadn't known that Adam was the name of a Polish developer, not a biblical character. That fact in particular annoyed him. It was like the universe of Adam Online had lost half its luster.

It was one thing when the name of a virtual world was linked to divine mysticism: a person dying in the real world to revive in the world of Adam, the first ever human being. It was another thing entirely to find out that you were in a world named after a mortal man. And a man with a high opinion of himself, at that.

The thought even flashed up; why the hell was he playing someone else's game anyway? But then he remembered what he'd learned from childhood. Adam Online wasn't just a game, it was the future of society. It might not be in this century or the next, but eventually, the Earth would become uninhabitable. A full departure for a virtual world was the only way to survive.

Other planets were too far away. So Earth was humanity's only home, the one they had to keep living in, even when it finally collapsed. People had already built a new home in the future ruins, albeit spectral and virtual. That new home was Adam Online. It wasn't perfect. But it was better than disappearing forever.

*But how will I perceive the virtual world now that I know it's just a bunker?* Grisha thought. *I didn't want to leave Adam Online before, but now I want to climb out of my pod to stupidly reassure myself that reality is just as terrible, dull and boring as it ever was... What have you done, Nika? Why did you make me think about all this shit?*

It was if Nika could hear him. Her call icon flashed in the chat. Grisha tore some gigantic multi-legged dinosaur bizoid in half to stop him covering the ground in thick acid, then turned into a cutting disk and shredded through a crowd of enemy mechanodestructors, slicing them into pieces. Only then did LeCube retreat behind the line of defense, handing the initiative in the battle over to Grisha's guildmates.

"What's going on, Nika? You don't usually call me first..."

Nika showed her image on the screen. Judging by her facial expression, she'd inserted her humanity chip.

"I'm worried. I don't want you to die."

"I know your how cunning you are," Grisha answered. "You're more worried about LeCube. But don't worry, I'm invincible with all this component nanomass. And it looks like we're winning."

There was a pause. Grisha rushed into battle, and Nika said nothing. She wasn't even looking at the screen, but off to the side somewhere.

"So what did you want? Only I have a war to get on with."

Nika livened up.

"Do you remember that you wanted make a suggestion before Fortunado interrupted us? What was it?"

"I wanted to say, why don't we just forget everything, leave our rotation and spend some time in real life? Together."

Nika shook her head.

"I'm afraid this is my last rotation, Grisha. I could die just a couple of days after leaving the pod. Stasis is saving me from death. The end of the rotation means the end of my life."

"I didn't know you had so little time. Your last rotation..."

"Not the last if I learn how to use that weird interface."

Grisha made a startling promise.

"We'll find out how. Just gotta deal with this coalition first."

Nika looked straight at him.

"Look after yourself. Increase your defense, don't overdo it. Do you remember what I said? You're working at the limit of your capabilities. The coalition isn't as weak as you might think right now."

Now it was Grisha's turn to prick his ears up.

"Tell me more. Do you know something?"

"I'm just guessing. They've already proven they can outsmart Fortunado. They're getting ready for something."

Grisha followed the course of the battle and saw that some enemy tanks had broken through the left flank where Fortunado had placed a Tesla tower. The tanks were cobbling together a replicator under the cover of a forcefield and two dragon bizoids. Judging by the blue and yellow flashes, several mages were also defending it.

The tanks crushed the Tesla tower, opening the path for more coalition forces.

"I gotta go, Nika. Without LeCube, our guys are going to get stomped."

Grisha hung up and rushed to help.

# Chapter 25
# Victory Day

THE ENEMY expected Grisha to make the replicator his main target, so they strengthened its defenses. Several mechanodestructors with advanced frames joined the mages and dragons. All the players were above average in level. Above them fluttered Camper the superman. His brand new red cloak and underpants stood out against the background of the smoky sky.

Grisha's old enemy no doubt said something in the chat, but he paid no attention. He wanted to hurry and end this battle, end the whole guild war. He was bored of it now. Grisha was already thinking of a way to convince his brother that they should forget Mariam and head into Rim Six. Hell, the whole guild could go there and take all the spoils.

Camper strained, trying to take LeCube down with his powerful telekinesis, but Grisha's reserve of component nanomass allowed him to simply ignore all the attacks.

*No, bro won't agree,* Grisha admitted to himself. *He's too close to the guild. He won't damage his reputation by breaking the contract with Mariam.*

Grisha split into four humanoid mechs armed with

kinetic mauls. Each strike of the maul was strengthened a hundred times. With those mauls, he crushed all the mechanodestructors into dust, then calmly went about slamming mages into the earth, breaking their cleverly woven magical defenses.

Merging back into LeCube, he then took on his disk form and rushed Camper. Camper sent Krypto Mouse to meet him. Grisha dealt with the mouse, but its kinetic explosion cost him a lot of CN. Camper took advantage of that. He simply turned and flew off.

Escaping a still undefeated enemy was the best measure of victory. Grisha took on the Grenika configuration and bombed the replicator and the tanks crawling in a column along Shoreline's streets toward the Black Wave base.

There was a lull. Grisha switched on the chat, looked at the tactical map and saw something unbelievable: the Black Wave had won.

Judging by the reports, all the remaining coalition troops were rushing to retreat. They abandoned the replicators that were still churning our military vehicles. They aimlessly crawled toward the base fortifications, but without the players to lead them, all the automatically created units got destroyed by the Black Wave's automatic units.

It was agony. The attack hadn't just failed. The coalition seemed completely defeated.

From his altitude, Grisha saw the mobile respawn towers working ceaselessly, swallowing up the retreating coalition troops. Black Wave jets circled above them, continuing to strike at the enemy. Magic transference portals flashed into life here and there. The coalition's magical forces were running even faster than their technological allies.

Grisha couldn't wait. He called Fortunado.

"You're a genius, bro."

"Half of this victory belongs to you."

"Yeah, but you planned it all perfectly."

"Maybe a little," Fortunado admitted humbly. "The Black Wave base defense withstood the attack. Its total durability is sixty percent. That means we can withstand another assault."

"But there won't be one, right?"

"I don't think so. Do you see them running?"

"So what now?"

Fortunado gave him a confident order.

"Now is the time to counterattack, to finish them off once and for all."

Fortunado's orders appeared in the neurointerfaces of all the Black Wave guild troops. He explained how to group up and which directions to attack in, which bases to capture first. Judging by the thorough detail of the counterattack plan, Fortunado had prepared it long ago. Nika was wrong to mock him after all. Developing a counterattack while the guild suffered defeat after defeat... That was a demonstration of true strategic talent.

According to the plan, Grisha was to return to the base and head to the respawn tower near Londinium. The coalition forces were concentrated there, so that was where LeCube was needed most.

Grisha first finished off the rest of the tank units and autosens lodged in a hastily built bunker. He wanted to leave a zone fully cleared of enemies behind him. Grisha's combat experience told him that even a single autosens or tank replicator forgotten in the rear could cause serious infrastructural damage.

The chat was full of victorious messages and

highlight reels from the battle. The Black Wavers bragged of their victory. Grisha gave into the overall joyous mood and posted a clip of Camper running away in the chat. It was a truly victorious day. Now the enemy guilds would turn into the defenders. A long and boring campaign to capture all the coalition bases stretched out ahead.

Grisha even found a positive in it: Fortunado would be so busy finishing off the guilds that he might not even get too upset when Grisha and Nika went to Rim Six...

The Fortunado tab started flashing in the chat. Grisha switched to it.

"The coalition is contacting us," Fortunado said. "Should we answer?"

"Of course, maybe they want a cease fire?"

"Would we agree to that?"

Grisha wanted to say "yes," but he realized that there could only be one answer to Fortunado's question.

"No, bro, let's finish them off, and if the siege draws out, we'll demand a king's ransom. They offered me a couple of billion for LeCube, so they have cash."

"Then I'll send you the feed."

"Sure." Grisha descended to the ground, took on his base configuration.

A screen appeared: the leaders of the coalition guilds standing in front of the respawn tower in Londinium.

Before them all stood Camper. His arms were crossed, his gaze strict, confident. His red cloak fluttered as always, even without wind. Grisha wasn't interested in the intrigues of the enemy camp, but he knew from Fortunado that Camper had been recently elected leader of the coalition. The role was purely honorary, of course. Camper wasn't even in a guild. The others stood by his sides.

Slippery Joe from the Golden Horde. Knight_Ivan from the Viatichis, shrouded in magical qualia armor and leaning on a broad two-handed sword, his brow knit in a frown. Knight_Ivan had a face with a disproportionately broad chin, and his enlarged bright blue eyes shone neon on his face. Jamilla stood next to the Viatichi, leaning on a spear fluctuating with streams of red energy. Members of Virtus.pro were also there, whose guild consisted exclusively of people from the Soldier of Fortune class, masters of firearms and precision group combat tactics. Grisha respected them, had even spoken to them in real life at player conventions.

He didn't know the rest, he could only identify them by their guild badges. And even then, not all of them; he was seeing some of the badges for the first time. He felt a rush of pride for the Black Wave. *We defeated guilds we didn't even know existed.*

"Well, nobody got anything to say?" Grisha asked.

Camper swept a lock of beautiful hair off his brow and spoke.

"We demand your surrender."

Grisha laughed, and Fortunado sent a picture of an ass to the chat, the same one he sent to everyone who said something idiotic.

"Don't you think you're the losers here, not us?" Grisha asked.

"Yeah," Fortunado agreed. "Actually, Camper, why don't you let Slippery Joe talk, or at least Knight_Ivan? You're a complete idiot. You weren't elected head of the coalition because you're a good player, it was because you're a waste of space."

"You..! You..! I'll waste you!" Camper shouted. "We're going to..."

Knight_Ivan clanked forward in his armor and moved Camper aside.

"Fortunado is right," he said, ignoring the superman's angry muttering. "But we really do want to offer a deal: you sign a peace treaty and give us LeCube. All the Black Wave bases we've captured will remain our territory. Apart from that, you sign a contract to pay us ten billion gold."

Grisha laughed and Fortunado spoke to him.

"Look at this, bro, they've all gone nuts."

"What happens if we refuse?"

Knight_Ivan clenched a gigantic fist.

"We will destroy you. We will wipe you out."

"Yeah? How're you planning to do that?" Fortunado asked carefully. "You already tried twice."

This time Jamilla spoke.

"Ivan, they don't believe us. Don't tell them. Let's show them."

Knight_Ivan nodded.

"So you refuse?"

"Of course," the brothers answered in chorus.

"Alright. You asked for it." Knight_Ivan turned his back and asked someone, "Have all the troops withdrawn?"

*Almost all* answered a voice from outside the video feed.

"Activate the nuclear bomb. Destroy our enemies."

"The nuclear... what?!" Fortunado shouted. Then the connection cut out.

Grisha didn't immediately comprehend Ivan's words either, but his reflexes kicked in. LeCube transformed into the Grenika and surged upward, just like the time it went into a near-earth orbit. If Shoreline was the target of the nuclear strike, he'd need to fly as far away and as high as possible.

Grisha kept the chat with Fortunado on the screen. His brother was in his Octopus frame, but the mechanodestructor's face showed such despair that even a human would have envied its expressiveness.

"Grisha... did you hear that? Are they serious?"

Grisha hadn't heard such helplessness in Fortunado's voice for a long time. Not since he'd found out that other players had taken the money they'd saved in the Liberty City bank.

Fortunado was defeated, lost. He didn't know what to do. This was a turn of events he hadn't predicted.

"They must be lying, Grisha, right?"

"I don't know... I don't think so. Listen to this order. Take your strongest frame and hide in the bunker where we grow bizoids. Don't try to get to the respawn tower, you won't make it."

"But where did they get a nuke?" Fortunado babbled.

"What difference does it make?" Grisha shouted. "Maybe the same place we got our last one? Maybe that Mariam of yours is doing just what I suspected, creating quests for high-level players? Playing both sides?"

"No, no," Fortunado muttered. "Mariam couldn't. She told me... secrecy... espionage..."

"Carry out your orders! We'll figure out who to

blame later."

Fortunado complied. Grisha switched to the guild chat and sent an urgent warning.

The Black Wavers picked out Grisha's order among his curses: get as far from Shoreline and the base as possible. Everyone near the tower should leave for any other zone. All mages should create the largest possible portals without concern for the mana cost, and use them to send their guildmates anywhere but there. Then...

The connection cut out. Grisha had flown up pretty high, but the shockwave hit him even there.

*Damage taken: -330,476, Big Pulowski II atomic bomb explosion.*

The Grenika software configuration lost its durability and switched off permanently due to the radiation. Grisha had no idea that the software configurations could be destroyed like any item.

LeCube reverted to its base form and began to fall even as the shockwave still pushed it away from the epicenter. The system warned him that he couldn't take on any other configurations for a certain time. The component nanomass itself was immune to the radiation.

The interface explained why everything had broken, but Grisha wasn't interested in all those science terms.

He switched off the detailed report. It didn't make any difference why he couldn't switch configs. The important thing was to keep an eye on the timer counting down until his abilities returned.

Grisha submitted to the will of the fiery whirlwind. He couldn't even control his flight. The strength of the shockwave was many times greater than Grisha's own.

LeCube turned somersaults in the ocean of fire, losing CN.

A long list of killed Black Wavers scrolled endlessly in Grisha's neurointerface. Everyone from his squad had died, losing their achievements and characters. Most Ancient Evil, Crusher, Blondie Lee... All the top players that had gathered at the base to regroup and counterattack.

Counters appeared in another part of Grisha's neurointerface.

*Available in storage: 1,540,555 CN.*
*Health: 9004.*
*Configuration cooldown time: 1 minute 02 seconds.*

Grisha was competing with numbers again. Which of them reached zero first — Health or Cooldown Time — would decide whether Grisha would be among the list of the dead or not.

Fortunado wasn't in the list yet.

# Chapter 26
# Dungeoncrawling

FIVE DAYS wasn't a lot of time in Adam Online. Just forty real hours. Sky sent progress reports. Constructing the search array was a slow process, as she'd promised.

    I visited the police arsenal again and bought some gear at a discount.

    *LESS Police UniSuit (Law Enforcement Special Suit)*
*Item class: Equipment.*
*Weight: 15 lbs.*
*Durability: 100/100.*
*Value: 100,000g.*


    *+4 Agility.*
*Increased resistance to damage from firearms and energy weapons.*
    *Full resistance to damage from stabbing and cutting weapons if the enemy's level is below yours.*
    *Your attack with any kind of weapon deals +6 (Strength stat) bonus damage to NPCs and/or players with a negative Reputation.*

    *Upgrade slot #1 (built-in): Police Standard Helmet, +1*

*Perception.*

*Upgrade slot #2 (built-in): Power Surge skill. Multiplies your Strength stat by ten for 6 seconds. This will help you break through locked doors, smash down walls or break concrete blocks with your head to astound onlookers.*
*Cooldown: 15 minutes.*

*Upgrade slot #3: Facepalm Neurointerface.*
*You can now control elements of the interface using your hands. Does not work without a tablet.*

*Upgrade slot #4: Autolooter I.*
*Automatically pulls in dropped items and places them in the inventory.*
*Effect radius equal to your Perception.*

*Upgrade slot #5: Durability Regeneration.*

You can't buy uniques like that in a store. All the upgrade slots were already full, so I wasn't spending any extra on them. However, in the city I preferred to walk around in the corrupt detective suit.

Since I was tied down by Sky's search time and was no longer in a hurry, I decided to play a little for myself. So I took a confiscated motorcycle from the police lockup.

I decided to just ride. First I fell off a few times, taking damage. In the end I lost control completely and dumped the bike in a river.

*Motorcycles skill learned: +10 XP.*

*Ahem, Leonarm, motorcycles aren't designed for underwater travel. To become a knight of the steel horse, you need to fall less and ride straighter.*

I took a second motorcycle from the garage. After that, things went quicker. I rode along the streets, gaining experience.

*Achievement unlocked: Urbanist — Liberty City. +10 XP.*
*You have explored 10% of the Liberty City metropolitan area. Keep exploring the city.*

While I was thinking of where to go next, that shyster Johnny Lane sent me a video message.

*Hey, tracker, still alive? One of my employees has found the location of the third musket. Don't ask me how, it doesn't matter now. He got eaten by liberats. Now it's your turn to die.*

*Marker added to map: third Lefaucheux musket.*
*Kuznetsov                                    portal:*
*#8429034AD85PO 119785FF34289*

It pointed to a part of Liberty City I hadn't explored. And it was underground, in the sewage system.

The Liberty City sewage system, called simply the Dungeon, had a peculiarity: multiverse portals. Legend had it that Kuznetsov the scientist built a space-time fluctuation generator in the sewers, which was meant to send him ten years back into the past to save his family from death in a car accident. Naturally, something went wrong. The generator exploded and killed Kuznetsov. After the explosion, the sewers were divided by portals. After crossing one, the player found themselves in the same sewage system, but another version of it.

This meant that it was impossible to fully explore the labyrinth sewers. Crossing a portal created a new maze layout for each player. Each version could be saved in the form of multiverse coordinates so that you could get back to the same place, or share it with another player, or, as in my case, organize a mission in a zone that had no map, nor guidebook.

That said, there was one guideline for all dungeons: move toward your goal, kill everything that moves, pick up the loot and try not to die. Almost like life.

After reaching the required point on the map, I opened a sewage hatch and climbed down. The Kuznetsov portal was ten paces away. It was murky, like the surface of a glass table. The veil covered one of the sewer tunnels. Next to the portal was an old Projectoria station. It activated as I approached and rose up from a pile of garbage, blinking its green light invitingly.

The control systems were excellent level designers. This station was here in case I died. So that I could continue my efforts to complete the dungeon after reviving.

When I crossed the portal, my map opened. All the generated worlds available to me were supposed to be marked on it. Right now, the only one I could access was the one with the coordinates that Johnny Lane gave me. This meant that I was thrown into a parallel reality with no preamble.

The only enemies here were the ubiquitous liberats and mutated humans, so-called fecal zombies.

The rats feared nobody in their own territory. They bravely jumped at me from out of cracks, from the ceiling, from pipes or just from under the water. Since their bites counted as stabbing and cutting strikes, and most of the creatures were lower level than me, I rarely took damage. The beasts' disgusting yellow teeth just glanced off my UniSuit, not even lowering its durability.

The fecal zombies were harder to deal with. They couldn't catch up to me, and the sound of splashing and groaning heralded their approach. But the zombies were well-armed with ranged weaponry — poisonous chemical blobs. They regurgitated a bright green blob into their hand and threw it at the enemy. It wasn't hard to dodge, but when you were in a narrow tunnel and five or six disgusting blobs were flying toward you, then no matter how quick you dodged, one of them would hit you and cover you from head to toe. The blobs slightly lowered my UniSuit's durability, so I had to be especially careful to listen out for splashing and breathing from around bends in the tunnels.

Although the mazes were unique, the algorithms for completing the dungeon were entirely predictable. I shot monsters, got achievements and upgraded my skills thanks to constantly firing my machine gun and my Tesla revolvers. I regularly got covered in poison from the fecal monsters, improving my Poison Resistance. Since all this often happened in the dark, my Night Vision also increased.

Moreover, Kuznetsov portal dungeons always had plentiful loot. Grenades, for example.

*Pearl Frag Grenade.*
*Fuse timer: 5 seconds.*
*Explosion damage: 3000.*
*Shrapnel damage: 80-100.*
*Frame material: pearlite (semi-transparent mineral).*
*Pearlite shrapnel quantity: 100.*
*Shard spray range: 65 feet.*
*This weapon has a special bonus. Requires Explosives level 1.*

I destroyed large groups of mobs with those grenades, increasing my Explosives skill.

Soon the tunnel brought me to another giant cave. It was lighter than the others due to the broad cracks in the ceiling, through which a sliver of the night sky could be seen. Dozens of pipes and tunnels led into the cave, spewing various degrees of filth into the lake of water. This made the cave murmur bewitchingly. If I closed my eyes and ignored the stench, I could imagine I was surrounded by waterfalls.

The water here was deeper than in the tunnels. At first it was just above the knee, then waist-high. The walls of old houses stuck out of the water, along with heaps of garbage and even a downed helicopter. A jolly skeleton sat in the pilot's seat. His hand was placed as if he was greeting me or beckoning me over.

I couldn't just refuse the dead man's hospitality. I decided to search the helicopter, stepped forward... and fell straight into the water. My head went under. Somehow I swam out, spitting out disgusting liquid. Now I looked like a fecal zombie.

In reality I knew how to swim. But in Adam Online, you had to learn again: I waved my arms in the water, splashing up brown muck.

*Swimming skill learned: +10 XP.*

*A lake of shit isn't the best place to paddle, but you have to start somewhere, right?*

On top of that, some rapidly shortening bars appeared in my glasses. As far as I remembered, the skill depended on Strength, which influenced how long I could stay afloat before I drowned. And Agility influenced movement speed while swimming. I had the right Agility for the job.

In a few strokes, I'd reached the helicopter and climbed into the cabin.

A giant creature similar to a seal immediately attacked me in silence. It grabbed me with its paws and pushed me outside. Out of the corner of my eye, I saw that the monster had made itself a nest in the helicopter cabin. Well done me for climbing in without looking.

We fell into the water. The creature dug its claws into my UniSuit and dragged me to the bottom. Unlike me, it could breathe underwater just fine. Now there was a bar indicating how long I could last without air under the water, which depended on my Health.

Ten seconds.

At first I tried to beat off the strange animal with my fist. Then it occurred to me to take out my knife and stab the beast in the stomach. Once, twice, three times. I felt the knife glance off without even cutting the creature's thick skin. Nonetheless, it started twitching, released me and swam away in a hurry. It was fat, and its webbed feet looked more like muscular flippers.

The air indicator disappeared and was replaced by a notification that repeated every second.

*Damage taken: -500, obturation asphyxia.*
*Damage taken: -500, obturation asphyxia.*

What a term! How was the average player supposed to know that 'obturation asphyxia' is a consequence of simple choking?

What were the workers at Glocon doing? This was one such case where the control systems, in choosing the perfect formulation to describe damage, delved into forensic science. Yes, it was succinct. But it was unclear.

The CSes are machines. Like people, they're imperfect. And when one imperfect creation helps out another — everything turns out great.

*Damage taken: -500, obturation asphyxia.*

*Get to the surface now if you don't want to drown in shit.*

I made a few powerful sweeps, caught up to the fat beast, dug my nails into its wrinkled skin and broke the surface. Once above water, I struck my enemy in the neck with my knife. It responded by hitting me in the face with a flipper as if clipping me round the ear for talking back.

"You started it," I said, plunging my knife into its throat.

The so-far taciturn monster seemed upset by my cruelty, and let out a loud roar. Blood sprayed from the wound on its neck.

I pulled back to attack again and inspected it in

more detail.

*Sewer Manatee*
*Level: 34.*
*Health: 8966/9000.*

*Another disgusting fecal creature from the sewers.*

*Natural Scientist: like all manatees, the sewer manatee is noteworthy for its calm and friendly demeanor. Can be easily trained. If you plan to live in the sewers, a manatee can be your best friend.*
*Natural Scientist: you invaded its nest! It just wanted to push you out, but you showed hostility. Careful, sewer manatees are terrifying when angered.*
*Natural Scientist: almost its entire body is protected by thick layers of skin and fat. Weak spots: throat and flippers.*

*Knife Combat skill increased: +10 XP.*

The sewer manatee quickly dodged to the side, avoiding my strike, and snapped its jaws.

*Damage taken: -230, sewer manatee bite.*
*An unknown and potent venom has entered your bloodstream. Its effect is unpredictable, but you'll have a really bad time soon (requires Military Toxicology level 1 and 20 Knowledge)*

*Natural Scientist: by the way, the sewer manatee also has a venomous bite.*
*Increase the Natural Scientist skill to level 2 to find out more about what the venom does.*

I hadn't noticed any changes in my body yet, but I decided to end the battle, turn around and swim away. The sewer manatee roared victoriously... And swam after me.

I made my way into the shallows and stood, taking out my revolvers.

"Swim back."

But the manatee roared again and stubbornly clapped its fins on the water, approaching the shallows.

I fired a warning shot. Two blue beams churned the water, creating clouds of steam, but that stubborn fatass wasn't easily scared. He made his way into the shallows and clumsily jumped toward me. He swam a lot better than he walked. And he looked so pathetic that I could barely make myself shoot him. When I did, the beam from the revolver bounced off the sewer manatee's skin and disappeared in the air.

I swapped my Tesla for a machine gun.

"Alright, if you don't want it the easy way, we'll do it the hard way."

I fired a short volley. Some of the bullets also ricocheted off his layered skin, but the rest pierced it, spraying out fountains of blood.

The sewer manatee yelped, stopped slapping its way toward me and began to turn around, slowly and carefully, like a truck on a narrow street. I decided to ignore the animal's endearing clumsiness and keep shooting. He wasn't even a person, at the end of the day. Why should I sympathize? He was more valuable as a source of loot than a pet.

I took a step forward and aimed at my fleeing enemy's back. But my finger didn't make it to the trigger. The machine gun fell from my hands, and my arms hung limp by my sides.

*You have lost the ability to control your arms. Who knows whether it's permanent or not. The effect of the unknown venom will last an unknown length of time.*
*Poison Resistance skill increased: +10 XP.*

It seemed the manatee had gotten me good under the water.

It was if this was all my enemy had been waiting for. He stopped retreating and turned to me again, clumsily shuffling and jumping his way around. Shaking his huge bulk, he began to move toward me. I stepped back, my arms immobile as if tied by an invisible rope.

"Come on, get back," I pleaded. "You won't catch me anyway."

But my enemy rose up, roared and slapped his front flippers together. He splashed down into the shallows and kept moving toward me. As if mocking my helplessness, he jumped straight at me and slapped me around the face with his right flipper. But the helmet held again, although its durability had surely fallen.

The monster pressed on, slapping me with its flippers, first my body and then my face. It looked as if I'd really offended him and now he was raining down angry slaps on me.

My answering strikes with the knife were so weak that they dealt almost no damage. Apart from that, every strike from the manatee shook me and I couldn't focus on using the Power Surge skill in my UniSuit.

The sewer manatee got tired of slapping me around the face. He dropped down on all fours and bit into my left leg, releasing another dose of venom. My Poison Resistance skill went up again.

*Congratulations, Leonarm, you leveled up!*
*Your level: 30.*
*Attention: you have unused stat points (1) and skill points (1). Spend them... somehow.*

Now that the manatee had stopped slapping me around with its flippers, I reached for the symbol of my neurointerface and clenched my fist, activating my skill.

The first order of business was to pull my leg out of the sewer manatee's mouth. The second was to give him a good kick. The animal flew backwards, flipping over onto his back.

Because my single strong kick dealt seven hundred damage at once, I got a message.

*Kick skill learned: +10 XP.*
*When words fail in arguments, fists prevail. But you have feet as well as fists. Also a good debating tool!*

The manatee stood on its flippers and began to run away, its fat skin gathering in folds whenever it jumped. Since my Power Surge hadn't ended yet, I caught up to the manatee and kicked him again.

*Kick skill increased: +10 XP.*

Screaming pathetically, the manatee flipped over several times and fell into the deep water. I picked up my machine gun. The stunned manatee flapped around in the water, preparing to dive.

"No way, you're not getting away," I said, then started shooting.

The bullets threw up little fountains of pink-tinged

water. The manatee stopped thrashing around and turned over, floating with its belly up. A weak current pushed it toward the bank.

I took out my knife and started cutting folds of skin off the sewer manatee. After a few attempts, I opened the creature's guts. Some items fell out of it along with its innards.

*Gold Emerald Ring.*
*A simple ring, with no magic or mysticism.*
*Value: 23,000-33,000g.*
*Knowledge: judging by the weight and thickness, this old ring is a collector's item. The manatee must have found some ancient treasure on the bottom and swallowed some of it.*
*Natural Scientist: since sewer manatees don't swim far from their nests, there can be no doubt that the treasure trove is somewhere nearby.*

*Sewer Manatee Liver.*
*This organ's value is unknown (requires Natural Scientist level 3). But since it dropped, why not take it?*

*Obtained knowledge: Sewer Manatee Venom.*
*Now you can create an antidote to the venom. Requires a Chemical Laboratory.*

"I'm not going to be doing chemistry in here," I said, continuing to cut up the corpse.

Nothing else dropped.

It goes without saying that I swam down a few times, diving up to thirty feet down, but I didn't feel the bottom. The treasure was deeper than I could dive.

On the other hand, I leveled up Swimming. During

one of my dives, a school of sewage nymphs attacked me. They seemed like harmless creatures, but the white worms filled the space around me, and I lost my bearings. Instead of swimming to the surface, I found myself right under the bottom of the sunken helicopter. While I was swimming out from under it, I took damage from obturation asphyxia.

I healed myself with a medkit. While waiting for the cooldown to finish so I could use another medkit, I climbed into the helicopter. I found another emerald ring in the manatee's nest, from the same treasure trove as before.

In a cupboard was the pilot's Wingover UniSuit. Its slots were full of upgrades that assisted in piloting aerial vehicles. The armory compartment was full of zombie skulls and bones that the manatee had dragged in. I dug through them and found an MGL revolver grenade launcher and twenty rounds for it. I dug through the junk a little longer and found four grenades.

Overall, I found quite a few theoretically useful things in the helicopter. For example, a low-level component adaptation machine (CAM). Unfortunately, it weighed near seventy pounds, or I'd have carried it off. If not to craft, then to sell it in the in-game auction house. I'd get more for it there than from NPC sellers like that conman Johnny Lane.

And... my hands were itching. I wanted to go back for the abandoned container from the repair set, pick it up and stick it in the CAM. I could split it into the components available at my level and try to craft at least a knife, just to see what I could make. Relive the good old days, as it were.

My UniSuit had already recovered. I marked the helicopter on my map in case I wanted to return. Or I could sell the coordinates of the Kuznetsov portal to another player who wanted to dive in shit for riches.

Carefully stepping through the shallows, I went further into the cave. Very soon, I smelled something: a serious monster was waiting for me ahead, the boss of the dungeon. At first I smelled it, then saw it.

The beast was huge...

# Chapter 27
# Huge Beast

THE BEAST was huge: a copy of a liberat scaled up to the size of a five-story building.

It stood on its hind legs, holding its front legs in the air, the top of its head brushing the ceiling of a cave with an underground lake at its floor. Far above, I saw a scrap of blue sky crossed with the bars of a grill. Dirty sewage water flowed in from it, adding more filth to the stinking lake.

The beast raised its face occasionally and, narrowing its eyes at the sunlight, lapped up some of the falling water. Then I saw its wet, bald belly, covered in dozens of leathery, semi-transparent growths in which I could see the fetuses of liberats. At least a hundred in each growth. A disgusting sight. Vildana would have liked it.

From time to time, the top of one of the growths opened, and a liberat covered in slime fell out of it. It hung by its umbilical cord and thrashed around until its mother noticed it and cut the cord with a claw. The newborn liberat flopped into the water and desperately paddled for the bank. A corpse of one such newborn floated by my feet. It seemed not all of them made it.

Apart from those relatively small growths, there were two huge ones that looked like monstrous breasts. The semi-transparent, blue-veined skin was so stretched and distended that I could see it clearly: two liberats rested within each growth. Larger than those I'd encountered before, and most importantly, their eyes were open. Nestled against the semi-transparent film, their red eyes roamed around, keeping watch on the space of the hall. I almost wanted to hide under the water.

They hadn't seen me yet. Taking cover behind a pile of bricks, I thought about how best to attack this creature. Or would it be better to sneak past it to look for the Lefaucheux musket? Judging by the marker, it was right behind the creature's back, in its nest.

The beast breathed loudly and dropped onto all fours, throwing up a wave of fetid water. The wave reached me, knocked me down. I had to hold on to the low brick wall to stay afloat. Still snorting and reeking, the creature turned and pulled a chunk of something edible out of a pile of rotting refuse.

The small liberats brought her food that turned up in the multitude of tunnels in the sewage system. Each held some sort of food in its mouth. A couple of zebra liberats had dragged in a human corpse. Others had brought a bizoid of a class I didn't recognize.

The mother examined each offering. The liberats that brought much were praised: the mother groomed them, and the small creatures gasped out happy squeaks. As for the ones that brought garbage, she gave them a slap, throwing them into the wall and letting them splash down into the water.

I took advantage while the beast was looking away. I started running, moving my legs with difficulty through the thick, disgusting water. Found some other ruined walls to hide behind. At this distance, I could read the creature's stats:

*Liberat Mother.*

*One of the giant creatures that lives in the Liberty City sewage system. They make their homes in stagnant underground lakes, after which they begin to produce a huge number of offspring. Destroying the mother will increase your Reputation with the authorities of Liberty City.*

*Level: 73.*

*Health: 120,000/120,000.*

*Natural Scientist: her thick skin is most likely invulnerable to small-caliber rounds. You'll need heavy artillery. Unless you find a vulnerability. Every creature has them.*

*Natural Scientist: the pups care for their mother, and the mother lives for her children (requires Natural Scientist level 3).*

*Attention: the Liberat Mother has an unknown battle skill (requires Natural Scientist level 2). Be careful.*

Hardy vermin in here. At least the vulnerability was obvious: I had to aim for those sacks of baby rats. That would anger her, but it would also force her to retreat to protect her offspring. But what did that mysterious reference to mutual caring mean? Never mind, I'd figure it out as I went.

*Natural Scientist skill increased: +10 XP.*

*Did you notice that the liberat mother doesn't just produce offspring, but also carries two guardian zebra liberats? They'll probably attack you in defense of their mother. There's a high chance that they'll be armed with a strengthened acoustic attack, not just teeth and fangs.*

The more I watched, the more I became convinced: I couldn't avoid a fight. Of course, I could try to find a way around, but... I wasn't sure one existed. And I also wasn't sure I could take the beast on. Was it better to retreat?

But all-powerful chance took the decision for me. I got a notification:

*Damage taken: -1, liberat bite.*

A few more of the little bastards approached me, baring their sharp white teeth. The liberat mother shuddered, opened her mouth and screamed. The fetid water of the stagnant lake began to seethe. Hundreds of the little creatures swam toward me, abandoning their offerings. Too late to retreat.

I took out my machine gun and thought for the last time that it was too soon for me to fight a mob of that level.

Hiding no longer, I climbed onto the brick wall and aimed my machine gun at the back of the nearest liberat. I took a deep breath, although in the virtual world this didn't affect my accuracy at all, nor the amount of oxygen going into my lungs. I began to fire.

The water foamed and bubbled. The bullets pinned some liberats to the bottom, after which they slowly floated up, their dead paws twitching. Others got their heads taken clean off. Those kept swimming for a few seconds, stopped and sank, flipping over so their rear ends faced up, their hind paws jerking.

Among the small gray bodies was the occasional large striped body of a zebra liberat. I kept my aim on them for longer and shot until I was sure the beast was dead. A zebra liberat that reached me unnoticed could knock me into the water with one hit, and I wouldn't come out again.

Occasionally, liberats that I'd failed to finish off swam to my little island, climbed onto it and limped toward me, leaving a bloody trail. I finished them off with my feet, crushing their heads or sending them back into the water with a swift kick.

I fought off the first wave of attackers without even going through a full magazine. Nonetheless, I took my chance to reload my machine gun. Incidentally, it was strange that I used it so much, but hadn't really looked closely at it. That said, I already knew that it was a standard cheap Kalashnikov or Maverik, without upgrades or improvements.

The liberat queen tore her face and screamed, mourning her many losses. Her children began to run to her call. In twos and threes, they appeared from tunnels and surrounded their mother. They were gathering strength for the next attack.

I aimed and fired a volley at the liberat queen. She just shrieked and took a few paces back, deeper into the cave. My attack forced her to stop assembling her army and instead attack me with what she had. The second wave of beasts was smaller than the first, and they didn't move quite as quickly, as if they were unsure of their strength.

I didn't shoot, I turned and jumped off the brick

island. Giving my enemies no time to get their bearings and detect me, I swapped my machine gun for the revolver grenade launcher and sent three rounds into the scurrying crowd. The first explosion through up hordes of small liberats, screeching and spreading their paws wide. The second swept away the large liberats. A third destroyed part of the island.

After the dust settled, I shot another couple of times, finishing off the rest and fully destroying the island. The piteous wail of the liberat mother sounded like a trumpet of my little victory.

I dragged myself through the water to the remains of the island so that my autolooter could pull in all the dropped coins and possibly valuable items. And I found such a rarity!

I doubted that it had dropped from a liberat. It probably dropped from the island I destroyed, which was once a structure.

*Obtained:*

*Automatic Salinger Rifle.*

*Can be used either as a medium-range sniper rifle or as an automatic weapon. But with your sniper skills, it'd be better used as a club.*

*You're obviously one of those people that hammers in nails with a microscope.*

*Magazine: 20 shots.*
*Ammunition: energy magazine with a capacity of 10 energy units.*

*Damage: 1570.*
*Energy Weapons skill level 2: +10%.*

*Total damage: 1727.*

*Optical sight: 4x.*
*Rate of fire in sniper mode: 3 seconds.*
*Automatic: 0.2.*
*Weight: 11 lbs.*
*Durability: 23/100.*

*This weapon can be upgraded to increase all its stats. Try it, you'll like it!*

The liberat queen continued her wails, but fewer and fewer of her children came to her call. A liberat occasionally came out of a tunnel. It seemed I'd killed most of her offspring in the area. The huge monster breathed noisily, shuffled through the water and followed me with her gaze. From time to time, the growths on her stomach opened, divulging more pups. The mother cut the cord and rumbled in pleasure. The newborns were weaker than the adult specimens, but fully capable of attacking me.

I brought up another grouped list of messages in my lenses. I'd killed quite a few liberats. My Explosives and Kick skills had leveled up.

After so many kills, my character had leveled up and I had a skill point. The progress bar to the next level was partially filled as well. That was good: a little more and I'd reach level 32!

I wanted to boost my Knowledge, but changed my mind. After level thirty, the Tracker class got a special stat — Accuracy. It didn't just affect firing accuracy, but also accuracy when throwing grenades, using knives or jumping across rocks.

Increasing the new stat by even one point provided a significant boost to accuracy when firing with the machine gun. Of course, that stat was more important for a sniper. I was far from that still.

At least I had a sniper rifle, even if it was beat-up.

*Rifles and Shotguns skill increased to level 1.*

*Firing accuracy with rifles and shotguns increased by 10%. You won't hit a squirrel in the eye, but you might at least hit the squirrel. Maybe.*

*Rifle and shotgun deterioration decreased by 50%.*

Improving this skill in combination with Accuracy and Eagle Eye, supplemented with a good dose of Luck, would eventually turn Leonarm into a precise and reliable machine when it came to headshots and single-shot kills. Just how Leonarm shot when I went down in the fight against the Black Wave.

I equipped the Salinger rifle. I got a large liberat in my sights as it swam toward me. The shot took its head off, and the body flew back a few feet in the water.

*Congratulations, Leonarm, you leveled up!*
*Your level: 32.*

*Attention: you have unused stat points (1) and skill points (1). Spend them wisely!*

I immediately upgraded my Knowledge and leveled up the Rifles and Shotguns skill, which gave me more accuracy and less weapon wear.

It was a shame I had only one magazine for the rifle. I couldn't spend my rounds on the little rats; I moved the crosshair onto the liberat queen, focused in on one of the growths full of pups and shot.

The growth burst and the babies spilled out, hanging off their umbilical cords like fairy lights. The beast's health immediately dropped by five thousand. Not bad, that meant I could...

The mother's scream was so piercing that I thought it'd damage my hearing. The growths housing the guard liberats opened, and the two creatures emerged, unfolding wrinkled wings. They split from the mother's body and soared up to the ceiling. The fine tails of their umbilical cords hung beneath them.

Since they didn't attack me right away, that meant they hadn't seen my position yet. I aimed my sight at one of the beasts:

*Winged Zebra Liberat.*

*Level: 30.*

*Health: 7,000.*

*Knowledge. An incredible symbiosis of two types of vermin: the winged rats defend the mother, and in return they get a nest and continuous feeding.*

*Natural Scientist. Don't let their weakness fool you. Their connection to the mother makes them stronger. And, as you can see, they don't fear the light and the properties of their skin are the same as those of their striped brethren. Even better.*

*Natural Scientist. And they're better armed.*

I aimed and shot one of the winged zebra liberats.

But they moved so quickly in search of my hiding spot that I missed. Incredibly, the cords stretching out from the mother didn't get twisted or tangled as the creatures flew.

I shot and missed a second time.

Only the third time, while the creatures hovered in place after detecting me, the blue beam of my rifle hit one of them right in the face. I saw its health drop to nearly zero, but then it instantly went up again, recovering over several seconds.

I had no more time to do anything else. They dove toward me and hovered between me and the bars. They opened their mouths and emitted such piercing shrieks that my helmet cracked, and blood began to seep from my ears.

*Damage taken: -1,000, acoustic attack.*
*Damage taken: -1,000, acoustic attack.*
*Police Standard Helmet destroyed, cannot be repaired.*

So much for my Perception bonus. I jumped back from the window and hid behind a wall. It was clear that while they were connected via the umbilical cord, their mother could heal them. I had to either concentrate my fire on the mother or somehow break the winged rats' umbilicals.

How could I break them? Hitting that fine thread with my rifle was unrealistic with my Accuracy, and trying to cut it with a machine gun volley would be ridiculous.

But I had no more time to think. The liberat mother finally figured out exactly where I was. Gathering her paws beneath her, she crouched and jumped, throwing huge waves into the shallows.

Her giant figure blotted out the light from the bars in the cave's ceiling...

*Damage taken: -22,041, crushing damage. The Liberat Mother squashed you.*

# Chapter 28
# Separate Ways

LeCube LAY in a mountain of debris and scorched earth left behind after the explosion. The system notified him that his ability to take on program configurations had recovered, and he had just under a million component nanomass left.

His health was another story — almost zero. Even the weakest enemy tank or soldier could have killed Grisha right then.

Instead of heading to the bombed-out remains of the Black Wave base, he needed to recover his health. Other surviving Black Wavers slowly begin to contact him. Less than ten in all. It was clear that even if the Black Wave hadn't been fully destroyed, it had been knocked down to the very bottom of the Adam Online leaderboard.

Fortunado was also alive, but not responding. Grisha guessed why — his brother had lost all hope. The remainder of the guild waited for orders, but they all knew that there was nothing left to do. To hide their despair, they had a lively discussion about where the coalition could have gotten an atomic bomb. If weapons like that became widespread, it would change the course of mass military conflicts.

"Now the game will be even more like the real world," one guild member lamented. "We'll be hiding in bunkers, building up arms, signing anti-nuclear treaties."

"What do we do now, boss?" another member asked.

"For now, go back to wherever you want. Sit quietly."

"But the coalition is going to attack and take our territory."

"Thank you, all of you, but there's no sense in fighting any more. Any of our guys who died and are leveling up new characters, tell them to just do their own thing."

The soldiers didn't argue with Grisha. They waited for Fortunado's decision. They didn't believe that the guild had come to an end.

Since none of the survivors could exist in the high radiation zone, Grisha set off for the epicenter. His health had already risen to an acceptable eighty thousand.

Grisha took on his disk form and flew to the black crater that had once been Shoreline. In pain, he looked upon the wreckage of his once mighty guild. It had taken them years to create it all: they'd spent so long building, buying, reinforcing... and it had all been destroyed in three minutes.

Grisha rarely thought of the past and the war that had transformed the Earth into the world in which he was born. He didn't know what the war was like, but he'd lived its consequences.

The ones who had made it hard to produce weapons like atomic bombs in Adam Online had been right. Even in that sense, the virtual world was better than the real one.

Grisha saw movement and a flash of energy at the respawn tower. The coalition had already sent a scout: a tank replicator and an autosen were already entrenched at the tower.

Fortunado was still in his Octopus frame. It was weakly armed, so the brother couldn't break through to the tower. Hiding behind a pile of melted earth, he shot the enemy with charges of plasma. The autosen quickly restored the damage, responding with volleys from a Tesla machine gun, but didn't withdraw from the tank replicator. It was a common tactic: first wait for two or three tanks to be created as reinforcements, then continue to advance.

Unlike LeCube, the Octopus frame was vulnerable to radiation. Fortunado's health was dropping at a shocking pace.

Grisha felt the urge to transform into the Grenika, but then remembered he'd lost that config.

"Shame," he thought. "The Grenika would have done this quicker..."

As the disk flew, LeCube switched to its robot spider config and crashed to the ground on all eight legs.

"Hold on, bro!" Grisha shouted as he joined the battle.

He fired missiles at the autosen and the replicator, which had already spat out its second tank. His legs a blur, he walked right up to them and finished them off in his usual style: tearing and cutting them into pieces with the tools on his legs.

Fortunado's octopus climbed out from behind the pile of earth and floated through the air to the respawn tower, its tentacles hanging beneath it.

Grisha was mistaken. Fortunado hadn't lost hope at all.

"Hurry, Grisha, we need to get to the base at Jamilla's Tomb and take a foothold there."

"So you finally agree that we need to go into Rim Six? That's right, broth..."

"Not at all. Mariam contacted me after the nuclear explosion. She says she didn't give the coalition that nuke."

"And you believe her?"

"Why not? She hasn't betrayed us yet. More importantly, when she heard of our defeat, she asked to meet in person. She says that..."

Grisha couldn't hold back any longer.

"Listen, you moron, Mariam is an NPC. All her tasks are just a quest for top-level players."

"No, no!" Fortunado's octopus waved all its tentacles. "This again?!"

"How do you think the nuke was created?"

"Well?"

"Nika said that there might be components required for creating nukes in Rim Six. She got it from there. Mariam's level is above four hundred. That's why she doesn't talk to you in person, so you can't see her stats."

"You're putting unrelated facts together to match your own assumptions..."

"And you're putting a bag over your head so you won't hear the truth. Whoever gets to Rim Six first is the victor."

"The victor of whom, and what? Adam Online? It's an endless game with endless worlds. Who do you plan on defeating here?"

Grisha always got lost in debates with his brother, because his arguments somehow always cleverly twisted together to make Grisha the fool. Just like Nika. Grisha had a way of ending such arguments.

"Whatever. Do what you want."

Fortunado slowed. The radiation had lowered his health to dangerous levels.

"So this is it, brother?" Fortunado asked. "We're going our separate ways?"

"Yes. You've had fun playing out your spy fantasies. You spent so long thinking strategically that you cracked. You see hidden meanings everywhere and ignore what's right in front of you: Mariam is a hidden quest. That's why nothing shows up in our interface."

"Alright, bro. You've made your choice. But let me tell you one thing first: remember that I've always been a better strategist than you?"

"Once or twice."

"And do you know why?"

"Because you have shitty reactions and you're no good on the battlefield?"

"Because I've always kept some of my knowledge hidden. Even now, I know more about Mariam than you do."

"How's that?"

"Bye, brother. If you want to believe she's a quest, that's your business. My business is to stop you. And take vengeance against... Nika."

"What does she have to do with it?"

"Ask her yourself."

His brother's words hurt Grisha. It was true,

Fortunado had always been secretive, had always kept things hidden. When he sent Grisha on missions, there was always something left unsaid, always a part of the plan that he alone knew. Like that time with Camper. If it weren't for the mages that Fortunado had sent after the group in secret, LeCube would have been lost along with Grisha.

But then Grisha got mad. How long could he suffer Fortunado's superiority complex? Some strategist he was. Grisha was sick and tired of it. It was high time he showed him that all his strategies worked only because they had an executor as good as Grisha behind them.

"Bye, brother," Grisha agreed. "This has been a long time coming."

"What has?"

"Brother against brother and all that. Now we'll finally find out who's stronger."

"I'll wait for you at Jamilla's Tomb. I'm stronger."

"Sure."

"Yeah. I always was."

With those words, Fortunado activated the respawn tower and teleported away. Grisha looked around one last time. This place had been the stronghold of his guild, his life's work up to this point. His garage with full of frames, his guildmates. His brother. All burned away in nuclear fire.

Grisha opened his stats, went to his guild settings, and...

*Player Grisha has left the Black Wave guild.*

Then he walked to the tower and selected Dimension X as a travel point.

As soon as he disappeared, coalition troops came spilling out of the tower. Camper flew in first in his gleaming red underpants and cloak.

Half a minute later, the Black Wave territory was captured.

Nika knew that Grisha had come to Dimension X, but didn't contact him, and hid her location on the map.

*Feeling guilty, rat?* Grisha thought angrily.

He transformed into the humanoid mech with powerful pincers on its left arm that could crush the most well-armored tanks.

Rumbling and clanking, Grisha walked from hangar to hangar, occasionally shouting into the ether.

"Hey, you little rat, enough hiding. It'll go worse if I have to find you."

But Nika wasn't hiding at all. Grisha found her in 'World 0.4+, Alpha Test.' She stood opposite her projector panel covered in icons. As always, she was immersed in crafting something.

She heard the clanking of Grisha's steel feet behind her, but she didn't move even when Grisha walked right up to her.

"Don't even try to deny it!" Grisha shouted.

"What, exactly?" Nika answered calmly, not turning her head.

Her fake calm enraged Grisha. He opened his pincers and grabbed the android by the shoulders, lifted her above the floor and shook her.

"I'll crush you!"

"Why?" Nika answered just as calmly.

Sharp locks of hard plastic hair fell onto her face. She tried to shake her head to get them out of the way.

"You made the nuke for the coalition. You destroyed the guild."

Nika wanted to shrug her thin shoulders out of habit, but the pincers stopped her. So she answered simply.

"Regardless of who made the nuke... Weren't you complaining that the guild was preventing us from going into Rim Six?"

"You rat, I never wanted you to kill them all!"

Grisha shook Nika so hard that damage numbers started falling off her. Before he crushed her in his pincers, Grisha called up her stats. He wanted to make sure that Nika didn't have any dirty tricks up her sleeve like a self-destruct function, which allowed a dying android to explode with massive damage. Neither LeCube's durability nor Grisha's health had restored enough to survive something like that if he killed Nika.

*Nika, Android.*
*Level: 396.*
*Strength: 8.*
*Perception: 62.*
*Agility: 2.*
*Knowledge: 332.*
*Health: 12.*
*Luck: 80.*

*Armor: 1675/2000*
*Health: 1200/1200*
*Reputation: —18, suspicion. A merchant of rare components in Londinium has put a price on her head. Don't miss this chance!*

That was it.

Nika was completely defenseless. She had no android skills or traps active. With Grisha's level and skills, he would have seen them.

Nothing.

It seemed she'd even whitelisted Grisha for the autosens and security systems in Dimension X. The guards should have attacked Grisha for grabbing their mistress in his claws.

Grisha's anger hadn't passed, but it had calmed a little. Still gripping Nika, he spoke.

"Hmm, you've almost reached four hundred..."

"Yep," the android nodded. "A little more and we'll be ready."

Grisha released his grasp, dropping Nika onto the floor. Almost unwillingly, he took on his base form. It recovered health more quickly. Nika rose, approached LeCube and placed a palm on its surface.

The regeneration sped up.

"There's one thing I don't get," Grisha said. "How did you make a nuclear bomb..?"

"You really think my guilt is proven?"

"Fine. If you did make that fucking nuke, then where did you get the components? They're only available in Rim Six."

"Someone would have had to bring me the materials from Rim Six."

"So who brought them?" Grisha asked quickly.

Nika removed her hand from LeCube. She approached the projector panel and swept off all the icons, opening a partner agreement. She threw it to Grisha's neurointerface.

"It's time to make our partnership official. As you

can see, I've put as many points as I can into Knowledge. Big guys like you could kill me with a single touch."

"So you want me to protect you in Rim Six. Like a bodyguard?"

"Yes," Nika replied calmly. "And also, I love you."

Grisha confirmed the agreement.

"I love you too, but I don't believe a single word you say."

"Then how will I tell you who brought me the components?"

Grisha switched back into the humanoid robot.

"I'm not an idiot. I guessed already. Mariam, right?"

Nika nodded.

"You guessed something else right too."

"That she's an NPC?"

"Yes, an NPC who knows that the real world exists."

"And you and Fortunado made fun of me. You said that doesn't happen, that I'm an idiot, that I just didn't get it."

"Sorry, but you really don't get it. Neither do I... I don't think anyone really gets what's going on. Especially the officials at Glocon."

"They don't even suspect that someone hacked into the base code of the CSes?"

Nika shrugged uncertainly.

"I think there's something more here than just an attempt by the CSes to rewrite themselves. That's the first thing that comes to mind, which means it's wrong. The exit interface was created to be reusable."

"Oh! Then I get it!" Grisha exclaimed. "The control systems have decided to use people to improve their architecture. To do that, they decided to create an interface and transfer into our bodies."

Nika sighed as if tired, which was strange. Androids didn't get tired.

"My Knowledge isn't just high in the game, but in life, too. For the hundredth time, the CSes are a set of algorithms, there's no way they can add anything to their code. Hell, Grisha, they can't even take decisions. They just react to the actions of players."

"But you said the Mentors created the control systems? And the Mentors..."

Nika cut him off.

"I was implying that there must be people behind all this. And they must be people who were able to trick or bribe officials from the Global Consortium of Standardization in Adam Online. These people have set things up so that it looks as if the Mentors or the CSes are plotting something."

If Grisha had eyes, they would have lit up with conjecture.

"What if..."

"No. Don't suggest ridiculous ideas about machines becoming sentient and deciding to conquer humanity. They can imitate sentience, but they'll never achieve it. And why would they want to conquer us when we already live inside machines?"

Grisha waved in annoyance.

"You're making fun of me again. So who are these people?"

"I don't know. And I don't care. All I want is to survive."

# Chapter 29
# Tumbleweed

NIKA AND GRISHA spent the next few days immersed in monotonous farming.

The leveling system in Adam Online was built on an incremental basis. Between level zero and a hundred, gaining one level required just a hundred experience. Between level one hundred and two hundred, it took two hundred experience. Then three hundred, then four hundred.

This meant that every hundred levels, leveling up slowed. But with enough stubbornness and professionalism, you could reach the level cap in a single taharration rotation, if only it weren't for the penalty system. The higher your level, the greater the penalty for dying. And if you died to an enemy who was even a single level beneath you, the penalty multiplied. This meant that players rarely reached level four hundred. And if they reached it, they didn't stay there long.

It wasn't just the fighting types who died, either. The ones with peaceful professions did too. If an engineer at level three hundred crafted some kind of fancy furniture or gear, an error in combining the components and processes could lead to an explosion or an energy surge that killed them on the spot.

The game provided balance, and there was no better balancer than death.

In short, Nika and Grisha farmed.

Nika leveled up by crafting constantly, creating numerous frames and then destroying them to create them anew. Some she sold, of course. Grisha even saw Nika making... furniture with unusual properties. Incidentally, furniture and clothing made by such a master at such a high level sold pretty well. Even faster than weapons.

Grisha used the Dimension X respawn tower to attack former coalition members. Predictably, after their victory, the allies steadily began to fall out. Although the Black Wave hadn't been fully destroyed, the Langoliers had regained control over their base and were actively expanding their influence. Nika sold most of her frames to them.

Grisha leveled up as usual, by finding juicy players and killing them.

LeCube had become a curse for top-ranking players. First Grisha tracked down and killed Camper. Then he tracked down and killed him a second time. He almost wanted to kill him a third time, but Camper's level was so low that it wasn't worth the experience.

In general, not much brought him enough experience to be worthwhile. Everyone in Adam Online was weaker than him, after all.

After Camper, he went after Knight_Ivan. He killed him until the guild leader of the Viatichis fell to position two hundred on the leaderboard and stopped providing experience to Grisha. He did the same with Slippery Joe from the Golden Horde.

After that, he put his personal respect to one side

and killed off all the top members from the Virtus.pro guild. He sent a standard audio recording with each kill: *You defeated the guild, but you didn't defeat me. Next time, choose the right side.*

He killed Jamilla once too. He ran into her somewhere on the border of Rim Five, where she was trying to find a path into Rim Six as usual. Plenty of players were seeking such a path, but none of them had found anything new yet. Many had even decided that Jamilla's Tomb was the only corridor into the new zones.

Grisha and Fortunado weren't speaking. Grisha heard through his former guildmates that his brother had gathered the remainder of the guild at Jamilla's Tomb. There he erected structures, strengthened his defenses. Over those two days, the Black Wave had risen from the lowest lines on the guild leaderboard to somewhere in the middle.

Yet again, Grisha found himself fighting numbers: the longer he leveled up, the stronger the defense became at Jamilla's Tomb. Sometimes it seemed like it would be best to attack straight away, before Fortunado turned the base into an unassailable fortress. He could gain the levels required to move into Rim Six during the battle.

But Nika rejected the plan.

"Sure, you'll level up easily. But I'm no fighter. How am I going to level up on the battlefield?"

"You could heal me?"

"That won't give much experience. Anyway, my Restore Life is already fully leveled. Using it won't give me any experience."

From time to time, Grisha opened the Adam Online (Asian Cluster) leaderboard and admired the top five:

1. *Grisha — 398 (Mechanodestructor).*
2. *Nika — 396 (Android).*
3. *Jamilla — 394 (Fallen Angel).*
4. *Joker JJ — 377 (Human, Black Wave).*
5. *Mikey Boy — 366 (Mechanodestructor, Langoliers).*

Apart from admiring his own position, he was keeping an eye on Jamilla. She was steadily catching up to him. From the scraps of information he received from his former guildmates, he learned that she'd left the coalition and begun harvesting her former allies. That was why she was leveling up so quickly.

Jamilla was still determined to make it into Rim Six.

After a few days, Nika reported that Fortunado wanted to buy some goods for her for five hundred thousand gold.

"What did you say?" Grisha asked.

"I refused, of course. After all, I'm no longer impartial. On the contrary, I have an interest in weakening the defenses at Jamilla's Tomb. We'll have to break through there soon."

Grisha guiltily admitted a misstep.

"Damn, then I was wasting my time killing the coalition. I'm their ally for now, I guess."

"No, you aren't allies, you're enemies with common intentions. Anyway, don't forget that we don't want everyone to get into Rim Six."

Grisha sighed.

"Fortunado's strategic genius would have come in handy now."

"Yes... we need to somehow break through the defenses, but not destroy them entirely. Maybe we can come to an agreement with your brother?"

"We've fallen out completely. I think we'll still be angry at each other even in real life. I tried — at first he ignored me, then blocked me."

"As if you spoke much in real life anyway."

"Damn, if killing coalition members isn't going to help us, then how are we going to level up?"

"By killing your former guildmates."

Grisha sighed and set off for Jamilla's Tomb. He wanted to visit his brother anyway. Maybe he'd speak if Grisha showed up in person? He had to travel a long way to the borders of Rim Five, avoiding skirmishes with squads of former allies in the coalition. He wasn't afraid of them, but he didn't want to waste component nanomass on fighting them.

He found the gloomy bluffs of Jamilla's Tomb shrouded in mist and buffeted by the wind underneath a heavy stone-gray sky. Grisha switched into the Moth jet configuration. Nika had created it to replace the lost Grenika jet. It was weaker and slower, but they'd had to choose between fast work and good work. Nika had created the Moth in two days, whereas the Grenika had taken several weeks to complete.

Grisha tried to rise above the cliffs, but the wind there was so powerful that his flight nearly ended in a crash.

Grisha called Nika and shared his intel.

"Got it," she answered. "The sky is inaccessible. Must be one of the ways they've made it harder to get into Rim Six."

"But Ozerg the Dragon flew around without issue."

"His level might have unlocked a skill to let him fly even in such strong winds."

Grisha continued to make his way across the chasms, switching to the disk config and tacking through the air currents with difficulty. The wind got so strong at one point that Grisha lost control. LeCube's disk flipped end over end and crashed into the cliffs. It all happened so fast that Grisha didn't even have time to switch to the ethereal creature config. When LeCube was in the cube or robot form, or the form of any other creature with a hard, interconnected structure, it took the same damage as anyone else.

"I get the message," Grisha said to the wind. "No flying, I'll crawl."

This time, to get across the crevasses, he had to plummet down them and brake before reaching the canyon floor. After landing, he switched forms to the robot spider, equipped with hooks and pins on its limbs, and climbed up the other side.

Several times he considered going back, finding the nearest respawn tower or Projectoria station and teleporting straight to the base at Jamilla's Tomb. But each time he stopped himself. The tower at the base would doubtlessly be well defended. LeCube would be torn to pieces as soon as it appeared.

"What if they don't tear it to pieces?" Grisha wondered. "What if I waste all of 'em as soon as I get there..?"

But then he remembered Nika chewing him out for his overconfidence, and he stopped fantasizing. He kept crawling along, dropping down to the bottom of the next gorge and climbing up the other side. Sometimes he took a detour to get around traps and vehicle generators that Fortunado had strewn around. That meant crawling through unexplored places. Once, he even got a notification.

*Pioneer skill increased: +100 XP.*
*You are the first to be in this area. What would you like to call this place on the map?*

A small pleasure, but a pleasure all the same.

Grisha looked around: the place was identical to the others he'd passed through. Rocks, little clouds of mist, some strange trees whose trunks gleamed like metal. A piece of tumbleweed rolled past LeCube, also made of metallic thorns.

"Guess I'll call this place Tumbleweed," Grisha decided, confirming the title on the map.

On the approach to the base, Grisha found a powerful defensive network of forcefields, fences, artillery and replicated military vehicles.

None of this represented any danger, but destroying it all drew attention. While Grisha was busy cutting down, blowing up and flattening the enemy vehicles, four Black Wave mages appeared as if from thin air. Grisha's Perception had been too low to detect them earlier.

By a quirk of fate, they were the same mages that Fortunado had secretly sent with Grisha during his skirmish with Camper near Londinium.

"How the tables have turned," said one mage in a black robe and mask. "We saved you before. Now we're going to kill you."

The mage extended his hands from the deep sleeves of his robe. They crackled with magical energy. Before Grisha knew what was happening, a Temporal Block covered the area. It was a spell that prevented or hampered the ability to slow time. Judging by the power of the spell, this mage had higher Perception than Grisha.

"You'd better think about who's going to save *you*," Grisha answered.

All four mages immediately began to cast a combined Phantom Explosion, a tried and tested method against LeCube. A dark orb began to form before them, growing in size and becoming brighter. When it turned white, it would be ready to use. LeCube wouldn't withstand an explosion from four mages at once. To preserve their strength, the mages stood behind the cover of a forcefield that the defensive structures at the base generated.

Grisha could have simply fled and taken a weak strike to the back, but he didn't want to retreat. Those four mages were too tasty a snack. A guaranteed level-up. Even if he killed two, he'd reach level four hundred.

While Grisha thought of how to respond and get all four of them, the mages... multiplied. An Astral Twin split from each of them. One held a sword, another a spear, another a mundane fireball. The astral projections inherited their properties from the originals, but with reduced stats. They also couldn't cast spells independently. Grisha realized that the mages didn't plan to defeat him with the twins, they were just trying to buy time.

Grisha activated his Invisibility skill. Invisibility was one of the skills available to all races, apart from angels. Invisibility was their normal state. Humans used the Optical Camouflage upgrade for the UniSuit to achieve it. Androids temporarily made themselves invisible using a special nano-skin. Bizoids altered the biochemical reactions in their bodies to achieve perfect transparency. Mechanodestructors switched on a masking device that changed the polarity of their forcefield, making the frame invisible to the enemy's eyes and sensors. Of course, invisibility always prevented defenses from working.

The duration of Invisibility varied between the races and depended on your Knowledge and Agility levels, and on the level of the skill itself. Grisha had all the required skills and stats. He could stay invisible for over two minutes.

The mages' astral doubles lost their target and aimlessly span in place. One of them even lost its fireball and had to cast another.

As Grisha expected, one of the mages broke off from casting the Phantom Explosion to cast an illumination spell that would make Grisha visible again. Paying no attention to the astral twins roaming the area where LeCube had just been, Grisha used part of his component nanomass to create the Diffusion frame. He didn't want to use his secret weapon so soon, but there was no other choice.

Diffusion worked similarly to Second Skin, with one difference — it was invulnerable to telekinesis and Matter Dispersion magic. The dust cloud filtered through the forcefield, losing half of its mass on the way, but with enough left to assemble into a small humanoid mech that Nika had named Bobby. There wasn't enough component nanomass left for firearms or energy weapons, so Bobby was armed with huge blades extending straight out of his arms.

The mage stopped casting the illumination spell and jumped back in fear, hurriedly casting armor on himself, but Bobby's sword blades lengthened rapidly and pierced through the mage. The robot folded his arms in a cross pattern, creating something like scissors, and joined the blades together, cutting the mage in half.

*Grisha (LeCube Mechanodestructor) killed Rowling (Human) with Bobby.*

The deceased mage's twin dissolved into thin air. Grisha's interface filled with a list of loot; dozens of powerful spell scrolls. All LeCube's carrying capacity was spent on component nanomass, so not all the items fit.

Then another mage broke off from casting the Phantom Explosion and cast a spell to raise elementals from the ground: earth, stone and fire. The elementals surrounded Bobby, combined into a single whole and absorbed the robot. The resulting notification in Grisha's interface made him wince.

*Damage taken: -12,556, Bobby destroyed.*

Maintaining his invisibility, Grisha tried to launch a second Diffusion through the forcefield, but the enemy's defensive systems had apparently diverted power from other places in the forcefield to the spot ahead of him. There was no time to search for a weak spot — the orb of the Phantom Explosion was now turning white. The mages dropped their hands and laughed. The orb flew beyond the bounds of the forcefield, lifted above the battlefield and began to grow.

*Damn...* Grisha thought. *I need to run... I needed to run five minutes ago.*

There was nothing left to do but switch to his base configuration, surround LeCube with a forcefield and hope that killing one mage and distracting another had weakened the Phantom Explosion enough.

# Chapter 30
# Rot, Decay and Corruption

THE PHANTOM EXPLOSION was strong. Too strong to survive unscathed.

Grisha felt himself losing control over LeCube. Just like during the nuclear explosion. He lost all data from his sensors, all sensations from his improved skills. Now he was just a cube with flat sides. And the cube didn't float in the air half a meter above the ground as it usually did, but instead lay on the ground, covered in dirt.

Grisha couldn't move, couldn't raise LeCube into the air. His system messages brought no good news.

*Damage taken: -60,000, Phantom Explosion.*

*LeCube frame structural integrity damaged. Primary CN cannot be used.*

*Lost: 1,520,000 CN.*

*You have no more consumable material. All program configurations are unavailable.*

*Warning! The explosion exhausted all your energy supplies. You need at least one energy unit for minimum mobility.*

*To create energy units, you must restock your*

*supply of component nanomass.*

This was it. A closed circle. Grisha couldn't convert CN into energy because he didn't have enough CN.

Clever mages. They predicted that LeCube would survive the strike, so they spent part of their efforts on an additional spell to extract his energy. It was actually quite a predictable move. In the war of magic versus technology, energy consumption was a classic weakness of mechanodestructors. If you could deprive a machine of its energy, you turned it into a sitting duck.

But the mages had fully exhausted their supply of mana as well. They couldn't finish off Grisha from a distance with fireballs or lightning. Their astral twins had long since disappeared. One of the mages tried shooting him with a bow, but the arrows either didn't reach Grisha or dealt no damage. Apart from that, shooting an ordinary bow at the highly advanced LeCube looked so dumb that the mages and Grisha all laughed.

"Fine," the shooter muttered, hiding the bow. "What're you laughing at? Let's go..."

The mages took out heavy weaponry: an axe, a sword, a hammer. They walked beyond the bounds of the forcefield and headed toward Grisha.

Grisha twitched in despair within LeCube. What if he abandoned the frame and tried to survive as a core? But then he realized that you couldn't get far through stones and crevasses on a monowheel. His death would be even more embarrassing — they'd chase him down and finish him off.

There was only one last thing to try.

"Let's negotiate."

"Nah," the mages answered in chorus. "We have plenty of cash. And we'll get even more for LeCube.

"Assholes," Grisha summarized.

"You're the asshole. You thought you'd keep crushing everyone? Never mind. Now it's your turn to bow."

The three mages surrounded Grisha and started hitting him.

*Damage taken: -163, iron axe strike.*
*Damage taken: -99, lead hammer strike.*
*Damage taken: -233, diamond sword strike.*

Grisha watched his health drop with indifference. What else could he do? Write Nika a death note? He imagined her anger when she found out that Grisha had died incompetently, having almost reached their goal. And lost LeCube too. Of course, there was a chance that LeCube would be destroyed, which would mean it wouldn't fall into enemy hands. It all depended on the Luck level of the mage that dealt the finishing blow. The higher the Luck, the better the loot, everyone knew that.

In any case, without LeCube, Grisha was a pauper — his garage of the best frames available had been destroyed in the atomic strike on Shoreline. Of course, he had an impressive sum of money left, but the mages would get that too after killing him. It was a good thing he had half his capital in a Londinium bank.

From time to time, Grisha changed his view point and looked at the figures of the mages surrounding LeCube. They steadily raised their weapons and dropped them, hacking chunks of health out of LeCube.

*Attention: Health critically low. You're about to die. Do something.*
*Health: 4,959/79,000.*

The column of damage notices scrolled on and on:

*Damage taken: -163, iron axe strike.*
*Damage taken: -99, lead hammer strike.*
*Damage taken: -333, diamond sword strike.*

The mage with the diamond sword was particularly annoying. Each fifth strike with that weapon dealt increased damage. Grisha switched his view point and started watching the gray sky. The heavy clouds curled, lightning flashing in gaps between them.

From the outside, the scene would have looked comical: three mages hammering on an immobile black cube. The sounds of their strikes melded into the thunder and lightning...

*Health: 1,789/79,000.*

"This is it, one more round of hits..." Grisha thought. "Yep, here it comes. And a last critical hit from the diamond sword..."

His health fell to zero.

A red mist covered his vision. Grisha lost the ability to change his view point. Now he saw the world through only one side of LeCube, but even that was quickly darkening and getting smaller. A blinking skill indicator remained.

*Last Chance! Save yourself!*
*Remaining: 1 minute 22 seconds.*

In this situation, more time merely extended the agony.

The mages stopped hitting LeCube, since there was no point continuing after his death. They just waited for Grisha to finally die.

*Last Chance! Well? Are you going to claw your way out of the grip of death, or finally give in?*
*Remaining: 1 minute 02 seconds.*

As if mocking, the system reported:

*Last Chance skill: +200 XP.*
*Last Chance skill leveled up to 13.*
*You can now live 1 minute 40 seconds after death.*

Ten seconds were added to the timer. Grisha sighed, vexed. Things always happened at just the wrong times. And he'd spent so much time leveling up that skill, he'd valued it. What was the point? Instead of extra time to fight, it was taking too long for him to die.

*Congratulations, Grisha, you leveled up!*
*Your level: 399.*
*Attention: you have unused stat points (1) and skill points (1). Spend them wisely!*
*Although what does it matter? You're nearly dead anyway.*

*Last Chance!*
*Remaining: 44 seconds.*

The ashen clouds parted, the lightning strikes grew more

frequent.

A flash broke the black sky and the opening of a magic portal appeared. The red mist had covered so much of Grisha's vision that he barely saw an indistinct humanoid figure appear from the portal.

Were the mages getting reinforcements?

*Remaining: 39 seconds.*

The figure leapt from the portal, spreading its wings. It seemed to be holding a sword. The wings extended... then the figure disappeared from Grisha's view.

His interface squawked:

*Jamilla (Fallen Angel) killed Joker JJ (Human) using the two-handed sword Rot, Decay and Corruption.*

The mage's crumpled body fell into Grisha's view, covered in the shards of his diamond sword. The mage's face was quickly covered in rotting wounds, then it dried out and the skin sloughed off the skull like dust. The death ended with the body fully decomposing and disappearing. The mage left behind a gleaming emerald surrounded by other loot.

The fact that Jamilla had killed a player so close to her in level so quickly was explained by the suddenness of her attack. She probably had the skill that provided increased damage in those situations. The mages had spent all their strength on casting the Phantom Explosion, and were almost defenseless against Jamilla with her triple-enchanted sword.

*Remaining: 35 seconds.*

The red mist had covered almost all of Grisha's vision, leaving something like a small spot in the middle.

He saw some sparks, heard the sounds of weapons. It ended with the message:

*Jamilla (Fallen Angel) killed* ⬥⬥⬥'⬥⬥⬥⬥⬥⬥ *(Human) using the two-handed sword Rot, Decay and Corruption.*

*Jamilla (Fallen Angel) killed Baby2102 (Human) using the two-handed sword Rot, Decay and Corruption.*

Then there was silence. Or had he lost his hearing as his life ebbed away? The crystal still span in Grisha's field of view, throwing spots of green light onto the stones. Jamilla's legs appeared, clad in qualia armor crisscrossed with veins of another metal to make it cheaper to produce the armor.

The crystal shook and soared away, emitting a glassy ringing sound. Jamilla swallowed it and gained some kind of magical bonus.

The fallen angel sat before Grisha, folding her wings behind her.

"How much longer?"

"Thirty seconds."

A red healing potion appeared in her hands. Jamilla poured it onto LeCube, but it had no effect. She tried a healing spell, but it hit LeCube and did nothing.

"Damn, my healing magic doesn't work on mechanodestructors. Alright, let's hope we have time."

"Time for what?" Grisha asked.

The portal was still open. A figure in a white suit appeared in the gleaming rift. She jumped onto the ground, flexing her fine, almost spiderlike legs. She swept a lock of plastic hair from her forehead and rushed toward Grisha.

*Remaining: 14 seconds.*

Nika struggled to cross the huge boulders and pits separating her from Grisha. Seven seconds. The red mist fully obscured Grisha's view, and it was steadily turning black. The final three seconds of the countdown appeared above it.

Grisha felt android hands contact the sides of LeCube.

His health recovered first:

*Health: 12/79,000.*

The number quickly rose. Nika was pouring all her strength into healing Grisha, or whatever it was androids did.

"Thanks for the healing," Grisha said. "But LeCube is broken somehow. I don't have enough component nanomass, I can't convert it into energy. So I can't move. Did you bring a pack of CN with you?"

*Health: 453/79,000.*

"I have something a little bigger than a pack," Nika answered. She moved a little to the side, keeping her hands on LeCube.

First one cargo transport flew through the portal, then a second, a third... The haulers bore the seal of Dimension X, so that nobody could doubt that Nika had finally taken a side in the battle for Rim Six.

Behind the haulers came autosens, battle mechs

and NPC infantrymen equipped in expensive Nevsky exoskeletons. They spread through the area, took up defensive positions. Some of them advanced and immediately entered into battle with the Black Wave's replicated tanks. Soon the tanks were destroyed, then the forcefield generators, and the way to the next line of defense was open.

Six rotary-wing machines emerged from the portal during the skirmish. But the helicopters couldn't join the battle; the strong wind forced them to descend. Anywhere above sixty five feet, the aircraft began to experience problems.

The portal spat out a group of android engineers in dark jumpsuits with the Dimension X logo on their back. Probably NPCs. Nika never hired players to work for her. After that, the portal hummed, rippled and slammed closed.

*Health: 4,453/79,000.*

The engineers began to unload the haulers, pulling out components and CAM (Component Adaptation Machine) parts. Nika removed her hand from LeCube.

"Heal yourself from here."

She approached the CAM assembled by the engineers, unfolded a projector panel with a million icons and threw them over to Grisha.

*Obtained: 1,520,000 CN.*

Grisha immediately began converting the CN and regenerating. He rose above the ground, shaking dust from LeCube's sides.

"I'm back in the game, brothers and sisters."

"Great. Now we have something to discuss," Jamilla said, standing next to Nika.

Jamilla spoke.

"I'm sure you know that I didn't save you so you could thank me. Although you could start with that."

Grisha switched to the humanoid mech and bowed low.

"Thank you, great lady. Get cocky and I'll reward your good deed with a bad one and take you out, like I did last time."

"Be more polite, Grisha," Nika intervened. "Jamilla is our third full partner."

"I thought it'd just be the two of us," Grisha said.

"Jamilla is a mage. It'll be useful to have magic in the party. Remember Ozerg. What if there had been ten of those dragons?"

"Yeah," Jamilla cut in. "If any of us get killed in Rim Six, then losing levels from the penalty will force us to revive in Rim Five."

"You're so smart, Jamilla," Grisha said. "You already figured out that dying is bad! Better than late than never, huh?"

Nika stepped between them.

"Before you kill each other... Jamilla, show him."

The fallen angel unfolded a partner agreement scroll before Grisha. Grisha read it, noting that Nika had already signed it.

"Making decisions without me again, Nika?"

"Sorry, but I don't need your opinion to make

decisions."

Grisha grumbled, but kept reading. He quoted:

"Second paragraph, agreement duration. 'This agreement remains in force until one of its participants reaches level four hundred and ten. After that, they are automatically excluded from the agreement, but it remains in force for the other participants.' Ooh, I like that, I'll level up faster than Jamilla and then I can take her out."

"Unless she gets you first," Nika answered calmly.

Grisha projected a screen on his chest and showed a middle finger emoji. He continued reading:

"Third paragraph. 'All the experience received by the undersigned when defeating an enemy will be distributed on a 50%/25%/25% basis, where 50% goes to the one who dealt the finishing blow to the enemy.' That won't work, change it. Not the one who does the finishing blow, but the one who deals the most damage."

Nika and Jamilla exchanged glances. It needled Grisha that Nika had some kind of secret relationship with her. But he didn't show his concern. Instead he called up a waiting emoji on his screen.

Jamilla nodded and ran her hand over the page, changing the condition.

"If you're so uncertain of your ability to finish, then sure."

"Hilarious." Grisha tried to convey more seriousness in his voice. "Thank you for saving me, Jamilla. If it weren't for you, Nika and I... We would have lost a lot. We're going into Rim Six becau..."

"Great," Nika interrupted him. "Sign and start fighting. That's all I need you for, remember."

Grisha signed and asked:

"We've started our attack before reaching level four hundred. Jamilla and I are only one level away, but what about you?"

"As the weakest link, let's hope I can level up in battle with help from you two."

Jamilla laughed and added:

"Kill as many as you can then, Gregory. For yourself and for Nika."

# Chapter 31
# Like a Horse in a Field

GRISHA PUT HIS STAT POINT into Strength to increase his carrying capacity and store even more CN. He used his skill point to upgrade his component nanomass storage. Each point increased his maximum component nanomass by ten thousand. That meant that he could store 1,540,000 CN.

His health had recovered. Grisha viewed his stats:

*Grisha, Mechanodestructor/LeCube.*
*Classes: Pilot, Defender.*
*Level: 399.*

*Strength: 128.*
*Perception: 78.*
*Agility: 123.*
*Knowledge: 39.*
*Health: 79.*
*Luck: 52.*

*Additional stats:*
*Balance (Pilot): 12.*
*Indestructibility (Defender): 6.*

Then he compared them with Jamilla's:

*Jamilla, Human.*
*Class: Blademaster, Healer, Wise One.*
*Master of Battle Magic at the Himmelbleu Academy.*
*Level: 399.*

*Strength: 102.*
*Perception: 56.*
*Agility: 99.*
*Knowledge: 77.*
*Health: 110.*
*Luck: 52.*

*Additional stats:*
*Cunning (Blademaster): 21.*
*Meditation (Healer): 9.*
*Wisdom (Wise One): 16.*

She had other stats too, like mana, spell levels, armor and so on, which became visible to him as a signatory of the partner agreement. It wasn't that Grisha disliked magic, but he didn't understand it. There were too many stats to keep in mind, to keep track of. Knowledge of spells and the workings of magical items. It was all too close to crafting. Grisha liked being a war machine, not a mathematician, calculating mana increase due to some magic gear or some crystal.

It was enough for him to know that Jamilla was crazy powerful. Almost as powerful as him. They were at the same level, but Jamilla was still in second place on the leaderboard. It was all due to the kill/death ratio. She'd died more often than Grisha, and at his hand. Even on her social network page, Grisha was noted down under her Nemesis section.

He switched his attention to Nika.

*Nika, Android.*
*Classes: Engineer, Scientist.*

*Strength: 1.*
*Perception: 101.*
*Agility: 1.*
*Knowledge: 342.*
*Health: 1.*
*Luck: 52.*

*Additional stats:*
*Genius (Engineer): 55.*
*Core Knowledge (Scientist): 43.*

Next to her bonus stats were Respec-T symbols, showing that the stats had been temporarily improved.

"Have you gone mad?" he shouted, reeling back from Nika. "One Strength? You have just one Health?"

"Yeah, I nearly died just jumping out of the portal."

"And you want to fight with those stats?"

"You and Jamilla will fight. My replicants will fight for me."

Nika pointed to a dozen replicators that her engineers had built.

"But you could die to a tiny piece of shrapnel!"

Nika approached Grisha, placed a hand on the gleaming black body of his 'most human-like robot.'

"I know. So try not to let them kill me. And I'll try to keep as far away from the fight as possible.

Grisha muttered.

"You've made this job a lot harder. Why do you need all that Knowledge?"

"It'll come in handy."

"Keeping me in the dark again..."

Jamilla separated them.

"Hey, enough chit-chat. Your former brother has been preparing for our arrival."

In the distance, a column of soldiers stretched out across the second line of defense at Jamilla's Tomb. This was the first time Grisha had gone up against his former guild. He hasn't yet seen the guild from that perspective... Of course, this version of the Black Wave was weaker than the one he was in. The soldiers had been assembled in a hurry. Many were mercenaries hired for the occasion. There was none of the old harmony in the ranks, nor the horde of mechanodestructors that had given the guild its power. Now Fortunado was even using medium-level mages that had nothing useful except high-level fireballs.

The landscape and weather conditions gave the Black Wave an advantage. Unassailable cliffs rose on two sides, and the insanely strong winds made aircraft useless. Nika's engineers even took apart the helicopters, distributing their resources to build autosens.

Nika marked out two autosens to escort her. Covering themselves with a forcefield, they took her as far away as they could, at the maximum range at which she could still control the replicators and engineers. Nika also took the cargo haulers with her, with supplies of component nanomass and the resources required to maintain constant production at the replicators.

"Look, Grisha," Nika said. "Fortunado has autosens, NPCs and other generated trash at the front of the line. But. It only looks like trash. Don't let his cunning get the better of you. I'm sure that Mariam has provided Fortunado with the very best replicators. They might even be better than mine."

"So?"

"So we have to act in a way that contradicts Fortunado's maneuver. We can't send our cannon fodder in first. You and Jamilla go."

"As you wish. You're our strategist, right?"

Grisha switched to his base form and advanced. Jamilla soon caught up to him. She took off her cloak and spread her wings, ready for battle. The vehicles began to move in behind them: two groups of mechanodestructors at level two hundred and fifty, and the same amount of autosens.

"Did I mess up your feathers bad last time?" Grisha asked.

"Pretty bad," she nodded. "I had to spend all my savings to recoup my losses just a little."

"That's good," Grisha responded happily. "By the way... since we're partners now, take a look a this..."

He took Ozerg's egg out of his inventory and showed it to Jamilla on a hand growing out of one side of LeCube.

"I can't read anything apart from the fact that it gives a fifty percent chance to defeat any opponent. But it has a bunch of properties, maybe you can see them...

Jamilla stopped in surprise.

"Ninety nine."

"Ninety nine what?"

"A ninety nine percent chance to defeat any enemy. And I can see the other properties. They won't mean anything to you, they're purely magical."

"Can you give me an example?"

Jamilla's eyes moved over the stats and she quoted one.

"'Can summon a dragon of the same species as the one who possessed the egg. Number of uses: five. Each time, the value of the egg and the power of the summoned dragon will reduce. The final use makes the item useless. By the way, since the item can't be destroyed, it can somehow be recharged, but I have no idea where to find a mage or source of magic strong enough to recharge it."

"How much is it worth?"

"At least five million. But considering that it's a legendary egg, you could ask for ten, or even more. Although nobody would buy it."

The hand extending from LeCube stretched toward her.

"Take it. I can't use it anyway."

Jamilla grasped the egg, but then immediately removed her hand.

"I don't have that much money."

"But I can't use the egg's full potential."

"Me neither."

"Why?"

"It requires level four hundred."

"Damn, just take the egg. What's wrong with you? Are we partners or not?"

Jamilla pulled the egg into her inventory.

"Thanks."

"Not doing this out of the goodness of my heart."

"I know..." Jamilla slowed and added. "Should we make a partner agreement between the two of us?"

"Why?"

"So that you know I won't kill you."

"Hah, who says you..."

"With this egg, I'll be invincible once a day."

Grisha tossed Jamilla a template agreement. The players agreed not to attack each other until the end of their current taharration rotation. Now Grisha felt like he'd avenged himself. He'd finally done something in secret from Nika.

The Black Wave began to fire on Grisha and Jamilla as soon as they entered the strike zone. It was a good thing that the strangely powerful wind knocked their missiles off course. They rarely hit their targets. But magical strikes that didn't use projectile charges reached LeCube. Jamilla stepped in then: she reflected strikes or blocked them using magical acts of her own. Out of habit, the enemy considered LeCube to be the most dangerous threat. Nobody knew that Ozerg's Egg now made Jamilla the strongest of the two.

Nika controlled her vehicles from a distance, along with the replicators. She was also clearly trying to preserve the vehicles, keeping them behind Grisha and Jamilla.

Grisha decided not to use ranged attacks. With those weather conditions, it would just waste energy. He poured all his resources into his shields and speed instead. His plan was to reach the defensive line as quickly as possible and start tearing his enemy to shreds in close-quarters combat.

"Why didn't you tell me?!" Nika suddenly shouted. "Why didn't you tell me you gave the egg to Jamilla?! Why didn't you talk about the egg? I forgot about it."

"What does it matter?" Grisha replied. "It's my egg, I can do what I want with it."

"Remember, Gregory," Nika said harshly. "Don't dare do anything without letting me know first."

"Fuck you."

"You're an idiot. That was stupid. That egg changes a lot in my plans."

The text of the partner agreement appeared before Grisha. Nika spoke.

"We're changing the agreement. For fifteen minutes, the experience distribution will be like this: seventy percent goes to Jamilla regardless of who does more damage."

"Fuck you!" Grisha said even more confidently. "Why?!"

"So that she reaches level four hundred more quickly and can use the egg, dumbass. You can't imagine what it can do. It's an item from Rim Six."

"Enough insulting me, dickhead."

"It's out of love."

Grisha signed the agreement. Then he switched to a config that Nika had dubbed "Multi-Limbed All-Destroying Robot." Its many arms ended in all types of close-combat weaponry: from titanic sledgehammers to pneumatic drills that spat out acid. Those made cracks in armor, spraying their corrosive substance inside mechanisms or armored bizoids.

In the meantime, Jamilla focused on destroying one of the forcefield generators. Nika gave her three tanks to help, but kept the remainder of her forces back.

The Black Wave engineers surrounded the generator, tried to repair the damage from Jamilla's spells.

The enemy still viewed Grisha as the most dangerous target, so they concentrated their fire on him. At short ranges, the missiles and shells had greater accuracy. LeCube started to feel the heat; its shields couldn't withstand such concentrated firepower, and its Health started to drop.

"Hey, do something. I can't fight alone. Nika, send me some tanks or something."

"No. Hold on. We still don't have enough to break through."

And Grisha held. He wandered along the forcefield, waving his limbs threateningly, buzzing his pneumatic drills, but unable to reach a single opponent. Then Grisha repeated his trick of slipping part of LeCube through the forcefields. He activated the Diffusion config, and a dark cloud of component nanomass pressed its way toward the enemy defenses. It had almost formed into another Bobby, ignoring the attempts of the mages and bizoids to interrupt the process. Neither spells, nor immobilizing slime helped them... but then the skies opened and a choral singing rang out. A column of light fell on the almost formed Bobby. The unfinished robot first quickly rose into the air like a spirit flying to the heavens, then exploded into burning sparks.

*Damage taken: -12,000, Bobby destroyed by Stairway to Heaven.*
*Lost: 30,000 CN.*

"Damn angels," Grisha and Nika said almost at once.

Apparently, aircraft couldn't work in this anomalous wind... but angels could. In general, the physics of the world barely affected them. They were invisible, ethereal creatures that barely got involved in battles.

After dealing with Bobby, the column of light moved toward LeCube. It moved slowly, Grisha could easily escape it, but the enemy continued to throw missiles and magic at him. He had to grow a shield on one of his arms to deflect the attacks. But each strike on the shield lost him a little component nanomass.

"Nika!" Grisha almost howled. "We need to either attack or retreat. They're chasing me like a horse around a field.

Jamilla laughed, and Nika replied unrelentingly.

"Hold on, horsey, I need to create some more vehicles and build more replicators."

Grisha switched to Jamilla. She was waging her own little battle for the generator.

"You were an angel, tell me how to deal with them."

"You can't, they're immortal."

"Thanks for the help."

"Angels can't die, but they can descend and become a fallen angel like me."

"What do they have to do for that?"

"Whenever angels harm other players, they

sacrifice their Reputation and Angelic Aura."

"I don't want to hear the rest," Grisha grumbled.

"Let an angel deal damage to you, then their Angelic Aura will fall."

"I didn't want to hear the rest," Grisha repeated. "Can I knock an angel out without sacrificing my own ass?"

"There are ways, like the Angelic Shepherd skill. Do you have that skill, or a config that emulates it?"

"No," Nika answered for Grisha. "I've never even planned a configuration like that for LeCube."

"You're a mage. Do you have any potions lying around for dealing with angels?" Grisha asked Jamilla. "Something to spray at them..."

"I have spells, but they take a long time to cast, I'm busy with the generator."

"Damn, you're all so busy and I'm the only one taking heat... Alright, come here, you divine piece of shit."

Grisha started running away from the forcefield to avoid the mass missile attacks and removed his shield. He waited for the column of light to move over him. He immediately felt the angelic force trying to lift him from the ground. He took on his base form, but added several long winding growths to the base like roots, and stuck them fast into the soil.

He directed all his resources to regenerating his Health and then froze, waited.

His component nanomass began to melt away, but Grisha kept his Health at an acceptable level, with no fear of dying from a missile or lightning ball that might suddenly hit him.

# Chapter 32
# Joy and Despair

I'D BEEN IN A SEWER in real life. Back in my student days, my class had been taken out on a practical assignment to study how QCPs worked in industry and city management.

I was assigned to study the architecture of the Moscow cluster of quantum platforms, which regulated life in the city. Traffic lights, the underground, power allocation, the construction of new microdistricts and calculating the number of taharration cells required for them in the Municipal Taharration Cluster. But they regulated the sewage system too.

We descended under the ground for a short time to see with our own eyes how the filtration systems worked, how they separated the dissociative electrolyte from the flow of refuse. The thing was, some careless users just flushed it down the toilet to avoid paying the recycling charges. The waste water was usually cleaned and put back into the sewage system. But dissociative electrolyte bound the water molecules together, creating hydrous dissociative electrolyte. It couldn't be used for washing — the water turned blue. It wasn't viscous enough to use in taharration pods. The waste water had to be cleansed three times to get rid of the stinking blue liquid. That meant that the filters had to work at triple speed, using triple the energy, which meant triple the cost.

In short, people who flushed dissociative electrolyte into the sewage system hurt everyone, including themselves.

Through a series of complex calculations, the QCP could determine not only the apartment that flushed the fluid, but also the time it happened down to the second. We students watched a map of the sewer with interest as flows with a mixture of dissociative electrolyte were highlighted. The blue threads led right to the offenders' apartments.

It was funny that people never learned anything. They thought they were cheating the system, then were surprised to get a fine for illegally discarding taharration waste. They paid the fine. Time passed, and they tried to con the system again, got another fine again, cursed the government, paid it... and threw dissociative electrolyte into the sewers again.

But what am I driving at? The fact that I didn't want to admit defeat. I'm a human being, and that means I don't learn from my mistakes.

I tried to take down the liberat mother fives times. I revived at the Projectoria station and repeated my path through the tunnels. Fortunately, the cleared areas rarely filled back up with new creatures. With those I did find, I just used my Glock or Power Surge to take their heads off or blow them up. I kept jumping across drops, arriving in the liberat mother's cave, picking up my items and rushing into battle again.

The mother had only one winged defender left, but he always defeated me. I tried various approaches: machine gun volleys, charges from the revolver grenade launcher. But the winged beast's health recovered through the umbilical cord, and my ammunition ran out. The beast reached me and screamed me to death.

I tried stealth, tried to shoot the cord from afar with my Salinger rifle. One time I got lucky. I didn't hit the umbilical, but I did hit the zebra liberat right in the head. That shot lowered the creature's health to one, but unfortunately the rifle's rate of fire was low; within three seconds, the beast's health was back up. It flew at me and started screaming. This time the acoustic attack came from such an angle that it didn't throw me to the side as usual, but pinned me to the bottom of the lake. The winged zebra liberat kept screaming until I choked in the shallows, with no strength to rise under the pressure of the sound... Fucking obturation asphyxia again.

I tried changing my equipment. Instead of the UniSuit, I switched to the corrupt detective suit from Joshua Culkin. It gave a big bonus to Health. And it almost helped. The acoustic attacks from the winged zebra liberat weakened long before my sixty thousand health ran out.

It took time for the attack to recover. The zebra liberat circled beneath the ceiling, and I shot it constantly with my machine gun. Thanks to my Accuracy, I was more successful than before. Of course, smaller creatures attacked me in the water, but I paid them no attention, occasionally just kicking one away. At some point, when I was down to my last box of ammo, even the umbilical cord couldn't help the winged zebra liberat. It screamed and twisted, its lifeless wings at the wind's mercy.

I was one on one against the liberat mother, again not counting the tiny rats at my feet. I took out my revolver grenade launcher and made sure the whole drum was full, then began to shoot.

The grenades flew from the barrel with a clapping sound, arced through the air to the liberat mother and exploded on her body. The damage was low when I hit her shoulder or legs, but sometimes I hit the growths on her chest, destroying two or three at once. That took a lot of health from her.

The liberat mother shrieked, calling her defenders, but there were too few to really threaten me. Finally, she stopped screaming or trying to cover herself from the grenades. She fell onto all four legs quickly, throwing up a small tidal wive, then crouched back and jumped.

This time I activated Sprint and ran. The skill worked slower in water. The safety of the tunnel entrance was too far away. The beast landed right on top of me, drenching me with filthy water.

Fortunately, this time she missed and failed to completely crush me. I even decided that I couldn't miss the chance. I was right under her gut. Above me boiled numerous growths full of pups. I grabbed the grenade launcher again and started firing without pause. Some of the explosions were so close that they damaged me too. Then the liberat mother just fell down onto her stomach, her legs splayed wide. In the first instant, the growths crushed me, and in the second I was plunged into the blackness of death.

*Damage taken: -35,000, crushing damage from*

*Liberat Mother.*

*Achievement Persevering Failure: +50 XP.*
*You tried to defeat the same enemy five times.*
*Planning to keep going?*

*Unlocked achievement Persevering Failure II.*
*Die 10 times to the same enemy.*

The achievement didn't sober me.

How much time had I spent in those attempts to kill the liberat mother? Almost thirty hours, it turned out. I was fully immersed in the game again, and time had no meaning for me. Thirty hours of life devoted to attempts to defeat a virtual creature. And I felt no regret. After all, back in the real world, my body hadn't even aged a second. It was this increased lifespan that had begun the chief marketing advantage of taharration over virtual capsules, gyrospheres or microwave emitters configured to affect brainwaves. For the sake of an increased lifespan, most were willing to suffer smelly blue liquid, an injection and a long comedown after leaving taharration.

Sky was soon to finish searching for all the data on Nelly, and I'd need to get started on other business. Which meant I could have spent a couple more days trying to defeat the Liberat Mother. The zone was tough, the enemy was higher level than me, I didn't get a penalty for losing to it. On the contrary, I leveled up, improving my skills and shooting the same mobs over and over.

I had no fear of time or sanctions. The simple lack of money was a problem. My weekly pension of five thousand gold had come in from my LCPD medal. I'd spent that too. And I bought the same thing: machine gun and rifle ammo, shells for the revolver grenade launcher, medkits and repair sets to quickly fix my weapons.

Now my wallet had just two hundred and thirty gold in it, not enough even to use the Projectoria station. I'd have to go back on foot, and then on the subway...

I made one last foray into the lake in the cave to pick up my equipment and guns before turning back.

It was a shame that I hadn't gotten the musket after all. Of course, I could spend a thousand hours trying to defeat the zone boss, but spending so much time searching for a single musket would be insane. It was clear that I wouldn't complete that dungeon alone.

But there was no reason to get down either. I'd entered the dungeon at level twenty four, and left it...

*Leonarm, Human.*
*Class: Tracker.*
*Level: 34.*
*UniSuit: LESS (Law Enforcement Special Suit).*
*Health: 10,000.*
*Armor: 1,400.*

*Main stats:*
*Strength: 7.*
*Perception: 6.*
*Agility: 10 (14).*
*Knowledge: 16.*
*Health: 10.*
*Luck. 7.*

*Additional stats:*

*Accuracy (Tracker): 1.*

*Skills:*

*Pistols and Revolvers (Racial) — 2.*
*Rifles and Shotguns (Tracker) — 3.*
*Eagle Eye (Tracker) — 4.*

*Automatic Weapons — 2.*
*Exorcist.*
*High Climber — 1.*
*Explosives — 1.*
*Vivisectionist.*
*Military Toxicology.*
*Battlefield Surgery — 2.*
*Decorator.*
*Motorcycles.*
*Natural Scientist — 1.*
*Knife Combat.*
*Night Vision — 3.*
*Pioneer (Passive) — 1.*
*Swimming — 1.*
*Insight — 2.*
*Jump — 2.*
*Close-Quarters Combat.*
*Handheld and Mounted Machine Guns — 2.*
*Seducer.*
*Radiation Resistance — 2.*
*Urgent Repair.*
*Trading.*
*Kick.*
*Poison Resistance — 2.*
*Energy Weapons — 2.*

*Achievements:*

*Open Book II.*
*All and Nothing.*
*All Thumbs.*
*Arachnophilia I.*
*Headhunter II.*
*Bombardier II.*
*Road Menace II.*
*Reveller.*
*Liberator II.*
*Beat Cop.*
*Urbanist — Liberty City I.*
*Sewer Hog I.*
*Zebraliberator II.*
*Barely Alive.*
*Persevering Failure I.*

I'd gotten the Sewer Hog achievement for killing fecal zombies, and the Barely Alive achievement for taking and healing a certain amount of damage.

That was another reason I'd left the dungeon with a light heart; I'd almost exhausted its potential for leveling up. I'd taken everything I could from it except my main goal, the quest item.

I decided to sell the loot I'd collected in the dungeon to the shyster Johnny Lane. It was better to choose a single trade partner and work with him, increasing my reputation and improving the relationship.

# Chapter 33
# Innocence, Beauty and Love

I HAD TO RIDE on the subway. Only the poor used public transport in Adam Online's cities. It was slightly embarrassing to ride in an expensive UniSuit, surrounded by players dressed in ragged armored vests. Three women in Adidas UniSuits were the most well-dressed among them. From what I remembered, those had no upgrade slots except the in-built ones: a boost to Agility and something similar to the Sprint skill my Doc Martens had.

It was noticeable that the women had spent money to boost their appearance, but hadn't had enough to finish it. One had a neat figure, but a gray pockmarked face. Another had it the other way around. A third had luxurious golden hair woven into a thick braid, but an emaciated and hunched body, no doubt the very same one she had in real life.

An exclamation mark hovered above the head of one of the NPC passengers. Skirting around me anxiously, the girls in the Adidas suits approached the NPC and started talking to him. I was killing time scrolling through social networks.

Hasty hadn't answered my request. Maybe he was

one of those snobs that ignored ordinary people. Or low-level players. It was funny to think that in real life, he might be poorer than me, might be a dirty MTC user, but in Adam Online he was far higher on the ladder.

I'd need to get to Swiftville to ask him in person about his involvement in the raid on the police department. And for what? To take vengeance for the death of Heylia Grant?

Yep, it looked like the lack of sex had bothered me so much that I'd fallen in love with an NPC. And I'd already forgotten what she looked like.

I browsed through player pages on social media. Ran into discussions of a so-called 'epic guild war' that had begun. The Black Wave had somehow become an enemy to all other guilds, who had united and decided to destroy the offender. Personally, I thought the reason for the enmity was the Black Wave's use of a nuclear bomb, which everyone considered a cheat.

Which could well have been the truth: if Rim Five had the components for a nuclear bomb, they would have been crafted long ago. That meant that the components were from Rim Six, which wasn't officially open yet.

The control systems had decided to use the approach that they'd used many years ago when opening Rim Four. The new zones were ready, but the players wouldn't know it until someone randomly opened the lone entrance to the new worlds.

Glocon had presented the access limitation as a kind of novelty, as if to say that not just any player was awesome enough to complete Rim Four. Olga had explained to me that in fact, it had been done simply to avoid overloading the CSes. After all, connecting one creative function cost multiple kilowatts of energy. This meant that the CSes output was ramped up slowly, and the CSes themselves regulated the load. It was far easier to limit the influx of players when you only had one entrance.

The fact that a coalition of guilds had been formed truly was an epic event. I couldn't remember a time when so many disparate groups had overcome their differences. Although, from what I understood, they hadn't overcome them yet. They intended to, but I doubted they'd manage it.

I couldn't help but visit the Black Wave guild page. But I didn't spend long there. For the first time in the last few days, I felt like yawning. There was nothing more boring than guild pages: pure bragging over captured territories, millions earned and endless images of top-class gear.

A mechanodestructor frame by the name of LeCube caught my interest. I'd never seen anything like it before. I would never have even thought that such a complex thing could be crafted independently.

Unfortunately, I had no information about where this LeCube had come from or who had made it. Just bragging posts that Grisha the mechanodestructor had killed however many top-ranking players and was surging his way up the leaderboard.

Not a single word about the Big Pulowski nuclear bomb that they'd used to wipe me out. Although the Black Wavers should have been threatening all the guilds: mess with us and we'll wipe you out too.

I tried to figure out at least a little of that dark

story.

How did players over level three hundred get into Rim Zero? It was technically impossible without the interference of someone from the real world. But I knew better than anyone that there was nobody in the world who could figure out the code of the control systems. They'd long since gone beyond the realm of human understanding.

I scratched my head.

What was going on? To unlock access to Rim Zero, the CSes would have to be reprogrammed. But that was impossible. To do so required the abilities of the CSes themselves. Theoretically, the control systems could have done it, but they would have had to do it... from the real world? As algorithms without physical bodies, how could they do anything in the real world? That same real world, incidentally, about which they had absolutely no understanding. They had no understanding of anything. They just worked with databases, modifying them for in-game situations using their past experience.

I felt like I'd almost reached an epiphany. But it was just out of reach. It was too soon to make any conclusions. First I had to find Nelly Valeeva, if she existed. And then find the Mentors... if they existed.

I returned to the tablet and opened the pages of my tentative friends, the bandits Offo and Ghost, thinking about inviting them to a raid for the liberat mother. Then a message popped up on my lenses:

*Damage taken: -235, knife strike.*
*Damage taken: -350, shot from silenced pistol.*
*Damage taken: -350, shot from silenced pistol.*
*Damage taken: -350, shot from silenced pistol.*
*Damage taken: -150, knuckleduster strike.*
*Damage taken: -150, knuckleduster strike.*

Without looking at my attackers, I used my improved jump, turning in flight to the apparent source of the threat and taking out my Tesla revolvers.

The girls in the Adidas suits had arranged themselves in a semicircle in the train car. One shot me with a pistol, a second was preparing to throw a knife at me, and the third, the one with the luxurious braid, was running toward me waving her fist clad in a gleaming knuckleduster.

"What are you doing, you dumbasses?" I shot the girl with the knuckleduster in the head several times. The scrapper flew back. The energy weapons had set her hair on fire.

The girl rolled around on the floor and screamed.

"My hair, my braid! Girls, help me, a-aa-ah!"

The girl with the beautiful face took a fire extinguisher off the wall and covered her burning friend in foam. She probably got the Firefighter skill.

Frightened NPCs ran from our car and players lazily stood up and left. I jumped behind some empty seats, but still took a bullet in the head from the girl with the fine figure. Since I had no helmet, I lost half my Health from that one shot.

The silenced shots kept coming, and the girl walked toward me, shouting.

"You're the dumbass!"

I took a few shots above the seats, forcing the enemy to duck down behind them.

I looked out and read:

*Innocence, Human.*
*Guild: Three Graces.*
*Class: Gunwoman.*
*Level: 18.*
*Health: 9,000/9,000.*

*Warning: Innocence has a negative Reputation: -12!*
*The authorities will be grateful to you if you arrest her or report her location to the police.*

The one rolling around in foam on the floor was just as aptly named:

*Beauty, Human.*
*Guild: Three Graces.*
*Class: Mixed Martial Artist.*
*Level: 15.*
*Health: 2,105/7,000.*

*Warning: Beauty's Reputation: —8! The authorities will be grateful to you if you arrest her or report her location to the police.*

The one that was still spraying Beauty with foam also had a wonderful name:

*Love, Human.*
*Guild: Three Graces.*
*Class: Blademaster.*

*Level: 20.*
*Health: 11,000/11,000.*

*Warning: Love's Reputation: —13! The authorities will be grateful to you if you arrest her or report her location to the police.*

The Three Graces — Innocence, Beauty and Love. Had to hand it to them. These girls had imagination.

Beauty put out her hair and crawled away behind a seat. Love did the same. I tried to shoot them, but the silent and accurate shots from the gunwoman Innocence kept my head beneath the seats.

In the end, we took up positions at opposite ends of the now empty wagon.

"What do you want from me, fine ladies?" I asked.

"Money. You're in the Whitelist."

Damn, I'd forgotten about that... I could deal with all three if them if I had any weapons other than the Tesla revolvers. Right now, we weren't even on an equal footing. The Three Graces looked a little stronger.

"How much are they offering for me?"

"You got two customers at once, making it three hundred thousand in total."

"Damn... who did I piss off that bad?"

"Some NPC by the name of Weinhardt and some player called Banshee."

"Weinhardt is the mayor of our fine city, you should know that."

"No difference to us," replied the mixed martial

artist Beauty.

"Alright, girls, enough, let's play." I switched my UniSuit to the corrupt detective suit that I wore with a pair of Doc Martens boots.

"Woah," one of the Graces said after my Health grew to fifty five thousand.

"Woah is right. But you asked for it."

Without waiting for an answer, I leapt from cover and sprinted through the whole wagon, barely stopping before imprinting myself in a wall. Now behind the Three Graces, I shot the MMA fighter point-blank. She had the least health.

*Leonarm (Human) killed Beauty (Human) with a Tesla revolver.*

*Your Reputation with the authorities of Liberty City increased: +1.*

The player dropped money, knuckledusters and a huge medkit. I also saw some bottles of pills, probably steroids or doping drugs that temporarily increased your strength and stamina.

I turned to deal with Love, but my head rang, the world disappeared and was covered in a bright white glow. Damn it. She was a blademaster, they had some kind of crazy obsession with chopping off appendages.

*Damage taken: -12,000, yataghan sword strike.*

Judging by the pain in my neck, the blademaster had decided to cut off my head. But she'd overestimated her strength. The blindness came from some secondary blademaster skill. But my vision soon recovered, and I managed to dodge the second strike at my neck.

The gunwoman Innocence didn't waste any time either. Bullets cracked off the walls, sometimes hitting me.

*Damage taken: -350, shot from silenced pistol.*

And another five times. Her pistol damage wasn't bad. And more importantly, it did the same damage wherever the bullet hit. A gunwoman class skill.

All my confidence disappeared. I turned, took a couple of bullets to the back and ran into the next car. The NPCs hurriedly moved out, freeing up space. The players stepped back too. Apart from one deadbeat in a torn armored vest.

"You're really in trouble, bro. I'm gonna help the girls..."

He took out a rusty pipe and rushed toward me. Did he want an easy kill? I stopped him by punching and kicking him.

*Close-Quarters Combat skill increased: +10 XP.*
*Kick skill increased: +10 XP.*

I didn't even bother checking the dead madman's name. Apparently some dumb scrub at level six. I took cover behind the seats again, and the other two Graces rushed to attack me.

All this was happening while the car was still moving, one moment speeding up, the next rocking from side to side in a bend, then slowing, approaching a station. I rose above the seats and opened fire on the Graces. The blademaster Love span her gleaming twin yataghans, reflecting the beams from the Tesla revolvers. Blue flourishes flew around the car, breaking windows.

One even hit a player. He screamed and ran away.

I managed to hit the gunwoman Innocence a few times. Actually, with my Accuracy and improved Pistols and Revolvers, along with Energy Weapons at level two, I should have been able to kill the persistent gunner far quicker, but she had another class advantage: reducing damage from enemy pistols and revolvers.

As for me, damage numbers were streaming off me as if from a broken fire hose. The Graces no longer hid their glee; it was clear on their faces that they felt they'd won. They knew I didn't have ammo.

The car stopped, the doors opened. I fell onto the floor and called up my police drone interface. A map came up. Two drones were standing guard at this station. I summoned them, holstered my revolvers and rose.

"Ladies, you're under arrest for disturbing the peace."

The drones flew into the car, surrounded me and attacked the Graces. The blademaster gave up right away, while the gunwoman Innocence shot a drone for some reason. In response, she was instantly paralyzed and fell to the floor, twitching.

I took out my handcuffs, turned Love over onto her front and clicked the cuffs closed on her wrists.

"Have fun in prison. They say it's a good place to level up Close-Quarters Combat."

"Please, don't," she begged. "I don't want to spend my rotation in prison."

I sat on the paralyzed Innocence and arrested her

too.

"There's nothing I can do, it's the rules of the game. And I don't think you'll be there long."

"Still sucks..."

"Why did you attack me anyway?"

"We're... we're a guild, we wanted to make some money."

"Bit of a shitty guild you girls make, I'll be honest."

"I see that now," Love sighed.

She told me the short version. They were three friends from Krasnoyarsk, and even worked together at the same factory. They'd visited Adam Online all their lives, but tended to level up more casual characters. I didn't ask which exactly. Once, Love came upon a reference to the amounts of money that guilds earned.

"Casual characters can never earn money like that!" she exclaimed. "So we decided to level up some battle toons and make our own guild. We want to make our millions, like the Black Wave."

"But you know nothing of the guild system, you have no mission, you haven't decided on a specific focus for your activities?"

"We figured, how could it be so hard? You get guns, level up, get paid for working." Love clarified, then hesitated. "Don't think we're just some silly girls. You know, Innocence opened her own chain of hotels in one of the magic worlds. First she made money, then she went bankrupt. And I've leveled up my crafting pretty well, I made wicker furniture in Londinium."

"Wicker furniture isn't quite what a guild needs."

The police drones confiscated the players' weapons. Holding the criminals on a forcefield tether, the drones led them out of the subway car. The doors closed and the train moved on.

I went back into the car where I'd killed the first Grace. It was clear. No corpse, no loot. Other players had taken their chance already.

I didn't get anything except credit.

*You arrested two criminals.*
*Your Reputation with the authorities of Liberty City increased: +2.*
*Your Reputation with the LCPD increased: +2.*
*Your current Reputation: 16.*
*Keep being a good boy.*

*Energy Weapons skill increased: +10 XP.*
*Pistols and Revolvers skill increased: +10 XP.*

*Congratulations, Leonarm, you leveled up!*
*Your level: 33.*
*Attention: you have unused stat points (1) and skill points (1). Spend them wisely!*

What a nice train ride. Profitable.
I put a point into my Knowledge and:

*Rifles and Shotguns skill increased to level 3.*
*Every fifth shot from a rifle or shotgun deals three times the damage.*

I sat down and took out my tablet. I searched for the Three Graces guild page, sent a voice message to the mixed martial artist Beauty, who was the guild leader.

*When your girlfriends get out of prison, message me. I have a Kuznetsov portal we can raid. I promise plenty of exp and a heap of loot.*

Beauty didn't answer right away. I'd left the subway and was walking to Johnny Lane's store when I got a text message back.

*OK.*

Short and sweet. Well done, Beauty.

# Chapter 34
# More About Asses

JOHNNY LANE hemmed, hawed, sniffed, chewed his wrinkled lips and adjusted his vest. He asserted several times that he hadn't seen 'such shitty rings with such tiny emeralds on 'em' for a long time. Nonetheless, he bought them at an almost fair price, making me forty six thousand gold richer and improving my Trading skill.

I decided not to sell the pilot's UniSuit I'd found in the helicopter.

"So how about the third musket?" he asked. "When you gonna bring it?"

"I'm working on it," I answered.

Johnny Lane shook his head skeptically.

"If I'd known you were so lazy, I'd have hired someone else."

He turned his back on me, sulking.

*Either fulfill your obligations or honestly admit defeat.*

*Reputation with Johnny Lane decreased: -1.*
Damn that old coot! I tried to explain myself.
"The job was harder than I thought."

"I'd have been better off hiring someone else," Johnny Lane repeated stubbornly.

*Sometimes it's better to be quiet than speak. You've heard that before, haven't you?*

*Reputation with Johnny Lane decreased: -1.*

At first I wanted to win the merchant over, maybe by giving him ingots of Yenav weapon steel... But then I remembered that trying to ingratiate myself with the driver had turned into a catastrophic loss of reputation. So I ran out of the store like a shot. I heard a grating voice behind me.

"Not even saying good-bye? You're not just a liar, you're rude."

*Silence is golden. But would it have killed you to just say a polite 'see you'?*

*Reputation with Johnny Lane decreased: -1.*

*Interesting*, I thought gloomily. *Is the requirement to be polite with some NPCs decided by the control systems, or did the developers build it in when Adam Mickiewicz was still alive?*

Both options begged the question: why? So that we wouldn't lose our human virtues? Or was it another corrupted emulation of 'realism'? As if whatever happened, an adamite had to be polite.

I was right on time. As I left the store, I got a message.

*From: LCPD Archive Manager Al Sky.*

*Hello, Detective. Your search has completed. I will share more detailed information on your return.*

Leaving Johnny Lane's store behind, I used the Projectoria station and moved to Central Park. Before going to see Sky, I stopped in at the Liberty City Police Department armory. A gray cop was stationed there. He was always reading the paper. Every time I visited, I saw sensational headlines:

*"Liberty City mayor suspected of property market manipulations!"*

Suspected? I arrested him myself at the crime scene!

*PCPD Third Detective Department chief killed! Primary suspects: the Yellow Piranhas!"*

That was just cheeky. And later:

*"Mayor no longer under suspicion. Yellow Piranhas confessed to attempt to sully Weinhardt's name!"*

The headlines made it clear: the bandits from the criminal districts were controlled by other bandits, the ones that sat in City Hall, the city's public service. If I'd followed that plotline through, I'd probably find fun quests with big money rewards. If, of course, the honest Mayor Weinhardt didn't kill me first. He managed to worm his way out of his last bind, after all, by putting all the blame on the Yellow Piranhas.

This time the gray cop's paper screamed out the headline:

*"Mayor promises to cleanse the city of all manner of liberats! Rewards offered for catching and killing liberat mothers."*

The gray cop rose from his chair and stood behind the counter separating the armory from the rest of the room.

"Hey, detective, how can I help ya?"

I nodded at the paper.

"What's the reward for a mother?"

"For you, a hundred and twenty thousand. Proportional to your reputation. Bring me her eyes as proof."

*Mother Eyes.*

*Bring the eyes of liberat mothers to the LCPD armory. By the way, why the eyes, huh? Do the cops want to look in the eye of the creature that fills the sewers with other creatures?*

*Additional and optional: find out why the liberat mother eyes are so valuable. Requires Natural Scientist level 3. Or a consultation with a specialist. Or find out some other way.*

*Even more additional: maybe the scientists will be interested in skins from the zebra liberats too?*

Funny. You could learn the value of liberat mother

eyes from any player or by searching through social networks. But only information obtained from a quest character or from leveling up a skill counted.

"Why are the eyes so valuable?" I asked the old cop.

"How should I know? They said take the eyes, I take 'em."

"Where did you send them off to?"

"Nowhere. Scientists come from the LCPD lab and take 'em. I wouldn't mind never seeing another of those eyes. They smell, they're covered in blood, ugh."

Just in case the player was too dumb to take the hint, the system clarified:

*Visit the LCPD laboratory and find out what they use the eyes for.*

"Thanks," I said to the cop. "I actually came for some ammo and a new helmet for my UniSuit."

The gray cop gave me all I need.

"And here," he added. "If you're thinking of hunting mother eyes, you'll need this..."

*Obtained: container for poisonous substances (5).*

"Thanks."

I said good-bye to the cop and walked back into the department corridor. Some cops I met on my way to the elevator nodded to me.

"I heard about how you arrested the mayor. Great job, detective."

Or:

"Careful, our mayor holds grudges. You might get hit by a car one day."

Or:

"Don't worry, plenty of officers have known for a long time that Weinhardt is dirty. If anything happens, we're on your side."

But all the cops were friendly.

When the elevator stopped in the corridor to the subterranean sections of the LCPD complex, a cute female officer blocked the exit. She had short brown hair, green eyes and full lips curved into a suspicious smirk.

"Don't let your guard down, creep."

With those words, she pushed me back into the elevator.

I flew to the wall and hit the mirror with my back and the back of my head, taking light damage.

*Linda Ray, Human.*
*Classes: Defender, Mixed Martial Artist.*
*Level: 63.*
*Occupation: LCPD Officer.*
*Health: 20,000/20,000.*
*Armor: none.*

The interface showed the stats of players and NPCs in a so-called 'intuitive format.' It hid secondary stats and showed the ones most important right now first.

The fact that I was seeing her Health and Armor meant that the NPC was in an adversarial state. A fight might start, and that meant that these lines were most important than Interests, Character or Mood. Otherwise my entire field of vision would have filled up with columns of text and I wouldn't be able to see what was going on. And the fact that my consciousness read the stats right away, instead of as ordinary text, didn't make the situation any easier.

Linda Ray moved quickly, far quicker than I could grab my weapons. She appeared before me and pinned me to the elevator wall. The glass even cracked. I was staring down the barrel of a huge revolver, twice as thick as a machine gun barrel.

"Tell me why I shouldn't just shoot you right now."

*Because you're another cute NPC. First tell me at least a little of whatever storyline is unfolding here,* I thought. I wanted to say something else aloud, like: *Why don't you shove it up your ass, gorgeous? I have revolvers of my own...*

But then my lenses started displaying possible answers that the Communicative skill from the LCPD badge provided.

*1 — Go to hell!*

*2 — I think you're mistaken, I'm not a target that escaped the shooting range.*

*3 — How dare you threaten me? I'm a detective, here's my badge.*

*4 — Sorry, there's a misunderstanding here. Have you mistaken me for someone else?*

*5 — (Seducer) Want to hold a bigger gun than that?*

*(Seduction probability: 2%).*

Nothing prevented me from answering in any way I liked. I could take out my gun and start shooting instead of answering. The control systems would link in a new creative function and figure out how best to advance the line of dialogs. Moreover, judging by the first answer option, I'd be acting according to the storyline even without hints.

But I liked the fifth phrase, even if the chances were minuscule. I said it to her. After she heard about my 'gun', Linda grabbed me by the collar and threw me into another wall.

"Joshua Culkin was right, you're an ass, rookie."

Communicative offered a few options for answers:

*1 — May he rest in peace.*

*2 — Joshua was a crooked cop, and now he's rotting in the cemetery.*

*3 — Leave me alone, crazy lady!*

*4 — Police, help, a cop is attacking me!*

*5 — (Insight) You're mistaken. Joshua himself was a crooked and immoral ass. But you're afraid of admitting that to yourself. You and Joshua were close, right?*

*6 — (Seducer) Joshua knew his asses. Yours is great, by the way.*

*(Seduction probability: 0%).*

I laughed and chose the sixth option. Linda Ray threw me into the last wall she hadn't yet thrown me into.

"I'd kill you, but I don't want to get my hands dirty."

Ignoring the hints, I used my own answer.

"Joshua teach you to throw people like that?"

Linda leaned over me, picked me up by the collar and threw me out of the lift.

"Don't you dare say his name, scumbag. I know

you set him up. You and that crook Mayor Weinhardt. Remember, worm, I'm going to bring you both out into the open.

*Communicative:*

*1 — Why follow me? Follow Weinhardt and you'll find out that Joshua was his main co-conspirator.*
*2 — Get away from me, psycho!*
*3 — (Insight) By denying Joshua's involvement in the real estate manipulations, you're denying the truth. You deny what you yourself believe. Joshua betrayed that belief, and that means he betrayed you, didn't he?*
*4 — (Seducer) Listen, sexy, don't you think we could think of better things to do in this elevator? Let's get to it, I'll show you a couple of comfortable poses.*
*(Seduction probability: 0%).*

The game was pulling me into an intricate storyline. I didn't want to get deeper into the Weinhardt stuff. Not now. It would have taken up too many game hours, taken me to too many new areas in Liberty City. It goes without saying that I'd end up with a ton of side quests...

So I chose option four, hoping to push the quest-giver away. Linda Ray chuckled contemptuously and walked into the elevator.

"We'll meet again, you ass." She pointed two fingers at her own eyes and then at me. "I'm watching you."

She pressed the buttons and the elevator doors closed.

*Powers of Authority.*

*Help Linda Ray move Weinhardt from the mayor's seat to the court's bench.*

*Seducer (optional): prove to her that Joshua Culkin wasn't the best lover in the world.*

I waved away the messages, not delving into the details of the quest conditions. I'd come back to it later. Maybe.

It was a shame the Communicative skill wasn't available with Johnny Lane. The old man's level might have been too high for me.

# Chapter 35
# Dandelion in the Wind

WHEN THE SKIES opened again, Grisha knew that he couldn't just withstand the angel's attack with a forcefield and regeneration. The angel became visible, turning into a bright humanoid figure in white clothes. Waving his giant wings, he descended slowly. He held a sword in one hand and a characteristic scroll of some spell in his other.

A bright light spilled from the angel as if a small sun was descending onto the gloomy land of Jamilla's Tomb. It was accompanied by the choral singing that came with all the angel's actions, announcing his presence.

*Logika, Angel.*
*Guild: Black Wave.*
*Class: Angel of Death, Hand of Vengeance.*
*Level: 353.*

"Worse than I thought," Jamilla said.
"What's that?" Grisha said in alarm.
"The Angel of Death class gets a smaller penalty to reputation and angelic aura for killing." And a Hand of

Vengeance can kill players with a negative reputation without losing any aura or reputation. It's the most combat-oriented setup for the angels, which aren't meant to fight at all."

"Damn. All I needed..."

As the angel descended, the Black Wave for some reason hurriedly backed off. Grisha realized that it wasn't a retreat. They were withdrawing their vehicles.

Jamilla confirmed his fears.

"The angel is going to use a powerful prayer. Probably the Trumpet of Jericho.

"What do I do?" Grisha panicked.

"You can't escape, so like Nika said, hold on."

"What am I to you, a whipping boy? Why am I always the one holding on?!"

Nika interrupted.

"Do you have a better plan, Gregory? Speak up if you do. If it's better than mine, we'll use it."

"You're as bad as Fortunado, always with your plan bullshit. I don't have any plan except taking out the enemy! But that's better than sitting and getting whooped by angels."

In the meantime, the angel had rolled up his scroll, turning it into a huge trumpet. He moved slowly, in no hurry. One of the drawbacks of that race was that the angels did everything slowly and majestically.

Now Grisha understood why Nika was keeping all her vehicles far away from the line of contact with the Black Wave. She'd clearly been expecting something like this.

The angel slowly, slowly lifted the trumpet to his lips. Grisha looked over to see what Jamilla was doing. Had she managed to break the forcefield generator? I couldn't see her.

"Have you assholes abandoned me?" Grisha wailed.

Jamilla replied, but not to him, to Nika.

"Is he always such a whiner?"

Surprisingly, Nika stood up for Grisha.

"No, he's a strong and brave warrior. He's just afraid that we've conspired to let the Black Wavers eat him so we can go into Rim Six on our own."

"And have you?" Grisha muttered.

Nika kept talking as if Grisha wasn't hearing them.

"It's like the idiot doesn't remember that we're bound by a partner agreement. If he dies, the penalty will be split between us too."

"Enough talking about me like I'm not here! Just tell me what this eric... Jericho's Trumpet does. What do I need to prepare for?"

"The spell... or really *prayer*, destroys all solid structures and splits them into their base components," Jamilla answered. "It's particularly effective against buildings and mechanodestructors."

"So LeCube will just collapse into a little pile of components?"

Nika interrupted.

"A 'little pile', is that what you think? I used the entire table of components and processes in Adam Online to create LeCube and its nanomass. LeCube is the height of crafting!"

"Alright," Grisha sighed. "I'll turn into a *big* pile of components, not a little one."

"In the worst-case scenario," Nika cut him off.

"But we'll try not to let it get to the worst case," Jamilla added. "Get ready..."

The angel filled up its cheeks with air and blew into the trumpet. Grisha didn't even know what 'get ready' was supposed to mean. He was already ready: he'd been regenerating his health constantly, even had enough component nanomass to keep regenerating for five minutes more.

The hills and the earth shook. An almost invisible flow of energy emerged from the trumpet, sweeping away stones and other small parts of the landscape. It happened with a roar and a shriek, a choral song and a thousand other sounds merging and flowing together into a deafening acoustic background. If Grisha had had eyes, he would have closed them tight. He sort of could, that reflex of his consciousness allowed him to switch off the image, stop looking at the world, but he didn't do that.

*What will be will be,* he decided, fearlessly staring into the flow.

Suddenly, several tanks emerged from the ground in front of Grisha in the path of the flow. They had drills mounted at the front. It seemed Nika had even equipped them with forcefield generators. Underground tanks didn't usually get those, since the generators demanded a lot of energy. Usually the tanks were left to fight for a few minutes before they went down. But Nika had given these tanks another mission. They organized into a thick screen in the path of the flow and took the first strike.

The flow swept away the tanks, which melted into a pile of precise cubes of iron, plastic, aluminum and a multitude of other components whose names Grisha didn't know.

When the flow reached LeCube, Grisha felt a

similar effect to that of Phantom Explosion or Kinesthetic Telekinesis. With the difference that he didn't doubt whether he'd survive or not.

*Damage taken: -39,500, Trumpet of Jericho acoustic attack.*
*Lost 300,000 CN*

His component nanomass and health had been halved. Then the second wave came from the Trumpet of Jericho and halved the remaining half.

"Damn you," Grisha said.

He switched to the disk shape and tried to fly away without climbing too high, but the third wave almost reached LeCube. Then Grisha took a risk and flew higher. The anomalous wind caught him, flipped him over and threw him like a plate against a cliff.

*Damage taken: -9,000.*

It was still better; the wind had saved him from the next wave.

It could be said that Grisha felt lost, but he was often in situations when his health dropped to dangerous levels. The lost feeling was quickly replaced by one of expectation; how would he get out of it this time?

Apart from that, he felt a small underground tremor through the bottom of the disk. The drilling tanks at work. Nika's presence encouraged him. Even though she was far from the battlefield, she was still controlling the tanks. Grisha rose and tipped the disk to the left and right, shaking off chunks of broken rock.

Logika the angel took the trumpet out of his

mouth. He slowly drew in air for another sounding.

The Black Wave troops were inspired by this possible victory over LeCube. The forcefields weakened and the Black Wavers moved to attack. Ahead of them marched weak, but well armed autosens, behind them — a column of troops in UniSuits. There were bizoids among them with the Shell DNA modification; sixteen-foot tall half-human, half-turtle creatures armed with cutting or crushing weapons. Next came those mercenary mages, all armed with identical fireballs. Rarely a mage rolled ball lightning or an ice orb in his hands. The last in line were the mechanodestructors, using the most convenient frames for the terrain — multi-legged giant spiders.

"Well... What do we do now, girls?" Grisha asked.

"Hold on," Nika repeated.

"Ugh, fine, I have a little left."

"Less than you think."

Jamilla didn't reply. It wasn't clear where she'd gone. And why wasn't she showing up on the minimap? Logika had already raised the trumpet to his lips... then he lowered it. If he blew it now, he'd deal damage to the Black Wave troops.

The Trumpet of Jericho disappeared, replaced with an Angelic Sword. Logika unhurriedly floated toward Grisha. His white clothes fluttered in the wind, his wings trembled, and his bright light penetrated even into the darkest cracks of the nearby cliffs. In this form, the angel was slow. Grisha could have easily fled, but Nika had ordered him to hold on.

Grisha sighed meaningfully, so that Jamilla and Nika could hear him. He'd agreed to be a decoy again, drawing the enemy's forces away.

*It'd be nice if they included me in their plans*, he

thought.

The earth shook more and two dozen underground tanks broke their way through the surface. Half of them dropped their drills and extended cannons, moving out to meet the enemy. A firefight unfolded, but even the trajectory of shells changed directory at random in that strange wind. Barely anyone was scoring any good hits. It was moving toward hand-to-hand combat.

The remainder of the tanks spread out in a semicircle in front of LeCube and, throwing off their fortifications, they transformed into artillery. Grisha was about to point out that they'd be useless; even their heavy shells would fall prey to the chaotic influence of the wind. But powerful blue charges flew from their barrels. The wind had no effect on energy weapons.

"Nice," Grisha agreed. "But plasma cannons need a strong power source. They'll only last minutes on batteries."

"That's all we need," Nika said.

Another dozen tanks and two transports burst out of the ground. One of them approached LeCube. The door opened, Nika climbed out.

"They'll kill you!"

Nika placed a hand on the disk.

"Who else is going to patch you up?"

Grisha got a full tank of component nanomass from the other transport.

Just as the transports and tanks arrived, so did Jamilla. She materialized from the air a short distance behind the approaching enemy army. She must have used a strong dematerialization spell and spent nearly all of her mana. That meant that neither the mages nor the humans with advanced Exorcist skills could detect her. If the Black Wave even had them.

With a few powerful strikes of her sword, Jamilla destroyed one of the forcefield generators. She disappeared again and materialized near the second one. Paying no attention to the fireballs raining down on her, she started hitting the generator. Soon it collapsed and exploded.

"Great," Grisha shouted. "Now they can't escape!"

A section of the Black Wave troops turned around and headed for Jamilla. Many of the enemy autosens were armed with plasma cannons or Tesla machine guns. Fortunado had studied the aerial anomaly in this location, after all. An energy generator stood far away from the line of defense. The soldiers that had spent their energy had to resupply. But now the place belonged to Jamilla.

Spreading her wings, she took wing and fired several feathers into the generator. It immediately exploded, firing off debris covered in plasma. Now the energy weapons of the partners and the Black Wavers would only last as long as their personal energy supplies did.

Even better than that — several of Nika's transports had arrived at the battle. The engineers unloaded parts and started assembling an energy generator. The Black Wave's engineers were doing the same.

Jamilla destroyed another forcefield generator to ensure that the enemy lost that advantage once and for all.

All the partners gained a little exp for the destruction of the enemy structures. They'd also gained a little for destroying enemy vehicles. But the fun part, and the part that earned the most experience, would start with Player vs Player.

Grisha was eager to fight. After recovering his Health, Nika patted the disk.

"Now go show them."

"What about you?" Grisha hesitated. "You're like a dandelion in the wind. We need to protect you."

"You're a real poet sometimes, Gregory. Go and fight. This dandelion will take care of herself."

Grisha switched to his previous Multi-Limbed All-Destroying Robot and launched himself into the battle. His powerful pneumatic drill had finally found a use! Smashing and throwing around enemy tanks and autosens, Grisha worked his way to the Black Wave players. But no matter how hard he looked, he couldn't see Fortunado.

He supposed that was no surprise. The commander controlled the battle from a safe distance.

"Never mind. I'll get to you, brother," Grisha said. "Let's see who has the bigger balls."

# Chapter 36
# Economy of War

THE ANGEL moved slowly. Grisha had time to destroy several enemy autosens and tanks. It wasn't even clear that Logika was planning. He could never catch LeCube. The edges of a second scroll slowly began to take shape in the angel's off-hand. Logika was creating a new prayer!

Grisha warned Jamilla and Nika.

"We see it..."

Nika had generated so many vehicles that her army slowly began to force the Black Wave army back. And her engineers worked faster. The Black Wave's energy generators weren't even half built, but Nika's were almost done. *Good thing I held on*, thought Grisha.

The three partners didn't have to discuss it to know that they couldn't let the enemy finish the generators. Grisha and Jamilla both concentrated on breaking through to the construction site. The Black Wavers had surrounded it with their vehicles. The battle turned into a violent slaughter, a confusion woven of smoke, dust and fire. The anomalous wind didn't carry the clouds far, just chased them from place to place, first covering the field of battle, then revealing it again. Only damage notifications dropping off killed enemies could clearly be read through the mayhem.

Soon the main forces of the Black Wave arrived. An indistinct enemy suddenly towered above Grisha, armed with a long staff.

The staff's strike hit Grisha's pneumatic drill and broke it into pieces. It fell onto the ground and split into components. This was a strike that permanently destroyed component nanomass. The enemy didn't give Grisha time to restore the weapon, he struck the other arm, breaking the second pneumatic drill.

*Damage taken: -25,000, qualia staff strike.*
*Damage taken: -25,000, qualia staff strike.*

His Health didn't take the damage, instead it went on the Armor the program configuration had. Grisha retreated and formed some tried-and-tested rapid-firing Tesla cannons on his arms.

Grisha's enemy turned out to be an old friend.

*Most Ancient Evil, Bizoid.*
*Guild: Black Wave.*
*Classes: Shell, Mixed Martial Artist.*
*Level: 302.*
*Health: 54,000/54,000.*
*Armor: 198,000/198,000.*

The Shell class transformed the bizoid into a creature that looked like a bipedal lizard from a distance, with four identical muscular legs, each with three thick fingers crowned in flat nails.

The Shell was one of few bizoid classes that allowed players to choose human subclasses like blademaster, mixed martial artist or soldier of fortune.

That made him dangerous, but also vulnerable. Hybrids like that had to use lots of energy to support their activities. And Most Ancient Evil's activity levels were currently pretty high.

Grisha opened fire from the cannons, spraying the space ahead of him with energy charges. But the bizoid tirelessly jumped from side to side, somersaulting and rolling to dodge the shots.

His movements were hard to follow even with all Grisha's skills. After performing a fast roll, Most Ancient Evil hit Grisha twice more with the staff, destroying his cannons again, then once more — in his hull, before backing off quickly to avoid counter strikes.

Grisha's Armor was gone. Any more damage he took would go to his Health. The bizoid built up to another successful attack, repeating his series of somersaults and rolls and landing before Grisha again. Grisha was ready. He dodged the staff strike and hit the enemy with both limbs in the chest. The shell cracked and sprayed out shards of bone, but it was still strong. The enemy was forced to back off.

Grisha jumped backwards too, started to recover his health and armor.

Sure, Most Ancient Evil's level was lower, but he wasn't to be underestimated. Bizoids were strong in close combat.

*I need to wear him out*, Grisha decided. He stopped regenerating, started converting component nanomass into energy units and created another rapid-fire Tesla cannon again.

Most Ancient Evil jumped, went into a bridge pose, somersaulted to dodge a hit, but it was all getting slower and slower. One strike hit the shell, throwing off sparks and fragments of bone.

"Tired?" Grisha asked.

"Not too much for you," Most Ancient Evil muttered. Sweat streamed down his green skin, betraying his fatigue and lack of energy.

Grisha spent more component nanomass to create another pair of limbs with Tesla cannons for LeCube, and increased his conversion.

"Then dance!"

The ninja turtle couldn't avoid such a rain of fire. More and more beams hit him, destroying his armor. It fell to thirty thousand. The many cannon shots had already started reducing the opponent's health. Most Ancient Evil stopped jumping, turned tail and fled.

"Where's the fire, buddy?!" Grisha shouted, giving chase.

Grisha shot as he ran and destroyed the remainder of Most Ancient Evil's shell, then took a long leap. He transformed his limbs into two axes in flight and crashed down on the fugitive. Two strikes with the giant axes lowered his enemy's health to thirteen thousand. A final hit sent Most Ancient Evil back to the respawn tower.

Grisha received a standard notification telling him of his enemy's defeat, but the experience boost was barely noticeable — most went straight to Jamilla.

"Well done, Gregory," Nika praised him. "Keep it up."

Jamilla stayed silent, busy with fighting the enemy players and vehicles. She spread her wings and rained sharp feathers down on her enemies, all the while waving that sword that seemed to be enchanted with everything it could be.

*Where are you, bro?* Grisha thought, casting his gaze around the battlefield. He wanted to dodge around the enemy and get further into the base. If he took out Fortunado, he'd get so much experience that it'd be enough for Jamilla and himself.

Nika was tougher. Her level progress was slow, although she'd sent dozens of vehicles out and taken part in building the new generators herself, risking death from random shrapnel.

All the same, Grisha saw that they were forcing the enemy back! And the Black Wave had started with both a numerical and positional advantage.

Their energy generators were being destroyed as soon as they started trying to build them. Soon the autosens would run out of energy both for their shields and their repetitive firing. At the same time, Nika's generators were happily spitting out new vehicles.

Sometimes Nika broke off from building new generators and started controlling the units, grouping them up, giving them minor upgrades, generally strengthening their attacking capabilities depending on the enemy's defenses.

Some of the troops went into battle in directions Nika indicated, while others went to the flank and patrolled. Some autosens went nowhere, staying with Nika, transforming into precision defense modules. Nika expected surprises from Fortunado, so she wasn't taking risks with her exposed position. She risked herself less and less.

Grisha couldn't stay quiet.

"Well done, Nika! You're amazing."

"So are you, Gregory."

"It used to annoy me when you called me that."

"And now?"

"Still annoys me, but I'm used to it."

The only thing bothering him now was the damned angel that was constantly healing his guildmates. Jamilla and Grisha didn't have that kind of support. They had to constantly think about preserving their health. Nika sent a transport to Grisha with a supply of component nanomass, but the angel used his Stairway to Heaven skill and redirected the transport to another area.

This loss of valuable resources had an upside: by using Stairway to Heaven, the angel had slowed the creation of his second Trumpet of Jericho.

Finally, Nika released her first harvester onto the field.

The harvesters were meant to completely turn the tide of the battle. The opposing sides had no access to resources. Nika's patrol units had captured all the transports sent by Fortunado, so he just stopped sending them. As for Nika, she had no resource mines in the area. That required time and free resources for building scouts and constructors. Trying to build mines during a battle would be pointless. The construction units were too weak and slow. Especially considering that you had to find mineral veins first.

The harvesters used another source of resources; they absorbed broken and weakened enemy vehicles, mechanodestructors or androids, processing them and producing components ready for use. The second and third harvesters were also ready and waiting for their escort units. Without their protection, the slow harvesters would be easily destroyed.

During the battle, the Black Wave retreated farther and farther, approaching the second line of defense at the Jamilla's Tomb base. Nika's patrol units had already discovered the base's first resource mines and begun to destroy them. The forcefield generators were subject to the same attack.

The harvesters started processing the enemy vehicle debris. The transporters trundled between the harvesters and the generators, unloading new components. It all worked cleanly, with no mishaps.

The generators worked at an increased speed. Nika had further reduced the durability of her new vehicles, preferring to create new ones more quickly. At that moment, quantity was more important than quality. The vehicles that survived in battle gained experience and automatically improved themselves, getting the components they needed for the upgrade straight from the harvesters.

*Look, brother, Nika has a better war economy than you,* Grisha thought vengefully. *Where's all your military genius now?*

The angel removed his healing ray from the area of the battle where Jamilla was and started healing those fighting against LeCube.

Grisha tore his way out of the heart of the battle and headed toward a generator. He'd decided to destroy at least one and reduce the forcefield's power. LeCube could slip through weak forcefields using one of its ethereal configurations.

Recognizing his maneuver, several players rushed to intercept him: mechanodestructors, mages and people in UniSuits. Without stopping, Grisha passed the group of mages, who were devoting all their strength to casting a strong dematerialization spell. It would work well against the robot that Grisha currently was. Grisha recognized their attempt too late, didn't have time to switch into a program configuration that would be immune to the spell. He panicked. He'd really put his foot in it!

The spell was already expanding, quickly extending toward LeCube, but at that moment, one of Jamilla's feathers pierced the center of the group of mages. As it landed, an explosion swept away the enemies, killing a couple of them. The rest used a fast teleport spell to get far away from Grisha. But even there, Nika's patrol units immediately started firing on them. Since the mages had spent almost all their mana on the teleport, they had to fight the autosens with axes, swords and arrows, retreating to the base's defensive line.

Logika the angel was forced to switch her blessing ray between two groups of Black Wavers. All that slowed the casting of the second Trumpet of Jericho prayer.

Grisha started cutting down enemy vehicles and defensive modules with redoubled enthusiasm. Then he entered into battle with several of his former guildmates at once, one of which was an old friend — the fallen angel Crusher.

Crusher tried to surround LeCube with a palisade of feathers that slowed movement, but Grisha was careful; he transformed into an ethereal being just in time, and rose right in front of the fallen angel's face. First he cut off his wings.

*Achievement Wing Clipper completed: +100 XP.*
*Cast fallen angels even further down by cutting off their wings.*
*Completed: 6/5.*

*Achievement unlocked: Wing Clipper II.*
*Cut off more wings.*
*Completed: 6/10.*

After that, Grisha brought his two axes together in Crusher's neck, sending him back to the respawn tower. Crusher was a lower-level player, but his death and the wing achievements were enough for some growth. Jamilla shouted into the ether.

"Yes, yes, Grisha! You did it! This is it! I'm ready."

Next I got a message that one of the conditions of the partner agreement had been completed; Jamilla had reached the agreed level. Experience distribution returned to the previous setup, with Nika as the priority.

# Chapter 37
## But...

CENTRAL PARK was immersed in the shadows of skyscrapers, but the tips of the trees were already starting to blush. The city simulated an early morning hour, so the streets were empty. Only police drones buzzed around the district.

I had a bunch of messages by the time I got there, but I couldn't wait to find out whether I'd managed to find Nelly with such a clever method that nobody at the MSB had figured out yet.

As I climbed up the broad stairs to the department building, I was deep in thought.

Ever since I logged into the game, I hadn't had time to get into any details. Events had happened so fast it was as if the control systems themselves were managing them, plugging in the maximum number of creative functions.

Maybe that was just what was happening?

A bot equipped with a downsized copy of Makarov's consciousness had barely had time to explain to me the essence of my mission before the Black Wave attacked us. The briefing was rushed and pointless.

A reasonable question occurred to me. Why

couldn't he have told me it all in real life, in a cozy office?

But I'd already asked that question to the Major General.

"Because, Anton, the information is too important," Makarov had answered then. "We aren't sure that it won't find its way into enemy hands. It will be better to introduce you to the mission details online."

Alright. I'd accepted that. The Major General knew better than me how to plan operations.

But even with all my loyalty, I couldn't explain why I hadn't been given any copies of mission materials. That scene of the conversation between Valeeva and the unknown girl would have been very useful in my search. More secrecy? Yet at the same time, somehow some players were able to get into Rim Zero and attack us. Some secrecy...

Sure, the fact that I hadn't gotten copies could be explained by the chaos caused during the attack. Makarov's bot was destroyed as a result, and the items that dropped from him were deleted by the controllers. Then the whole zone was wiped clean by a nuclear strike, a weapon that had never been used before in any Rim.

All of Adam Online was talking about the nuclear strike. So not so secret after all, in the end.

That happens.

But...

I walked through a corridor, then descended into the basement.

I froze before the door to the archive where Sky awaited me.

For the first time, I think, I had a vague sense of some kind of setup. The haste of the briefing felt like an attempt to distract me, and thereby distract the whole MSB. Without giving me time to think, I'd been pressured into accepting the situation, and I hadn't asked the questions: why is it like this, and not different?

If you want to draw attention from the right flank, start a fire in the left. Or toss a group of high-ranking players into Rim Zero.

That was just how action-packed quests in Adam Online were planned. That synopsis author I was acquainted with had told me that.

When you had to give a player a strange twist in the storyline, you had to limit the time the player had. Start a timer, start taking valuable resources away from them, organize a 'sudden' attack... Fearing to lose the initiative, the player would act like a frightened deer and run along the route already set for him.

Incidentally, time wasn't the only way to limit a player. There were other maneuvers. You could hang a sword of Damocles above the player, reduce all their choices to two options: either do what you're told, or fall and die.

That's what had happened to me.

After the inevitable fiasco with the Black Wave, I'd had only two choices. Quit the game or continue. Damn it! I chose...

I chose wrong!

I didn't leave and start the game over. Yes, it would have been stupid. But stupidity is unpredictable. Stupidity doesn't run along previously set routes, it forces its way through the bushes and takes the bumps and the bruises.

Suddenly it started to seem as if the loss of Leonarm's levels was inevitable. I'd been blaming myself for something that hadn't depended on me at all... Maybe that was why I was killed in Rim Zero, so I wouldn't be able to just hang around? But I couldn't think of who that might benefit.

It didn't seem logical that the MSB itself would bring down its own operation. Too many people were involved in it. Millions of rubles from the organization's budget had gone on buying the services of professional adamites. They couldn't all have been in a conspiracy against themselves, could they?

Makarov's bot was also above suspicion. He was working according to a program upon which dozens of experts from several MSB departments had agreed. Secret instructions couldn't have been hidden within it.

Even if I supposed that it was possible, the bot could have just killed me in the tent and deleted Leonarm. Why give me a leveled up character? That was like a killer giving their victim a pistol.

I had suspicions, but no explanations.

And if you can't find an explanation, that means there are no real problems. Just your own groundless suspicions.

As I was about to press the button to open the door to the archive, a message appeared. I jumped a little in fear, and my heart started beating faster. More precisely, my memory of a faster heartbeat started beating.

Just as I was thinking of distracting maneuvers...

here one was:

*Stükke the Great quest completed: +500 XP.*
*The Vildana — Leonarm contract has ended.*

*Message from Vildana:*
*Lazy, good-for-nothing ass! I died a hundred times fighting dragons. Mages tried to rape me with stony... I fell into crevasses, drowned in rivers and burned to death in volcanoes. The giants of the Craggy Mountains crushed me under their heels, and avalanches swept me off mountains I'd spent days climbing up! I have been pierced by arrows and spears. Then those damn mages again with the stony...*
*Enjoy your money, slacker. Hope I never see you again.*

*Obtained:*

*Bar of qualia: 17.*
*Maiden's Tear ruby: 1.*
*Room key at Giant's Sister hotel in the town of Scarewar, in the Himmelbleu Empire in the world of Goldivar.*
*Obtained award: For Loyal Service to the Himmelbleu Empire.*

*1,000,000g.*

*Attention, you are overloaded!*
*Stop stuffing your pockets with everything you find. They're not bottomless, unlike your greed.*
*Carrying capacity: -12.*

As always, Vildana had appeared at just the right moment. At the moment when I wanted least of all to deal with game business.

Another message came in:

*Achievement Millionaire completed: +10 XP.*
*You got your first million.*

*Achievement unlocked: Millionaire II.*
*Money begets money, right? So turn the million in your account into two million.*
*Completed: 1,215,032 / 2,000,000.*

Next I got notifications about achievements and leveling up to thirty nine, about available points that I should spend wisely...

Enough, that was it!

I threw away all the qualia bars. I even angrily kicked them across the corridor. Qualia was a valuable material. Each bar was worth at least ten thousand, if not more. The next player to wander the LCPD basement would have a lucky day.

As if mocking me, I got another notification.

*Kick skill increased: +10 XP.*

I grabbed my tablet, opened my interface settings and switched to Do Not Disturb mode. All the notifications and icons disappeared. There was just a green dot barely visible in the corner of my vision.

That was a long time coming. Now I wouldn't have notifications constantly trying to grab my attention. I opened the door to the archive and went in.

Sky's hologram appeared without any lag. She

even looked nicer somehow. Maybe she had a new haircut.

"Hello, Detective."

"Hey, artificial intelligence. Show me what you found."

The hologram froze. Sky was downloading data. Then, in a glitching voice, she asked for permission to remove her hologram.

The holographic icons of the search result popped up around me and multiplied. Within a second, there were so many of them that I was surrounded by a confused mass of garbled symbols.

"Query r-r-r-resulted in three milllllll... resss... c-c-clusters of infor...mation."

"Hey, don't dump it all on me! Switch on filtration."

The millions of information clusters disappeared.

"By which criteria?"

A good question. As if I knew which!

I thought for a moment.

The scrap of conversation between Nelly Valeeva and the unknown entity that Makarov showed me in the tent was not a two-dimensional stream, like messages from players about their shenanigans. It was a snapshot of Adam Online. Like a cast of the virtual reality, one that preserved a specific state of the world in set coordinates.

The snapshots allowed a moment of existence in the world to be reproduced in all its detail. And the depth of that detail depended exclusively on the observer's requirements. Theoretically, every snapshot of Adam Online could provide information about the state of the entire world of Adam Online.

For example, if somebody, or I myself, had possessed the required debugging tools, they could have saved a snapshot right here and now. Of me sitting in the archive and thinking about how I was sitting in the archive and thinking...

A stopped moment or fragment could be assembled with any degree of detail. But the detail wasn't the main feature of the snapshot. That was the opportunity to infinitely produce data.

In debugging a snapshot, the observer could not only view the state of the archive, Sky's haircut or the folds in my jacket, they could also 'look through the window,' meaning fully move from the current coordinates to others. Leave the bounds of the archive, walk through the department building, then go to the park, then stroll through the city, leave it entirely, go up into space or even move to another Rim. Everywhere, they would have found the same degree of faithful detail.

It's a paradox, but having created a snapshot of one moment of virtual reality, the observer could view the entire world of Adam Online.

Theoretically.

In practice, a snapshot of a single moment of reality across all of Adam Online would have equaled all the data that existed in Adam Online at that moment in time. Which made the creation of such a snapshot unrealistic, because it would require double the computing power needed to store the currently existing information. The planet would simply not have enough resources to create such a snapshot.

The support infrastructure of Adam Online was

already the most resource-intensive of man's industries. Sixty seven percent of all global energy use. Almost fifty percent of chemical and electrical manufacturing. Metallurgy, electronics, nanoassembly factories, medicine, water and bio resources, all this worked to support an improved illusion of reality. Even as beggars, modern people produced and spent as many resources in a single day as all humanity spent in one year at the start of the twenty first century.

Anyway, creating a snapshot like that was a purely theoretical exercise. When you were within the game, you had no tool to create it. You could only track game traffic when you were in the real world by taking data from the control systems. It was impossible to do in the traffic itself. But in reality, you couldn't read anything in the data. To do that, you had to transfer your consciousness to the virtual world inside that snapshot.

So experts from the special agencies captured streams of traffic at random, packed them into snapshot containers, and later, undergoing taharration to transfer their consciousness inside the snapshot for research. It was a very long process with an unknown result.

The process was called 'fishing', because nobody knew what would turn up in the hazy traffic of an illusion shared across all humanity. You could catch a piece of a secret UN meeting, or the antics of some random player in the brothels of Liberty City's Redlight Splash district.

Judging by the fact that the snapshot of Nelly and the unknown entity was so corrupted, it could be that most of the intercepted traffic involved something else, and the fragment with Nelly was found at random.

But...

I wanted to shout that 'but' at the top of my lungs...

How could a modern game session acquire data from a time when taharration didn't exist yet? Nelly Valeeva was the first person to test out this technology. What was in the snapshot was probably a fragment of that very test.

It was like looking at an old photograph of a person who wouldn't be born for another hundred years.

"Detective?" Sky interrupted my dead-end thoughts. "I m-m-must make you-you-you aware th... th... that maintaining the d-d-data arrayyy requires an increased equipment load, which will lead to-to-to overheated systems. You must hurry."

"Sorry. Alright, the search criteria..."

# Chapter 38
# How to Throw Smoke
# Bombs on Mirage 2047

I GOT READY for a long question-and-answer session. I had to sift through mountains of information to narrow down the criteria. Even the control systems managing Sky felt the weight of such large volumes of data.

They struggled for the first thirty minutes. All queries related to Valeeva led to user-made content. Most of it was pornographic or crazy fantasies of gore, cannibalism or eating feces. It was crazy what some players came up with!

Then I ran into a curious fact.

On the guild page for Dead Face, I saw a video presentation called:

*"Reality doesn't exist, or why our world is a spoo(n/f)"*

I had no idea how this could relate to Valeeva.

It turned out the guild wasn't just a guild, it was a religious sect.

That wasn't news for Adam Online. Many religious

groups had moved their activities into the game, where they could reach a wider audience. Since there were no other forms of inter-player collaboration, all religious organizations were forced to become guilds. And so appeared the guilds of the Jehovah's Witnesses, Krishnaites, Catholics and Muslims.

But the faith of Dead Face wasn't based on any known religion. They had their own mythology.

These sectarians declared that the world beyond Adam Online was also a simulation. The reality to which we departed at the end of the game was another game created by certain powers with an unknown aim. Of course, the signs of it being a game had been kept out of humanity's attention.

Only a chosen few could master the game's interface.

The goal of each human, the Dead Faces said, was to try to become a chosen one. This meant first accepting a certain fact: that our consciousnesses were wandering between two identically harmful simulations. Humanity must find a real exit from its double-ended dead end.

*Alright,* I thought. *All this is ordinary nonsense augmented with theories from the subculture of the past. Every sect thinks itself chosen. But what does Valeeva have to do with this one?*

I had to look deeper.

The next thing the sect says was that both simulations were created with the support of an intelligent, but non-humanoid life form...

"I knew it," I laughed. "Aliens, of course! How could we do without them?"

But I was wrong. The sect's imagination went further than that old chestnut.

An unknown form of life existed on Earth long before humanity came to be. The Dead Faces called this life form the 'gray slime,' since it lived exclusively on the ocean floor. And it looked, hmm, kind of like gray slime.

After humanity came into being, the two civilizations existed in parallel. They didn't know about us, and we didn't know about them. The gray slime had lived for a billion years, and people had been around for less than a hundred thousand. We simply had no points of contact. Since the gray slime existed exclusively in the form of information housed by the molecular structure of the slime itself.

We couldn't understand the meaning and aims of their civilization. Just like they couldn't understand us.

But in the second half of the twentieth century, when human information technology became to develop at a rapid pace, the gray slime felt our presence. In a way, they discovered humanity. As if humans had suddenly realized that trees were intelligent life forms...

Listening to this insane theory, it occurred to me at once that it would make a decent plot for some mission. Alright, next... I needed to find out what connection Sky had found between this nonsense and Nelly Valeeva.

The gray slime tried to contact us. Naturally, without any success. But since the gray slime could perceive only the informational presence of humanity, it was via information that they tried to make contact.

That's right. They wanted to talk to us on the internet, in games, on television channels. But the effort led to nothing but interference and white noise. The humans remained certain that they were the only intelligent form of life on the planet.

But taharration changed all that.

The human consciousness transferred into the virtual world was a form of life that approached that of the gray slime. It was Nelly Valeeva, who had first transferred her consciousness into the field of interaction with the gray slime, who had become a catalyst for a relationship between the two civilizations. However, the relations remained one-directional. As before, we knew nothing of the creatures, but the gray slime was already feeling out a method of communication.

*Yep, there's the mention of Nelly. I don't need to read the rest...*

But I gave the nonsense another few minutes. And didn't regret it.

The presentation said that after taharration spread throughout the world, and Adam Online evolved, the gray slime tried to achieve large-scale contact... and killed all humans on the planet.

I even cracked up. The person that created this pseudo-theory could have made a good career for themselves as a quest writer. If they'd sent their imagination down that road, they'd be getting five hundred bucks in royalties per month. They'd be living in the Golden Billion.

But the presentation went on to explain that the slime didn't intend to kill humanity. It had no idea that we even had fragile physical bodies. For them, we were weak flashes of alien data. In trying to 'talk,' the gray slime filled the planet, destroying the humans' bodies and absorbing their information into their own structures... That information was our consciousness.

The gray slime had completed a total taharration, resettling our consciousnesses within themselves.

According to the Dead Faces, the real Earth was a desert. All those of us that lived in Adam Online and left for 'reality' had been dead a long time. The gray slime held our souls in this prison, continuing to study us. Our enemies didn't even know that they'd destroyed our physical bodies...

Next the presentation's author spoke of the rites that must be executed to escape this double prison and tell the gray slime of the evil it has wrought.

The rituals were dumb, like all fanatic rituals. But in the description of one of them, I ran into an idea that I'd encountered before.

The Dead Faces insisted that the gray slime existed in the virtual world of Adam Online. Here was the place to contact it. These creatures could only be contacted through NPCs. After all, the gray slime had melded into them.

NPCs were the only almost intelligent creatures of Adam Online that weren't human binary arrays.

That idea led me to what Amy McDonald had spoken of when she told me about the neohikki movement, those unfortunate psychopaths that nurtured 'companions' for themselves.

Of course, that bore no relationship to Valeeva. But it related to me in a distant way. I liked Amy.

I opened the list of Dead Face guild members. There were around two hundred thousand of them. That was an insane number. But the guild's leaderboard position was low. They weren't developing, weren't fighting in guild wars. Although with that many members, they could have taken out whoever they wanted in Adam Online. Even the current war with all the guilds against Black Wave seemed a petty thing by comparison.

There were four Amy McDonalds in the guild list. One of them was my acquaintance. She'd joined the guild recently. But so what? What did I gain from knowing that?

I ordered Sky to delete this and similar data clusters from the search material.

"Please clarify the 'similar' parameter," she asked.

"Anything related to sects and religion."

"Done."

"And cut out the porn! And those shit eaters."

"Done."

Oh, wow... How many of Adam Online's inhabitants possessed a 'magical consciousness'? Conspiracy stories like these weren't nonsense at all to them. They didn't know anything about how QCPs worked, about the control systems, about the huge real infrastructure that maintained this virtual world.

I wasn't an expert in Adam Online either. You couldn't become an expert in such a huge phenomenon. You could only have a professional knowledge of a piece of it.

But even I knew the huge amount of work that had been done by prior generations. Adam Online didn't appear by the will of some gray slime. It went through all the development stages, from simple game sessions in a virtual capsule to an all-encompassing virtual taharrated world that could no longer be called a simple 'game.'

It took a special kind of idiot to believe that someone had 'melded into' NPCs, that they'd achieved consciousness and all that crap.

Judging by the Dead Face guild member list, the real world was the same as it always had been; mostly comprised of morons. Truly, a dead desert.

I sighed and looked around in despair. I imagined how much more crap I'd have to look at, sift through and throw away before I found anything useful. If I ever did.

But I turned out to be wrong again.

I thought back to the shirt on the girl talking to Nelly. It bore the lettering Darknet, plus some kind of emblem that I couldn't remember. I formed a query with that data.

Of course, it wasn't a solid lead. Plenty of scrubs had created guilds called Darknet. And hundreds of new scrubs came to Adam every year, adding to the list. That turned into millions of mentions of the word, many of which somehow even correlated to Nelly Valeeva.

The data was arranged by type: streams, text messages, replays, three-dimensional reconstructions and much more. I started with streams. There were over three hundred thousand... Why would players be mentioning historical figures in their streams?

Incidentally, streams differed from snapshots or three-dimensional reconstructions in the fact that you, the viewer, were as if inside the player's head as they streamed their experience to their social network page. You didn't just see what they saw, but also saw their interface. This meant that streams were popular among those studying the abilities of a certain class or weapon.

I myself once had a stream for crafting energy weapons. It goes without saying that you could offer paid subscription to your streams and earn while you taught scrubs. I was a cool crafter and I earned a decent amount. Those subscription payments were enough to pay for dissociative electrolyte of the highest quality.

"Sky... how can we sort through three hundred thousand entry points?"

"By coordinates, by time, by number of participants, by era, by Adam Online version number, by..."

"Alright, stop, I get the picture."

I drooped again. No matter how much you sort a pile of shit, whether by color, by smell or by hardness, it'd still be a pile of shit.

I wasn't an expert in deep searches or data analysis. I was a programmer for low-level QCP components. They say that in the old days, almost everyone knew how to use searches. But of course, back then, the search systems were primitive and weren't operating on such huge databases.

"Sky, can you apply excluding filters?"

"Of course, detective."

Her tone of voice let me know that she wanted to add "Why the dumb question, detective?" Apparently, the control systems had analyzed my interactions with this creature and given her a creative function.

"Exclude everything that doesn't include words, images or any other features that could be identified as an 'anomaly, something unclear, a glitch, an error.'

"Done. Two thousand and twenty entry points remaining."

"Exclude the ones that don't mention Darknet."

"Done. Two entry points remaining."

"How many?"

I stood up from the chair, wondering if I'd misheard her. Although that was impossible in Adam Online. Especially for those with the improved hearing of a Tracker.

"Two streams, detective. Both created in the same zone. The first was forty years ago, the second — six months ago."

Sky projected two holograms in front of me.

After the first rewind, I knew this was it. I couldn't even believe I'd done what nobody else had thought to do in the MSB. Dozens of analytical departments, hundreds of experts across all industries concerned with virtual worlds and control systems. None of them had even thought of what I did?

Gratifying. But I couldn't believe it.

My suspicions took root.

Why had the everyone in the MSB decided that Nelly Valeeva should be sought out in the most distant Rims? Not only decided, but also convinced me and Makarov of it?

Sky broke the silence again.

"Detective? I repeat, soon I will have to clear all the search request links.

"Yeah, yeah, sorry."

I waved my hand over the hologram, starting the first stream to watch it in detail.

The streamer and the other players were in a battleground in the Rim One Arena.

Five players against five, all Soldiers of Fortune. Split into groups of 'terrorists' and 'counter-terrorists,' they played a reconstruction of a game even stranger than DotA 5. I didn't remember its name.

The rules of the mini-game were simple: the

terrorists placed bombs, the counter-terrorists tried to stop them. An alternative strategy was to completely eliminate the enemy team. There were no respawns. Losing one soldier significantly lowered the team's chances of winning.

In this mini-game, accuracy with firearms was key, and the choice of guns was limited. Also, the game maps themselves weren't randomly generated, but specially designed to keep the gameplay balanced. If the counter-terrorists had a terrain advantage in one part of the map, then the terrorists had one in another. In short, although it was a 'mini'-game, it still provided rich combinations of gameplay.

My streamer stood on the sunlit street of an ancient city and held some gray cylinder in his hand. He spoke in a hard to understand mumble.

"Hi all, today I'm going to tell you how to throw smoke bombs on the Mirage Two Thousand and Forty Seven" map...

The streamer turned into a narrow passageway between houses and continued.

"Throw the first smoke bomb at the start. To do that, you need to stand on this ledge..." He jumped onto a step. "Then you need to aim at the gap between the two sticks..."

He threw a smoke grenade and jumped off the stone. He swapped his knife for a grenade. The streamer ran into some archway and ended up on a square full of big boxes.

A cloud formed on a ledge with steps and the letter 'A' drawn in red paint.

"Look, now the smoke will stop anyone who tries to take up a position on the stairs where it's easy to fire on the corridor we just came out of."

The streamer took out a second grenade and returned to the dark corridor... And stopped.

"What's that? Do you see that? Some kind of glitch. What happened?

I paused the stream and looked closer. There it was! The conversation between Nelly and the girl in the Darknet t-shirt played out in the darkness.

# Chapter 39
# Waiting Time

THE RIM ONE ARENA was between Liberty City and Swiftville. It went without saying that I had no access to that zone's Projectoria, so I had to get there myself. Thankfully, I had a huge choice of transportation: from skateboards to electric scooters, from helicopters to airships.

I decided to catch a passenger airship. I wanted to fly in peace and comfort.

I ignored the exclamation marks above the NPCs' heads, hid myself in a corner and nestled up to a view port. The suburbs of Liberty City floated by beneath me. I even saw a piece of the abandoned district where I'd met Vildana.

I tried not to think about two things as I traveled. About the fact Irene was waiting for me at my apartment, and about why the snapshot with Nelly ended up in some random game so many years ago? The very same conversation somehow turned up in a second stream, in which people were playing DotA 5.

Maybe... these bugs happened a lot more than we thought? Just not all of them made their way into streams or into the MSB 'fishing' missions. On the other hand, how likely was it that I'd run into this bug?

If it was a glitch at all.

The charter of the Global Consortium of Standardization for Adam Online stated that the game universe was practically free of bugs. Which was untrue, of course. Nothing was perfect, even a perfect virtual world. It was just bugs were fixed so quickly in the system that users rarely encountered them. If there were no problems in the game, then why did tech support bots exist?

...Damn, I'd just decided not to think about it and then found myself thinking about nothing else. I remembered Irene again. Sure, she could wait, of course... Anyway, she wasn't sitting in my apartment, and she wasn't waiting. She didn't exist at all. And wouldn't exist until I entered the apartment.

I stood up from my chair, crossed the spacious passenger deck and sat at the bar. The airships interior and exterior had been done in a steampunk style, so a steam-powered retro-futuristic robot stood at the bar. It had a cast-iron barrel-shaped body, a bronze head with thick lenses instead of eyes, and leather gloves over wooden hands.

The barman emitted a puff of steam, his gears squeaking.

"Good day to you, sir. What would you like?"

I looked over at the shelves full of hundreds of varieties of alcoholic beverages. When you need to distract yourself from a woman, even if she is just a set of algorithms controlled by software, you won't find a better medicine than alcohol. The important thing was not to overdo it, or you'd achieve the opposite and go looking for a woman. Any woman, not just the one you were trying to forget.

And there were enough cute NPCs on the airship. Some of them looked invitingly toward me. No, not today, girls. I had no time for your invented stories. I needed to figure out my own real one.

I touched the green dot at the edge of my vision and it unfolded into my interface in Do Not Disturb mode. I opened the Reveller achievement. I checked its requirements and started ordering drinks. I took a swallow from each order and then switched to another. Why worry about money? I was a millionaire, after all.

I kept tasting until I got a message:

*Reveller achievement completed: +10 XP.*
*Y-you still \*hic\* standing? Let's sing a song?*

*Achievement unlocked: Reveller II.*
*M-m-m-m, I love you, buddy. Let's have another drink?*

*Alcoholic brands tried:*
*Moonshine: 0/1*
*Tequila: 0/5*
*Gin: 0/5*
*Calvados: 0/1*
*Sake: 0/1*
*Rum: 0/5*
*Schnapps: 0/1*
*Cider: 0/5*

Trying not to fall over, I staggered over to my spot by the window. I couldn't continue the alcoholic challenge.

Nothing killed time as well as digging through stats.

Although there was sleep too, but I had a terrible fear of it. And I wasn't the only one — few in Adam Online used 'character sleep.'

The problem was that during sleep, you fully disconnected. It was difficult to even call the state 'sleep.' You didn't have nightmares, because what dreams could a digitized consciousness in a virtual world have? In the end, Adam Online itself was full of nightmares that you successfully fought against.

No, in sleep mode, you just disappeared.

Taharration itself was like death. A disappearance from the real world. We left our bodies as ethereal sets of data. But we didn't lose our sensation of life: people thought and existed.

After the sleep timer activated, the control systems stopped actively servicing your binary array, marking it suspended, in hibernation mode. The last thing you realized before the disconnection is that you'd lost your soul as well as your body.

I'd rather read my stats for the tenth time, or even game logs, than willingly disappear. Even the avatar of a sleeping player disappeared for other players.

Of course, you couldn't just go to sleep at any time. That would be a cheat for people wanting to escape from battles or avoid dying when the scenery collapsed.

I rose from my seat again and approached the multitude of trade machines arranged along one wall. Among the Tenshot and All-Seeing Eye machines, I searched for a Stylish You machine, which offered various skins for player avatars.

After examining the homogeneous assortment, I chose.

*Brutal Buck.*
*Skin set, beauty standard B+.*
*Contains 10 skins that transform you into, uh... a brutal buck.*
*Number of uses: 10/10.*

The box was small, about the size of a make-up box. I opened the lid and ten projections shone before me: men standing at full height.

All the projections were roughly similar, muscle-bound and bearded men who differed from each other in the size of their beard or color of their hair. I could select one and spin it to see more details. These skin sets were a quick way to change your appearance for the better without messing around with settings.

There were special establishments for fine-tuning your appearance; beauty salons, hairdressers, barbers and so on. There special skins were created for players, either based on their real appearance or something completely different. Or the players themselves could gain the skills required to play with their appearance settings forever more.

Some changed themselves so much that they transformed into grotesque things, parodies of humanity. Disproportionate heads, huge genitalia, unimaginable haircuts. Remembering players like that made me think that bizoids are a perfectly natural evolution of madness for people in Adam Online. Hmm, even entropy wouldn't scare people like that. They were already touched.

There were skills for it, like Stylist, which, at a high

enough level, would allow you to fundamentally change your virtual body, including changing its sex. I had no idea how to get the skill. But certain non-combat classes had it by default, like the politician or businessman.

The Brutal Buck set didn't have any settings, you just got what you chose. I chose the brute with the long ginger beard and bald head. He looked good in a bandana.

True, after applying the skin, I didn't look quite as good as the guy on the projection. My muscles were smaller because of my low Strength. My height and bearing weren't particularly impressive due to my Agility and Health.

But even this 'me' was far better than the one based on my real appearance. Reality lost to virtuality again.

When the airship reached the Arena, I was dropped below on a fast elevator built into the mooring tower. I was the only person departing at this zone.

Each Rim had an Arena. It was the place that hosted all the mini-games for which there was no space in the cities. Most of the mini-games were reconstructions of classic games.

In itself, the Arena was small and was apparently a copy of the 'Coliseum,' some historical stadium in real life that was destroyed many years ago in a war. At the entrance, the player or player group was invited to choose a mini-game, and then separate locations were generated to host the mini-game.

But some of the games couldn't be called 'mini' at

all. The zones could be as big as a DotA 5 map, or huge like the worlds of the city building simulators.

Plains stretched out around the Rim One Arena, the grass shaking in the wind. The sun already stood high, its bright light and heat exceeding the acceptable comfort parameters for players. Which was why there wasn't a soul in sight. No players, no NPCs.

It made sense. The mini-games in the Arena weren't a very popular entertainment. They interested fans of the archaic, or those who were bored of the overabundance of possibility in other zones in Adam. They interested those who sought simplicity; the mini-games didn't try to imitate reality, their intentional playfulness was an attractive quality.

Guiding myself with the player stream, I entered the required arch in the Arena building. I didn't really know what I was doing. It was obvious that I needed to reproduce all the actions of the streamers in the mini-games. I started from the Mirage 2047 map, where Nelly had appeared before.

But I still didn't quite believe that repeating their actions would lead to the same result. Even if the 'glitch' repeated, what would that give me? This time I had no plan of action.

A screen with mini-game settings popped up in the chill darkness of the arch. Since it was a team game, I'd need to invite friends or load some bots. That was a question: if I went into the game with bots instead of players, wouldn't that contradict the original actions? Whatever, I'd try going into the game alone.

I chose counter-terrorist, the same as the streamer. I took a step forward, passing through the settings screen, and found myself in the sunlit map of Mirage 2047. Although the sun there wasn't hot at all. I felt no temperature, no wind, no scent.

I immediately felt changes in my virtual body. My stats, which were important in Adam Online, stopped meaning anything. In this mini-game, all the characters had the same size, strength and speed.

Moreover, I stopped feeling that I was in a comfortable body. Movement felt more like walking in an exoskeleton. I saw my hands, but I realized that they weren't mine, although I was controlling them using whatever my hands were feeling.

A virtual body inside another virtual body.

First it was tough, I couldn't move normally. I kept running into the corners of buildings or getting stuck between boxes. It was hard to even walk — my legs weren't going where they should. It took half an hour for me to jump onto the ledge from which I needed to throw the smoke grenade. Jumping here was unnatural; before jumping, you had to run and... slightly crouch. It was a very stark contrast to my capabilities in the main world of Adam Online, where I could jump how I pleased.

Nonetheless, I appreciated the game's limitations. It wasn't character skills you leveled up here, but your own skills as a player. You trained your own 'accuracy' or 'reaction speed.' In this mini-game, you could spend hours improving your aim, but it still didn't guarantee that you'd get experience and level up. You have to learn to fire accurately. There was no way other way to improve.

Incidentally, that seemed to me to be one of the main drawbacks in the role-playing system of Adam Online, and in any role-playing system. It wasn't the player that got better while playing, but their character. No matter how much I, Anton Brulov, practiced with a machine gun, I wasn't improving myself... I was improving Leonarm.

Gradually, I got used to the blocky body of the counter-terrorist. I learned to run, jump and crouch. The character wasn't capable of more. Nothing happened when I tried to lie down; the body didn't react to those commands. Damn it, I couldn't even look round a corner! I had to move my whole body out like a mobile target on a shooting range. My head wouldn't turn separately either, I had to turn my entire body to look around me.

All these ancient games were made for gyrospheres or virtual capsules. In these devices, contrary to the marketers' talk of 'full immersion,' the player controlled their character as if from outside, without fully immersing themselves in the body as happened with taharration.

It was time to throw some grenades...

# Chapter 40
# Little Brother

IN LARGE-SCALE military clashes, when a soldier was in the heart of the battle, he felt a sense of confusion and chaos. It seemed to him as if everything was going wrong, that the commander had made a mistake, that other maneuvers or other units should be used on this section of the battlefield.

That's how it looked to Grisha, although he trusted Nika's suddenly appearing gift as a general. He imagined that all his enemies were ganging up on him. On the map itself, who knew what was going on. Grisha glanced at Jamilla and confirmed his suspicions; it was the same for her, the same chaos, only she was dealing with it better.

*You're both doing great*, Nika encouraged them, but it seemed to Grisha that she was comforting him in particular.

There were also short quiet spells when Grisha looked at the map and saw no chaos or mess. Both sides acted distinctly, each with a plan that they tried to hide from their enemies.

Grisha watched LeCube's stats with alarm. Too many resources had gone on defense. Although the enemies themselves were no longer attacking, but defending.

Without reading his own stats, Grisha felt that his mastery had grown. Previously he'd always tried to give LeCube a form familiar to a mechanodestructor, like a robot, a tank or a jet like the Grenika, but now he wasn't afraid to stay in his base configuration, as a cube or a disk.

The transformation from the base configuration took mere seconds, while moving from a complex program configuration to another took two seconds or more. And LeCube was highly vulnerable in the meantime.

Grisha was no longer afraid to stand against the enemy in the form of a simple cube, and not a threatening transformer armed to the teeth with all kinds of weapons. After completing his combat mission and killing the enemy, Grisha took on his base configuration and moved to the next target. One instant, and a mechanodestructor towered above the enemy in the black cube's place.

But the sharpness of the battle was lost. The Black Wavers had entrenched themselves and were taking fewer losses.

"Come on, Jamilla!" Grisha shouted. "What are you doing with that magic egg? Roll it into battle!"

It was as if Jamilla had been waiting for his command.

The earth trembled. It didn't just tremble, it shook. Some of the buildings with forcefield generators inside couldn't withstand it and collapsed. The anomalous wind temporarily died out, and the clouds parted, revealing an intolerably blue sky. Slowly flapping her wings, Jamilla rose above the battlefield, holding Ozerg's Egg in an outstretched hand. Pulsing circles of energy emanated from it, shaking the earth itself.

"Now we could do with some airplanes," Grisha said.

"The clear sky is a temporary event," Jamilla replied.

The Black Wave troops retreated under the protection of the heavily weakened forcefield. Nobody knew what to expect from an unknown magical item in the hands of a level four-hundred player. Grisha even thought that he could phase through the defenses, but Jamilla warned him.

"Relax, I'll handle this."

Grisha moved farther back from Jamilla and stood next to Nika. She placed her hands on him, healing him, and a transport approached and deposited some component nanomass into LeCube.

"That's the last of the CN," Nika said.

"What do I do now? Abandon LeCube?"

"I think it'll be easier to craft in Rim Six. I'll have higher skill levels. Maybe even new skills too."

The enemies concentrated all their fire on Jamilla, but she took almost no damage. Whether from the egg or one of her own skills that she'd been saving for a special occasion. The pulsing energy of the egg seemed to neutralize the enemy's strikes.

And each wave that hit the Black Wave warriors dealt some damage. Not a lot, but it was regular. No matter which defensive measures they tried, none of it worked, or it worked only slightly.

The blessing from the angel couldn't cope with the damage.

The next wave emerged in a blinding circle, for a moment covering everything with a white light, and when it ebbed, over half of the enemy units had died. All the generated vehicles had simply disintegrated, leaving piles of components behind. The strongest players remained, but their health was so low that they could be killed by sending Nika's generated vehicles after them.

According to the agreement, all three partners got an equal amount of experience.

"I reached four hundred," Grisha said casually.

"I'm still at three hundred and ninety nine," Nika answered.

Jamilla didn't say anything. Holding the weakly pulsating egg in her hand, she attacked the remainder of the Black Wave.

"Come on, girl, craft something," Grisha said.

"I've already maxed out everything in crafting."

"Then I'll help our little mage," Grisha said.

Grisha rushed into battle, but a message in the chat stopped him. It was Fortunado.

"Let's talk."

"No, all we can do is fight to the end!" Grisha answered instantly.

"I'll let you into Rim Six. Stop killing us and wait..."

Grisha, Nika and Jamilla all got a partner agreement sent.

It was brief. It had just three clauses. The first, 'Good Bye Weapons,' prevented either side from dealing damage to the other, and the second, 'Availability,' allowed the sides to see each other on the map. The last one was a 'Duration' of a hundred hours.

Fortunado invited all three into the fortifications of Jamilla's Tomb to discuss the details.

"Sign it. And... welcome..." he sighed and closed the commlink.

"Doesn't look like a trick," Grisha said. "But it would be dumb to have mercy on Fortunado. I think we should punish him in full.

Jamilla supported Grisha.

"I'll wipe them all out myself... Although the egg is a consumable resource. Shame."

Nika summarized.

"Although I do not share your bloodthirsty urges, I wouldn't mind punishing Fortunado either. But... is our goal really to destroy the Black Wave?"

"No, our goal is to..." Grisha sometimes took rhetorical questions seriously. But then he stopped, realizing that nobody had asked his opinion.

"That's right, Gregory," Nika said. "More than that, it makes sense for us to let the guild keep guarding the entrance to Rim Six. Don't forget, other players will want to get there too."

"Agreed. Then let's sign it and move on!"

"If you want my opinion," Jamilla said thoughtfully, "I wouldn't sign it."

"Why not?"

"The Availability clause doesn't agree with me. Why do we need to know that Fortunado is in his base? But he'll know about all our movements and new zones."

Nika agreed with Jamilla.

"We'll remove the Availability and increase the duration to a thousand hours."

The partners changed the agreement clauses and sent it to Fortunado. After a small delay, he returned the agreement approved. Nika withdrew her forces to the generators and put them into patrol mode.

"We can expect tricks from Fortunado," she explained. "There are ways to circumvent any agreement, especially such a short one."

Grisha and Jamilla went first, with Nika behind, escorted by four precision defense modules. They formed a square and protected her with a forcefield.

"One of the easiest ways to circumvent an agreement," Nika said, "is hiring third-party players. I'd choose snipers and I'd station them on those cliffs. One volley and I'd be toast. You'd both survive, of course."

Jamilla and Nika looked up at the peaks. They really could see the figures of humans in UniSuits up there. None of them were Black Wave members. Nika continued.

"Against you, I'd use mines, traps or the most expensive autosens that the guild craftspeople could make."

As if to confirm her words, the partners walked by a whole unit of autonomous sentinels. All were level two hundred and bore no guild markings.

Even Jamilla's enthusiasm was curbed.

"Why... why didn't he send them into the battle? There are almost fifty super advanced autosens here!"

The deeper they went into the fortifications of

Jamilla's Tomb, the greater their surprise; a compact defense of forcefields with generated vehicle squads swarming behind.

Particularly discouraging to Grisha was the presence of several jets, calmly hovering in the flows of the anomalous wind.

"How did he... why are they flying... and why can't ours?"

Nika was the only one to show no surprise.

"It's just as I suspected. Fortunado was saving his strength."

"Saving it?!" Jamilla shouted. "He didn't even use it properly, look!"

At the top of a short cliff, a giant dragon sat as if on a roost.

"Oh, my old friend," Grisha said. "That's Ozerg, whose egg you're carrying, Jamilla."

"Yeah, I got that," she spat back. "Only this one is at level four hundred and twenty. I wonder, did they find the egg or did it fall from a slain dragon?"

"These Ozergs are funny," Grisha said. "Their eggs are stronger than the dragons themselves."

Nika added.

"It all makes sense. The loot should be more valuable than the object it dropped from. Otherwise, why fight for it?"

Jamilla added:

"It looks like Fortunado, in defending the passage to Rim Six, has been taking advantage of some of the loot that comes out of there into Rim Five."

Nika corrected her skeptically.

"Someone is delivering the loot to him, but the anomalous wind isn't blowing it in at random."

The partners passed all the lines of defense. They

saw a multitude of vehicle generators and plants for manufacturing autosens. Nika noted that the vehicles were being crafted slowly. Fortunado was focusing on quality, not on speed. Mines jutted out from the ground here and there. He was harvesting resources.

All the partners had already forgotten their recent victory.

"But then why did Fortunado let us in here?" Grisha said in amazement.

Nobody answered his rhetorical question.

When the partners entered the building in which Fortunado had set their meeting, their amazement reached its limit: at the center of the empty room was a white orb. The size was the same as LeCube's base form. Its sides nebulously reflected the room's walls.

The partners read its stats.

*Fortunado, Mechanodestructor.*
*Frame: LaSphere.*
*Guild: Black Wave.*
*Classes: Engineer, Politician, Defender.*
*Level: 388.*
*Member of contract 'Black Wave — Grisha — Nika — Jamilla.'*

*Health: 89,000/89,000.*
*Armor: 99,000/99,000.*

LaSphere began to move, floated toward the trio.

"Hey, bro," Fortunado said.

Ignoring his brother's greeting, Grisha switched to the humanoid mech and quickly spoke to Nika on a private channel.

*Been working for both camps again, cunning rat?*
*Grisha, I swear, I had nothing to do with this.*
*I believed you!*

LaSphere descended gently to the floor and then rose in the same humanoid mech shape. It was as if Fortunado was demonstrating to Grisha: look, my frame is just as good as yours.

"If you're blaming Nika right now, let me intervene. She wasn't involved."

"But the frame..."

"Our genius Nika didn't invent that frame herself."

"I beg to differ," Nika said.

"Differ as much as you want. But I have something similar now too."

Nika approached LaSphere and slapped a shining white side.

"You've only made things worse for yourself, Fortunado. When the players find out that the complex components required to create component nanomass can only be found in Rim Six, your defenses won't hold."

"Well, well," Grisha said, with the tone of a detective who'd solved a crime. He suggested to Fortunado and Nika that he was listening closely, although in fact, he didn't really understand what was going on.

"So you've arranged deliveries from Rim Six?" Nika asked Fortunado.

"Yep, only you were working with my supplier before I was."

"We-e-ll!" Grisha said even more confidently, feeling even more confused.

Nika walked away from LaSphere.

"You're downplaying my skills. Mariam contacted me to create a nuclear bomb not because she felt like it, but because I'm one of very few who can do it. Crafting is a job for the diligent."

"We-e-e-e-ll, now I get it," Grisha said. "So it was Mariam? Uh-huh."

Grisha switched off the automatic emoji display on his chest so that the 'confusion' emoji wouldn't give away his true understanding of what was going on.

Nika shook her head.

"I don't believe you made it yourself."

"Of course not. But you aren't the only android in Adam Online, are you?"

Grisha formed a thought a little late.

"Hey, bro, it isn't the frame that matters, it's who's using it. My cube would crush your little circle. I'd crush you."

"It's not a circle, it's a sphere," Fortunado corrected him. "And I don't plan on fighting you. I want you to go into Rim Six."

Jamilla had kept out of the conversation. She'd moved into a corner and started doing some magic or other; fixing her armor, refreshing the mana charges in her crystals, upgrading her weapon enchantments and so on. But after she heard what Fortunado said, she came closer.

"Why the change of heart?"

"Yeah," Nika said. "And what does that Mariam of yours have to say about it?"

"Yeah, what will she say?" Grisha joined in, without even the slightest concern for what Mariam might say.

"We don't have to tell her anything. She doesn't

need to know that you got there with my help. To support the fiction, I imitated a long and difficult battle. It'll look as if you defeated me and fought your way through."

"If it weren't for the contract, I'd have messed up your little orb so bad that there'd be no need to fake anything."

"Don't, Grisha," Nika said strictly. She addressed Fortunado. "Have you lost trust in Mariam all of a sudden?"

"I didn't trust her. I've nev..."

"Sure, sure," Jamilla interrupted. "You're awesome and not at all gullible, etc. You don't trust anyone. We get it. But you said that we should trust you?"

"I suggested the contract myself," Fortunado answered. "What else do you need?"

"That's suspicious too..."

"Yeah, real suspicious," Grisha interjected, seeing nothing suspicious at all in the contract.

Nika interrupted the stream of words from Jamilla.

"Why did you change your opinion?"

"Why are you all ganging up on me?" LaSphere hopped, showing Fortunado's annoyance. "My intentions from the start were to use Mariam as much as possible. I want to get into Rim Six as much as you guys."

"So come with us, bro!"

"I can't. I have a contract with her. She made me sign to say I wouldn't move into Rim Six without her. On top of that, I'm getting lots of loot from her. You saw it yourself."

Nika wrapped her arms around her thin shoulders.

"I get it. You want us to explore Rim Six and keep you appraised of what we find?"

"Exactly. That's why I'd like us to add the

Availability clause back into the contract."

"We agree," Nika said.

"Sure, sure, great idea," Grisha agreed. "Enough chat, let's get into Rim Six! It's time!"

But Jamilla expressed doubt in the partner chat. *What if there's some kind of level five-hundred one-shot[1] superboss right behind the entrance to Rim Six? Or an anomaly, or a trap, or a pack[2] of Ozergs?*

*Then we'll fight it,* Grisha answered

Nika wanted to give a long speech, but she laughed. *Yeah, perfect, you'll fight it, that's what you're looking for in new zones, right?*

The partners returned the Availability clause to the contract and signed again.

Grisha turned into his disk and flew to the exit.

"Come on, let's go, let's go!"

Nika mussed her plastic hair.

"Where're you going? I'm still not at level four hundred yet."

"Oh, I can solve that problem," Fortunado said.

A projector panel appeared along a wall in the room, filled with thousands of icons and connecting lines.

"I have the required components," Fortunado said. "You craft another unique item and get a bunch of experience for it. It goes without saying that the item stays with me."

Nika slowly approached the projector and dragged her fingers across the icons, creating and

---

[1] One-shot — killing with one hit.

[2] Pack — a collaborative group of social mobs which responds in unison to an attack on any individual of the group.

breaking connections.

    "A nuclear bomb?"

    "That's the one."

# Chapter 41
# The Hundred-Year-Old
# Woman

I AIMED a bunch of times, moved my crosshair to the space between the rafters, threw my smoke grenade, jumped off the ledge and ran through the corridor into the square. Then I turned, ran back... but there was nothing in the darkness of the corridor.

But for some reason I didn't think I was doing anything wrong or that I couldn't reproduce the glitch this way. I just felt like I needed to keep trying. Of course, it was hard to keep track of my progress without getting reinforcement in the form of experience and achievements...

On the millionth throw, it worked. The familiar spot with the two figures appeared in the darkness of the archway.

The mini-game stopped working due to an error when the snapshot appeared, just like in the player's stream. I found myself in my body again.

I stood in the Coliseum arch, and the spatial cocoon in which the conversation between Nelly and the girl in the Darknet t-shirt didn't go anywhere. On the contrary, against the backdrop of the ordinary Adam Online, the snapshot became clearer, the voices became audible.

I came closer and waved my hand. It passed through the whole scene without resistance.

Damn, what now? I'd found something like Nelly...

"Good time of day, player!" an Arild said joyously, walking into the archway. "Bugs have been detected in this zone. Please wai..."

I interrupted him with a shot from my revolver. The bots would quickly fix this 'bug,' if I wasn't careful, and I'd have to repeat the mini-game again.

Since my interface was in Do Not Disturb mode, I didn't see any notifications about losing Reputation. But I didn't care about that anyway. What was I supposed to do next?

"Good time of..." The blonde head of another Arild dissolved in a beam of energy.

I estimated that with such frequent appearances, the bots would destroy my Reputation within three or four minutes. I needed to use that time to at least figure out what the conversation was about. I went into almost the very center of the spatial bubble, stood right between the ghostly Nelly and her interlocutor. The sound came interrupted, with the syllables swapped around in some words.

I snapped my fingers in front of Nelly's face.

"Hey, hundred-year-old woman. Can you see me? Can you hear me?"

The hundred-year-old woman looked only at the girl.

*"Who are you?"* Nelly asked.

*"I'm like you; a copy of a copy,"* answered the

Darknet girl.

"I've heard this before, ladies. Hurry it up, come on."

"Who gave... create... network... under?"

The snapshot trembled, changed its proportions.

"Good time..."

The third bot's corpse fell by those of his comrades. The bots didn't use creative functions. They could only show three emotions: smiling, confusion and rejection. Even now, falling to the ground, they took on identical 'dead' poses, folding up into even heaps. As if I was playing an ancient mini-game where the model animations always looked the same.

Nelly Valeeva broke the silence.

"Mentors... Helper characters that teach new players? I never used them."

"... you ...that feat... about," the girl answered. "The Mentors were created to analyze the game situations of beginner DotA players. They are pseudoartificial pseudointelligences that interact with the player, studying and becoming more complex alongside them."

I waved my revolver.

"Come on, girls, reveal some secret. I don't know how long I can hold here."

"We are a virtual consciousness..." Then a stream of strange noises, and: "But we didn't know it until you appeared."

Nelly also answered with a set of unintelligible syllables. It was a little comical, even; a historical figure with an extremely serious expression on her face, talking absolute nonsense.

"What do you intend to do?"

"Well done, Nelly, you're finally asking the right

question," I said encouragingly.

"Good time..."

"There's nobody good here," I answered, firing my revolver.

*"Are you asking if we want to rule over humanity?"* the Darknet girl said. *"That won't happen any time soon."*

"Did I hear that right? That's a twist."

The Darknet girl said, clearly, as if specially for me:

*"Nelly, notice that I'm confirming all your guesses. I could be a harmful program from Moscovian Rus. Or China. Or even India. Why not?"*

"Don't believe her," I laughed. "She's probably lying."

"Good..."

I didn't even look or turn around, I just shot toward the entrance to the arch. The new bot folded up nearly by the others.

Nelly's interlocutor continued.

*"Do you dream of immortality? One day, you will all digitize your consciousness."*

*"...dren ... liv ... under here?"* Nelly inquired. *"The Mentors will inhabit our bodies instead of merging the copies?"*

"Ooh, ladies..."

*"But for this to work, you must stop coming back here. I wouldn't have told you this, but you're getting in our way."*

Nelly's eyes widened.

*"What do you mean, coming back? This is my first time here..."*

"Good time..."

"You too, pal."

Was that the fifth or sixth bot today? Why had they added the option to kill tech support anyway? Maybe... Could it be for cases like this? To allow things that were forbidden in Adam Online?

If something was taken as a bug by the control systems, bots were sent out to fix it. That's the way it used to be. Now you could prevent them from doing so. Of course, there were also the controllers. They wouldn't stand on ceremony and wish you a good time of day. But before the matter reached them, rulebreakers had enough time to achieve what they wanted! Yep, reading sectarian conspiracy theories had definitely been well worth the time. The imagination was a powerful thing.

In the meantime, the conversation drew to a close. The cocoon suddenly lightened. Now Nelly and her conversation partner weren't standing in front of a vague gray fuzz, they were in a circle of light. Well, and so was I.

"Is that all?" I asked Nelly, not expecting an answer.

An expression of confusion and fear appeared on her face. It looked like she'd learned something that had scared her. But for me, it was all a mystery.

The Darknet girl had dissolved into the white background.

I scratched my forehead with my revolver barrel. No, my forehead wasn't itching, but old habits died hard.

"Who are you?" Nelly suddenly asked.

The gaze of her dark, slightly almond-shaped eyes was pointed straight at me.

"You can see me?" I said in amazement.

"And you can see me? Who are all you people? What are you doing in the Darknet? Are you an artificial intelligence too?"

"Not exactly. It's hard to explain..."

I looked at the archway in alarm. The bots had stopped appearing. Did that mean the controllers would be here soon?

"In the name of Allah, what's going on here?"

"Nelly, firstly, I've been searching for you to get an answer to that very question... Secondly, none of my explanations will make much sense to you.

Nelly frowned.

"Stop babbling. Tell me, who are you?"

This hundred-year-old woman was pretty sharp when it came to talking to strangers.

"It doesn't matter who I am. What matters is who you are."

"And who am I?"

"A binary array which, it seems, has been stuck in a recursive loop in Adam Online's control systems for a hundred years, replaying one and the same scene over and over."

"A hundred years? What is this crap?"

"Well, maybe a little less. Eighty years. Years have become kind of complicated, you won't get it."

Nelly swore in Tatar and added:

"I want to get out of here right now."

I switched to Tatar as well.

"I'm afraid, Nelly-khanum, that you'll never get out of here."

"Why is that?"

"You have nowhere to go. You died a long time ago."

Nelly Valeeva looked around as if seeking a door so she could leave the snapshot. It continued to exist. Now I was there, a player who had made note of it, and that meant I was supporting its existence. Although the snapshot contained nothing but the white mist and Nelly.

I tried to think of a way to pull Nelly out into the real... I mean, into the virtual world. How could I achieve control over the snapshot? I opened my interface and dug around in my settings, but found nothing.

"What do we do?" Nelly asked, switching back to Russian.

Although Nelly tried to look confident, it was clear she was upset. Hell, it must have been stressful. According to her memories, she'd only just transferred her consciousness to the extranet, where an unknown creature in a Darknet t-shirt had dumped a bunch of strange facts on her. Then a dude appears with two huge revolvers, claiming that she, Nelly, was long dead.

To be honest, I was trying to look confident too, but I didn't know if I was successful. I had absolutely no understanding of the situation whatsoever.

"Where are we?" Nelly asked.

"In Adam Online. More precisely, at the Rim One Arena."

"Is that a new game? I've heard of it. Its creator got it wrong, it won't take off."

"Oh, ma'am, you can't even imagine how far it took off."

"Pfft," Nelly answered.

We fell silent again.

The situation had become completely idiotic. The snapshot had existed for precisely as long as I'd been watching it. If I left the cocoon, it would instantly disappear, resetting the current state of Nelly Valeeva's binary array. If I threw more grenades and caused the snapshot to appear again, Nelly wouldn't remember our conversation. Like an NPC that had died and respawned.

"What are you thinking?" Nelly asked suspiciously.

"Oh, khanim... I don't know where to start."

"Start with yourself. Are you human?"

"Yeah. I'm Leonarm the Tracker. I mean, I'm Anton Brulov, offi..." I nearly told her my rank. "Just an Adam Online player."

"So you still insist that I'm in a game?"

"I know it for certain."

"Why is everything white here? Although..." Nelly gazed into the white. "I can make something out. Before the conversation with the Mentors, I saw some cities, buildings or mechanisms..."

Nelly waved her hand below her as if trying to find a seat to sit on.

"I explained it already. You're the binary array of Nelly Valeeva, owner of the Labsetek company. Many years ago, you sent your consciousness into the extranet."

"I'm a copy of a copy..." Nelly repeated.

"If you want to know, your experiment turned into a huge breakthrough in human history. You were the first person to undergo taharration..."

"Tahar... what?"

"'Taharration,' that's what you named the process of transferring a human consciousness into a virtual world. It came from a word that translates as 'ablution.'"

I stopped talking. Dumbass! I was explaining the meaning of a word from Nelly's own native language.

"I... I named it? What a dumb name. When was this? I never named anything like that."

"Well, after you got out of the pod. And it wasn't you who named it, it was... hmm, your original."

I hesitated over a sudden thought. What if Nelly Valeeva hadn't departed into her body, but the Mentors themselves? What if the historically famous Valeeva wasn't the original at all, but was a copy? Or even a Mentor? That could explain the sharp shift in her character that many of her colleagues had noted.

Yep, the conspiratorial thinking from the Dead Face guild had definitely made itself at home in my brain.

"I haven't logged out yet," Nelly cried.

"You haven't. But your original... or a copy, left almost a hundred years ago."

The woman buried her face in her hands.

"This is all crap. I'm creating all this with my mind."

"No, ma'am... I mean, yeah, but not quite. If you mean that I'm just a nightmare, a figment of your imagination, you're wrong. It's all a lot more pedestrian than that."

Nelly shook, looked as if she wanted to hit me.

"Who are you anyway?! What do you want from me? You say you're just a simple player? Who are you playing for? The CIA? The NSA? The MSB?"

I was amazed. The woman was so stressed, but she didn't lose her professional grip of herself. That's what it meant to be a person of greatness.

"Nelly, I won't lie... I was looking for you, I found you and..."

"And?"

"And I don't know what to do."

Nelly tried hard to laugh to show suspicion.

"Now I know you're an MSB agent. You guys are

amateurs. Losers."

I wanted to remind her that all I had to do was leave the snapshot to return her to a state of informational non-existence until another bug revived her copy and started the conversation with the girl in the Darknet t-shirt.

But I looked at her sad face and felt pity for this copy of a person. Surprising myself, I said:

"I'll try to help you."

"I don't need help from a dirty MSB agent. I'll figure it out myself."

Her eyes told a different story. There I saw hope and gratitude.

# Chapter 42
# Medicine

LIFE HAD TAUGHT ME a rule: never promise a woman that which you can't provide. Sometimes I broke that rule. I'd promised Olga that we'd grow old together, but she left first. I broke the rule this time too. How could I help Nelly Valeeva?

I switched my interface from Do Not Disturb mode. I waved away my new messages and looked at Nelly.

*%Unknown%, %Unknown%.*
*Class: %Unknown%.*
*Level: %Unknown%.*
*Health: %Unknown%.*
*Armor: %Unknown%.*

*...*

All her other stats were the same, all %Unknown%. Only one message stubbornly floated before me:

*Attention, reading the stats of the game world element %Unknown%, %Unknown% (UID OOOOOOOO-*

*183923-1980-54010S...) caused an error. Instruction block absent or damaged. Data array type undetermined or unknown. Corresponding warning sent to tech support.*

*An error report has been delivered to your account.*

*We would like to apologize for any inconvenience this may cause.*

*Attention: username cannot be %Username% (Error! Check taharration system settings).*

*Error report could not be delivered due to lack of address.*

Heh, one error crashed into another.

Fine, the game tool wasn't very useful. What did I need to do? Find Valeeva and find out how she managed to spend decades in Adam Online without falling prey to informational entropy?

It seems I'd found the answer to that.

The Mentors, or some other program, or even a control system, supported her existence by constantly reproducing the same snapshot scene. Nelly Valeeva's consciousness existed in that cycle with no concept of what was happening. She relived that scene time and time again. Then the CSes either copied her, or restored her to her initial state to repeat the cycle.

They couldn't erase her, but they could return her to a kind of respawn point and 'reset' her progress.

Why was the unknown program or CS doing this? It didn't seem likely to be some kind of nefarious action. Nelly Valeeva was the binary array of a human, it shouldn't be wiped and destroyed. So the CSes were conscientiously distributing resources to reproduce an isolated snapshot. The fact that a human consciousness was stuck in permanent recursion didn't bother them. They'd done their job.

The more important question wasn't how it worked now, but how it worked before? After all, for Valeeva's binary array to appear in Adam Online, someone would have had to transfer it there, right? The fact that the snapshot appeared in ancient mini-games seemed to indicate that the transfer had happened back in the era of those games. Probably right after Nelly appeared in the virtual world.

Nelly broke the silence.

"If I... If I've been here for a hundred years, then what have I been doing all that time?" She covered her face again. "God, have I been repeating the same thing all that time?"

"You know your field. You guessed it. I've been thinking about that too. That's how you avoided informational entropy."

"What's that?"

I didn't answer.

I was thinking; should I tell her everything? About my mission, about what happened to people when they stayed in the game for longer than they should? If necessary, I was allowed to share secret information...

"Well?" she demanded.

"I was thinking of how to explain the modern world and its technology to a person who hasn't seen the world for a hundred years."

"Start somewhere. I'm not an idiot. Judging by you, humanity hasn't gotten that much wiser in a hundred years. Maybe the opposite."

Another sarcastic lady. Although, according to accounts from her time, Nelly Valeeva was exactly that. A decisive and harsh executive. According to one study, under her direction the Labsetek team was involved in deadly experiments on people. Without their consent.

Of course, this version of Nelly hadn't yet transformed into that cold-blooded bitch that Valeeva remained until the end of her life. But the seed was there.

"I'll start with myself. Like I said, my name is..."

I stopped. The space of the snapshot was beginning to stir and fade.

Nelly looked at her hands.

"What's happening? What is this?"

I didn't feel any changes. I just saw that Nelly was rapidly melting away, as was the whole snapshot.

"It must be the controllers.

Nelly didn't bother asking who or what they were. She caught on quick. She realized there was no point in knowing the details of the nightmare she'd found herself in. She just nodded.

"Controllers. Fine. This has been some day."

I upbraided myself for my helplessness.

*Come on, think! Didn't you want to complete this MSB mission with flying colors? Weren't you proud to be sent to find a digital cure for death? Here's the cure, right in front of you.*

Nelly Valeeva put her hands to her chest and gazed into the void. I figured the controllers were about to reset her binary array to its previous state. What should I do then? Throw more grenades? Call her back and watch again as she disappeared?

On the other hand... I no longer believed that

Valeeva's binary array was the key to the problem of entropy. Who needed immortality when you get reset and lose all the feelings and experiences you had? Sure, if you threw every human consciousness into an endless loop, it would exist for as long as the equipment supporting the virtual world existed. But was that living?

Certain religious leaders may have been right. Death is unavoidable.

But I couldn't let Nelly Valeeva be reset either. No, not because I pitied her. In the end, she wasn't a human, she had no body she could return to. She was something between myself and an improved version of Irene Laggan.

I didn't want to keep Nelly for humanity, but for myself. Without her, my activities in Adam Online had no meaning. The rest of my life had no meaning. I thought that with Valeeva...

I didn't have time to finish the thought. Nelly was almost invisible. She moved her ghostly gaze from the emptiness and cast it on me again. It broadcast an open plea.

"What's going to happen to me? Will I... die?"

"The controllers have taken you for a cheat or virus. You don't have an entry point to Adam Online, or even a player name. And you're not an NPC."

"So what will happen to me?"

"You'll return to your previous state."

"But I'm... a person."

"For me, maybe, but for them... you're just a glitching NPC or a nefarious program. I don't know how to help you..."

As soon as I said it, I knew how to help. Nelly's image wavered and rippled ever more strongly. I hurriedly called up my inventory, found the Contract section and sent Nelly a standard contract between a player and an NPC.

I wasn't sure it would reach her, but it worked. Human or not, Nelly was a data array that was identified as part of the game world. Nelly sprang back, examining the interface elements that appeared in front of her.

"What's this? Some contract?"

"Sign it quick if you want to live."

Nelly signed the contract, and everything stopped. The snapshot disappeared, but Nelly stood opposite me, dressed in a standard gray vest and jeans. Only she had no bag on her shoulder.

"What happened?"

"Nothing special. By signing a partner agreement with you, I kind of confirmed your existence in the world as an NPC. You have a job that justifies your existence and the resources required for it."

"Is that so."

"Congratulations, hundred-year-old woman, now you're officially a non-person."

"So who am I?"

"I'd say you're an NPC, but that's not right either. You're an NPC to the system right now, because you have a partner agreement with a player. But in fact, you're a person. At least I think so. You're a hybrid of a person and an NPC."

"How is that possible?"

"No clue. Nobody knows anything about situations like this. All I can suggest is that due to the absence of the block that limits the data type, the CSes didn't understand how to treat you. Now they know, even though there's still no block.

"So if you or I break the contract, the controllers will come back?"

"Yep."

I didn't tell her that the controllers would drag her off anyway when I left the game at the end of my taharration rotation. But there were thousands of hours until then. We'd think of something.

We sat on one of the stones that had fallen from the Coliseum wall. There was no need to sit. In contrast to a real body, a virtual one could stand as long as you liked. But people were more used to having long conversations seated.

And considering what I was planning on telling Nelly, I wanted a bottle of whiskey sitting between us.

Nelly listened attentively to my comprehensive report. Especially the parts that touched on Adam Online, the Global Consortium of Standardization in Adam Online and how taharration works.

"The technology hasn't changed significantly," she noted.

"Yep, only the computers have gotten faster, and even the cheapest dissociative electrolyte is higher quality than the stuff you used."

"Does it stink the same?"

"Sure does. But the expensive brands have special perfumes added. Although additives slightly decrease the electrolyte's life span, so it reduces the taharration duration."

Nelly laughed.

"During the first experiment, I thought of doing exactly that, adding fragrance to the dissociative material."

"Your Labsetek wasn't just the first company to suggest a commercial usage for taharration, but also the first to sell the products for it; designer pods, fragrances, medical robots, special mixtures of dissociative electrolyte... you can even change the liquid color."

"You say 'my Labsetek,' but I'm just the manager of the network security department. How did I become the company owner?"

"Well... It's clear that you were promoted by people who kept in the background. It's clear that you were the company leader in name only. The taharration process became an important technology, powerful governments couldn't resist taking control of it. You're not such a blind patriot that you believe the Kazan Republic independently controlled the technology? Of course you were being watched."

"So as I understand it, in the end my technology was taken for the benefit of all humanity?"

"But before that, you managed to make a hell of a lot of money. You were one of the top ten richest people on the planet."

"That doesn't surprise me."

Nelly asked about her future... or rather, her past self with hesitation. The subject seemed unpalatable to her.

I would have been out of sorts too. It isn't a lot of fun to find out that you're a copy of someone who was more successful. Her name had been given to streets, squares and even a city in the Kazan Republic. And here she was, the potential heroine, a copy of a consciousness that couldn't imagine what it was doing in a virtual world...

It was like a school reunion. You were proud of your career, proud that you could buy an electromobile without a loan, but then you realized that one dumb nerd from school didn't even turn up for the reunion because he was living in the land of the Golden Billion. His mere absence turned all your achievements to dust.

Sometimes Nelly interrupted me, asking precise questions. I left some of them unanswered, since the answers would reveal secret information. But I realized that she wasn't asking them just to uncover secrets, but to assess me. My access level and my place in the MSB hierarchy.

I told her of my doubts and guesses.

As for how her binary array had reached Adam Online when she'd transferred her consciousness to the extranet before the virtual world reached its modern state, she explained it like this:

"It's simple. I transferred it."

"How's that?"

"I don't know what stories you guys have invented about me in turning me into a historical figure... but we didn't invent taharration to expand the horizons of human consciousness, or give people immortality, or create a new game for people to waste time on."

"Hmm..."

"Uh-huh. You forgot who I was when I went through this, what did you call it, taharration? A network security specialist. There were unusual anomalies in a subnet of the extranet. This anomaly arose in some DotA 5 game traffic. Then... then the opportunity presented itself..."

Nelly clearly stopped herself, not wanting to give up secret information. I encouraged her.

"Come on, it's been a hundred years. Enough secrecy. Anyway, you're not even Valeeva anymore, you're her copy. So you're not bound by any nondisclosure agreements."

"My difficulty is from something else. It would mean telling you something that has nothing to do with your mission. Superfluous information that will only distract you. Just trust me, I didn't digitize my consciousness for the sake of humanity, I did it for work. There was no other way to study the suspicious anomaly."

"Sounds kind of weird. You mean to tell me that Labsetek created a breakthrough technology just to catch some hackers?"

"We didn't create it at all. It already existed, the inventor just didn't realize its capabilities."

"Woah. I'm confused. You stole it?"

"We stole nothing, we took someone else's work and split it off in another direction," Nelly answered haughtily. "I'm not going to argue with you, I've done great things. If it weren't for my theories, the technology wouldn't have gotten any funding and would have ended up unused. Its author had no plans to transfer human consciousness anywhere. He'd just created a tool that could possibly be used — I repeat, *possibly* — to digitize our consciousness. I made that possibility a reality."

"Let's say you're right..."

"There's no 'let's say' about it. I'm sure your bosses at the MSB know the truth."

Another jab implying my rank was low.

"You're unlucky, Leo... Anton," she gave an exaggerated sigh. "You've completed your mission and found me, but to no benefit."

"Seems so."

"What do you plan to do?"

"Find the Mentors. Only they can explain why

you've been floating through virtual worlds for a hundred years, wandering from archive to archive. And I still don't have a final answer to the question of informational entropy."

"I see... And I'll be forced to follow you?"

"Got other plans?"

"Firstly I'd like to explore Adam Online. It's my only reality now, after all."

"Oh, believe me, this place is a lot better than reality."

Nelly gaze lost focus. She was looking at her interface.

"Strange. I'm not new to games, but... Wow, have games really become so easy?"

"What do you mean?"

"My interface has incredibly abilities... I don't fully understand what they mean, but I can choose any race and any class... any weapon... any equipment... I can give myself any level and choose skills matching my class and level... This Adam Online of yours isn't a game, it's a piece of shit... Why bother playing if you've already unlocked everything?"

I jumped up from the stone.

"That's not the player interface!"

"What is it, then?"

"It's the NPC console."

# Chapter 43
# Aladdin's Magic Lamp

"A NON-PLAYER CHARACTER console?" Nelly asked. "Tell me..."

I told the hundred-year-old woman about the fact that there used to be no difference between NPCs and players, which hackers used to access the console instead of the player interface.

"Your binary array has no limitation instruction block, since it was created long before Adam Online came into existence."

Nelly corrected him.

"Not that long at all. I met Adam Mickiewicz at some conference. He was presenting his game idea then. Nobody listened to him, his Adam Online didn't offer anything new. Just some garbage action game..."

Nelly went back to studying the interface.

"So I'm an unwilling cheater?"

"More than that, you can't be caught cheating. For the CSes, you're not even a player."

Nelly thoughtfully passed her hand in front of her face.

"It's not all as rosy as that. Since I'm an NPC, I'm supposed to fulfill the demands of these... CSes? But I have my own will and I won't be following anyone's commands. What will happen to me then?"

I shrugged.

"I don't know."

"But I do. First they'll send those guys in the jumpsuits..."

"The tech support bots."

"Then the controllers again. And nothing will save me. So I'll need to behave with humility. And, unfortunately, stay close to you. At least for now. That'll make me look busy to the CSes. Without you, they'll suspend me to avoid wasting resources."

I was amazed at how quickly this hundred-year-old woman had the virtual world figured out. And the cheat console had nothing to do with it. Valeeva was a top-class expert, even if her knowledge was a hundred years out of date.

I didn't sing her praises in public. I'd already realized that Valeeva was one of those people who I'd always be disagreeing with. She was self-confident and inflexible. She'd always put her own opinion above everyone else's. She'd only listen to someone else's opinion if they were an expert in their field. It was entirely obvious that I was an expert in nothing as far as she was concerned.

That bitch didn't even thank me for saving her.

She could have at least remarked on my clever maneuver with the partner agreement, which allowed her to finally live instead of just existing in a recursive glitch.

We were still in the same dark archway of the Arena. I

approached the exit, looked at the sunburnt plains and sighed.

"Now we need to get to the nearest Projectoria station. Would be nice to know which way around the Coliseum to go."

Nelly walked over to me.

"Are the stations marked on the map?"

"No, first you need to find a station, then it shows up on the map. I came here on an airship. There was no station at the mooring. Wait! The console!"

"That's right, nubcake."

I vengefully committed her acidic behavior to memory. No problem, I didn't have to think hard to come up with insults either.

Nelly messed around with the interface a while, then sent me a map.

*Obtained Rim One Map.*
*This map is a rare item.*

In spite of the mark of rarity, you could easily buy a map like this on the in-game market or find one by completing missions for the authorities in the large cities.

You could also buy maps on the market that were created by players themselves. But they had a significant flaw; the maps didn't integrate themselves into your interface, meaning you couldn't place markets on them, set routes, select a Projectoria station and travel to it. User maps were purely supplemental. You had to take them out of your inventory to look at them.

*Achievement Cartographer completed: +10 XP.*
*You got a map of all of Rim One. That's a lot easier*

*than exploring an exciting and mysterious world yourself, right? You don't even have to leave your apartment.*

*Achievement unlocked: Cartographer II.*
*Create, find or buy a map of Rim Two. Incidentally, you can also take maps off players who are weaker than you.*

I turned to Nelly.
"Can you..."
"Sure," she laughed.
Maps of all the other Rims suddenly appeared in my inventory, except Rim Six. The messages grouped into one.

*All levels of the Cartographer achievement completed: +40 XP.*
*You collected all the available maps. There are no more maps.*

*Congratulations, Leonarm, you leveled up!*
*Your level: 40.*
*Attention: you have unused stat points (1) and skill points (2). Plan well and spend them wisely! All signs point to you knowing what you're doing.*

Now that was good! With Nelly's help, I could get whatever I wanted. The hundred-year-old women realized where my thoughts were going and spoke sarcastically.

"What is your wish, master? Behold the genie of the lamp."

I read her stats.

"First, give yourself a name. Then choose a class...

Choose something useless as a test. Try choosing businesswoman for now."

*Nelly Valeeva, Human.*
*Class: Businesswoman.*
*Level: 199.*
*Health: %Unknown%.*
*Armor: none.*
*Occupation: %Unknown%.*
*Interests: %Unknown%.*
*Character: %Unknown%.*
*...*

*Nelly Valeeva shares skills with you:*
*Decorator, level 30.*
*Trading, level 30.*
*Insight, level 30.*
*Exorcist, level 30.*
*Seducer, level 30.*
*Battlefield Surgery, level 30.*

"Great, you can teach me a level of any skill. I choose Seducer..."

"How about you calm down and get what you're given? Here, take this."

*Decorator skill upgraded to level 1.*

*You're an experienced buyer. New goods unlocked in furniture stores. Time to start shopping, huh, millionaire?*

*May your home be beautiful. You've unlocked the Construction Market. Hurry and see if there are orders for interior design there!*

This was starting to annoy me.

"I don't get it, why are you treating me like an enemy?"

"How should I treat you? This is the first time I've met you. I can't verify your story. You think I should be your best friend?"

Hard to argue with that...

"But still, we're stuck together. You're stuck with me, that is. If you want to live, cooperate."

"Listen, what was your name again, Leotard? If you think I'm going to be your obedient slave, you can think again. Don't try to blackmail me with your shitty contract. Either my biographers didn't research my life too well or you didn't pay attention in school. I'm not someone who will leap at the chance to live a life as pathetic as this. I don't know about you, but I don't feel like a person. I don't feel like you're one either. This whole fucking virtual world is a joke. I see all its bullshit from the inside."

"But..."

"Have you people from the future convinced yourselves that this is life? Great, each to their own. But I'm a hundred years old. I've seen real life."

"Well, you're..."

"I'm not done yet. Shut up and listen to what the great historical figure says. If you think you can saddle me up and ride me with that contract, then you're an idiot. Now I'm totally sure you're from the MSB. You've forgotten, Leotard, it was *you* who came here to look for me *me*. Not the other way around. We're going to go where *I* say. We're going to do what *I* say. You're going to get from me only that which *I* believe should be given. I'm not your bitch, you're mine. Don't like it?"

"No."

"Then cancel the contract.

"No."

"Then don't talk to me like an NPC who has to serve your interests."

"You have it wro..."

"I have it exactly right. Don't make excuses."

I fell silent, thinking over what I'd heard. Nelly was both right and wrong. Of course I was rushing her with my demands, but I didn't expect such an explosion of emotion.

As if dropping a bunch of insults on me wasn't enough for Nelly, she wanted to prove her power too.

Her gray vest and trousers disappeared and were replaced by ornate armor that greatly enhanced her figure. An axe with a sinuous handle materialized in her hand. It had a living dragon's head in place of a blade.

The axe descended onto my head.

*Damage taken: -10,999. Dragon's Tooth axe strike.*

*You have one health point left! You made a will, right?*

Incidentally, that wasn't a joke about the will. A partner agreement could include a clause that after death, all your items would go to the partner. It kept them from enemy hands.

One inconvenience was that only the items described in the will could be handed down through it. So players were often too lazy to make one. A will wasn't included in the standard contract, so there was none between me and Irene. I should have included it. Might have come in handy.

Next, she really got started.

*You have been cursed with Unhealable. Medicine*

*will not have any effect on you.*
*Duration: unknown (Requires 70 Knowledge).*

*You have been cursed with Stone Statue. You cannot move at all.*
*Duration: unknown (Requires 70 Knowledge).*

*You have been cursed with Wooden Soldier. All your weapons have turned into wooden planks.*
*Components obtained: 1,022 wood.*
*Attention, you are overloaded!*
*Carrying capacity: -129.*

Nelly debased him even further.

*You have been cursed with Riches to Rust. All your equipment has been split into its base components.*

Entirely naked, I stood before Nelly surrounded by a pile of little boxes; cloth, metal, plastic, glass... Everything my gear had been made of. And the hundred-year-old woman was still furious.

*You have been cursed with Fake Wealth. All your money has been turned into worthless paper.*
*Components obtained: 1,215,032 paper.*
*Attention, you are overloaded!*
*Carrying capacity: ...no point in calculating how far it is in the red — this is untenable!*
*The scale of your greed is simply astonishing.*

*You have been cursed with Frailty.*
*-5 to all stats.*
*All skills lowered to level 1.*

*Duration: unknown (Requires 70 Knowledge).*

*You have been cursed with Noiselessness.*
*You cannot speak or talk.*
*Duration: unknown (Requires 70 Knowledge).*

*Exorcist skill increased: +10 XP.*

In the sudden darkness, I watched as Nelly walked around me, waving her dragon-head axe. Then her armor slid off and Nelly was back in her old clothes.

The hundred-year-old woman sat down on the stone, covered her face and burst into tears.

# Chapter 44
# A Hardware Problem

EVERYONE LEFT the building to give Nika the space she needed to craft a nuclear bomb. Jamilla went to look at the dragon, Grisha and Fortunado were left alone.

A black cube and a white orb.

Fortunado said that a delivery came in from the 'other side,' as he called Rim Six, every twelve hours.

"There's a random set of items in those loot boxes. Sometimes there are chunks of cheap ore alongside powerful magical objects. We can't read some of the item properties, you have to be over level four hundred to see them all."

"Then why does Mariam send them to you?" Grisha asked.

"I don't think Mariam herself is sending them."

"Why not?"

"I've met her here, in the base. So she isn't in Rim Six."

"Who is she?"

"An NPC. But she's very odd. She's only somewhere around level two hundred, but her class is Overseer.

"What's that? Never heard of it."

Fortunado paused.

"Yes, there's no such class even among those available only to NPCs."

Because Fortunado faltered again, Grisha realized something. He displayed triumphant emojis on all LeCube's sides and shouted in glee.

"Aha! So I was right. She's a character who is part of the quest to open Rim Six."

Fortunado quickly agreed.

"Yes, yes, bro, you're the sharpest of all of us, yup."

Grisha didn't catch the sarcasm.

"Just going to roll over and accept I was right? You made fun of me. Said I was dumb, that I didn't get it. And all the while all your ideas about the special forces and a conspiracy were just fantasies."

"Exactly right, Grisha, without a doubt."

"Alright, I forgive you," Grisha declared. "Now tell me, where do you get program configurations for your little ball?"

"I make simple configs myself. I buy the more advanced ones from an android that Mariam introduced me to. He's an NPC too, around level three-hundred and eighty."

"And how much did it cost you to get a config to transform into a fighter jet, for example?"

"Loose change. Why would I remember? A hundred, two hundred, three hundred thousand at the most."

LeCube jumped, showing anger and upset on its walls.

"A hundred?" Grisha groaned. "Oh, Nika, oh, you cunning rat. She charged me a million for each. And she said it took her three months to make each config."

Fortunado burst out laughing.

"I would have done the same. What did you expect? It's payment for hating crafting. If you had even a medium level of skill, you would have known the cost of the components."

"Shove your crafting up your asses, nerds."

Suddenly, the white LaSphere turned red, and Fortunado said to Grisha:

"We've detected scouts from the Viatichis and Free Adamites. Jamilla's Tomb will have guests soon."

"Well, with this many soldiers, you'll deal with them. The Ozergs can do it on their own. How many do you have?"

"Three. But we can't afford to relax. Our mages can't use them to their full capabilities."

Grisha was surprised.

"If you have dragons, why did your soldiers lose it when Jamilla used Ozerg's Egg?"

"We got the Ozergs as little dragonlings in cages. We didn't even know they drop powerful eggs."

"I don't get it, why is the guild getting rare units and crazy items?"

"I don't get it either. I suspect that whoever is filling the loot boxes is doing it at random without even knowing the value of the items. So a wooden block and an ultradense bar of qualia are both worth just as much to them."

Fortunado went to the front lines of defense to organize his forces against the potential upcoming attack.

"Need help?" Grisha asked.

"Under no circumstances. You three sit quietly! Mariam can't learn of our agreement."

"Damn... That's boring. How much longer until

Nika finishes the nuke?"

"Ask her."

The white orb zoomed away, and the black cube slowly drifted toward the building.

Grisha was angry at Nika for her deception. She'd taken him for a ride to the tune of over ten million for configs that cost ten times less!

He started dreaming of grabbing her android body in his steel arms and tearing it in half.

"And I'll play football with her chip-filled head with the other mechanodestructors," he threatened aloud.

Nonetheless, he floated silently into the room in which Nika worked. He hovered in a corner, hesitating to interrupt her crafting.

"Bad idea to come in here," Nika said. "Before I crafted the first charge, I got killed several times."

"Never mind, I'll survive."

Nika confidently moved icons around the surface of the projector panel. Each icon indicated one component or another, or a set of components. A new set could contain up to ten thousand components.

If an icon was lit up, that meant there was enough of that component in storage. If it was gray, then the components were there, but not enough of them. If the icon just had an outline, then there was none of that component. If it had an outline and an exclamation mark, that meant there wasn't enough Knowledge to use the component and its links or that an unknown component was required.

And that was just the basic knowledge about the component indicators. An experienced crafter or a player with the CAM Operator skill saw far many more supplementary symbols and explanatory notes.

Many factors had to be considered in the process of crafting. For example, the position of the icons relative to the others, or the position and length of the links, or the position of the links relative to the icons.

Some components couldn't get along with being close to other components. Some links between components couldn't pass near other components. That incompatibility was often delayed: the craftsman could make all the connections between the components, then some time later — something broke... and the item didn't turn up anywhere, or the craftsman died and the expensive components were wasted.

Apart from that, crafting was regulated by the crafting tools themselves. It was one thing to make a knife out of wood, steel and a smelting process using a simple workbench. It was something else entirely to craft complex devices and mechanisms when the craftsman was using a component adaptation machine, a CAM.

That was what Nika was using then.

The CAM allowed her to operate on symbolic representations of the components on the projector panel without touching or even seeing the components themselves. Those were kept in storage. Which made sense, because creating frames for mechanodestructors required tons of materials. You couldn't pile them all up into your own personal little hill and sort through it all.

Crafting complex items was an intricate puzzle that couldn't be solved without advanced logical thinking and skills. The puzzle threatened to destroy the craftsman if they incorrectly assembled its parts.

Crafting levels allowed you to see dangerous or incorrect connections and juxtapositions. With a high level CAM Operator skill, you unlocked defense against incompatibility — the icons pushed each other away slightly to show you that they couldn't be placed near each other. But even then, you had to be careful and not miss the hint.

Even attentiveness didn't guarantee anything. Crafting some items required a temporary connection between two incompatible components. In cases like that, the craftsman had a limited time to complete connections or move components in the right order to prevent the incompatible components from detonating.

Or if they missed the moment, then just run away.

When Grisha realized that he was out of the danger zone for the crafting process, he spoke.

"So you were talking to Mariam long before she became a client of the Black Wave?"

"'Talking' is too strong a word. She just contacted me. She gave me money, components and step-by-step instructions to craft a nuclear charge."

"If someone had step-by-step instructions, couldn't they craft it as well as you?"

"Assuming they had the same Knowledge and corresponding skills. And my patience. So that means not just anyone. It took a lot of time and effort to create the nuke. It was that process that taught me the links and references I needed to craft LeCube. Which is a hundred times cooler than some dumb nuclear bomb."

"And the second charge?"

"The second was easier and faster. I don't know

whether it was deliberate or accidental, but Mariam gave me more components than I needed to make one bomb. I gave one to her, the other I kept a while and then sold to the coalition later."

Grisha wanted to ask how much Nika had earned. A billion? But he asked something else.

"So if we got the required components, we could start manufacturing nuclear bombs and take over all of Adam Online?"

"Well, apart from zones with different laws of physics. But those are few."

Grisha thought for a moment.

"I mean, for example, could we bomb Liberty City? Would all the players and NPCs die there?"

Nika's turn to think.

"Without Liberty City, the game mechanics would be broken."

Grisha chuckled.

"You're always talking about mechanics and logic, but I don't see any logic in this. It's like, now we can create bombs that can destroy whole cities in the game, but we can't use them against cities?"

"But cities can't disappear, you know. Maybe if we detonated a nuke in Liberty City, the game would show us the explosion and the destruction, and even generate some kind of instance,[3] 'Ruined Liberty City' or something, but the original city wouldn't go anywhere."

"But doesn't that contradict the principle that you can do what you want?"

"You incorrectly interpret the phrase 'do what you

---

[3] An isolated location individually created for each group that enters it.

want.' There are rules. Cities can't be destroyed."

"Well, I don't know, that seems like a bug or a development flaw. Like when you did the experiment and everything broke down and the system rolled back."

"Anything's possible, Grisha..." Nika was busy crafting and responded without thinking.

"You claimed that the great Adam Mickiewicz thought of everything. That Adam Online would be persistent precisely because our binary arrays help create the world, or something like that. Where did that error come from?"

"In Mickiewicz's time, nobody expected the game to become a refuge for humanity. Adam Online's game logic became more convoluted with the introduction of each new Rim. Meaning it became more difficult for us to perceive. For the CSes, there was an order to it all. But now..."

Nika fell silent and ran to the other end of the projector panel, where she started rapidly moving icons and connections around.

Grisha realized that this was an important moment in the process, and stayed quiet. When Nika turned around, he asked her:

"Now what?"

"It seems that things have reached a critical point. It's no longer possible to keep all the rules, zones, game events and laws of physics in balance. The virtual world has become more complex than the real one. Or in other words, real life has run out of computing power to maintain the growth of the virtual world."

"You mean Adam Online is broken?"

The abominable toothless smile of an android appeared on Nika's face.

"Not the world of Adam Online itself, but the

equipment it runs on. It's a hardware problem, not a software problem."

"Are you sure?"

"Of course not."

"But since we're a part of the hardware that supports Adam Online, does that mean we're the problem?"

Nika's suddenly lowered her hands from the projector panel. The icons trembled angrily, getting ready to explode.

"Grisha... sometimes you're a genius."

"Ahem..."

"Why didn't I think of that?"

"Nika, the components... they're shaking."

"What if the problem really is us, the players, not the QCPs or the rest of the infrastructure?"

"Nika!"

"And is it a problem at all? What if it isn't a bug, but a feature?"

LeCube span and floated toward the exit in panic.

"It's going to explode!"

The android turned back to the projector panel and quickly calmed the icons, wrapping them up in other icons and connections.

Nika said nothing else until the very end of the process.

It was hard to say whether she was thinking about what Grisha had said or about crafting. Grisha passed the time scrolling through the animations and emojis for LeCube. Right now he was showing a firework on his side to celebrate an event for the ages; wise Nika had called him a genius.

Nika walked away from the projector panel again and waved her hand over the compile button. The icons merged into each other and grew larger. The process connections also melded into thick threads and disappeared.

Soon, a diagram of an atomic bomb span on the empty projector panel, surrounded by lines of text.

Nika got a message.

*New unique item Big Pulowski Nuclear Bomb created: +1,024 XP.*
*Fireball diameter: 5000 feet.*
*Damage in fireball area of effect: 15,000,000.*
*Area of effect: 14,000 feet.*
*Damage in area of effect: between 8,000,000 and 45,000.*

There were lots more lines, like 'shockwave damage' or 'radiation damage,' but Nika didn't bother reading them. It was clear enough that this nuke was even more powerful than the last two.

*Congratulations, Nika, you leveled up!*
*Your level: 400.*
*Attention: you have unused stat points (2) and skill points (2). Spend them wisely!*

Nika shook out her hands as if they were dusty and spoke.

"There we go. Now it's time."

# Chapter 45
# 100500

GRISHA WAS a giant black cube, his black sides showing a blurry reflection of mountain peaks. The first player to master a new type of mechanodestructor frame.

Nika was a tall, thin android with a sophisticated humanity chip and incredibly high-level crafting skills. She was so weak that she could have died to a rock dislodged from a cliff by the anomalous wind. Both fragile and mighty.

Jamilla was a beautiful fallen angel. She was equipped in shining armor of qualia and 'erstel,' a new component from Rim Six. Fortunado had sold her his only bar of it for five hundred thousand gold. One unit of erstel gave plus one hundred mana regeneration per second, higher than any other known component. The component had a few more properties, but they required high Knowledge. The required level could only be reached in Rim Six. Jamilla kept silent about how much regeneration she had in total. On top of that, she had a mighty weapon — Ozerg's Egg. Maybe she wasn't the only one that had such an egg, but she was the only one that could use it.

All three were at level four hundred. All three

stood before the entrance to the cave that led to Rim Six. Fortunado said that if a player below level four hundred walked into the cave, they were simply thrown back out.

The partners exchanged glances. They were finally there. They'd be the first to enter the new Rim. The nicknames of those players would be written into the encyclopedias of Adam Online. They'd immortalize their names themselves as they named new zones. The first hundred players to enter Rim Six would get so-called 'unique player items,' the ability to add weapons, armor or other devices to the game and have them named in the player's honor. There were five hundred unique user items in the game. They could rarely be found on the open market, and they were ridiculously expensive.

Grisha embraced the moment and shouted:

"Friends! We should make a guild."

"I don't join guilds," Jamilla reacted sharply.

"I don't want to either," Nika answered.

"Damn, you guys are so boring."

Jamilla began to move into the dark of the cave first, but Nika stopped her.

"Wait! Grisha is right. We need a guild."

*Always the way,* Grisha thought. *First these smartasses don't listen to me, then it turns out I'm right....*

Jamilla turned.

"I don't join guilds."

"Wait and listen," Nika repeated. "We know nothing about moving into new Rims. I don't know about you, but Grisha and I are from the younger generation, no new Rims have opened in our lifetimes."

Jamilla, who was many years old, wasn't about to start explaining that she'd seen the openings of Rim

Four and Rim Five in her time. If she'd been born a little earlier, she would have seen the introduction of Rim Three too. She'd only been seventeen years old then, just a little shy of adulthood.

"I've been playing a little longer than you..." she said. "There's no difference between the Rims. I see no reason to create a guild."

"I understand, I'm the same way..." Nika answered. "But right now, we're better off in a guild."

"Yeah, yeah, a guild!" Grisha echoed her. He wanted the achievement: the first guild to be created in a new Rim. Awesome!

"Why do we need a guild?"

"It unlocks the ability to create a home base. We'll be able to set up a respawn tower, respec stations, hangars... I'll build warehouses for CAMs."

"A solo player can do all that too."

"A guild contract unlocks guild skills. What if a strong enemy kills you, Jamilla? You'll lose at least one level. You'll be back at three hundred and ninety nine. You'll respawn in Rim Five, not in Six."

"So?"

"The Guild Assist skill allows guild members to give their experience to another guildmate," Grisha recalled. "Useful sometimes, although we rarely used it. People were usually too greedy."

"So what?" Jamilla asked. "You guys are at level four hundred too, what do you have to share with me?"

"Grisha has nothing to spare," Nika agreed. "But when I crafted a unique item, I got enough exp for two levels at once. I have one spare level point. I can save at least one guild member."

"What do we do with the partner agreement?"

"It can stay active. We can make a guild

agreement with the minimum clauses. No experience sharing, no skill trading. And we'll give it a short duration."

"Fine, I give in," Jamilla said.

Nika wrote up the guild contract and sent it.

"Now we need to think of a guild name and choose a leader and three guild skills."

Jamilla spoke up immediately.

"You're the leader. As for the name, I don't give a shit. We should discuss the skills."

Nika turned.

"Grisha, you come up with a name. You like making up names, right?"

LeCube's walls lit up with exclamation marks and question marks. Grisha asked:

"Jamilla, is 'I don't give a shit' a suggestion for a name, or just how you feel?"

There was a rumble and a gust of wind behind the players. One of the Ozergs had taken off from its perch. Watching as the giant dragon blotted out half the sky and flew off somewhere, Nika spoke.

"Looks like Fortunado's war has started. I hope my army comes in handy to him. Come on, Gregory, hurry and think of a name!"

"Grenike, Nikjagger," Grisha started throwing out options. "Nigreja, Jagreni, Gremilla..."

"What the hell are you doing, Grisha?"

"Making a word out of our names."

"Why make it so complicated? Come up with something simple, like 'Fiery Demons of Rim Six' or 'Ultrasmashers'..."

"But that's so cliché. Why not go further and just use numbers like you always do? Guild One Fiddy."

"Sure, I'll put that."

"No! Wait! I was joking! Noooo!"

"Too late. Next. Guild skills."

They all started reading through the list. After a short negotiation, they settled on the most necessary skills for a small guild.

*Incontestable Leadership.*

*+20 to all guild members' Health when within 3300 feet of the leader (depends on guild leader's Perception).*

*Mobilization.*

*Moves all guild members to the leader. Mobilization works even on guild members currently in battle.*

*Area of effect: 3300 feet (depends on guild leader's Perception).*

*Cast time: 10 seconds.*

*Cooldown: 12 hours.*

*Guild Assist.*

*Guild members can donate level points to one guildmate. No more than 5 at once. No more than 50 in a single rotation.*

*Cooldown: 24 hours.*

Nika finished creating the guild and chose a guild crest by tapping on a random image from the thousands available — some plant wrapped around a shield with a skull on it.

All three walked into the cave.

The cave was big enough for even a large bizoid or mechanodestructor to walk into it.

Nothing happened as they walked.

"Feels like we should get attacked by at least a couple of monsters," Grisha muttered. "This emptiness isn't exactly exciting."

Then the partners arrived at an entirely ordinary Respec-T station. Next to it was a so-called Obelisk of Virtue, which did the same as the respec-tification station, only for magic classes. A small pond full of murky thick liquid bubbled away nearby. That was a Coacervate, in which bizoids could redistribute their stats and upgrade or purchase new DNA modifications. A little farther away was a shining Altar for angels and fallen angels.

All Temples had Altars. They were basically a variation on CAMs, with the difference that they didn't just work with components, but also with creatures. A certain number of animals or people were brought to Altars as a sacrifice, and they provided powerful angelic spells in return. For example, not just anyone with a magical class could create something like Solar Pillar, but any mid-level angel could. The main difficulty was collecting enough sacrificial material. Angels couldn't kill, after all.

Humans and angels worked together to achieve it: the all-seeing angel tracked the prey and teleported a player with a combat class to it. Sometimes they would teleport a whole group of players if the victim was a strong bizoid (and bizoids were always strong) or a high-level human. While the hunters fought, the angel supported them with blessings. If they won, the angel would received the required creature for the altar, and the hunters got experience, loot and level-ups. Everyone was a winner. Apart from the people getting hunted down and killed. The stronger the player brought as a sacrifice, the more powerful the spell or prayer.

"I don't need to change my stats," Grisha said.

"I'm happy with mine too," Jamilla said.

Nika approached the Respec-T station and touched it.

"I need to lower my Knowledge and increase my Health and Agility. Had enough of taking risks."

The path continued to be quiet and empty. The partners casually left the cave, finding themselves in the same kind of terrain they were in before it, with gray cliffs rising in the mist around them, the sky shimmering with the anomalous wind. Spiral clouds span furiously, melted away and appeared again.

"By the way," Jamilla said. "We've all leveled up now, so let's cancel the experience sharing?"

Nika canceled that clause in the contract and everyone signed the new one.

The partners walked a little further, then all got the same message.

Grisha read his.

*Congratulations, Grisha, you discovered Rim Six.*

*Pioneer skill increased: +100 XP.*
*Keep exploring new areas. Don't forget to mark*

*them!*

*Achievement One of a Hundred completed: +100 XP.*

*You are among the first hundred players to discover the new Rim.*

*A surprise awaits you... When? Nobody knows. It's a surprise!*

A few steps later, all three players were suddenly taken to the game settings, above which a video message window opened. The Glocon logo span in the frame.

The logo disappeared and a video of Adam Online gameplay began. A voice spoke.

*Congratulations, player! You have become one of the first to unlock a new world of incredible adventures and surprises prepared for you by the control systems and hundreds of quest writers. This new world comes with a few new additions. Please familiarize yourself with them in the updated user manual that has just been delivered to your inventory.*

*Attention, you are entering a game zone of Rim Six. Please be aware that from this point on, Rim Five is considered a low-level zone. Players over level 400 cannot move to zones in Rim Five or other Rims. All your property remains under your ownership, but you cannot visit it while playing as a level 400+ character.*

*To visit old player zones, you must lower your level using a Respec-T station or other facility for redistributing stats for your race. Thank you.*

Next, the message:

*What would you like to do?*

*> Keep playing as this character.*
*> Return to Rim Five.*
*> I don't get it, I need help!*

*> Leave Adam Online (Attention, this will end your current taharration rotation).*

Grisha chose to keep playing. At once, the user manual leapt from his inventory and opened itself unbidden. Grisha read:

*The first edition of this manual was written by Adam Mickiewicz himself. It has been refined and expanded with the addition of each new Rim.*

*On the threshold of the launch of Rim Six, we are pleased to present an updated version of the manual. Nobody at Glocon knows what awaits players beyond the borders of Rim Five. We're just as ignorant as you are of the control systems' plans. Even the writers who worked on some of the missions and quests in Rim Six don't have a complete picture of the adventures that await you.*

*And so, friends, refresh your knowledge of the Adam Online world and forge ahead, into Rim Six!*

*Radzhesh D. Smirnov, Glocon Director.*
*Global Consortium of Standardization in Adam Online.*

The next section appeared before Grisha.

### 1.1. WORLD COMPONENTS

*All entities in Adam Online consist of components managed by processes. The player's binary array is not an entity. It is a separate category in the world that influences all the other categories.*

*The binary array is read-only to the control systems. All changes in the data of the binary array are performed by the binary array itself. It is a cast of human consciousness. But the Player entity has an avatar that can be edited by the control systems. Just like any component or process of Ada...*

Grisha didn't read the manual. He was a practical person, and had learned the subtleties of the game in the game itself. So he closed the manual and tried to trash it from his inventory, but he couldn't — the manual couldn't be deleted.

"I don't want to read, I want to play," Grisha said, turning to Nika.

She held a material copy of the manual in the form of a brochure.

"You plan on reading all that?" Grisha asked in horror.

"Yeah."

He turned to Jamilla... she was sitting on a stone too, with the tome of the manual open on her knees.

"Damn nerds," Grisha sighed.

Grisha got so annoying with his constant requests to

keep going that Jamilla finally gave up. She rose from her rock, threw away the tome. It vanished into thin air.

"Fine. I'll start exploring. But first I want to be clear: everyone goes their own way. I'm going left, you guys go right. Nika, don't use Mobilization unless there's an emergency. If some monster starts eating you, rely on Grisha, not on me. Ideally don't use Mobilization at all, I might get mad. We might be in the same guild, but I don't want to see you guys. Please don't message me, I don't want to keep in contact. I want to explore the world myself. I hope you understand. I don't want to discuss it. See you later."

Jamilla turned her back with no intention of listening to their answers. A black hooded cloak appeared on her. She threw the hood over her head and disappeared.

"Fine, go then," Grisha answered a little too late.

After hearing out Jamilla, Nika had returned to her reading.

"Well, guild leader, what's your plan?"

"To find the border of Rim Seven."

"Wh... what?"

"I'm sure that those who created the reality transfer interface must live somewhere far from here. Somewhere at the edge of this world."

"What makes you say that?"

"They're running from players. Running from the expanding universe of Adam Online. Their existence doesn't depend on our binary arrays. They don't need us at all."

"Who are 'they'"? The Mentors?"

"Maybe."

"But..."

"Save the questions for later, Grisha. I don't quite

know anyway, I'm just guessing. So we'll start doing what you want most of all."

"Hot mechanodestructor and android sex?"

"No, idiot, playing the game. Exploring the world, leveling up, upgrading our skills.

Grisha cheerfully transformed into a jet and tried to take off, but the anomalous sky wouldn't let him fly above thirty feet.

"Well, looks like I'll be upgrading my piloting skills."

"And I'll work on my Knowledge and crafting skills. Firstly, I need to get back to my previous level, and secondly, I need to find out why flying machines don't work here and how to get around that.

Grisha transformed into his humanoid mech and scooped Nika up onto his shoulder. They walked off to the right, like Jamilla had asked.

There were still many thousand hours until the end of their taharration rotation. They'd only joined the game a little before Leonarm had. Those had been the conditions required for getting into Rim Zero. You had to start a clean game session with a new character, then get your old characters back, which someone had moved to Rim Zero by transferring them to the ownership of hacked NPCs. It annoyed Grisha that Fortunado had refused to name the people that pulled all that off. But now he realized that Fortunado didn't know.

In short, Grisha and Nika had enough time to build themselves a base and complete the first quests. They left the mountain zone without adventure. The cloudy veil disappeared and they saw the buildings of a huge city in the distance.

A city where they would be the first players among a million NPCs.

# Chapter 46
# Aggro Range

ALL THE SPELLS Nelly had cast on me disappeared. Now I was dressed in a standard vest and jeans. On my shoulder was a bag in which, I was certain, there was another undeletable copy of the 'Guidebook on Rim One of the Adam Online Universe.'

I was in no hurry to console the crying hundred-year-old woman. Firstly, I was angry at her. Secondly, I had no idea what to do when strong women cried. I intuitively felt that it was best to do nothing. If you tried to console them, you were lost. They'd finish crying and make as if nothing happened, but they'd hide hatred toward you. You saw their weakness.

I discarded from my inventory the million sheets of paper that had been my capital. The paper stacked up in columns, filling the whole arch of the Arena to the top. The wood joined those columns. I wondered how long the stacks would last before the CSes expropriated it all.

On the other hand, paper cost one gold per hundred sheets. Which meant the arch contained twelve thousand gold worth of paper.

Fortunately, the Riches to Rust spell had destroyed only my clothes, armor and UniSuits, not my

LCPD badge, medals or amulets. Although it did sting to lose the corrupt detective suit. I doubted that Nelly could return an item created specially for a quest.

But figuring out the capabilities of the NPC console would come with time. For now, I needed to restore peace and cooperation.

I approached Nelly. She sat on a rock, hunched over, her face in her hands. Her shoulders had stopped shaking, and I heard no more crying. Since even the heaviest crying didn't affect your avatar, nobody had to worry about getting red eyes or a swollen nose.

"You..." I began. "That..."

Nelly rose and answered in a way I didn't expect.

"Sorry. I shouldn't have done that to you."

"I shouldn't have threatened you either. You're in a stressful situation."

"Well, you didn't threaten me that much. I'm a god in this world."

"Not a god, a bug."

We both fell silent, realizing that our attempt to make peace had led to another argument. Nelly turned away and looked at the stacks of paper and wood.

"Woah. Guess I owe you a million."

"A little more... Can you..?"

*Obtained: 100,000,000g.*
*Achievement Millionaire II completed: +10 XP.*
*Achievement Millionaire III completed: +10 XP.*
*If you sold your soul to the Devil, you sold it too cheap.*

*Achievement Millionaire IV completed: +10 XP.*
*You know how to make money from money. A million here, a million there...*

*Achievement Millionaire V completed: +10 XP.*

*How are you feeling, sir? Would you like to take a bath in gold?*

*Achievement Millionaire VI completed: +10 XP.*

*Bathing in gold? Ugh, so basic. I'd rather sail a Golden Ocean on my yacht!*

*Achievement Millionaire VII completed: +10 XP.*

*The power of millions is in their zeros. Just don't get them mixed up.*

*Funds in your account: 100,000,000g.*

*Congratulations, Leonarm, you leveled up!*

*Your level: 41.*

*Attention: you have unused stat points (2) and skill points (3). Spend them wisely!*

Nelly slowed, digging around in her interface.

"I can't give you any more."

"You stingy?"

"The total for a one-time transaction is limited to a hundred million per twenty-four hours. Probably some fraud protection."

Studying the console excited me. Nelly too, it seemed. At least we had something in common.

"I have an idea!" I said. "What if you try throwing another hundred million out of your inventory?"

"Haha, sure, what happens if I..." Nelly delved into the interface. "How do you want it? Sacks of gold coins, banknotes or a check?"

"A check, of course."

A piece of paper appeared in the air in front of

Nelly and slowly fluttered down to the ground. I picked up the check and moved it into an inventory slot, but the amount in my account didn't change. A second later, I got a message:

*Why do you need so much money? Not got enough already?*

*Service has ceased for your account for twenty four hours.*

*Please note, suspiciously frequent and large monetary transactions have been detected. The problem has been dispatched for analysis. Do not worry, you might not be guilty.*

As soon as I read the message aloud to Nelly, another one appeared.

*The control systems have confirmed the non-game origin of 100,000,000g.*

The check disappeared from my inventory.

Nelly laughed.

"Those control systems are smart. And you claim they work autonomously, without human interaction?"

"Pretty much."

"Now I do believe I'm in the future. Alright, let's stop the financial machinations before we get audited."

I won't lie, the smiling and laughing hundred-year-old woman was a pleasant sight. Far cuter than when she was hating me.

I carefully asked:

"You don't mind if I decide what we should do next?"

"For now, sure."

I decided not to focus on her 'for now.' At least it was something.

"First I want to get the best equipment and weapons."

"You'll need to be a little more specific. I don't know anything about the gear in the game."

"Hmm, but you chose a good axe, and somehow managed to pick out the most painful spells to cast on me..."

"I didn't choose anything exactly, I just... how can I explain it? I turned into another NPC temporarily. Anyway, Ant... Leonarm, you have nothing to fear while I'm with you."

"I'm not afraid of anything except you. Still, I'll feel better in good gear."

"Alright, say what you need and I'll try to find it. By the way, from what I understand, I have only common and rare items, but there are empty slots for unique and legendary items. I think it's because the control systems or the players themselves create those items. Apparently NPCs get them during quests or from trading."

"I wonder, can you hand out quests?"

Nelly thought for a moment.

"Shaitan knows, to be honest I'm finding it difficult to navigate through the interface... So many strange things. There are no names or tooltips... Sometimes some code shows up, but it's so crazy that I can't figure out a single line. Is all the code in Adam Online machine code?"

"Exactly right."

"Machine code was widespread in my day too, but programmers could still read it. Although not always."

I asked Nelly for a pencil and pulled a sheet of paper from a nearby stack, then started writing down a UniSuit build. That's when I hit the first limitation. I couldn't just take the best UniSuit from all the standard UniSuits in Adam Online. There was a level limitation. In addition, you had to have the right stats to equip it. For example, my Strength wouldn't let me equip the heavy models, or even the medium ones. I could only use light UniSuits without too many upgrade slots.

So the best I could build was a UniSuit I could have gotten even without Nelly. Only it would have taken a lot longer to get.

So to start with, I distributed the points I'd gained. I upgraded my Strength by two points at once. I opened my Skills... and realized that I didn't need to worry any more about what to level up or what not to. My cheater partner could not only teach me what I needed, but also give me rare books that upgraded any skill.

I put all three points into:

*Pistols and Revolvers skill increased to level 3.*

*+10 to magazine capacity of all pistols and revolvers.*

*+5 to damage from all energy weapons with infinite ammunition.*

*Pistols and Revolvers skill increased to level 4.*

*All pistols and revolvers and ammunition for them cease to weigh anything.*

*+5 to damage from all pistols and revolvers.*

*Pistols and Revolvers skill increased to level 5.*

*Hand-made. Now you can build your own pistols and revolvers. To create weapons, you need model diagrams, the required components (which vary from model to model) and a workbench or a CAM.*

*Pistols and revolvers that you craft will receive:*
*+5 Durability.*
*+5 Damage.*

Hey, I'd gotten some crafting skills... only I really didn't need them. It was a problem: it was one thing to level up a character in tough conditions, to value every point earned and take joy in gaining experience. But when your level was the only thing stopping you from accessing a multitude of possibilities, you lost yourself.

I needed all of it. A UniSuit with a dozen upgrades, a weapon, useful items... Nelly was waiting for my list, but I didn't even know what to start with." But I had to start with something, right?

"Please find me the Tesla revolvers I had before."

The search took several minutes. Nelly kept getting lost in the interface, which hadn't been designed for people. But in short order, I had two shiny new revolvers in my inventory. A quick glance at the item descriptions showed me they were better than the last ones. But as I expected, they had no upgrades. Just a naked model of the highest quality, as if I'd bought them in a store.

Even with a cheater friend, there was plenty to dream of.

"I haven't figured out the interface yet," Nelly suddenly said. "But some players are approaching us."

Nelly and I left the dark archway and walked out into the burning sun. Two transport jets hovered in the sky. The model had a teleporter at its base which allowed it to instantly land troops or vehicles.

"I never would have thought," Nelly said, "that at age thirty three, I wouldn't just get a little cellulite, but also an aggro range."

"Maybe it's someone here to play in the Arena?" I asked.

"I doubt it..." Nelly closed her eyes. "Aside from the interface, I keep getting strange commands. Not even commands, but images... Not like I'm hearing voices or anything like that. No. I just sometimes start to know what's happening. These players are somehow linked to something called the Whitelist. Yeah... I have access to the list now. I see, it's some kind of target board..."

I got it too. I took out my revolvers and regretted that I hadn't had time to get a UniSuit from Nelly.

"Woah, you have nine hundred thousand on your head," Nelly reported.

"Hmm, last time it was somewhere around three hundred. My head is getting more valuable by the day."

The teleporters in the jets flashed, and a dozen players materialized before us. Naturally, Banshee stood at the front. She'd gotten herself two broad-bladed sabers to replace her katanas. Each was the size of Banshee herself. In the real world, she wouldn't have been able to pick up even one of them. But the blademaster easily pulled them along the sand with her.

Stopping opposite me, she waved her giant swords, raising a whirlwind of sand.

"At first I wanted to put a price on your head myself, but you managed to get yourself some rich enemies. Killing you isn't just a pleasure anymore, it's a profitable one."

*Banshee, Human.*
*Guild: Tong.*
*Class: Blademaster.*
*Level: 61.*

*Health: 55,000/55,000.*
*Armor: 100,000/100,000.*

Banshee had changed her appearance somewhat, turning into a young and beautiful version of who she'd been in Rim Zero. She'd kept her bald head and decorated it with tattoos. She was dressed in strong armor with broad shoulders. The armor shone slightly; it was either enchanted or affected by a blademaster skill.

Her escorts were a little lower level and not as well equipped, but they were all blademasters from the Tong guild too.

"Wondering how I found you?"

"No." I feigned a yawn.

"You shouldn't wander around empty zones with a reward like that on your head," Banshee said.

"It makes you an easy target." I calmly walked toward her. "It's a shame you found me. You didn't do yourself any favors."

Instead of answering, Banshee swung her swords. I jumped back, but it was like trying to run away from lightning. The broad blades of the sabers collided with my legs.

That familiar pain from cut-off limbs again... I fell

into the sand and turned to Nelly.

"Why are you just standing there?"

She shrugged.

"I felt like standing."

But Nelly at least through some UniSuit into my inventory. I activated it. It had a medical upgrade built in that stopped blood loss and switched off pain receptors.

At that moment, Banshee made a mistake. Believing that Nelly was who she appeared to be, meaning an NPC, she attacked her. Her soldiers followed her maneuver. Some of them attacked me, some my personal cheater.

In response, Nelly put on a real show of transformations.

First a huge slug appeared in her place and instantly sucked Banshee inside itself. I watched for a couple of seconds as the blademaster floundered within the slug and screamed dimly. Then her body dissolved, and the slug spat out her armor, sabers and a few other items.

The soldiers lost their courage and nervously swiped their katanas and sabers, but dealt little damage. Having killed Banshee, Nelly transformed from the slug into a super, complete with a red cloak that fluttered in the absence of wind. Grabbing two of the soldiers by the collars, she launched into the sky, piercing the veil of clouds. She dropped the warriors and descended back to earth just as fast, but now in the form of a fallen angel, a pair of gold wings on her back.

The two warriors hadn't fallen half the distance to the ground before Nelly spread her wings and fired a spray of feathers into the group of frightened blademasters. That one shot tore all their bodies into multiple large chunks. It was a confusion of heads, arms, blades and scraps of armor.

Fountains of blood sprayed the whole area. Component cubes span here and there, created from destroyed armor. To finish, Nelly raised her clenched fists over her head, sending a charge of energy at each transport jet. Electric threads wrapped around the jets, after which they exploded, showering the battlefield in components: steel, plastic, titanium and more.

The two warriors in the air finally finished their fall and crashed into the pile of sundered bodies, spraying out blood and damage units. Nelly switched back to her usual form and sighed.

"Shame there were so few of them. I had more ideas."

# Chapter 47
# %Unknown%

"YOU SHOULDN'T have done that," I said. "You should have killed them more simply instead of bragging about your cheater skills.

Nelly landed before me and touched my body. My amputated legs grew back. All my health restored at the same time.

She floated up again and spoke.

"I'm just a veteran player. I'm a hundred years old, heh-heh. You have to play with elegance. An elegant victory is better than just a victory. Remember that, newbie."

"Now the players will complain and demand you get a strike for cheating."

Nelly answered haughtily:

"Don't you get it yet, Leonarm? I'm not some poor maiden you've swooped in to save. When you're with me, you're the maiden. Here, take this, dress accordingly."

*Obtained:*
*Princess Outfit.*
*Beauty standard: A+.*

*Whoever you are, whatever you've done, you can always become the most beautiful girl in town. A prince on a white horse will gallop up any day now, milady.*

I threw the outfit out of my inventory.

"You know what? If you weren't such an arrogant bitch, I'd have made a pass at you."

"Remember something else, newbie. You'd have tried to make a pass at me precisely because I'm an arrogant bitch."

My annoyance at Nelly came back. Her confidence, arrogance and... grinding attitude were taking their toll. Damn it, she was even more arrogant than I was. So this was why Amy and Vildana got angry at my lectures. At least this was a good lesson.

I decided to put this ghost of the past in her place.

"Hey, hundred-year-old woman, enough acting like a know-it-all."

"Hundred-year-old? And how old are you? At least I'm using my own image, not some skin of a bearded dude. Your real face is probably so gross that you don't want to show it to me."

Damn, she even knew I was using a skin. NPCs did have access to exactly that kind of information. I decided to remove the Brutal Buck skin.

Nelly looked at my true form.

"I thought it'd be worse."

"What's wrong, Nells, scared to admit that you're not a person?"

"Are you a person?"

"I have a body. It's waiting for me to return from taharration. You have nowhere to go."

Nelly laughed.

"You have nothing right now. You're a binary array locked in a game just like me. Only do you know the difference between us?"

"I'm not a hundred years old?"

"I have the NPC console. I can kill you every second. And since I have nowhere to go, I could do that until your rotation ends. Would you like that?"

"I'll just quit exit the control sys..."

"I checked the timings. You wouldn't be able to quit before I kill you again. And then again, and again..."

We fell silent, glanced at each other and then burst out laughing at the same time.

"We're like children," she said.

"Yep. Especially you, old lady."

"Enough, I'm not just long-lived, I'm a hero too. You studied my path through life in school. Appreciate the fact that now you're having an adventure that the biographers don't know about."

We exchanged barbs in a well-meaning tone. Sometimes it happens that two people who seem to dislike each other at first glance can be capable of working together.

We left the battlefield and set off for the Projectoria station.

I examined the enemy corpses a few times.

"Did you drop something?" Nelly asked.

"I feel like I've left something unfinished. Thanks to you, I have infinite access to any resources, but I still feel the need to go back and collect the loot. How can I abandon sabers that are worth a hundred thousand each? Human nature is strange. Even when we have everything we could ever need, we strive to collect, save up, store..."

"Taking up a career in armchair philosophy, huh?"

I wanted to answer sarcastically, but something in her stats caught my attention. My Seducer and Insight skills added additional lines to NPC stats, like Character, Interests or Seduction Probability. With Nelly, they all showed the same — %Unknown%. Which didn't seem that odd, she was a person, after all, not an entity controlled by creative functions.

But now I could clearly read:

*Mood: Inspired, Displeased, %Unknown% and %Unknown%.*
*Seduction probability: %Unknown% or 2%.*

I was so surprised that I even stopped.

"What're you staring at?"

"Do you notice any changes in yourself? In your mood? Any desire for anything?"

"I'm a copy of my own consciousness abandoned in a future game world. What kind of changes are you expecting exactly?"

I opened the description of the Seducer skill and confirmed that it was at level three, which provided:

*Non-verbal Communication. Now you can increase the Seduction Probability stat by touching parts of NPCs.*

"Please take this seriously," I asked.

"I can't, we're in a fucking game."

I touched Nelly's shoulder.

"Don't move, I'm checking something."

I lifted my hand and put it on her neck. There it was!

*Seduction probability: %Unknown% or 8%.*

"Do you feel any change now? Do you feel... attracted to me?"

Nelly pushed my hand away.

"Touch me again and I'll kill you."

Damn, why couldn't women answer a direct question directly?

"So you don't, then?"

"What difference does it make? What are you, some kind of pervert? Don't you have anything better to do?"

I decided not to tell her about the strange things happening with her stats. I theorized that the control systems were working as usual, connecting new creative circuits to an NPC that was talking to a player. That meant Nelly's consciousness was now accessible to them. Something incredible was happening before my eyes: the control systems were influencing the binary array of a human being.

It was clear that they couldn't display her 'interests,' but the patterns of an NPC's emotional behavior were copied from human behavior, so the CSes could identify a few of them.

Theoretically, I could influence Nelly the same way I could other NPCs — using my skills.

Or I couldn't.

Once we reached my apartment, I'd check the affect my tacky decor had on her.

When we reached the Projectoria station, Nelly asked me:

"Why are we going to your apartment? You tired? Need to shower and eat? You need to play house?"

"Someone is waiting for me there. Apart from that, it'll be nicer to discuss our next steps in a calm environment. With your help, I can get to level four hundred quickly, and we can go to Rim Six."

When I opened the door to my apartment, it was in half darkness. Candles burned here and there, a fire crackled in the hearth. The Sixth Sense lamp stood out in particular. The one in the shape of a girl on her knees. A burning red light came from her open mouth.

"Finally, I've been waiting for you so long!"

Irene came out to meet us, dressed in a transparent negligee. At first she rushed to embrace me, then backed off and frowned. Her seduction probability stat fell from a hundred to eighty percent.

"Who's this?" she asked jealously.

Nelly examined the Sexodrome bed. Stopped at the lamp. Cast a glance over Irene.

"You're some fresh kind of loser, Leonarm. This is the 'calm environment' you were talking about?"

I ignored the insult, keeping watch on her seduction indicator. When Nelly looked at the lamp, it rose to twelve percent! What more proof did I need?

At that moment, Irene whispered in my ear hotly:

"You want a threesome?"

*Group Sex skill learned: +10 XP.*
*The more, the merrier.*
*Irene Laggan suggests having a threesome. Upgrade this skill to increase the number of participants.*

Nelly walked into the kitchen as if she owned the place.

I followed her and Irene followed behind me. Nelly materialized a hookah pipe and put it on the table. She looked at my elegant and stylish furniture with disdain and transformed one of the stools into a heavy wooden armchair. She dropped down into it, put the mouthpiece of the hookah to her lips and released a cloud of peach-colored smoke.

"Shaitan curse you, everything in this world feels so real... I remember in real life, my doctor told me to smoke less. Here I can smoke as much as I like."

A walked to the cupboard and got out a bottle of Penny Packer whiskey, part of my gift from the driver. While I was pouring a glass, I got lost in thought. It wasn't even that long ago that all that had happened. The bus, Three Bucks, meeting Vildana... I wondered, how was she doing? Had she stopped being a good witch and turned back to the dark side?

I sat opposite Nelly, and Irene, still in the transparent negligee, stood next to her. The NPC always had to be in the player's field of vision, after all.

"Let's talk."

"What about her?" Nelly waved the hookah mouthpiece at Irene.

"Well, later she and I..."

"May Shaitan take you, as my grandma used to say! I don't care about you getting your rocks off, I care about her hearing what she shouldn't."

"Don't worry about that. Non-player characters don't react to conversations that don't concern them. Especially when the conversation concerns the world beyond taharration."

"Wait. The control systems manage the NPCs. So they filter out references to the real world? Which would mean that the CSes themselves know about the real world? Otherwise how would they filter information about it?"

"No. The control systems don't know. They're not even player characters, they can't know something or not know it. They're faceless programs. If they don't find any triggers from their database in our conversations, they won't do anything."

"Alright, but NPCs are programs too, right? What if she gets hacked? What if she's bugged and people are listening through her?"

I sighed. The hundred-year-old woman was living on last-century ideas.

"If there's time, find some history books or game manuals. You'll get it. I want to talk about something else. Who was that girl in the Darknet t-shirt?"

"A Mentor. Or their avatar. Hell, I don't even know if the Mentors are a single entity or multiple different ones."

"How did the Mentors come to be? Did they just emerge, or did someone create them?"

Nelly snorted, blowing out pink smoke.

"You're not much of a scholar, huh? You must realize that an intellect, even an artificial one, isn't a fly that appears above any old pile of shit. It can't give birth to itself."

"How do you know?" I smirked. "What about our human intellect? Did someone create that too?"

It was her turn to smirk.

"Of course, Allah created man. Didn't you know that? We're going off track. The Mentors were created before the invention of taharration..."

"But as if in the expectation that it was coming? I've already thought about that. A coincidence."

"A coincidence it may be," Nelly readily agreed.

"But in my case, the Mentors tried to convince me that they created themselves after interacting with people. Moreover, they told me their plan to take over our bodies."

"I heard something about that in the snapshot fragment."

"They said that when taharration became widespread and most of humanity moved to the virtual world, they would go out into the real world and take the place of consciousness in our bodies."

"What do they need from the real world? They like dancing in acid rain? Or cooking our former bodies with radiation?"

"I don't know why the Mentors want to get into the real world. But every artificial intellect has a goal for which it was created. And the goal of the Mentors is to find a way to move any binary array from this game into any body in reality."

So far, I was in agreement with Nelly. She didn't seem to be hiding anything, although a cloud of thick pink smoke often hid her face, preventing me from seeing her facial expressions.

"Listen, you say that someone made the Mentors," I continued. "But that would be a huge amount of work, right? Not something you could do in secret in a garage with materials you had lying around. The Mentors couldn't have been created without someone knowing about it."

"I don't know which myths they've accrued in your time. But in my era, Mentors were supplementary programs that taught scrubs how to play DotA 5. It was then, in the process of communicating with humans, that they became intelligent. Well, as intelligent as a self-teaching algorithm can become."

"Bullshit."

"Agreed. That's why I believe that we need to find the reason for the Mentors' existence elsewhere, not in the game."

"Then where?"

"Offline, of course."

"But my mission was to find you, and then..."

"Don't you get it? There was no point in finding me. My knowledge of the Mentors is a hundred years out of date."

"Eighty..." I automatically corrected her.

Nelly continued.

"And more importantly, since the Mentors are still working and growing, that means someone offline is keeping them going."

# Chapter 48
# Harem

DURING THE CONVERSATION, Irene stood opposite me and next to Nelly. I could see the differences in their body language clearly; a player controlled a character, the control systems controlled a skin.

Of course, if it didn't occur to you to look for differences, NPCs looked just like players. Some even surpassed idiots or school children taharrating into Adam Online for the first time. Apart from that, with the Seducer or Insight skill, you always knew if you were looking at an NPC.

That was why the adamites that didn't want a game, but a reality simulator instead, they switched off the interface and spoke to NPCs as if with real people.

The NPCs had no mixed states. They could express only one emotional state at once. Joy, distrust, suspicion, sarcasm or hatred occupied them fully. A person, always, even in sleep, was a wild mix of all feelings at once. It was just that sometimes, one feeling got stronger than the rest.

We cried out tears and laughed ourselves to tears, whereas NPCs just switched through those states.

Nonetheless, NPCs never looked completely

happy or sad. To imitate a real person, the 'emo-mix' algorithm was used. The NPC quickly swapped 'happiness' for 'sadness,' then immediately for 'sarcasm' or 'playfulness.' The speed of these switching emotions was such that they melded together, successfully emulating humanity.

I had no idea how those emotions worked with bizoids. The players that chose such alien creatures probably weren't sensitive types.

Mechanodestructor skins conveyed feelings like any humanoid skin. Especially if they were anthropomorphic mechanisms.

But the facial expressions of robots looked so awkward that players preferred symbolic signals. They projected the corresponding emojis. There was even an option to automatically project them. The system 'guessed' the emotional state of the binary array and independently displayed the correct emoji for it.

Of course, like any automation applied to such a chaotic creature as a human, it often failed. In the early stages, instead of the 'fuck off' emoji, the automatic system invited the conversation partner to have sex. This was doubly strange coming from a robot.

But the control systems constantly updated themselves and their creative functions. Such miscommunications were swiftly fixed, the database grew.

In the past, I'd played a mech a few times. The automatic emoji streaming had never made a mistake.

Nelly interrupted my thoughts. She pulled the mouthpiece away from her lips and spoke.

"One, two, three... And a knock at the door."

Then someone really did start knocking.

"Nice to be an NPC with a human consciousness,"

she added with a grin.

I took out my revolvers. Irene also reacted by taking out her pistol.

"Well would you look at that," Nelly commented. "Just as I was admiring the realism of this world, your whore pulls a gun out of thin air. I don't think she had it up her ass."

The knock at the door sounded out again.

"Leonarm," an unfamiliar voice said quietly.

I put my finger to my lips, signaling for silence. Nelly started blowing bubbles loudly with the hookah.

The door handle rattled. I heard a sniff and a whisper.

"Do you have the lockpicking skill?"

"No."

"Me neither."

"Why don't I smash it with my fist..."

I crept to the door and opened it quickly. Three stunningly beautiful girls stood at the threshold.

Irene emitted a baffled murmur behind me:

"Who are these ones?"

The girls from the Three Graces guild had gone to quite some effort over their appearance. Far more than on their stat levels.

The gunwoman Innocence was a brunette with a white face, bright red lips and long straight hair gathered into a ponytail. She wore a UniSuit that looked more like a bikini. At least a UniSuit's appearance didn't affect its functionality. A broad leather belt completed the outfit. The same Tesla revolvers that I had hung from it.

The blademaster Love was a green-eyed ginger beauty dressed in a tight leather suit open wide at the chest. The pommels of two swords stuck out above her shoulders, and two more short swords and a set of throwing knives hung at her belt.

The mixed martial artist Beauty had kept her thick braid, but that was the only familiar thing about her. Now she was a blonde with very exaggerated features bordering on the grotesque. Her eyes were too big and too blue, her lips too pink and puffy. If she kept upgrading herself like that, she'd turn into a caricature of beauty. She wore very short shorts, a tight white t-shirt and fingerless gloves.

I heard Nelly laugh behind me.

"We got the makings of a harem here. I'm amazed that your bosses chose such an irresponsible loser for this mission. I think I can guess the reason. You won't like it."

Nelly wanted to offend me, but I just found it funny. She seemed to think that all I did was slack off work to play on my Sexodrome with NPCs or players. When in all this time, I hadn't even... But what was the point in explaining that? It didn't matter what she thought.

The guild leader Beauty walked into the room, clenching her fists in her gloves.

"Why are you showing up here without warning?" I asked. "Trying to ambush me? Didn't you learn your lesson last time? Did you forget that my head cost you your lives and freedom?"

"Not at all," Love hurriedly explained herself. "We didn't warn you because we were afraid that you might set up an ambush."

Even Nelly laughed at that explanation.

"We wanted to find out what your raid was all about," Innocence asked. "You promised heaps of loot."

I helplessly looked at all the girls. Nelly bubbled away at the hookah with a wide grin, filling the room with smoke. The more time she spent in my apartment, the higher her Seduction Probability meter got. Now it had reached fifteen percent. Keep laughing, hundred-year-old woman. We'll see who's laughing when I put on some Seducer's Underwear and you fall at my feet without even knowing what's going on.

Strangely enough, I mostly felt bad for Irene. She was still in that negligee, clutching her pistol... and had been crowded into a corner of the apartment.

"Listen, girls," I finally said. "I have stuff to do, I don't have time for the raid right now."

All three of the Krasnoyarsk graces started chattering angrily. How's that? What stuff do you have to do? You promised! You signed a contract. You can't do this. All talk and no walk!

Love looked at Irene in her negligee and at Nelly with the hookah mouthpiece at her lips.

"You seem to have plenty of time to hang out with NPCs, but you don't have time to raid with players?"

"I see no reason to delay," Beauty supported her. "Let's go right now."

There was a weak and indecisive knock at the door. I ordered everyone to sit quietly and stay in the kitchen. I went to go open the door. On the way, I waved away a message that had been blinking since the Three Graces arrived.

*Achievement Hospitable Host completed: +10 XP.*

*You have five guests in your home.*

*The doors to your home open to all who knock. It's a good thing you live in a nice area...*

*Achievement unlocked: Hospitable Host II.*

*There are two types of guests: the ones that want to drink a lot and the ones that want to eat a lot. And they all want to do it at their host's expense.*

*Gather 25 guests in your home.*

*Completed: 5/25.*

*Attention, the Lakeview Estate apartment can only contain 10 guests at a time. You must expand your apartment.*

Well, if guests kept coming at this rate, I'd complete it sooner than I thought.

I opened the door.

Amy McDonald stood at the threshold.

She'd changed since we'd last met. She'd also made some upgrades to her appearance. Changed the line of her nose and size of her eyes a little. But in contrast to the Three Graces, she hadn't fully changed the way she looked. She was still the same Amy, just slightly improved. Although as far as I was concerned, she was cute enough before. Dressed all in black, her lilac hair peeking out slightly from under her black hat.

Judging by the fact that she was a level thirty nine bandit, Amy had abandoned her attempts to level up to a super.

"Sorry for turning up like this," she said quietly. "I need to talk to you. It's hard for me to admit this, but... damn."

She fell silent and stepped back.

"Yeah, I have a bunch of guests, come join in," I sighed.

Amy stepped in tentatively. I could see that it took a huge effort for her not to turn and run.

"Oh yeah, I forgot you're a neohikki. People are hard for you."

"It's not quite like that," she forced out. "Actually, I'm trying to overcome it..."

An idea suddenly struck me.

"You know, it's good that you came. I want to introduce you to an NPC who is going to really surprise you."

I led Amy McDonald into the kitchen. The Three Graces were already sitting at the table and had found the champagne that Vildana and I had drank at our ill-fated meeting. Nelly was sitting in the same spot, her feet up on the table, still puffing away at the hookah. She observed and assessed the players' behavior.

"Who's this one?" Irene piped up, going back to reacting to my actions.

Amy's glance slid across the Three Graces, held a little on Irene and stopped on Nelly. She noticed the humanity in her face, saw details that would have missed other players.

Nelly pulled the hookah pipe out of her mouth.

"You another one of this superlothario's broads? NPCs are obliged to service players, sure, but you're a person, right? What do you want with this goon?"

Amy even took her hat off in surprise.

"The virtual world has unlocked huge possibilities for you," Nelly Valeeva continued arrogantly. "Your lifespan has increased, you have time for intellectual pursuits. To improve your digital soul. And what do you make? Some dress like whores, others craft things out of components and sticks. A hundred years of progress, and you can't wait to get to a world that imitates the games of the past."

Amy answered unexpectedly.

"Aren't you the one who can't wait to judge people? It's as if you don't know what it's like to live in the real world."

"Whatever the case may be, reality can't be worse than Leonarm's brothel." Nelly blew out another puff of smoke.

Amy walked up to Nelly and touched her hand.

"Has someone hurt you? Tell me, maybe I can help."

Amy's touch wiped away Nelly's brave face in an instant. She even began to resemble Irene for a moment; just one emotion at any given time.

I grabbed Amy by the shoulder and led her to a corner of the kitchen.

"Out with it, what's your seduction probability with her?"

"Seventy seven percent," Amy whispered. "Weird, some of the her stat lines are just full of strange symbols. And it's strange that an NPC knows about reality, but hasn't killed herself yet."

"Oh, that woman is unlikely to kill herself," I said. "She's lived a hundred years, she'll live another hundred."

"She isn't an NPC..?"

"Hey, Leo, when're we raiding?" Love asked.

"He has one raid planned — in his bed," Beauty laughed.

I joined in with the banter.

"That's right. Let's go try out the Sexodrome. We can level up some sex skills."

The Graces exchanged glances.

"Well?" Innocence said. "Why not? Could be fun."

At that moment, Amy left me in disgust and returned to Nelly. She poured herself some champagne and had a quiet conversation with her. I hope it wasn't about the garbage from the presentation of the Dead Face sect. At this point, Nelly was ready to believe in any nonsense about the future she'd found herself in.

Love stood up from the table.

"I'm in too."

"Not me," Beauty replied.

Nelly laughed meaningfully behind my back. I was lost. I didn't think the girls from Krasnoyarsk would take my offer seriously. Sometimes it's better to be quiet than speak, as the game had advised me many times.

Love and Innocence walked into the bedroom.

Innocence, the brunette, sat on the Sexodrome and let down her gleaming black hair. The red reflections of the sleazy lamp played across her body beautifully. The ginger, Love, climbed on after her. All the knives and sabers disappeared from her close-fitting leather suit.

Love climbed on top of Innocence and they kissed.

It looked incredible. The A+ beauty standard skins were doing their job.

"Where are you, Leonarm? We're waiting for you."

I walked awkwardly toward them.

"I didn't mean right now."

"Excuse me?!" the MMA fighter Beauty said angrily, slamming her fist into her palm. "You weaseling out again? Don't want to raid, don't want to fuck. Make up your damn mind!"

What could I do? Part of me begged to let it onto the Sexodrome. Sex with a player was always cooler than with an NPC. Anyone could sleep with an NPC. But the gurgling of Nelly's hookah reminded me of my duty. I doubted that getting into an orgy would raise me up in the hundred-year-old woman's estimation. And I... I wanted to make a good impression on the historical figure.

Maybe that was my main problem. I was always trying to make an impression on people who didn't give a damn about me.

The two Graces were already taking each other's clothes off. Their perfect bodies shone invitingly in the semidarkness. Irene walked past me into the bedroom and took me by the hand.

"Come on, Leonarm, let's join in."

*God dammit!* I wailed internally. *Why can't things happen at the right times? Why right now? How could this get any worse?*

Something heavy suddenly thudded against the door, accompanied with a metallic ringing.

"Open up, my precious friend! Don't stress, I ain't here to kill ya."

# Chapter 49
# Game's End

VILDANA WAS in the same erotic and impractical armor that she'd wore when she visited my home the first time. Apparently she remembered that I'd liked it.

"Leonarmy!" she shouted at threshold. "You won't believe it, but I've missed you. I thought, why did I act that way? You're no model, but you're not bad. And you might as well be drooling when you look at me. So I decided..."

When she saw Vildana, Nelly burst out into loud laughter.

"The greatest special agent in all Rus. He was sent to save humanity from death, but he misunderstood the mission and decided to fuck all the players and NPCs in Adam Online."

"Who's this killjoy?" Vildana asked. A spear covered in gemstones appeared in her hand. Her sexy armor was swapped out for impenetrable black plate mail which seemed to absorb light.

When the black plates activated, the interior items that were protecting the apartment from magic exploded, showering the floor in shards and small component cubes.

*Items destroyed:*
*Saberwhip Flower.*
*'Ghost Busters' Magic Interceptor.*
*Your home is now defenseless even against magicians!*

In response, Nelly jumped up from the seat and turned into a warrior in huge armor, a Dragon's Tooth Axe appearing in her hand. She kept holding the hookah pipe in her other hand. She drew on it and released a puff of pink smoke.

"Just try it, girly."

Vildana looked at her enemy's equipment and put her spear away.

"How much for the axe?"

Nelly also quickly returned to her previous form.

"I value rational behavior. You can have it for free."

"Thanks, friend."

Vildana read the properties of the axe.

"Wow, rare. These weapons are called near-oneshotters. One hit and any enemy's health and armor drops to one."

"Don't wave weapons around in here," Irene said suddenly.

Vildana put away the axe, looked at Irene in her negligee, at the two Graces on the bed, then moved her gaze back to me.

"You haven't been wasting any time, friend. So you let me make you into a millionaire and now you're having yourself an orgy? Well done, maybe I'll join in."

I just waved my hand. I had no more energy for explaining that I had no orgies planned. At least not today.

Vildana poured herself some champagne too.

"To renewed acquaintances!"

Nelly Valeeva grinned and watched me, adding to her cloud of pink smoke. Amy stood next to her and stared into space, still as a stone. Amy was having another attack of social phobia.

Alright, since I couldn't make an impression on the hundred-year woman, I'd try not to damage the players' opinions of me. I raised my glass of whiskey and waved to the two Graces on the bed.

"On my way!

I drank the whiskey in a single gulp and took a step toward the bedroom. Is there any point in saying that I never got there?

The world plunged into darkness, then appeared again. I was thrown up. My body froze a short distance from the ground. The familiar sensation of losing my body came to me. Against all my interface settings, a message popped up before me.

*WARNING!*

*The controlling QCP has initiated an emergency exit from the local Adam Online control system.*

*Likely cause: threat to integrity of taharration pod, loss of power, closed access point. Contact the administrators as soon as you can after your rotation ends.*

*This emergency message has been relayed to all services. Remain calm. You are perfectly safe.*

*Searching for insurance policy...*

*Attention: username cannot be %Username%
(Error! Check taharration system settings).*
*No insurance policy found.*

*Exiting system in 45 seconds... 43... 41...*

What happened? Was there a power cut in the bunker? I knew that landlord was an idiot...

Both the Graces stopped stroking each other and came back into the kitchen. The entire harem watched me with alarm. I looked at them just the same.

Vildana was the only one who didn't lose her cool. She sipped her champagne and asked:

"What's up with you?"

"Emergency exit."

"Where're you going? Or are you afraid of us now? Can't handle all these gorgeous girls?"

The Graces laughed. Amy overcame her anxiety and joined them. Only the loyal NPC Irene Laggan remained impassive. Player technical difficulties were beyond the limits of her perception.

"Nah, seriously, what's with you, dammit?" Amy was really worried about me. "What do you mean by emergency exit? Exit to where?"

"It's not the where to, it's the where from," I answered.

*30 seconds...*

I glanced at the players. It occurred to me that they were just ordinary people. If they knew anything about illegal entry points to Adam Online, then it wouldn't be any more than they knew about trading in black market organs, radioactive materials or weapons.

For them, the world of real criminals and underground landings was far more distant than the fantasy zones of Himmelbleu and Goldivar. They were simple adamites that didn't ask "how does this work," they just accepted the virtual world in all its beauty and absurdity.

With the exception, of course, of Nelly. She'd been an outstanding individual in real life, and in virtual life, she'd become an outstanding hybrid of a person and an NPC. Some get all the luck...

"What happened?" Beauty asked.

"Problems with my taharration pod," I said.

"How can that happen?" Beauty said in shock. "Pods don't break."

"Everything in the world breaks," Love argued philosophically.

Innocence spoke up.

"Hey, so are you going to log back in? You promised to show us a dungeon with piles of loot."

"All men are like that," Love stated. "First all the promises, then they gotta leave for an emergency."

I wanted to shrug my shoulders, but the log-out process had already locked my body, and I couldn't cancel the forced exit. I could only move my eyes and speak.

"Girls, I know where we can get a pile of loot," Love said, gesturing at the decor in my apartment.

"Hell yeah, let's loot this dive!" Beauty agreed.

My emergency exit concerned me more than the safety of virtual objects of doubtful value. Nonetheless, I was grateful to Amy and Vildana.

Without a word, they both took out their weapons. Vildana waved her axe, finished her glass of champagne and threw the glass to the floor.

"Careful, three vultures. Hands off my friend's

property."

Amy pointed a short machine gun at the Graces.

"And mine."

The Three Graces jumped back and each took out her own weapon.

"You're the vultures."

*10 seconds...*

I wanted to tell them to go outside and fight there, otherwise there'd be no property left to save, but none of them could hear me anymore — my speech function had turned off.

Soon my vision would switch off and I'd live out my final seconds panicking in an abyss of non-existence.

I turned my attention to Nelly. Something strange was happening to her too.

Nelly Valeeva was frozen with her arm raised, still holding the hookah pipe. The sound of a distorted voice emerged from her half-open mouth along with the smoke. She was like Sky, when she froze while searching through huge databases.

Nelly's figure flickered, parts of her started to turn transparent, collapsed into components and then reformed.

What was happening to her? Was there some global bug in Adam Online? But the NPCs seemed to be operating normally, and not glitching. Irene assessed the circumstances and joined my apartment's defenders. Now the fight was fair; three on three.

The series of strange flickers ended. Nelly dropped the hookah pipe, rose and took a step toward me.

"Anton... I just learned..."

Nelly looked at my immobile figure in confusion. The hundred-year-old woman had no idea of the timer, or about the emergency exit from the local control system.

*What did you learn?* I wailed silently. *Idiot, can't you see? I'm about to disappear!*

Nelly shook her head.

"The Mentors. I learned about the Mentors. Somehow I was taken to another zone... or somewhere else... I just spoke to them. Or to her. Or to him..."

*3 seconds...*

*Damn it, keep talking!*

Nelly looked at the harem preparing for battle. Then back at me.

"The Mentors... they need me. And they need you too. More precisely, the Mentors need us. You and I together.

*1 second...*

The world plunged into darkness. From far away, I heard Nelly's distorted, fading voice.

"Don't fear reality... And come back, you hear? We need to decide together how we're going to..."

Her voice cut off before I could find out what we needed to decide. A clap — and the darkness turned into the blue mass of dissociative electrolyte.

I had experienced an emergency exit from a taharration

pod before, while training at the MSB. But before then, we were told many times that taharration complexes were flawless. Errors in the operation of pods weren't that rare, but they represented no threat to the subject. After all, the body could always be relocated (by literally pouring it out along with the electrolyte) into another pod without being disconnected from the access point in Adam Online.

The manufacturer maintained the operation of domestic pods. They also provided guaranteed equipment replacement while the client was connected to the virtual world. In Municipal Taharration Clusters, MTC operating personnel replaced the pods.

Underground landings were another matter. Nobody gave you any guarantees there. Any hint at the smallest functional problem, even a slight drop in pressure, and the QCP started the emergency exit procedure.

The period for the consciousness to adapt to its old body was disabled during an emergency exit. That meant that for the first minute, you just lay in a pool of dissociative electrolyte without the ability to move so much as a finger.

Swimming in the thick blue liquid, I thought of all the choice words I wanted to say to the landlord. Amy had taught me a few.

The feeling in my arms and legs was starting to return. My old arms and legs! I strained and sat up in the pod. My head was pounding, and clumps of jellied electrolyte stuck to my face. I leaned over the side and threw up the pints of blue liquid that had filled up my stomach. Then I threw my arm over the side, awaiting an injection.

But the medical robot didn't come. What was

happening?

Somehow, I managed to unstick my eyes and clean out my ears. I heard distant sounds that made the liquid in the pod tremble. It wasn't my head that was pounding, the noise was coming from outside!

I tried to pull myself to the edge of the pod to look around, but my arms were still weak. I sat back down and listened... Then realized with horror: the banging noises weren't just noises. They were explosions! And there was the staccato cracking of a machine gun... There was the whoosh of a flamethrower on a military vehicle.

What was going on, God dammit!? Had nomads attacked the landing? But how did they defeat the combat mechs that the landlord had promised would be guarding the approaches?

My vision still swam, my eyes were covered in a blue film. I needed to wash them with a special solvent. But the robot usually brought it along with the injection.

Of course, I wouldn't die without the injection, but I'd have a particularly bad hangover. The later you took the injection, the more painful it was for your body to rid itself of the electrolyte, and the longer it took. I tried to get to the edge again. This time I managed to lift my elbows over.

What I saw made me fall right back again. The whole landing was in chaos, covered in debris. Daylight streamed in from above. Someone had broken through right from the surface! That meant they weren't nomads. They didn't have the technology for this.

They might have been competitors of my landlord. They sometimes warred between themselves, finding opposing landings and raiding them. But... They never did it if a client was using the landing.

It wasn't some code of honor that made them spare people, it was just that it was unprofitable for landlords to kill prospective clients. After all, there weren't that many people who needed illegal access to Adam Online. The landlords' client base was limited.

My conscious quickly took control of my body. I sat on my heels and looked out carefully again. Behind the glass surrounding the pod's little room, I saw the rear sections of two Cassies, those robots the landlord had promised would protect me. One was shooting in bursts at something inside the room, the second was smoking with a scorched hull. The Cassie span on a broken track, sometimes firing machine gun volleys back at an unseen opponent. I was no expert in combat robots, but it was obvious they wouldn't last long.

I pushed off and swam to the other side of the pod. I threw one leg over the side and heaved my body over. I didn't fall to the floor, but onto the chair where the landlord had placed a tablet showing Olga's face before I went into Adam Online.

The chair broke and then I fell to the floor. A piece of debris pierced my stomach.

I raised my head and my glance found the medical robot. It was frozen in a hospitable gesture, extending a tray holding syringes and a bottle of liquid for clearing out the dissociative electrolyte. The power light on its head was off. That dumb landlord had forgotten to charge the medbot. The dock station must have been in another part of the building. The medbot couldn't leave the 'patient's' room. So its algorithms decided to stay where I'd be most likely to find it when leaving the pod.

I fought for control over my heads and grabbed the syringe, injecting it into my arm, then a second with vitamins, a third... I started to feel better.

I crouched down and looked out again.

Alright. What was going on?

# Chapter 50
# Endgame

FROM WHERE I was crouched, I could see a projector panel full of technical information. The attackers had broken into the landing and destroyed the power equipment, forcing the controlling QCP to switch to emergency power. Those batteries were in the pod room too, protected by armored glass.

For the time being, I was safe. The first line of defense were the barely alive Cassies, who were fighting off an attack from an unknown enemy. The second line was the armored room with the pod inside.

The robots would hold on for a few more minutes. As for how long the glass barrier would hold, I had no idea. That depended on the attackers' weapons. If they could break through such a thick layer of earth, my defenses wouldn't hold long.

On top of that, the enemies had destroyed the building's infrastructure: from the dissociative electrolyte feed to the ventilation. It was a good thing the landlord hadn't skimped on defenses. My room had automatically locked down, cutting off the outside world and protecting me from radiation or poisonous gases.

I crawled around the pod on all fours and looked out from the other side. Beyond the glass, under the smoke and dust, I could just make out... feet. One was bare, the other wore an ordinary slipper. It was my landlord, lying between the Cassies under a pile of stone. Strange. Why had he stayed at the landing so long? He was even dressed as if he was at home, he must have spent several nights here.

Whatever. That wasn't my biggest problem.

I reached out for the tablet with Olga's photo on it. I waved her image away and called up the QCP control interface. The platform didn't respond. The landlord had probably disabled wireless access for security reasons. My opinion of the landlord changed again. Sure, he'd made a mistake by putting the medbot's charge station out of reach. But by cutting the connection before he died, he'd basically saved me. I just wasn't sure for how long.

I coughed, throwing up more clumps of electrolyte.

"Platform, activate voice control. Access... Anton Brulov."

All the technical info on the projector panel minimized and a loading icon started spinning. Thank God the landlord hadn't forgotten to grant me access.

"Repeat request for verification," the QCP said in a soft feminine voice.

"Access for Anton Brulov."

The icon flashed green. Then the platform said:

"Attention, environment beyond protected zone is extremely dangerous. You are likely under attack by intruders. The following chemical compounds have been detected in the atmosphere...

"Cancel environmental assessment. Show me the camera feeds."

"All cameras have been destroyed," the platform

said.

I wanted to ask her to show me a recording of the incursion, but there'd soon be no need.

First one Cassie exploded, then the second was thrown back by some unseen shadow hiding in the smoke and flames. A few agonizing seconds of waiting later, and I sighed; an arm clad in a Nevsky exoskeleton descended on the armored glass. Another hit, and another. The entire soldier emerged from the smoke, although the pilot's cabin was covered in impenetrable black glass.

I wasn't seeing so well myself. The blue film of electrolyte on my eyes still blocked my vision. I kept rubbing my eyes, but it didn't help.

The soldier stood right by the glass and hit it with both arms. Then the black glass faded slightly. I could see the pilot clearly. It was Makarov.

He pointed to his head, making a funnel shape with his hand.

"Platform..." I said. "Enable external audio."

"In the current situation, it is not recommended to..."

"Just switch them on."

The room filled with the crackle of flames. A voice boomed out.

"I had high hopes for you, and you let me down, sonny."

"What do you mean I let you down? I found Valeeva."

"Now we'll have to kill you before they get to

you."

"Who are 'they'?"

"Sorry, Ant. You'd be better off just opening the door and dying now. I'm going to break in there and kill you anyway. Although I have to admit, I'm pretty fu... I'm pretty tired. I'm too old for working in the field."

While he talked, Makarov struck the glass with his fists. I jumped with each strike, and the projector panel rippled.

Bang — the first cracks appeared in the glass.

Bang — smoke started pouring through the cracks.

Bang. Bang. Bang. A piece of glass fell from the web of cracks.

Very recently, I'd fought giant monsters, jumped off a motorcycle, had limbs cut off and even been at the epicenter of a nuclear explosion. But all those threats paled in comparison to the cracking of that armored glass.

"But why? Why?!" I wailed helplessly. "I did everything just as we discussed in the briefing. The highest ranks of the MSB know!"

Makarov stopped hitting the glass and condescended to answer. He really did look tired from the physical demands of all this.

"Our colleagues have nothing to do with this. They truly believe that we can find Valeeva and reach the Mentors."

"But I did find her! I did it..."

"The leadership and Mr. President were not meant to learn that you found her, but that the mission failed. That our agent's character was killed by unknown attackers. That the character was lost, and the operation delayed for an undetermined length of time, while our department took measures against the attackers. That was what they were meant to hear."

"But I..."

"You would have left the pod with honors, gotten a medal, ten thousand dollars and a yearly holiday on a tropical island at the expense of Moscovian Rus."

Makarov renewed his attacks on the armored glass.

"You would have lost, but would have emerged a victor. Now you've just lost."

I stood naked, on my knees on the other side of the glass. I didn't even know what I was saying. I begged.

"But we can talk about this, I'll agree to stay quiet!"

Bang!

"I'll sign a contract... Please, Major General!"

Bang!

"Valeeva's binary array will be frozen by the controllers soon. She won't survive without me. Nobody will find anything out."

I was ready to sacrifice the last remnant of a historical figure's consciousness to save my own skin...

Bang!

"Please, I beg you!"

Bang.

The Major General dropped his arms again. He was far from young. Even in the exoskeleton, he was struggling. He stopped hitting the glass and touched the head of his heavy infantry exoskeleton as if wiping away sweat.

"I don't like this any more than you do, Ant. I'm not a monster. So please, help me. Let me kill you without all this serious talk."

Bang! This time it was me hitting my forehead against the cracked glass.

"Please... General... Sir..."

"I'm sorry you didn't calm down, Ant!" Makarov shouted. "I'd hoped that after you lost it all in Rim Zero, you'd abandon the mission. I counted on you to take advantage of your chance to live for a while in Adam Online, sleep around, eat some nice food, have a play, and then return to me and report that the mission had failed with a clear conscience. But no. You started over from nothing. You started completing a mission that I'd deliberately assigned to an unreliable failure like you. Champion of losers."

"But I won't say anything! I can tell them I failed the mission."

"Your silence has nothing to do with it. They need you now. And we can't allow that."

"Who's 'we'? Who are 'they'? What do I have to do with any of this?!"

Bang! Bang!

These new strikes against the glass were so powerful that they threw me backwards into the pod's side. I hit the back of my head. As if because of the strike, the blue clumps of electrolyte finally left my field of vision, but instead, I saw:

*WELCOME TO ADAM OFFLINE!*

*Performing preliminary calculations for body characteristics...*

I just lay on the floor, dimly staring at the blue messages floating before my eyes. Like in the Adam Online interface, the meaning of the words seeped into my consciousness. I didn't read them, but instantly understood them.

I must have gone mad in my desperation. I was seeing a game interface. My insane consciousness, having just returned to its real body, refused to accept its inevitable death. Especially after such a long time of death being a minor stumbling block.

Bang! Bang! Another few chunks of glass fell into the room. The Major General tried to push a grenade through the hole, but it wouldn't fit.

Bang! He started widening the hole with his fingers.

*Preliminary calculations complete.*
*Your compatibility with this body: 100/100 (Perfect).*

*Searching for nano-scale components (NC).*
*Components not found in set range.*
*Expand range?*

Bang! Bang! Like a stubborn NPC, Makarov kept hitting the glass.

"Expand range? Go for it, expand it," I said to who knew what.

Even Makarov paused in his strikes.

"What did you just say?"

"I want to live."

"Oh no, sonny, sorry. You know too much."

"I don't know shit..." I sighed.

Makarov started beating on the glass again, and my nonsensical interface reacted:

*Attention, cannot expand range without changing spatial coordinates of body.*
*Change coordinates?*

"Yes, please," I asked, still lying on the floor.

*Attention, the value of 'change coordinates' is equivalent to moving the body in space.*
*Move your lazy ass and try taking a stroll, player!*

I watched all this as if from afar. The ludicrous interface was challenging me to get up and go to find some so-called nano-scale components. It was probably a visualization of my subconscious need to find a way out of this situation.

I didn't care. I was trapped. And there was no way out...

Then an idea hit me, and I jumped up, even hitting the top of my head on the edge of the pod. My rapid movement made Makarov jump back from the glass, thinking that I had some weapon.

I laughed wildly.

"You're an old moron! I've wanted to say that to you for a long time."

I kept insulting him, borrowing from Amy McDonald's rich vocabulary.

"That's it, son," Makarov whispered kindly. "Let it all out. I deserve it."

I leapt to my feet.

"You think I'm trapped here? You're the one in the trap."

I ran to the projector panel and initiated the taharration procedure. While the platform gathered data, the weird interface flashed up again.

*Components not found in set range.*
*Expand range? (You already know how to do that).*

"Fuck off already."

I waved my arms wildly in front of myself. I didn't know what I did, but all the messages collapsed into a barely noticeable blue dot in the corner of my eye. Just like the Adam Online interface in Do Not Disturb mode.

Bang! Bang! The hole in the glass expanded. Soon he'd be able to shove a grenade through it.

The projector panel of the controlling QCP lit up with red warnings: dissociative electrolyte not fresh, battery charge insufficient for full taharration rotation. That's where the landlord had let me down. Whatever. Rest in peace.

One of the advantages of an illegal access point was that you could get around all the prohibitions in the system. A legal entry to Adam Online would have been interrupted as soon as the QCP detected old electrolyte. My account would have been fully blocked from logging in. I'd have had to contact Glocon and explain the reason for the technical fault.

I ordered the QCP to ignore all the warnings and continue preparations. I rushed over to the medical bot, roughly turned it onto its back and started searching through its medicine storage. I found the syringe I needed and plunged it at once into my leg.

Now there was no way back. Even if Makarov suddenly decided to leave, the second syringe had killed my body entirely.

A familiar drowsiness immediately overtook me. At the same time, a fierce pain began to course through my body. Just as my body had begun to get rid of the electrolyte, it had gotten a second dose!

Makarov shouted something, realizing my intentions. I climbed into the pod and sank down into the cold electrolyte. The major general and I both watched the taharration process. The old man beat on the glass while I just lay in the pod, trying not to think about the fact that I was leaving the real world with no hope of coming back.

The controlling QCP suddenly squawked:

"Integrity breach in synchrotron emitter housing. It is highly recommended that you cancel consciousness taharration and await inspection of the housing by a qualified expert. Continue?"

"Of course, my dear," I answered.

My thoughts raced feverishly, but I recognized the irony: I was talking to a computer named in honor of the person for whom I'd been searching. Even the voice of QCP NELLY ver. 6.2 was reminiscent of Nelly's. The real one, from Adam Online... or the unreal one, or her copy? What a mess.

The projector panel lit up:

*Process complete. Ready to taharrate.*

That was that. Good bye, world. I'd have over eight thousand hours of life in the virtual world. Then informational entropy would do its job.

I reached over and picked up the tablet from the floor. I looked at the photo one last time.

"Hey, Olga. I've thought of your fate so much that now I'm following in your footsteps."

Seeing the tablet in my hands, Makarov roared. "You bastard!"

"That's me, grandpa," I answered weakly, almost unconscious.

Makarov turned and started running away. He recognized the tablet model. The MSB armory had them. Who knows why I'd brought it with me. Maybe I wasn't as big a failure as Makarov had thought.

With a wet blue finger, I touched the icon that launched the hidden self-destruct program. The explosion would be big enough to leave nothing but a crater where the bunker stood. The tablet's frame was made of a condensed tetryl-RDX explosive.

I set the timer for twenty seconds. That would be enough time for me to escape. As for Makarov, he was going nowhere.

I'd wanted to be a hero, right? The moment had finally come!

"If you want to survive, die," I said in farewell.

I threw the tablet and dove into the blue liquid of the dissociative electrolyte.

I would never again emerge from it.

END OF BOOK TWO

Want to be the first to know about our latest LitRPG, sci fi and fantasy titles from your favorite authors?

Subscribe to our *New Releases* newsletter:
http://eepurl.com/b7nilL

Thank you for reading *The City of Freedom!*
If you like what you've read, check out other LitRPG, fantasy and science fiction novels published by Magic Dome Books:

*Level Up* LitRPG series by Dan Sugralinov:
*Re-Start*
*Hero*
*The Final Trial*
*Level Up: The Knockout* (with Max Lagno)

*The Way of the Shaman* LitRPG series
by Vasily Mahanenko:
*Survival Quest*
*The Kartoss Gambit*
*The Secret of the Dark Forest*
*The Phantom Castle*
*The Karmadont Chess Set*
*Shaman's Revenge*
*Clans War*

*Dark Paladin* LitRPG series by Vasily Mahanenko:
*The Beginning*
*The Quest*
*Restart*

*Galactogon* LitRPG series by Vasily Mahanenko:
*Start the Game!*
*In Search of the Uldans*

*The Bard from Barliona* LitRPG series
by Eugenia Dmitrieva and Vasily Mahanenko:
*The Renegades*
*A Song of Shadow*

*The Neuro* LitRPG series by Andrei Livadny:
*The Crystal Sphere*
*The Curse of Rion Castle*
*The Reapers*

*Phantom Server* LitRPG series by Andrei Livadny:

In order to have new books of the series translated faster, we need your help and support! Please consider leaving a review or spread the word by recommending *The City of Freedom* to your friends and posting the link on social media. The more people buy the book, the sooner we'll be able to make new translations available.

Thank you!

Till next time!

www.ingramcontent.com/pod-product-compliance
Lightning Source LLC
Chambersburg PA
CBHW020457020726
47493CB00001B/70